Before the Rains

DINAH JEFFERIES

VIKING

an imprint of

PENGUIN BOOKS

VIKING

UK | USA | Canada | Ireland | Australia
India | New Zealand | South Africa

Viking is part of the Penguin Random House group of companies
whose addresses can be found at global.penguinrandomhouse.com.

First published 2017
001

Copyright © Dinah Jefferies, 2017

Grateful acknowledgement is made for permission to quote on page 9 from
André Malraux, *Anti-Memoirs*, © Editions Gallimard, Paris, 1967 and on
page 301 from *Rumi*, selected and translated by Raficq Abdulla, published
by Frances Lincoln Ltd © 2015. Reproduced by permission of Frances Lincoln Ltd.

The moral right of the author has been asserted

Set in 12/14.75 pt Dante MT Std
Typeset by Jouve (UK), Milton Keynes
Printed in Great Britain by Clays Ltd, St Ives plc

A CIP catalogue record for this book is available from the British Library

HARDBACK ISBN: 978–0–241–28708–8
TRADE PAPERBACK ISBN: 978–0–241–29750–6

www.greenpenguin.co.uk

MIX
Paper from
responsible sources
FSC® C018179

Penguin Random House is committed to a
sustainable future for our business, our readers
and our planet. This book is made from Forest
Stewardship Council® certified paper.

For Richard

Delhi, India – 23 December 1912

Anna Fraser stood waiting on the ornate balcony of one of the *haveli* mansion houses lining the route. At eleven in the morning, the streets had been washed and sprayed with oil, but still the wind-swirled dust irritated the eyes of the gathering crowd. The rows of wide-spreading neem and peepal trees along the centre of ancient Chandni Chowk blew about wildly, as if in defiance, while crows added their voices, cawing and cackling high above the narrow lanes fanning out from the main square.

Anna held up her white parasol and nervously glanced down at the vendors selling everything from fresh sherbet to fried fish with chilli. There were strange-looking fruits, chiffon sarees, books and jewellery, and, behind fine latticed windows, women losing their eyesight embroidering delicate silk shawls. Where the smell of sandalwood permeated the air, apothecaries made fortunes from oddly coloured oils and potions. Snake oil, David called them, though Anna had learnt that some were obtained from crushed lizards and the colour was that of the pomegranate. It was said that whatever you desired you could find it here in the heart of the city.

Whatever you desired! Oh the irony of that, she thought.

She turned towards the spot where the Viceroy would soon appear seated on an elephant, accompanied by his wife the Vicerine. Bursting with pride, Anna's assistant district officer husband, David, had informed her that he too would be riding an elephant, one of fifty-three, all picked to follow immediately behind the Viceroy at the head of the procession. Delhi was to take over from Calcutta as the centre of British Government, and this was the day Viceroy Lord Hardinge would be sealing the deal by making a ceremonial state entry into the old walled city, starting from the main Delhi railway station on Queen's Road.

Anna identified the sound of canaries and nightingales hanging in dozens of cages gracing the frontages of the shops below and, further away, the harsh noise of the few tram cars still running. Then she looked down at the riot of oriental colour as the teeming crowd continued to assemble. She called to her daughter, Eliza.

'Come now, darling. They'll be here in a few minutes.'

Eliza had been sitting quietly reading to pass the time, but rushed out at the sound of her mother's voice.

'Where, where?'

'Ants in your pants? Again. Just be patient,' Anna said and glanced at her watch. Eleven thirty.

Eliza shook her head. She had been waiting too long and with this level of unprecedented excitement it was hard when you were only ten.

'It must be nearly time to see Daddy now,' she said.

Anna sighed. 'Look at you. Your dress is already crumpled.'

Eliza glanced down at her frilly white dress, especially made for today. She had tried her best to keep it nice, yet somehow she and dresses never quite got on. It wasn't that she didn't try to keep them clean but there were always such interesting things to do. Luckily her father never minded if she ended up in a mess. She loved him ferociously; handsome and funny, he always had a warm hug for her and a wrapped sweet lurking in the fluff at the bottom of his shirt pocket.

Behind the natives the British, arrayed in pale cottons and linens and seated in stands lining the street, seemed colourless by comparison. Despite the splendour of the day Anna couldn't help thinking that many of the Indians looked listless, though perhaps it was because of the bitterly cold wind blowing in from the Himalayas. At least the British looked suitably excited. She wrinkled her nose at the smell of ginger and ghee in the air and, drumming her fingers on the railing, continued to wait. David had promised so much when he suggested she come out to India with him, but with each passing year the magic had soured. Down below, fidgeting children began to break free. A very young toddler had stepped out of the line and into the path where the procession would pass on its way to the fort.

Anna tried to work out who the child's mother might be. How careless to allow such a young child to be so far from her, she thought. She spotted a woman, wearing a bright emerald skirt and matching shawl, who seemed to be lost in thought while staring up at the balcony, and it crossed Anna's mind she could be the child's mother. It was almost as if the woman was looking directly at her and, as their eyes met, Anna raised a hand to alert her to the child's plight. Just as she did, the woman dropped her gaze and stepped out to draw her wayward child back into the safety of the crowd.

As Anna watched the hordes flowing in below, she was glad to be set apart from the complex mix of toothless hags, their heads and faces covered, the lone beggars in threadbare blankets, the mixed traders and their children, plus the local residents wrapped up in shawls, all of whom seemed to be screeching at each other. As cats prowled the street, heads raised to watch the pigeons flocking in the branches of the trees, middle-aged men looked on importantly, casting their eyes now and then on the so-called dancing girls, and in the background the voices of children singing lifted Anna's heart a little.

She couldn't help but be aware of the past pervading every inch of the historic square, seeping even into the bones of the buildings. Everyone knew this was where the processions of the emperors had taken place, where the Moghul Princes had pranced on their dancing horses, and where the British had come flaunting plans to build a powerful new Imperial Delhi. Since the King's arrival in Delhi a year before, peace had triumphed, with no political murders at all; hence it had been deemed unnecessary to engage special precautionary measures to police the day.

She heard the loud boom of guns signalling the imminent arrival of the Viceroy. The guns sounded again and a roar went up from the crowd. Now people hung from all the windows and balconies, heads turned towards the repeated booming. Anna experienced a jolt of something unaccountable, almost a premonition, she would think after it had happened, but for now she shook her head. She glanced at her watch again, then glimpsed the biggest elephant she had ever seen, carrying a splendid open-topped silver *howdah*, or seat, from where Lord Hardinge and his wife viewed the scene. The blue-grey elephant itself was decorated in the flamboyant native way, painted with coloured patterns and covered in trappings of velvet and gold. The procession had already passed through the Queen's Gardens, where the public had not been allowed to collect; now, as they entered Chandni Chowk, the cheering reached a crescendo.

'I can't see Daddy yet,' Eliza tried shouting above the din. 'He is there, isn't he?'

'Goodness, are you not the most impatient child who ever lived?'

Eliza gazed down at the street, where dozens of children were attempting to surge forward. She raised her brows. 'I don't think so. Look at them, and their fathers aren't even in the procession.'

She leant out as far as she dared, pressing her hand into the railings and jumping, and, as the long line of elephants gradually came into sight, she could hardly contain her joy.

'Be careful,' her mother scolded. 'If you insist on leaping about like that you'll fall out.'

Behind the Viceroy were two specially chosen district officers, then the Princes of Rajputana and the Punjab chiefs on even more elaborately decorated elephants. They were surrounded by their own native soldiers, carrying swords and lances and wearing the usual ceremonial armour, and behind them would come the rest of the British Government on plainer elephants. Eliza knew the order off by heart. Her father had explained every moment of the day and she had insisted that he pause and look up to wave at her as his elephant reached the spot beneath their balcony. The wind had now dropped, the sun had come out and it had turned into a perfect morning. The moment had finally come.

Anna glanced at her watch again. Eleven forty-five. Bang on time. Across the street the woman in emerald now held the small child in her arms so that it might see. That's better, Anna thought.

Loud cheers broke out from the British, with shouts of *Hurrah!* and *God save the King!* While Lord Hardinge saluted back, Eliza spotted her father. She waved excitedly and, as the Viceroy's elephant took another few steps forward, David Fraser's animal was made to pause so that he might fulfil his daughter's wish. As he glanced up at the balcony to return her wave, a shattering explosion, just like the massive roar of a cannon, instantly silenced the crowd. The buildings seemed to shake and the entire procession came to a shuddering halt. Anna and Eliza stared in shock as flying particles and white smoke belched outwards. Feeling as if she'd been punched in the chest, Eliza rubbed her watering eyes and leapt away from the rail. She couldn't see what had happened, but as the air trembled and the smoke cleared a little her mother gasped.

'Mummy, what is it?' Eliza cried out. 'What is happening?'

No reply.

'Mummy!'

But it seemed as if her mother could not hear. All Eliza knew was that something had flown through the air and now she didn't know what to do. She gazed at the stunned crowd in confusion. Why didn't her mother answer her? She pulled Anna's sleeve and saw that her mother's knuckles were white as she gripped the railing.

Down below the crowd had now surged forward, and through the cloud of dust Eliza saw soldiers running towards the Viceroy from every direction. A terrible smell of burnt metal and something chemical made it hard to breathe. She coughed and then pulled at her mother's sleeve again.

'Mummy!' Eliza shrieked.

But her mother was staring, white-faced, wide-eyed, completely frozen.

In a strange state of suspended animation, Anna seemed only aware that across the street the woman in green had fainted. Eliza saw her too but didn't know why her mother kept pointing at the woman. All she knew was that a horrible feeling in her stomach was making her want to cry.

'Daddy's all right, isn't he, Mummy?'

Finally, Anna noticed her. 'I don't know, darling.'

And though it seemed as if she only had eyes for the woman across the street, Anna had seen her husband stagger in his seat, then lurch forward. For a moment he had seemed to straighten up and even smile at Eliza, but then he had slumped forward again and this time remained motionless. The servant holding the state umbrella for the Viceroy had fallen sideways too, and was now hanging tangled in the ropes of the *howdah*.

Eliza, meanwhile, only had one thought and that was for her father. He was all right. He had to be all right. Suddenly she knew what to do, and giving up on her mother she turned on her heels, ran down the stairs and out into the street, where she collided with a young Indian boy who seemed not much older than her. Unable to find the words, she stared at the boy in a state of disbelief. 'My daddy,' she whispered.

The boy took her hand. 'Come away. There isn't anything you can do.'

But Eliza had to see her father. She shook the boy off and pushed her way through the crowd. When she reached the front she froze. The elephant was so terrified it refused to kneel, and Eliza watched in utter dismay as another English officer positioned a ladder on a packing case from a nearby shop so that her father could be lifted down. After they had done it they laid him on the pavement. At first his body looked unmarked, though his face was translucent like ice, and his eyes were wide open in shock. Eliza tripped over her feet and almost fell as she ran to kneel by his side. She stared in horror, then flung her arms around him, her dress soaking up the blood now seeping from the one person in the world she loved above all others.

'I'm afraid he didn't stand a chance, poor bugger,' someone was saying. 'Screws, nails, gramophone needles, glass. It looks like that's what the bastards used in the bomb. Something got him straight in the chest. Almost a fluke, I'd say. But if we have to tear Chandni Chowk to the ground we'll get the so-called freedom group who did this.'

Eliza continued to wrap her arms around her father and with her mouth to his ear she whispered, 'I love you, Daddy.' And forever afterwards she would tell herself that he had heard.

Then, above the growing whispers of the crowd, the young boy gently spoke. 'Please, Miss, let me help you up. He is gone.'

As Eliza glanced up at him, everything seemed to have become unreal.

PART ONE

'Far away from us in dreams and in time,
India belongs to the ancient Orient of our soul.'

– André Malraux, *Anti-Memoirs*, 1967

I

*The princely state of Juraipore, Rajputana,
in the Indian Empire*

November 1930

For just a moment Eliza caught a glimpse of the façade of the castle. It shocked her, the way it shimmered – a mirage conjured from the desert haze, alien and a little frightening. The wind stuttered and then picked up again and, for a moment, she closed her eyes to shut out this trembling extension of the sand. No matter how far from home, and without the faintest idea of how things would work out, there could be no turning back, and she felt the fear in the pit of her stomach. At the age of twenty-nine this would be her biggest commission since setting up as a professional photographer, though it was still unclear to her why Clifford Salter had chosen her. However, he had explained that she might be better placed to photograph the women of the castle, as many were still nervous of outsiders, and especially men. And the Viceroy had particularly asked for a British photographer to guard against conflicted loyalties. She would be paid monthly, with a lump sum for successful completion.

She opened her eyes on air thick with the glitter of sand and dust, the castle hidden from view once more, and above her the seamless blue sky, merciless in its heat. The escort leading her towards the city twisted round to tell her to hurry. She bowed her head against the stinging and climbed back into his camel-pulled cart, clasping her camera bag to her chest. Above all else she must not allow sand to damage her precious cargo.

Closer to their destination she raised her eyes to see a fortress stretching across the mountain top, dream-like. A hundred birds swooped across the lilac horizon, threads of pink cloud tracing delicate patterns high above them. Almost drugged by the heat, she struggled not to fall victim to the enchantment; she was here to work, after all. But if it wasn't the wind calling up the distant past as she hunched up against it, it was her own more recent memories.

When Anna Fraser had contacted Clifford Salter, a wealthy godson of her husband's, she had thought that with his connections he might find her daughter a position as a clerk in a solicitor's office in Cirencester, or something of that kind. She had hoped it would prevent her daughter from trying to make her way as a photographer. After all, she would say, who wants a woman photographer? But someone did and that had been Clifford, who said she'd be ideal and would suit his purposes perfectly. Anna couldn't object. He was the British Crown representative, after all, and answered only to the Rajputana Chief Political Officer or AGG, who exercised indirect rule over all twenty-two princely states. He, the Residents, and the minor political officers from the smaller states all belonged to the political department directly under the Viceroy.

So now Eliza faced a year inside a castle where she knew no one. Her commission was to photograph life in the princely state for a new archive to mark the seat of British Government finally moving from Calcutta to Delhi. The building of New Delhi had taken much longer than expected, and the war had delayed everything, but now the time had finally arrived.

She'd heard her mother's warnings about the sufferings of the people and saw that outside the huge walls of the castle urchins played in the dust and dirt. She spotted a beggar woman sitting cross-legged near a sleeping cow and gazing ahead with empty eyes. Beside her bamboo scaffolding leaning against a high wall blew perilously, with two planks of wood coming loose right above a naked child squatting on the ground beneath.

'Stop,' she called out and, as the cart rumbled to a standstill, she leapt out, just as one of the planks began slipping from its tethers. With her heart pounding, she reached the child and pulled him from harm's way. The wood fell to the ground and splintered into several pieces. The child ran off and the cart driver shrugged. Didn't they care, she wondered, as they climbed the ramp.

A few minutes later the cart driver stood arguing with the guards outside the fortress. They were not obliging, even though he'd shown them the papers. Eliza looked up at the forbidding frontage, and the enormous gated entrance wide enough for an army to pass through; camels, horses, carriages too. She'd even heard that the ruler had several cars. Meanwhile the vehicle she had been travelling in had broken down, and continuing by camel cart meant Eliza was tired, thirsty and coated in dust. She could feel it in her sore eyes, and in her itching scalp. She couldn't help scratching, though it only made things worse.

Eventually a woman appeared at the gates, a long wispy scarf covering her face and revealing only her dark eyes.

'Your name?'

Eliza told her who she was and shaded her own eyes against the piercing afternoon sun.

'Follow.'

The woman nodded at the guards, who looked disgruntled but allowed them both through. It had been eighteen years since Eliza and her mother had left India for England. Eighteen years of ever-decreasing possibilities for Anna Fraser. But Eliza had made the decision to be free. To her it seemed like a second birth, as if a hidden hand had brought her back, though of course there was nothing hidden about Clifford Salter. He might have been more attractive had there been, but a more ordinary man it would be hard to find. Thinning sandy hair and moist, myopic pale blue eyes reinforced the impression of dullness, yet she was indebted to him for arranging this job for her in the land of the Rajputs, noble warrior clans in this cluster of princely states in the desert region of the Indian Empire.

Before walking through a series of glorious archways, Eliza dusted herself down as best she could. A eunuch led her through a maze of tiled rooms and corridors to a small vestibule. She'd heard of these castrated men in feminine dress and she shuddered. The vestibule was guarded by women who stood glaring at Eliza as they barred her way through wide sandalwood doors inlaid with ivory. When, after some explanation from the eunuch, they eventually allowed her to pass, they left her to wait alone. She glanced around at the room, every inch of it painted in clear cerulean blue with the patterns picked out in gold. Flowers, leaves, filigree scrolls rose up the walls and trailed across the ceiling; even the stone floor had been carpeted in matching blue. Although the colour was bright, there was a delicate beauty about the overall effect. Wrapped up in the blueness she felt almost a part of the sky.

Was she expected to announce her arrival in some way? Cough politely? Call out? She wiped her clammy hands on her trousers and put down her bag of heavy photographic equipment, then, after a moment of uncertainty, picked it up again. Hair knotted at the nape of her neck, and drab khaki trousers with a crisp white blouse – now limp – only magnified her feeling of being out of place. She'd never fit in with so much alluring colour and pattern. She had spent most of her life pretending to fit in, talking about things that didn't matter, feigning interest in people she didn't like. She had tried so hard to be like the other girls and then other women, yet the feeling of not belonging had followed her even into her marriage with Oliver.

In a glowing orange room, beyond the blue vestibule, streams of sunshine from a small rectangular window lit the dust motes floating in the air. Beyond it she could see a corner of another room; that one deep red in colour and where the carved walls of the *zenana* proper began. She knew the *zenanas* of the royal Rajputana palaces had long been forbidden to non-royal men. Clifford had explained how these women's quarters – he called them harems – were steeped in mystery and intrigue; places of scheming, gossip and unbridled eroticism, he said, all the women having been trained in the 'sixteen arts of being a woman'. Rife with multiple copulation and moral degeneration, he'd said with a wink, even with the priests, or maybe especially with the priests, though the British officers who preceded him had worked to eradicate the darker sexual practices of the *zenana*.

Eliza wondered what the sixteen arts were? Perhaps if

15

she'd known them her marriage might have been more of a success, but, remembering the solitariness of her life with Oliver, she snorted at the thought.

A cloying oriental perfume, surely containing cinnamon, and maybe ginger, plus something intoxicatingly sweet, wafted from the red room, confirming everything she'd heard about the *zenana*. Because of it she felt trapped and longed to step forward to the window, pull back the white billowing curtain and lean out to breathe fresh air.

Her arms were beginning to ache and she bent down to place the heavy baggage on the carpet, this time against the wall where a peacock-shaped lamp sat atop a marble column. At the sound of a deep cough Eliza glanced up and then quickly straightened and smoothed down the strands of hair escaping her carefully placed pins. Her thick long hair, inclined to frizz, was a lifetime's battle to keep under control. She swallowed a flash of anxiety at the sight of an extremely tall man standing in silhouette in front of the window.

'You are British?' the man said and she stared, startled by his impeccable English.

As he stepped forward the light fell across his face. The man was Indian and looked immensely strong. His clothing was covered in red and orange dust, and some kind of large hooded bird rested on his right elbow.

'Should you be here?' she said. 'Isn't this the entrance to the *zenana*?'

She stared at deep-set eyes the colour of amber, fringed by impossibly dark lashes, and wondered why he wasn't wearing a turban. Didn't all Rajput men wear them? His dark skin was gleaming and his shiny chestnut hair was pushed back from his face in a loose wave.

'I think you should look for the tradesmen's entrance,' she added, wanting him to be gone and thinking he must be a merchant of some kind, though in truth he looked more like a gypsy or travelling minstrel. A trickle of sweat ran down under her armpits; now it was not only her hands feeling sticky.

At that moment an older Indian woman entered the room wearing the traditional garments: the long full skirt known as a *ghagra*, with a neat blouse and a billowing scarf, or *dupatta*, that floated as she moved, the colours a clashing mixture of vermilion, emerald and scarlet threaded with gold, and yet together they worked beautifully. A cloud of sandalwood wafted around her, along with an air of hushed calm, and, as she pulled a rope behind the marble column, the peacock lamp sprang to life, showering blue and green light to glitter over her hands. Then she took a few steps towards Eliza, and made a slight bow with hands pressed together, palms touching and fingers pointed upwards, with dozens of jewelled rings, and the manicured nails polished in silver.

'*Namaskār*, I am Laxmi. You are the photographer, Miss . . .'

'I . . . I am Eliza Fraser.' She bowed her head, not certain if a curtsey was in order. After all, this woman had been Maharani, or queen, and was mother to the ruler of Jurai-pore. Clifford had told her that the woman's beauty and intelligence were legendary and that along with her deceased husband, the old Maharajah, she had been responsible for modernizing many of the customs of the state. Her hair was plaited and then wrapped in a coil at the nape of her long elegant neck, her cheekbones were pronounced, and her dark eyes sparkled. Eliza saw that the woman's reputation for beauty was based on truth but wished she'd asked Clifford to explain more about protocol. All he'd said was keep an eye out for moths and white ants. The moths would eat her clothes and the ants the furniture.

Laxmi turned to the man. 'And you? I see you have brought that bird in here again.'

With a shrug that had the look of familiarity, the man raised his brows. Eliza noticed they were dark and thick.

'You mean Godfrey,' he said.

'What kind of a name is that for a hawk?' the woman said.

The man laughed and winked at Eliza. 'My classics master at Eton was called Godfrey, and a fine man he was too.'

'Eton?' Eliza said, in surprise.

Laxmi sighed deeply. 'May I present my second and most wayward son, Jayant Singh Rathore.'

'Your son?'

'Do you only repeat what is said to you, Miss Fraser?' Laxmi said with a rather arch look. But then she smiled. 'You are nervous, so it is understandable. But I'm happy you are here to photograph our lives. For a new archive in Delhi, I'm told.'

At the mention of her work Eliza came to life and spoke with spirit. 'Yes, Clifford Salter wants informal shots to show what life is really like. So many people are fascinated by India and I hope I might get some pictures into the better photographic magazines. The *Photographic Times* or the *Photographic Journal* would be perfect.'

'I see.'

'A complete guide to life in a princely state over the course of a year. I'm so looking forward to being here. Thank you for inviting me. I promise not to get in the way, but there's so much I want to see and the light is incredible.

It's all about the light and shade. You know, the chiaroscuro, and I hope to be able . . .'

'Yes, yes, I'm sure. As for my son, you'll find that once he's cleansed the desert dust from his clothing he is not as forbidding as he looks at present.' She laughed. 'Admit it. You thought he was a gypsy?'

Eliza could feel the blush creep up her neck at her own dust-coated appearance, and though it wasn't the hottest season she felt the heat.

'Don't worry, when he's been out in the desert for days on end, everyone thinks that.' She sniffed. 'Thirty years old, addicted to danger and prefers the wild to us civilized folk. Hardly any wonder he's not married yet.'

'Mother,' he said, and Eliza picked up a warning note in his voice. After that he went to pull aside the curtain and lean against the window with a look of indolent disinterest on his face.

Laxmi's frustration with her son showed in the quiver of her chin, but she recovered herself quickly and turned to Eliza. 'Now, your equipment?'

'This is some of it. The rest is following in a cart.' Eliza waved vaguely in the direction where she assumed the cart might be.

'I'll have it taken to your rooms. You'll be staying here where we can keep an eye on you.'

Suddenly daunted, Eliza must have shown her anxiety, for the woman laughed again. 'I'm teasing you, my dear. You shall be free to come and go within the castle just as you please. We have followed the Resident's requests to the letter.'

'That's very kind.'

'It is nothing to do with kindness. It's in our own

interests to try to oblige the British Government when we can. Relationships have been tricky in the past, I admit, but I am trying to bring my influence to bear on certain factions within the castle. Anyway, enough of us. You have your own darkened workroom with access to water as requested, and you'll find your personal rooms are most comfortable and overlook a pretty courtyard full of potted palms.'

'Thank you. Clifford told me he had made the arrangements with you. But I was expecting . . . well, a small place of my own.'

'That wouldn't do at all. In any case, our guest house in the town is undergoing renovation. And not only that; we may have removed purdah here in Juraipore, but there are many who still believe women should remain behind the veil. We can't have you scampering about in the wild on your own.'

'I'm sure I'd be all right,' Eliza said, though she was not sure at all.

'No, my dear. The British think they alone are responsible for bringing us women into the light but, to be perfectly frank, I only ever paid lip service to the custom of purdah and, after his mother died, my husband readily acquiesced to my requests for its removal. The submission and ignorance of women suited most men. Luckily for me my husband was not one of them.'

'What will I do outside the castle walls?'

'Be accompanied at all times, of course. And that brings me to your first assignment. Now that we are well into the month of Kartik, Jayant here has kindly offered to accompany you on a trip to the Chandrabhaga camel fair. The day after tomorrow. You will be accompanied by servants following behind. I'm sure my son will enjoy using his English and you'll enjoy the fair. I understand there will be camels of many colours and many interesting faces to record. And tomorrow you will accompany Mr Salter to a polo match.'

Eliza's nerves got the better of her. She wasn't keen on the polo match or the camel fair. She wanted to get settled and find her feet before dashing off anywhere else and especially accompanied by this Prince, if that was what he really was. She attempted a smile but her mouth tightened. 'I was hoping to see more of the castle first,' she said, noticing that the Prince was watching with a curious expression, the hawk still on his arm.

'Mother, I think you might have met your match,' he said.

While he was speaking Eliza thought she heard something new in his voice. Was he teasing her? Or was he teasing his mother?

Laxmi made a ladylike sort of a splutter and Eliza had the distinct impression that she considered meeting her match to be highly unlikely. 'Plenty of time to see the castle. The fair is not to be missed, you will see something of the countryside and you will meet Indira there. I'll get the maidservant, Kiri, to show you to your quarters.'

'You allowed Indira to go on ahead, mother? That's trouble in the making.'

'I've sent a reliable man and a handmaiden with her, and in any case the girl knows her camels.'

The sun must have moved, because now long rays of light had fallen across the floor. Laxmi had been open and amicable but Eliza could sense you wouldn't want to cross her. When she left the room, every inch a queen, the man bowed quite formally. And now that Eliza was the one observing *him*, she took in a strong face, defined by high

cheekbones, much like his mother's, but much more mas-
culine, an intelligent brow, the eyes as before, wide set and
amber, plus a moustache. When he glanced her way with a
stern expression she dropped her gaze.

'We didn't invite you,' he said quite calmly. 'We acquiesced to an order that we must allow you access to the castle
and escort you to other locations. There are many such
orders from the British.'

'Ordered by Clifford Salter?'

'Indeed.'

'And you always accede to his orders?'

'I . . .' He paused, then changed the subject, but she'd had
the distinct impression he'd been on the verge of saying
more. 'My mother wants a chocolate-coloured camel.'

'There are chocolate-coloured camels?'

'Mainly at Chandrabhaga. You'll like it. Few British go.
And with your camel-coloured hair you'll fit in nicely.'

He smiled, but she stiffened slightly and ran a hand over
her hair. 'I prefer to think of it as honey-coloured.'

'Well, this is Rajputana.'

'And Indira. May I ask who she is?'

'There's a question . . . just nineteen but a law unto herself. You'll find Indira very photogenic.'

'Your sister?'

He turned to look out of the window now. 'No relative at
all. She is a very talented miniaturist. An artist. She lives
here under my mother's protection.'

Eliza heard the sound of children's voices as they laughed
and shrieked somewhere out beyond the window.

'My nieces,' he said, and waved at them before twisting
back to look at Eliza. 'Three of the little darlings, but no
nephews, much to my brother's eternal shame.'

A youngish woman padded into the room and indicated that Eliza should follow. Eliza picked up her bag, feeling annoyed. How could he say such a thing right in front of her? Did he really believe that having only girl children was somehow shameful?

'Leave it. Someone will bring it to you.'

'I may only be a woman but I'd rather take it myself.'

He inclined his head. 'As you wish. Be ready at six the day after tomorrow. Not too early for you?'

'Of course not.'

He appeared to be scrutinizing her. 'Do you have any female clothing?'

'If you mean dresses, yes, but when I'm working I've found trousers to be far the best.'

'Well, I shall enjoy getting to know you, Miss Fraser.'

His indulgent smile irritated her more than it ought. Who was this arrogant man to judge her? Lazy, spoilt, aimless no doubt, like all the Indian royal men. And the more she considered it the more irritable she became.

Eliza woke early the next day. Her curtains were flimsy and the sun was already bright enough to force her to shield her eyes as she jumped out of bed and went to gaze out of the window. She had the strange sensation that, despite all the intervening years, something of this oriental country still coursed through her blood and had remained deep inside her. Just the smell of its soil stirred distant memories, and she had woken many times during the night feeling as if something was calling her. The air carried the fragrance of the desert sands and she breathed in the chill morning, feeling exhilarated and nervous.

The view of the courtyard was as promised and she

smiled at monkeys leaping from tree to tree and playing on the most enormous swings she had ever seen. Because the castle – just one part of the gigantic fort – sat high on the vast craggy sandstone hilltop rising above the gilded city, the vista across the flat rooftops below took her breath away and she hugged herself in delight. Small cubic houses, snuggling close to the fortress walls, were shining a deep burnished ochre, but the more distant houses faded gradually to pale silver at the horizon, where the town gave way to desert. It was a child's paintbox of every sublime shade of gold and honeysuckle under the sun. Dotted in among the houses, dusty trees reached up to the light, and above the whole city great clouds of birds swooped and dived.

It was cool now, but Eliza suspected that by the afternoon the temperature would reach the mid-seventies or even higher and there would be little chance of rain. She wondered what to wear for a polo match and decided on a long-sleeved shirt with a heavy gabardine skirt. What to pack for India had troubled her for weeks before she began the long journey by ship. Her mother had been hopeless, and seemed only to recall the evening dresses she had used to wear during their time in India before her husband, Eliza's father, had been killed. Eliza remembered so little of those days but even now a lump came into her throat when she thought of him.

Life hadn't been easy, and then, after her husband Oliver died, Eliza had returned to live at home, where she'd found Anna constantly hiding secret gin bottles, usually under her bed or beneath the kitchen sink. Anna persistently denied her own behaviour and sometimes could not even recall her episodes of heavy drinking. In the end Eliza had given up hope. That they knew Clifford Salter had been a lucky twist of fate, and by coming to India Eliza had sought to move forward, yet here she was still looking back, and not just to thoughts of her mother.

She glanced around her room. It was large and airy, the bed hidden behind a screen, and one corner had been set up as a little sitting room with a large armchair and a comfy-looking sofa, behind which an arch led to a small dining room. There was no sign of moths or ants. Another decorative archway in the wall opposite her four-poster bed led through to a lavish bathroom. The door to her dark-room was outside in the gloomy corridor and she was happy that it had been confirmed that only she would have the key.

As she laid out her clothes she thought about her arrival the evening before, just as a brilliant sunset had reddened the sky. The temple bells had been ringing and two girls, zooming along on roller skates, had almost taken the legs from under her. They shrieked and giggled and apologized in Hindi, and Eliza, pleased she had more or less understood them, was grateful to the old Indian ayah who had taught her. The lessons she'd recently taken to bring the language back had helped too.

Soon after that an immaculately gloved servant, wearing a white uniform and a red turban, had brought her bowls of dahl, rice and fruits on a silver tray and, after unpacking, she'd been grateful for an early night. Had it not been extraordinarily noisy she would have fallen asleep instantly, tired from the long journey from England, plus the ongoing trek to Delhi, and then another day's journey to Juraipore. But noisy it had been. Music, laughter, birds calling, frogs belching and children up until all hours: all of it drifting through her window along with the shrieking of peacocks – a sound more like cats howling – and all of it punctuating her night.

She had lain awake helpless beneath the intoxication of a Juraipore night: the drums, the reed pipes, the smoke in the air, but more than anything it was the ever-present sense of life being lived to the full in spite of poverty and the harsh desert world.

Unable to stop her mind spinning, she thought of her father and her husband. Would she ever be ready to forgive herself for what had happened? She must if she was to make the most of this chance in a lifetime, and she could not risk having to crawl back to her mother with her tail between her legs. Eliza hardly dared admit that she had come to rediscover something within herself, something she'd lost the day they had left for England.

2

The day was blazingly hot and Eliza soon felt sticky and overdressed. This was a day for muslin summer dresses, not heavy linens, though Clifford wore a linen suit with collar and tie. It was a smaller affair than she'd been expecting, rather more like a garden party than anything else, but with a sprinkling of supporters already gathering on both sides – some sitting on chairs – there was a definite air of excitement. Eliza had never been to a polo match before and the ground, surrounded by trees and iron railings with a view of the hills in the background, was idyllic.

'At least it's dry here,' Clifford said. 'Unlike England, where muddy fields are a problem.'

He told her the British team consisted of army officers from the 15th Lancers, and they appeared to have brought with them a crew of highly vocal supporters, many of whom seemed to have already been drinking. There were a few other military types too, complete with their servants, and also a couple of kitted-out additional players should the day's play require them.

Eliza waited beside Clifford and watched the small crowd. Just past the main group of British supporters, a man and a tall woman stood arm in arm. The woman glanced across and smiled. Clifford, noticing, whispered that she was Dottie Hopkins, the doctor's wife. 'You'll meet them both later,' he added. 'Good people.'

The woman looked friendly and Eliza was pleased at the

thought of them being introduced. In the other direction a large noisy group of Indian supporters were gathering, again accompanied by a swarm of servants in formal dress, and now Eliza's eyes were glued to them.

'Although this is known as the game of kings, Anish, the ruler, rarely attends these days,' Clifford was saying. 'Prince Jayant is the one to watch. He has superb horsemanship skills and is a great team player. If he's in the team today we'll have a match on our hands.'

'Do these games take place often?'

'The big ones are part of a regular tournament, but this is just a small friendly for our own entertainment. Jaipore have the best reputation, you know. Won the Indian Championship this year, but Juraipore are coming up fast behind.'

'That's wonderful.'

'And we still aim to triumph. Wave the flag and all that.'

Soon after that the players arrived, looking smart and straight-backed as they walked on to the field. Then the proud-looking grooms led the ponies on, and the crowd began to clap, though Clifford was quick to explain that these were not really ponies but full-sized horses.

'It's a terribly expensive sport. The ponies are worth thousands.'

Eliza watched the team members mount – they all looked incredibly powerful – and just as she spotted that Prince Jayant was among them, he began to seat himself on a magnificent black horse. Now a roar went up from the delighted crowd, followed by persistent cheering and whistles from the Indian supporters.

Clifford drew closer to Eliza. 'He always draws a crowd. And his pony has a brilliant temperament. You really have to rely on the animal not to become over-excited. Now see those two chaps?'

Eliza looked in the direction he was pointing.

'The umpires. There's a referee too, in case of disagreement. Polo is all about fair play.'

So far this was good fun, and Eliza was pleased to be out in the open air and enjoying the novelty, despite her earlier reservations. She watched as the two teams lined up facing each other, their polo sticks at the ready, and then, as soon as the ball was struck, the game began. An intense atmosphere developed as clouds of dust rose up from the hard ground and the horses thundered along, but among the swooping and dipping it soon became apparent that the Prince's pony seemed to be pulling back.

'Is that supposed to happen?' she asked.

Clifford frowned. 'Does seem a bit frisky.'

She continued to watch the men on their ponies and then, glancing at the Indian crowd, saw that a couple of men in formal dress and with curved swords at their waists had stepped forward as if in expectation of trouble. She held her breath, but after that nothing happened and the game went on. Eliza watched in fascination, barely listening as Clifford explained the rules of polo to her and the different terminology.

It was only a few minutes later that something seemed to be really going wrong with the Prince's horse.

'My God!' Clifford exclaimed as it began to trot back and forth in a prancing, out-of-control manner, and then to actually buck.

Eliza noticed the mixed expression on Prince Jayant's face – annoyance, though puzzlement had the upper hand. There were murmurings among the British and the Indians too and then loud shouting as Jayant's saddle began to slide to one side and, within seconds, he was lying on his back on the ground, the horse running wild. The rest of the players stood completely still and everyone watched in horror as two grooms ran after the panicking horse. Eliza held her breath and clutched Clifford's arm as it bolted into the crowd of Indian supporters, many of whom shouted and flapped their arms in shock, while others ran to escape. Suddenly there was a high-pitched scream and a woman fell backwards against the railings. As the horse kicked out again and again, Eliza could feel the fear; people were still running to get out of its path, but the woman, now lying on the ground silently, was not moving at all.

Eliza saw the doctor, whom Clifford had pointed out earlier, run to lean over the woman. Then he squatted by her side.

While the grooms eventually caught and then quietened the panicking horse, two men arrived with a canvas stretcher and the woman was carried off, followed by the doctor. Meanwhile the Prince was scrambling to his feet and dusting himself down, apparently unhurt, but looking absolutely livid, and then he left the field with the horse in tow. The two men with curved swords at their waists went after him and Eliza realized they must be his bodyguards.

The photographer in her was trained to see the details of a scene and she spotted an Indian man, probably a stable boy she thought, though he seemed to almost be sneaking from the stables and around the back of the Indian crowd and then over towards another man. The second man was tall, with a regal bearing. He clapped the stable man on the back and grinned broadly. It struck her as odd, considering their Prince had just been hurt. Despite the tense atmosphere, Eliza noticed two of the British supporters sniggering as they exchanged glances and winked at each other.

'What idiots! There's nothing amusing about this,' she said. 'For all we know that woman might be dead.'

'I'll hear soon enough from Julian Hopkins,' Clifford said.

Meanwhile the British were talking among themselves, untroubled, not seeming quite as shocked as they ought to have been, and without a hint of making a move to leave. But the Indian supporters were shaking their heads and muttering, several just turning their backs and walking away from the grounds.

'So the game will have to stop now,' Eliza said, sure that it must.

'No,' Clifford said. 'Look. A substitute for the Prince is already coming on. It's allowed in cases of injury.'

'Really? Isn't that rather callous?'

'The show must go on, Eliza.'

As she glanced around Eliza could feel the anxiety that had gripped the crowd begin to lessen, and she hoped the woman had survived.

'But this is a rum thing,' Clifford continued. 'Very rum. I've never seen anything like it. Though with the Prince gone I expect we shall now win the day. So that's something. I doubt he'll ride a different pony after all this.'

3

The following day Eliza and Jayant Singh left the marble halls and walked out into carved pink sandstone courtyards, gleaming and glittering in the pale early morning light; then on through interconnecting pavilions to a place where cooler breezes blew through scented gardens. Although Eliza was still thinking about the polo match, something about the grandeur made her stand up straighter, elongate her neck and walk with pride, and as she threw her scarf over her head it billowed out. With just that simple feminine action she felt as if she had momentarily stepped into the embroidered shoes of an Indian queen.

'This place almost looks as if it's made from sandalwood and not sandstone,' she said, as they reached a formal garden bordered by a wall where the culprits of last night's racket were strutting. Peacocks! When one took off from the wall and flopped its way to the ground, she laughed. Who knew beauty could be so ungainly?

'Planted in the eighteenth century,' the Prince said, indicating the rose bushes, cypresses, palms and orange trees.

They left the castle by way of a ramp that passed through seven arched gateways. On their way through one of the gates Eliza spotted five rows of hands sculpted on one of the side walls.

'Made from the *sati* handprints,' the Prince said, seeming utterly unconcerned. 'On their way to the funeral pyre the women dipped their hands in red powder and pressed their hands against the walls to express their devotion. Then later the prints were sculpted.'

Eliza gasped. 'That's horrible.'

'We call the woman who dies a *sati* and you British call the actual act suttee. It has been illegal in British India since 1829 and here in the princely states after that, with a ban for the whole of India issued by Queen Victoria in 1861. But still . . .'

She already knew about the ritual immolation of the widows of Rajput Princes, and the ordinary women too, but felt sick at the thought of it. Could they have truly believed widow-burning was an honourable way to die? It was almost impossible to comprehend how the women must have felt.

She gazed at the sandy lanes of the medieval city, packed tightly with craftsmen of every kind, and thought of her first sight of the immense walls with all these bastions and towers. She glanced back at the fort. Rising impregnable from a rocky hill, it was clearly built from stone chiselled out of the rock on which it stood. Who knew how many women from within those walls must have died on the fire?

They climbed into the car and after a while, as they left the city behind, Eliza gazed at the desert, where winds lifted the burning sands and thickened the air. For mile after mile of flat plains, the road ribboned through a sun-bleached landscape, with sparse acacias and thorn bushes only intermittently punctuated by patches of lush green. It was a lonely, empty place, and Jayant Singh was silent, clearly concentrating on driving along barely distinguishable roads. Eliza excused his silence; however, a man who took up so much mental and physical space was not somebody you could wholly ignore. She sensed a kind of wildness in him. It bothered her, and she felt tense and awkward, but tried to make conversation; only his taciturn responses meant she eventually gave up and sank back into reverie, allowing the assault on her senses to engulf her. Then, just as she was slipping into a daydream of palaces, gardens and swinging monkeys, and at the precise moment the face of her father was about to appear, Jayant began to talk.

'My saddle had been tampered with,' he said, and, at the sound of his warm smoky voice, she came to with a jolt. 'I saw you at the polo yesterday. I'm sure you must be wondering.'

'I was sorry to see what happened. How do you know? About the tampering, I mean?'

'The billet strap had been split. I checked it the day before but arrived too late to check again yesterday. The billet is the most vulnerable part of the girthing mechanism. I should have checked again.'

'And that caused the horse to buck?'

'No, that was down to the prickly acacia hooks some idiot placed under the saddle.'

'Oh God! You mean actual sabotage.' She thought of the two Indian men who had looked so shifty. 'You might have been killed.'

He smiled. 'Broken something more like, but as you can see I'm fine. However, my horse might have been killed. I can't forgive that, and as for that poor woman . . .'

'How is she?'

'She has concussion, I believe. Thankfully it wasn't worse.'

'That makes me so angry. It's horrible to think it was done wilfully.'

His voice deepened. 'Childish is what it is. My horse is a beauty, with stamina, agility and speed. That's what I care about, and God knows what more might have happened in the crowd. It gives polo a bad name.'

'What can you do about it?'

'I've complained to Clifford Salter and the polo authorities but we can't prove who did it. I have my suspicions, but they were just a motley visiting team and have departed now.'

Eliza kept her thoughts about seeing the two Indian men laughing to herself. Although the Prince had looked furious at the time, he seemed relatively philosophical about it now.

'So what is your interest in us, Miss Fraser?'

'You know what it is. I have a job to do.'

'Strange that Mr Salter chose an unknown woman.'

Eliza bristled. 'I'm not entirely unknown.'

A few moments of silence as she inwardly fumed.

'This is a journey of several days,' he continued, carelessly interrupting her thoughts.

'Well, I wish you'd told me. I've only brought one change of clothes.'

'As have I.'

'Do you not wash?'

He laughed out loud. 'If I had a pound for every time I've been asked that by a European. Tonight we will camp and tomorrow too. So no.'

'I didn't mean it like that.' She was sure he'd understood her perfectly but let it go. 'So? Camp where?'

'In the desert. But don't worry, you won't be alone, a servant girl will be with you. She and others are following.'

'And the tents?'

'Already organized. Some men have gone on ahead to set up. Every year, the Chandrabhaga fair of Jhalawar takes place in the Hindu month of Kartik. It is a state largely unexplored by the British, which is why my mother thought you might like to see it.'

'What about fuel for the car?'

He took one hand from the wheel and waved at the great outdoors. 'Here and there. Stopping points. It is arranged.'

'You normally come so far for your camels?'

'Very perceptive. And no, we go to Pushkar or Nagaur.'

'Then?'

'Business to attend to. During the fair pilgrims gather on the banks of the sacred river Chandrabhaga. You will also see forts, palaces, wildlife, and a peaceful lake where we have a summer palace left to us by a cousin. It's where we will eventually stay. You might also want to visit the ancient city of bells.'

'I'm not a tourist, it's people I want to photograph,' she said, feeling irritated. 'And anyway, that's what the Viceroy has asked for. Not amateur snaps. We are setting up archives in New Delhi. Clifford says it's about comparing life in the princely states with life in British India.'

'To our detriment, no doubt.'

She bristled. 'Not at all. Anyway, I'm hoping to be able to mount a small exhibition of my own if I can find sponsorship.'

'Well, be careful. Chatur will no doubt think you're a spy.' He laughed. 'Are you?'

Eliza felt her skin prickle with irritation. 'Of course not. Anyway, who is Chatur?'

'The *dewan*. He runs things.'

She remained silent.

'Traders from distant parts of Rajputana, Madhya Pradesh and Maharashtra meet at this fair. You will get your shots of people.'

'And Indira?'

'Yes, indeed.'

'Do you want to tell me about her?'

'Best you should see for yourself. By the way, I take back what I said about your hair. In the sunlight it is reddish or maybe gold, not camel-coloured.'

'Honey,' she muttered, but couldn't resist smiling.

They passed a few settlements huddled around their own wells and, now and then, small villages where peasants grew maize, lentils and millet, and when they passed herds of goats, sheep and even camels grazing on nutritious grasses, he spoke again.

He pointed to the land beyond his window. 'Where you see those grasses, *khimp* or *akaro*, you can tell that deep beneath there is water. Sometimes vast reserves of water. But it may be more than three hundred feet below.'

'I suppose drilling is expensive.'

He nodded. 'Some of the women walk miles every day to the big water tanks and reservoirs. I am interested in water. We are dependent on monsoons to fill reservoirs and this year we had little rain, not much last year either. Life can be harsh. You cannot conquer a desert, you can only do your best to protect it.'

'I need water to develop my photographs.'

'And that very thing may be your downfall.'

That night Eliza and the Prince sat cross-legged around a campfire with dignified men wearing colourful patterned turbans. The air was cool and soft, with a slight breeze carrying the scents of sand and dust that mingled with the spices from the cooking pot suspended over the fire. Surprised to be so readily accepted by them, she realized it was only because she was with Jayant. As he offered her a tall glass of milk, she noticed that his skin shone amber in the flickering firelight.

'Camel's milk,' he said. 'Very nutritious, but it sours rapidly so you have to drink it straight away. They never make it into cheese.'

She sipped the milk and agreed that it was good.

'But don't drink the *asha*, whatever you do.'

'What is it?'

He laughed. 'A powerful fermented drink. It'll knock your head off. I speak from experience.'

One of the men was playing some kind of drum, another softly ringing some prayer bells and, as smoke rose into the air, Eliza felt intoxicated by the utter timelessness of the scene. The servant girl who sat beside her would also be sharing her tent, so although Eliza felt a little nervous of being out in the wilderness with so many men, she didn't actually feel threatened.

The next day, after a surprisingly cool night sleeping on one of two *charpoys*, traditional woven beds, Eliza woke to a silvery dawn and the sound of voices. She stretched out, intending to enjoy the moment, but the aroma of food was too enticing and, as she was absolutely ravenous and the girl was already up, she threw on her clothes without a thought for washing and made her way out of the tent. And in those few moments the light had changed. A morning of extraordinary beauty greeted her, the sky blushing deepest pink on the horizon, rising to pale peach, with not a cloud in sight. The delicate light cast a gentle glow over the flat land that seemed to stretch for miles, filling her with a sense of endless spaciousness. She spotted what she assumed was a temporary goatherd's dwelling constructed from wooden poles, with just a tarpaulin of some kind thrown over for shade. It was surrounded by dozens of goats chewing on the sparse bushes and though the nomadic life must have compensations, Eliza thought it must be very lonely too.

She was pleasantly surprised to be greeted by a smiling Prince Jayant, the proud angles of his face softer than before. He held out a hand to indicate where they were to eat. But it wasn't just his face, everything about him had changed and she realized that this new relaxed person was a man born for the outdoors. He wore dark European-style trousers with just a loose open-necked shirt in deep green. Later she would ask if he minded her taking a photograph of him.

During a satisfying meal of dahl and rice cooked over the fire by one of the men, he laughed and joked with the others, didn't stand on ceremony and was clearly well liked. Eliza noticed the laughter wrinkles fanning out from his eyes, and thought the increased stubble on his chin and jaw added something that made him seem more accessible.

'Do you often camp?' she said.

'As often as I can. It's my escape, you see.'

'You need to escape?'

'Don't we all?'

She realized how true that was, but also how different he was today. 'You don't stand on ceremony. I thought you might, but you're no ordinary Prince, are you?'

He inclined his head. 'Maybe not, but one never really forgets where one comes from.'

'That's unfortunately correct.'

'I think you should see Udaipore at the start of the rainy season. It would be the best place to see the dark clouds rolling in. It's the city of lakes.'

'I've heard.'

'Maybe I'll accompany you there to take photographs,' he said. 'It is one of the most beautiful places in Rajputana.'

When they reached the foothills of the forested Aravalli range, Eliza stiffened at the sight of blue bulls wandering freely.

He laughed. 'Don't worry, Miss Fraser. They won't come near us. They're long accustomed to caravans of goods and people passing through since ancient times. We are part of the old trade routes that crossed this desert bringing goods from afar. In exchange we sold our sandalwood, copper, camels and gems.'

'I wish I could have seen it back then.'

'They were dangerous times, with the states constantly at war with each other. And life can be harsh out here.'

Eliza spotted a group of vultures on a rocky outcrop.

He grinned. 'See what I mean. You'd never have had a chance if you were taken ill back then.'

'Golly, perhaps I'm lucky to be here now.'

'No doubt about it. But look at how beautiful the landscape is. These hills stretch for miles and miles. The vegetation is mainly tropical thorn, and mixed deciduous and dry teak species, but I worry about future deforestation.'

'Is that likely?'

'It's already happening.'

As they talked more about life in Rajputana, the Prince seemed very relaxed. He clearly loved the land of his birth and, despite his British education, it was obvious that this was where he belonged. The early tension she'd felt when they set out the previous day had completely dissipated and by the end of the second day in his company, Eliza was feeling relatively content.

*

As they approached the fair on the final day they passed a man with an enormous handlebar moustache and a haunted look in his eyes. He was leading a camel on which a woman sat side-saddle, her red scarf billowing out but still covering her face and hair and with tinkling bangles circling her ankles. Clasped to her side was a tiny child with black hair sticking up around its head. The bright colours of their clothing stood out in sharp contrast to the incredible blue of the sky.

'Can you stop,' she said. 'I have to take a picture.' Though sadly the colours could never be seen in her monotone photographs.

'Ask the man's permission first,' Jayant said, and put his foot on the brake. 'I was told you speak the language. Though I have no idea how.'

'I lived in Delhi as a child.'

'No, wait,' he said, as Eliza opened the car door. 'Better if I ask. The dialect is different here.'

Prince Jayant climbed out, and after a dialogue with the other man during which both were smiling he handed over some coins and came back to the car.

'All set,' was all he said.

She took the photograph using her Rolleiflex, hoping she'd caught the haunted look of the man, and they continued on past a lake, disturbing enormous white birds with impossibly long beaks. As they took off in unison from the surface of the water, she gazed in wonder at their huge wingspan and the beautiful black feathers at their tips.

'How incredible!'

'Pelicans,' he said. 'You've not seen them before?'

'Not in the Cotswolds,' she said and could see that he smiled.

'The level is lower than it ought to be,' he said, as he gazed at the water.

When they neared the fair Eliza gasped at the sight of hundreds of camels spread across the flat land. Men sat in small groups beside smoking fires and, when the Prince stopped the car and she climbed out, the smell of smoke and dung was overpowering. She had expected to feel conspicuous, but the place was heaving and nobody noticed her.

'Don't stand near the back side of a camel,' he said with a grin as he pulled her aside. 'They are windy creatures. Grumpy too.'

On the other side of a narrow track she saw cattle, goats and horses. 'I didn't realize they traded all kinds of livestock here. How does anyone ever find what they want?'

'Camels have different qualities. If you know what you're looking for it's not difficult.'

'What are you looking for?'

'Ah,' he said, and with a wry smile on his face he paused. 'That might take a lifetime to understand. And another lifetime to explain.'

She glanced at him. There really was something of the philosopher about this man. When she looked back at the animals she saw that they were an assortment of different sizes and different colours and mentioned it to him.

'Just like us, wouldn't you say? There are hardy breeds and more delicate animals too. Let us look for Indira.'

Eliza stuck close to the Prince, wondering how she should address him. So far he insisted on calling her Miss Fraser and it made her feel uncomfortable. She had avoided calling him anything at all, so decided to ask.

'Call me Jay,' he replied. 'Everybody does.'

She frowned.

'Well, not everybody, but you may.'

'Isn't it rather informal?'

'I didn't expect you to be bound by tradition. You certainly aren't in your manner of dress. In fact it almost seems to me as if you dress with disregard.'

He was looking at her with an intent gaze and she was shocked to realize she felt indignant that he had somehow seen inside her. 'That's rather . . .'

'Not very British, you mean, but I am not British, despite the attempts of Eton to make me so.'

'Is that what they did?'

'What do you think?'

She looked at the ground before lifting her head, realizing that the shadows of the past could still be present even on the sunniest day. 'It's Mrs Cavendish, by the way. But I'm using my maiden name, Fraser, instead.'

He glanced at her ring finger.

Though shocked by the loss of Oliver, it was not the loss of true love. In the circumstances, how could it have been? But her father; that had been a knife to the heart; so deep she couldn't function. Couldn't eat. Couldn't sleep. And for several months could not even speak. And the knowledge of her own culpability had left her the victim of terrible nightmares.

'I'm a widow,' she said.

He raised his brows.

'I didn't intend to dissemble. It just happened.'

'Best keep it between us, I think. People still believe widows bring bad fortune and things have a way of getting out.'

'I'd prefer to tell Laxmi. She's been so kind and I don't want her to find out later and think I came here under false pretences.'

He shook his head. 'People believe that outliving your husband means you didn't look after him properly and that it's generally your own bad karma at fault.'

'As if I don't already feel bad enough.'

'You are expected to do penance for the sin, you are meant to eat only plain rice and never remarry, even though the law does now permit remarriage. It's antiquated, I know, but it could make life difficult for you. They would also expect you to wear white and shave your head.' He grinned at her.

'I thought those beliefs were dying out.'

He inclined his head and shrugged as if to refute what she'd said. 'And even though the British made suttee illegal it still happens. Old habits die hard, Miss . . . I mean Mrs Cavendish.'

'I think you'd better just call me Eliza.'

As he nodded a young woman brushed past Eliza and ran up to Jay, where she gave an exaggerated curtsey and then laughed. She was very slight and at first Eliza thought she must be a child, a relative of some kind, but then she saw the young woman's face: paler than Jay's, it was a face of such extraordinary beauty Eliza could only stare. The girl's loosely tied long hair floated down to her waist and her eyes were the most incredible green, not unlike Eliza's own greenish-grey eyes but lined with something dark. And yet where Eliza's were soft gentle English eyes, the colour of ponds, this girl had emeralds for eyes. They sparkled, catching the light while she laughed and chattered with enthusiasm. And joy, Eliza thought to herself. Sheer effervescent joy. She wore a nose jewel and was covered in bangles and necklaces. After a few moments Jay took hold of her hand and, smiling broadly, came across to Eliza.

44

'Indira,' he said. 'This is Eliza, Miss Fraser to you. Eliza, this is Indira.'

'Namaskār,' the girl said, and placed her palms together close to her chest.

Jay interrupted. 'She was educated at the castle and speaks good English, Eliza, so don't let her fool you.'

As the day faded, Jay drove the three of them back to the summer palace beside the lake. It wasn't as Eliza expected but was in rather a poor state of repair, with peeling walls within and crumbling walls without. He told her he owned a palace in a similar state of repair in Juraipore state, and that he was thinking of having it restored for the day when he would have a family of his own.

'It is called Shubharambh Bagh.'

Eliza knew *bagh* meant a place with a garden and orchard, specifically one containing fruit, and *shubharambh* meant auspicious beginnings.

'It could be beautiful there,' he continued. 'But it might be useful if you would consider taking photographs of it as it is.'

She nodded her agreement.

As he showed her around the predominantly blue and dusty arched hallways she gazed with genuine astonishment at beautifully crafted latticed screens with a design of foliage rising from a tall vase.

'The *jali*,' he said. 'These were the women's quarters. The openwork screens allowed the women to see out without being seen themselves.'

Eliza's first thought was that far from being kept behind a screen, Indira seemed keen to lead the way, occasionally placing a proprietorial hand on Jay's arm. Nothing demure about Indira, she decided. Was the girl signalling her prior claim on the man? She certainly had no shame about touching him occasionally and Eliza wondered if the two might be lovers, or if Indira was some kind of concubine. Or maybe they were just behaving as if they were siblings? Then she remembered Laxmi had said the girl was a miniaturist, an artist of great talent.

'We rarely use this place,' he said. 'So I am meeting a potential buyer while we're here to raise funds. On my brother's behalf. He doesn't like to travel.'

'You seem to have palaces everywhere.'

'My family does, but I have just the one. You will love the arcaded loggia there, or perhaps I'm exaggerating and should call it a porch. The floors are white marble, but are now sadly crumbling.' He sighed. 'The whole place needs much restoration.'

'It sounds beautiful.'

'I need light and air with room to breathe, which our main castle with its maze of corridors and dark staircases doesn't allow. On this point I fully agree with the British.'

On the terraced roof someone had laid out large cushions surrounded by flaming torches and on one side a screen of diaphanous curtains. The three made themselves comfortable and a feast of fruits, dahl, rice and meats was carried up by two young girls. Beneath the scattering of stars the scents of night drifted over and mingled with the aroma of food and their warm bodies. Touched by a disquieting sense of magic that surely had no place in the real world, Eliza gazed up. If anything the night shone brighter than the day, and, as the breeze gently blew, the screen of curtains fluttered. At risk of wanting to linger for ever, she had to remind herself she was not here to be seduced by the enchantment of

India, but rather to capture it, and that the romance of the desert could, at a moment's notice, be blackened by harsh sandstorms: that it could become the desert of death in the blink of an eye. And although the pulse of life beat strongly, if death lived on your doorstep it was little wonder you'd want to believe, as the Hindus did, that your life simply completed one leg of a journey towards oneness with the universe. At that moment Indira began to sing a sad lyrical-sounding song that touched Eliza so deeply, she couldn't prevent a rising sense of envy at yet another of this girl's talents.

4

'I'm sorry we didn't get to say hello at the polo match but I am so pleased to meet you,' the tall, dark-haired woman was saying as she held out a hand, her bright blue eyes shining with pleasure. 'Anyway, I'm Dottie. Dottie Hopkins.'

Eliza had arrived at a cocktail party consisting of a small gathering of British people, held at Clifford's villa on the smarter side of town. The interior, as she had expected, was elegant and filled with sunlight. The large French windows had been thrown open, the scent of freshly mown grass drifting in and mingling with cigar smoke. But for the heat she could have been in a British country house on a summer's day.

'Your husband did a good job with that poor woman,' Eliza said.

'Yes, it was all a bit awful really. She was incredibly lucky it wasn't worse. Did you stay to the end?'

'Yes, but because Clifford had to rush off when it finished, so did I.'

'He needed to investigate foul play, I imagine. My husband tells me there had been. Though it's all blown over now. They think it was something to do with those British hangers-on. Anyway, Clifford won't want a fuss made if it was down to one of us.'

Eliza remembered what she had thought she'd seen. It was probably nothing, but she would certainly keep her wits about her at the castle.

'Now, I hope we will become great friends. We live next door.' Dottie gave a little smile. 'So you know where to come, you know, if . . .'

'Indeed,' Eliza said, and returned Dottie's warm smile. The woman was possibly in her late thirties, had kind eyes, and a firm handshake.

'Clifford has told us so much about you.'

'Has he?' Eliza said and felt surprised.

'I do admire you. I'd be terrified to go off on my own as you have. I didn't even know women could be photographers. How did you get into it?'

Eliza smiled. 'We were on our honeymoon in Paris, my late husband, Oliver, and I, when we went to two or three exhibitions.'

'I'm so sorry for your loss.'

'Thank you . . . One of the exhibitions was photography. Something just clicked inside my head when I heard a woman photographer talking about her work, and when Oliver saw how enamoured I was he bought me my first camera as a wedding present. I owe it to him really, though I still have a lot to learn. Anyway, I hope to make a decent fist of it here.'

Dottie smiled. 'I'm sure you will.'

Eliza didn't speak but gave a little nod to acknowledge Dottie's comment.

'Well, you're brave. I can see that. What's it like? I'm positively itching to know.'

'The castle?'

'We haven't lived here that long but I've been there, of course, though just as a visitor, usually when there's a *durbar* or something like that. It must be utterly fascinating to live there.'

'I've not seen enough to be able to say much. People have been kind, so far.'

'Well, you know Clifford would do anything for you. He's so good like that. Helped Julian and me out so much when we first arrived . . . finding servants, that sort of thing.' She paused and pulled a bit of a face. 'Have you met the Maharani yet?'

'The Prince's wife?'

Dottie nodded. 'Priya.'

'Not yet.'

'I've heard gossip about her, and if the rumours are right, you'd better keep an eye out. For a man called Chatur too. From what I hear he manages the entire castle affairs.'

'Oh?' And Eliza remembered that Jayant had mentioned the man.

'Clifford does such a good job and, if you ask me, has the patience of a saint, but he's had endless trouble with this Chatur chappie. Digs his heels in. Won't follow orders. You know the usual type. Hates the British.'

They moved across to the window, where a table had been laid with canapés and jugs of fruit-filled punch. Dottie poured two glasses and then held up a plate of canapés. 'Shrimp all right for you?'

Eliza bent her head slightly to look at them.

'They're fine. Canned, of course. We're too far from the sea for anything else. You'll be offered mutton here and there, but of course it's actually goat. Stick to the vegetarian food at the castle. That's my advice. My husband has had to deal with a lot of upset British stomachs over the years, so I should know.'

'Thanks, but if you don't mind, I think I'll give the shrimp a miss,' Eliza said, and turned to survey the room, where she spotted a sturdy-looking man with a neat moustache smiling across at them.

Dottie clapped her hands. 'Oh look, there's Julian. You must meet him in a minute. He and Clifford are great pals and, as I get the impression Clifford thinks the world of you, I rather think we'll be seeing lots of you here.'

Eliza frowned. 'Really? Clifford knew me as a child but I've hardly seen him for years. At least, not until recently.'

Dottie smiled. 'Well, anyway, now you know where we are, do feel you can drop by. Any time.'

'That's very kind.' And Eliza really felt that it was, and, who knew, from time to time she might well need an escape into a familiar world she did, more or less, understand.

'The men often get up a table for poker,' Dottie said, then smiled again, almost apologetically. 'Well, it's awfully dull for me so you'd be most welcome. There are so few English-women in these parts.'

'I had rather intended immersing myself in the Indian world.'

'You'll need breaks. I'm sure of it. Now come and meet Julian. I'm sure you'll get on like a house on fire.'

The day after the cocktail party, Eliza developed her first photographs and was delighted by the results, especially the early shot of the man with the haunted look in his eyes and the child with its black hair sticking up. There had been something eternal about the man, dignified and yet sad too. She loved the way a photograph could tell an entire story and preserve it in a single moment. She hoped she'd be able to take more pictures inspired by her heart and not just by her head, and, if she could manage to get out and about and grasp something of the mysterious quality of the ordinary people, she'd be happy.

She had received a hand-written message from Chatur, whom she still hadn't met, informing her that the first photographs had to be of the royal family, as anything else would be most disrespectful. She had been planning to do that anyway, so she didn't mind. It would be a clear record of who was who before she attempted shooting in the more intimate recesses of the castle. And while Clifford would probably only be concerned that she captured everything for the archives, she was determined to use her creativity.

A red-turbaned courtier wearing white directed her to a spacious courtyard surrounded on three sides by the screened balconies of the *zenana*. While the women of the *zenana* were no longer restricted by the veil, many still remained behind the screens, and a tingle of apprehension ran through her when she realized everything she did was being watched.

A tall upright man with an impressive moustache, heavy untrimmed eyebrows and baggy shadows under his eyes walked towards her. She could have sworn this was the same tall man she'd seen laughing at the polo match after the Prince's accident. She had wondered about mentioning it to Clifford, but, worried she was probably adding two and two and making five, hadn't wanted to look naïve.

'I am Chatur, the *dewan* or senior court official,' he offered in a haughty tone of voice. He didn't wait for her to reply nor hold out a hand, but carried on imperiously. 'I have the final say on what does and what does not have a place in the castle. I organize everything. Do you understand? Everything you wish to do must go through me.'

Though a commoner, the man had the stern bearing of a king and, Eliza decided, he was clearly a man who thought a great deal of himself. She held his gaze, though it wasn't easy, and she had to force herself not to shrink from something shady in his dark eyes. That he had a reputation she'd already heard from Dottie, and his attitude now seemed to prove it. He looked as if he was scrutinizing her, though she had no idea if there was a particular reason or not.

'If you follow my guidelines you will find I can be very helpful, Miss Fraser. If not, well . . .' He spread his hands in a shrug.

'I understand,' she said, deciding that to acquiesce was the best policy, at least for now.

'We shall be seeing a lot of each other,' he said, giving her something resembling a half smile. 'I expect you to ensure the association is a harmonious one. We don't appreciate strangers poking their noses into castle affairs.'

'I can assure you I won't be poking my nose, as you put it. I'm only here to take photographs.'

'So you say, Miss Fraser. So you say. I shall be keeping a strict eye on you.' And after that he spun on his heels and left.

The short exchange hadn't helped vanquish Eliza's nervousness, but she resolved not to brood.

She had considered a number of locations that might provide the right light, but had been told this was the only time and place she would be allowed, and she had been given just a thirty-minute period in which to take the shots. She'd also needed to consider the background, preferring something simple to allow the eye to focus on the subjects of the picture, the people. It turned out most of her ideas had been vetoed by Chatur as 'highly unsuitable'. The result was that the photographs would have to be taken against an elaborately decorated wall. This would require care.

As soon as she had identified the optimal position for the camera, she began to assemble her equipment. Today she would use her large field camera, a Sanderson 'Regular'. Though not large compared with many plate cameras, she had brought it with her as the best compromise between a lighter weight, and obtaining the quality of image she sought. She also always carried her trusty Rolleiflex for hand-held opportunities. Luckily the Sanderson's rise and fall, while tilting the front plate, gave her control over perspective and the plane of focus she needed to enable her subjects to stand out.

It took a while to set up, as it required a heavy mahogany and brass tripod, and possibly the use of flash powder to provide a bright burst of light. She mounted her Agfa flash lamp on a second tripod and attached the remote release, consisting of a long rubber tube with a rubber bulb that she would squeeze. That bit of pressure would trip the flint-striking mechanism to ignite the flash powder. She walked around studying the location to decide on the amount of flash powder she would need. She might only have time to take three or four, no more than six photographs, so she decided to mix the flash powder in advance to save time, rather than mix it for each shot. This had its dangers, as once mixed it could go off unexpectedly. A combination of magnesium powder and potassium chlorate, it had singed her hair more than once, but if she placed her subjects under the shade of the tree it would fill in the shadows.

Once it was done and as if on cue – confirming that feeling of being under continual observation – four servants came out carrying what looked like a throne. She'd heard of these sumptuous cushioned seats. It was a showy red and gold *gaddi*, not to Eliza's taste at all, and if it reflected the Maharajah's personality she couldn't help thinking that Jayant and his brother Anish must be as different as chalk from cheese. She pointed to a place beneath the tree and they set the throne down alongside several other chairs. Another servant came out to sprinkle rose petals around the spot.

She heard the lyrical sound of a flute, followed by the heavy beat of a drum, and she recalled being told that in Indian mythology the drum beats creation into existence. Then she heard a rustle of silk and glimpsed the royal family entering the courtyard by way of a semi-concealed ground floor archway. Eliza felt awed by the grandeur as they solemnly walked over, and that increased her nervousness. The Maharajah seated himself and only then acknowledged Eliza's presence.

Anish, the Maharajah, was a large man who was dipping his chubby fingers into a box of Turkish delight that his sour-faced wife, Priya, kept open on her lap, sending clouds of sugar powder flying as he popped one piece after another into his mouth. His eyes were a little bloodshot and Eliza wondered if he might be a drinker as well as a glutton. Her mother used to say she believed the excesses of the Indian Princes were due to the appalling practice of polygamy. Her mother despised polygamy with a passion.

Both Priya and her husband wore multiple rings and further jewels about their clothing, and for once Eliza was glad she could not record the scene in colour. If she'd thought the *gaddi* was ostentatious, these two were a hundred times worse. Probably in her late thirties or early forties, Priya was not a beautiful woman in a traditional sense; she had a stiff expression on her face, with no trace of a smile, but she was arresting, with deep-set eyes and a slightly hooked nose. Her clothing consisted of a blouse, a gold and red embroidered skirt or *ghagra*, with a matching silk shawl covering her hair, a string of sparkling rubies at her throat and, part of the way up her arm, *poonchees*, heavy silver and gold bracelets.

Eliza glanced to her left as Jayant entered the courtyard together with a broad-shouldered shorter man with ink-black hair and dark eyebrows. Wearing a long fitted coat to the knees, made of black satin with delicate gold embroidery and a stand-up collar, and black trousers, Jay was also in his finery but it was of a more restrained style. It was the first time she'd seen him wearing a turban, but what really surprised her was how dignified and elegant this 'outdoors' man could look. When he smiled at her she realized she had been staring and, embarrassed to have been caught, turned to fiddle with her camera. At the sound of footsteps behind her she twisted round. Indira had entered from yet another semi-concealed archway and now came to stand beside Eliza.

'I am instructed to offer assistance should you require it,' she said. '*Theek hai?*'

'Yes, that's fine,' Eliza replied.

But this was a different Indi: the effervescence gone and with eyes lowered, her demeanour was much more cautious. By the look on the Maharani's face it seemed clear that the older woman was the reason why; Priya didn't acknowledge the girl's arrival but gave her a pitying look, then pointedly turned her back on her. While Eliza was wondering who the other man was, Jay's mother, Laxmi, and the Maharajah's three daughters were the final members to join the group. Jay's younger brother was at school in England and would not be joining them.

Eliza grouped them together closer than it seemed they wanted to be, while the Prince's friend stood out of view. Priya sighed repeatedly and after only a few minutes got to her feet. With her back to Eliza she turned to Laxmi.

'Surely the Englishwoman has finished? I need to go to prayers.'

'Her name is Miss Fraser,' Laxmi replied gently. 'The agreement is that she should be free to do whatever she wishes.'

'Your agreement!'

'Let's have no arguing on this beautiful day,' the Maharajah said. 'The sky is blue, the air is fresh, the birds are singing. She may do whatever she wishes, but naturally . . .' He smiled at Priya. 'Within reason, my dear.'

Priya gave her husband an aggrieved look, curling her lip in a sneer. 'And, of course, you always do what your mother wishes.'

Anish frowned. 'I'm sure Miss Fraser will not be much longer.'

Eliza swallowed her nerves. This lot were tricky. 'Not long now. If you don't mind taking your seat again, Princess, I'll hurry along.'

She was aware that during the preceding few minutes Jayant had completely ignored the argument and had been whistling quietly under his breath. He stood nonchalantly, framed by the sun, and as if without a care in the world. But the divisions within the family and the contradictions gathered there were becoming clear. Eliza couldn't afford to make enemies, not now that she'd sunk so much into buying her equipment. Her continuing progress was slow, as for every picture the plate had to be changed. She fumbled more than was usual and, with a sensation of immense relief, finished the job without anything jamming. It was a small blessing, because otherwise she'd have had to retreat to complete darkness to try to sort it out, and that would have delayed the shoot. She preferred using her Rolleiflex outdoors, and would do so for more candid shots, but today had been designed for formality. It was what the royal family were accustomed to and she didn't want to scare them off at this early stage by taking the kind of informal pictures she really wanted and that she had specifically been asked to produce. Clifford had said right from the start that it was to be as true a picture of life in Rajputana as possible and should not be dictated by the royal family's penchant for formal, unsmiling shots.

As the family wandered off, Jay took Anish aside and Eliza could hear that they were disagreeing about something. She heard the name 'Chatur' mentioned several times and, looking out of the corner of her eye as she dismantled her equipment, she could tell Jay was fuming. At one point he placed a hand on his brother's arm and seemed to grip him tightly. Anish shook Jay's hand off and then spoke in a raised voice. 'Do not interfere. How Chatur chooses to run castle affairs is up to me, not you.'

'But you give him too much power.'

At that point Eliza moved her tripod and they noticed her, lowering their voices, but it was clear to her that Jay didn't approve of Chatur.

Anish then left and Jay stood quite still for a few moments before coming across and assuming a normal voice. 'Not bad. In fact quite impressive,' he said.

'You've not seen the pictures yet,' she said, bristling at the opinionated tone in his voice.

'Professional.'

'You expected something different?'

'Well, by sending a woman photographer . . .' He paused and looked at her searchingly, and now he seemed gentler. 'What I mean to say is that it is unusual, is it not? And we are less accustomed to seeing a woman of class doing a job of work.'

'A woman of class?' she said and blinked.

He nodded.

'I'm an oddity at home too, but I intend to make a name for myself,' she said, privately thinking how much she valued the release of work. 'And I won't be deterred.'

'Your desire for recognition may well be your downfall.'

'Along with my use of water, I suppose.'

He gave her a half smile.

'You think I shouldn't try?'

'There needs to be balance. A filtering out of what matters from what does not.'

'And you've achieved that?'

He glanced away. 'I wouldn't say that. By the way, this is my old friend, Devdan. Dev for short. We met at a camel fair when we were boys. I like to go incognito when I can. It gives me a greater sense of freedom.'

'Not to mention that if the traders don't know who he is he gets a better price. I had no idea who he was when we met,' the shorter man said with a broad smile. 'Anyway, gift of the Gods, that's me, or, at least, it's what my name means.'

'Firebrand, it should be.' Jay laughed and thumped him on the back.

'And here to do a spot of hawking, hunting antelope, and camel racing with my Rajput friend here. Honour above all, that's the Rajputs, isn't it, Jay?'

Jay smiled, but Eliza could see his amber eyes had darkened, his thoughtfulness concealing something that made her feel that beneath the confidence lay something less certain. She waited for him to speak and kept her eye on the noisy monkeys in the orange trees.

'Indeed. Those were the days! Suicide rather than defeat,' he eventually said, and only after a slightly awkward pause added, 'Before we became so timid.'

'Timid! You don't strike me as being timid,' Eliza said.

'Ah, but once we were ferocious,' Dev chipped in, and judging by the look on his face Eliza could believe it. In fact, though shorter than Jay and despite his flippant manner, there was something about the man. He had been friendly enough, but every now and then she caught him staring at her with a wary look and it made her feel uncomfortable. It might just be curiosity but, whatever it was, she found it hard to look him in the eyes. They were very deep and Eliza found them difficult to read. He didn't at all seem like the kind of man she'd have expected to be a friend of Jay's.

'You speak of balance,' she said, turning from Dev to look at Jay. 'So what about work? If your old role of warrior has gone, why not find something useful to do?'

'Hear that, Jay, she thinks camel racing isn't useful.' Dev laughed at his own comment and, relieved that the mood had lightened, she smiled.

'She may have a point,' Jay said.

'So how did you become interested in photography?' Dev asked.

'My husband bought me my first camera when we were

on our honeymoon.' She had spoken without thinking and glanced at Jayant.

'You must miss him,' was all he said.

The guilt over Oliver knotted somewhere deep in her chest. The slow tightening, the feeling of not being far from foolish tears. But now, as always, she clamped down on her emotions and gave a curt nod.

'And what in particular intrigued you about photography?'

'It was so exciting.' She smiled. 'I saw pictures of the work of Man Ray. It's highly experimental, and he worked with surrealist artists like Marcel Duchamp. And then, when I tried for myself, I found I could see things differently through my lens. I learnt to focus on the unexpected. It was like seeing the world anew. Of course my husband didn't imagine it would lead to a career.'

There was a slight pause.

'It was only after he died that I had the funds to buy more equipment and pay for lessons.'

'I'm sorry, I didn't realize,' Dev said.

'And now . . .' She glanced down. 'It's my whole life. For me photography is not just about what I see, it's about what I feel.'

But her response had lacked the strength of passion she really felt. She didn't tell him that only through her camera lens could she really express herself, nor did she say that photography had become her solace. She didn't tell him that she believed success in her career might relieve her of her guilt. She wanted to make her father proud of her, and believed that if she worked hard she could rise above her pain. But the truth was she would lay down her life rather than end up like her mother, even if it meant she had to accept a lifetime of loneliness as the price of pursuing a career. And one thing was certain: never again would she compromise who she was for the sake of feeling less alone, nor would she feel ashamed of insisting on having a voice.

'You look different,' she said to Jay, putting aside her thoughts, and pointing at his coat.

'Ah, this. It's called an *achkan*. Mughal in origin.'

She glanced up at the lacy *jali* screens carved from marble and experienced again the sensation of being watched.

Eliza spent much of the rest of the day immersed in her darkroom. In the heat of Rajputana undeveloped photographic plates would easily deteriorate, so her plan was to always develop the plates quickly. What she hadn't bargained for was how the extreme heat of the afternoon sun intensified the oppressive atmosphere of an enclosed darkroom with no ventilation, especially as she wore gloves of nitrol and a face mask. The developing fluid was a mixture of chemicals, the most toxic being the white lustrous crystals of pyro, and that was the main reason she had insisted on there being only one key. Just a little pyro ingested or touching the skin could have nasty side-effects. But she loved working alone like this, and although the smell from the acrid, vinegary chemicals made her head ache, she carried on and ended up with a series of contact prints. These she'd show to Clifford, who would hopefully give permission for them to be sent on to Delhi with the plates for the final printing, along with Eliza's marked-up instructions and notes about the desired size too.

5

Surprised by a knock at her door, Eliza called out to whoever it was to wait and that she wouldn't be long. She had
thought it must be a servant bearing some kind of refreshment, but when she opened the door she saw Indira leaning
against the opposite wall.

'Would you like to see my work?' the girl said, her eyes
darting about and looking as if her high spirits had returned.
'We are both artists, if you can call photography an art.'

Eliza nodded politely. 'Surely if pictures make people
want to look that's all that matters.'

She was quite keen to see Indi's artwork, though if she
had been asked she'd probably have said she was more curious about the girl herself. There was something about her.
Something that didn't quite add up. Who was she? Where
had she come from, this young woman who appeared to
enjoy the freedom of the castle with few of the constraints?
And, at the back of Eliza's mind, she continued to wonder
what was the nature of this lithe young woman's relationship with Jayant.

Indi's diaphanous scarf floated as she sailed with liquid
beauty through labyrinthine corridors and cramped rooms,
but Eliza found it hard to breathe freely. The feeling was
deepened by the darkly claustrophobic passages, shadowy recesses and countless narrow staircases. The *jali*
screens were everywhere and, having lost her way on
two occasions, it was easy to understand why the British

had described these palaces as rife with intrigue and gossip.

And yet the magnificence of the golden pillars when they arrived at an opulent *durbar*, or reception hall! When Eliza gazed up at twenty-foot-high doors made of brass and beyond them a mirrored ceiling sparkling with light and inset with jewels, she gasped. Rubies. Sapphires. Emeralds. It was quite insane. There was a proud lilt to Indi's voice as she pointed out each member of the family hanging on the walls. She had painted them all in the old Mughal style, and as Eliza took them in she marvelled at the girl's talent.

'You painted all these?'

Indira nodded, and with a touch of pride in her voice said, 'Yes.'

'You don't see the need for a photographer, do you?'

The girl chewed her lip while Eliza waited for an answer. 'Painting is *mera pyaar*,' she eventually said.

'Your love. I do understand.'

'I feel as if I enter a secret inner world when I paint.'

'That's how I feel about photography. It's all about how I see things,' Eliza said, and held Indira's gaze, weighing every word she was about to say. 'I'm not here permanently. I promise I'll be no threat to you.'

'And that's really all you're here for? To take photographs?'

'Of course. What else?'

The girl narrowed her eyes and something flitted across her face, but she didn't speak.

'And I'm certain not everyone approves. The Maharani, Priya, doesn't seem to like me.'

Indi chuckled. 'Priya doesn't like anybody. She blames the way Jay is on his British education. You're British.'

'The way he is? What does that mean?'

'On the one hand he avoids displays of emotions, which is very Rajput, and also he will never own up to any kind of vulnerability. On the other hand he's self-reliant and wayward, often not listening to his family! He is a man who refuses all opportunities to marry a pretty young Princess and has friends who favour civil disobedience, especially since the salt tax and Gandhi's march against it. As I said, Priya is no friend of the British, but there has been growing unrest and her fear of violent revolution is even greater than her anger at the British.'

'She's frightened, I suppose,' Eliza said, thinking that behind Priya's hard edges there might be an underlying fragility.

'She'd never admit it, but probably yes.'

'People who have a lot to lose often are. Maybe she's scared of what will happen if India becomes self-governing?'

'Maybe. But I think Anish will have already made plans to hide his wealth somewhere in one of the old tunnels under the fort.'

'The wealth is incredible.'

Indi nodded.

'What about Dev? Is he one of Jay's friends who favours civil disobedience?'

'Possibly. He has not been given licence to own a typewriter. That should tell you something. He believes ordinary people should be educated so they can speak with one voice.' Indi shrugged. 'Or something like that. You never know with Dev.'

Eliza let out her breath in a long sigh and decided to change the subject. 'How did you learn to paint?'

'I was taught by a Thakur at my village.'

'A nobleman?'

'Yes.'

'You aren't of high birth?'

Indi shook her head and looked at her feet. 'No.'

Eliza hoped the girl would reveal more, but her face had closed so she decided not to pry about the past, instead asking what she liked about being at the castle.

Indi looked up, seeming relieved at the new direction the conversation was taking. 'I love everything about it, of course. But I'm more interested to hear about you. Did you never want to marry?'

Eliza smiled internally. Did she seem so very old? As she gazed up at Indi's beautiful miniatures she thought about how photography had come to take over her life. When they had been in Paris she'd met a woman who was on her way to becoming a photographer in her own right. It was then Eliza had realized that such a thing might be possible. And after one of her early amateur prints of a lone ragamuffin child had made it into an illustrated magazine, she was certain she too could become a competent photographer.

She hesitated but then decided to speak. She might need this girl's friendship one day. 'I was married, but my husband died in a traffic accident.'

Indira's face wore an expression of shock and her mouth fell open. 'You are a widow?'

Bewildered by such a response, Eliza experienced a sinking feeling in the pit of her stomach. She hadn't fully grasped the gravity of telling anyone. Jay had said she should keep it quiet, but she had blurted out something about a husband in front of his friend Dev, and now Indi too. What had she been thinking?

6

One night soon after her meeting with Indi, Eliza glanced out of one of the corridor windows not screened by *jali* and saw a courtyard dotted with utensils, the pale moon silvering the bowls, pots and all manner of cooking containers lying on the ground outside the kitchens. This nocturnal display amplified her feeling that she might never understand her new world or what it meant to be a Rajput.

And in the morning when she heard that Clifford had arrived at the castle, she couldn't avoid thinking he was about to further upset her tender equilibrium. After she was shown into a small day room further along the corridor dividing the men's and women's quarters, he breezed in carrying a large flat box and in a most unprecedented way made himself immediately at home, with his feet up on the plush velvet day bed.

'I'm here to help you prepare for the state *durbar,*' he said in his clipped manner of speaking, and pushed back the wire spectacles that had been sliding down his nose. It was clear he was a man inclined to sweat, especially when wearing a heavy linen suit, and his forehead was shining now. He took out a white handkerchief and wiped his skin. 'It's a rather showy spectacle in a couple of days' time. A giddy affair really, with all the usual ceremonial trappings, and a high turnout.'

'I have to go?'

'I was under the impression you'd enjoy it. Dottie will be there.'

She took a breath and, feeling brave, decided to state her case. 'Well, it would be nice to see her again, but actually I want to move out of the castle.'

'Into the town?'

She nodded.

He shook his head, though it didn't seem to be with much regret. 'Sorry, no can do. Guest house is closed.'

She sighed deeply. This wasn't going to be easy. 'There's no privacy. I feel as if I'm being watched the whole time.'

'That's because you are. It's always an uphill battle with these types.' He paused and lifted up the box. As he did, his trouser leg rolled up and Eliza saw that his skin was milky white and the hairs were ginger. He was clearly a man who would burn badly.

'But you must always remember, it is we who are the Empire builders.' He paused for a moment as if to let that sink in. 'Anyway, I have something for you.'

'I don't understand. From whom?'

He smiled, looking pleased with himself. 'Let's just call it a little settling-in gift from me to you.'

She took the box, laid it on the table, slowly undid the strings and then opened the lid. She couldn't prevent a slight gasp at the sight of a gown in the most beautiful vibrant shade of blueish-green.

'Your mother told me it was your favourite colour.'

She frowned. 'How did you know my size? Was that my mother too?'

'It's silk,' he said, ignoring her question. 'Do you like it?'

'It's beautiful.'

'If you feel it's a trifle too revealing, there's a matching shawl, embroidered by hand with gold thread, no less. You can throw it around your shoulders.'

'I really don't know what to say.'

There was a momentary silence as he got to his feet and went to look out of the window. If it was to allow her time to think, she felt grateful; maybe she'd been wrong about him, maybe he was more sensitive than she'd thought. But she couldn't accept this dress from someone she barely knew. What would it say about her if she did? And yet she'd never owned anything so glamorous and the temptation was strong.

'Tell me about this *durbar*,' she said to give herself time. 'What's it for?'

'There was a time when the princely states would hold two important *durbars*, one a political event where the Maharajah and his ministers would hold court to determine the affairs of the state; the other social, a spectacle to entertain and display the wealth and magnificence of the Prince's court.'

'And this is the second kind?'

'Yes. Since we manage most of the administration in co-operation with Prince Anish, there's now only a need for a lavish *durbar* to remind folk of the splendour.' He beamed proudly. 'We have successfully separated the administrative from the ceremonial. We can't have these people creating chaos.'

Eliza still didn't understand why the Princes had relinquished so much of their power by signing treaties with the British, and longed to ask, but she'd had enough of Clifford for one day. All she knew was that British India took up about three-fifths of the country, and that the rest was made up of 565 princely states under 'indirect' British rule.

'I can't accept a gift like this from you,' she said flatly.

'I think you will find you have to.'

Rather than argue, she changed the subject. 'Do you know why they put dozens of cooking pots out last night?'

'I don't give a hoot for their weird and wonderful customs. But probably moon's rays, that sort of tosh.' He walked over to the door. 'By the way, what do you make of Laxmi?'

'She's very kind.'

'Be a good idea to keep eyes in the back of your head. Just report anything that makes you feel suspicious direct to me.'

'Goodness. Like what?'

He shrugged. 'Nothing in particular. Just a friendly suggestion.'

'Clifford, I was thinking of using some of the better photographs to mount a small exhibition. Would that be all right? Perhaps in October, towards the end of my year here?'

'I don't see why not. Have you thought of where you'd mount it?'

'Not yet. I thought you might be able to advise me on that.'

'Well, we'll see. Just run the ones you want to use past me first. Wouldn't want you to give the wrong impression of the Empire. Anyway, see you on the night. Don't let the side down.'

'I won't.'

'Frankly, the way you'll look in that, well, it's just as well the *zenana* and *mardana* are kept separate.'

'*Mardana?*'

'Men's quarters, my dear. In my eyes you are already

70

beautiful enough but in that, well, you'll be a sight for their sore eyes. I'll have to keep a watch on you.'

As Clifford had given her some idea of what to expect, she took time over her appearance on the evening of the *durbar* and, once she was dressed in his silky gift, the handmaiden Kiri came to brush her hair. One hundred strokes, Eliza whispered. No more. No less. She could almost hear her mother's demanding voice in her head as Kiri threaded glittering crystals through her hair.

A memory came racing back of brushing Anna's hair. When Eliza had asked why she looked so sad, there had been only silence and then her mother's warm tears had dripped on to Eliza's own hand. She hadn't known what to do or how to comfort her mother but had tried to reach out. Anna had swept her hand away and nothing more was said. It had swollen in Eliza's mind, that small moment, though she never understood what triggered her mother's ongoing melancholy, except for the death of her husband, of course.

As Eliza gazed in the mirror now she hadn't expected the way the peacock colours of the silk dress lit her eyes so they sparkled as brightly as the crystals in her hair. And indeed, waving freely beyond her shoulders, her hair shone like burnished copper against the creaminess of her complexion. The woman tied up her hair loosely, then gave her a subtle version of Indian-style make-up, outlining her eyes in grey and dabbing a touch of colour on her lips and cheeks.

Just as Eliza was set to leave the room, Laxmi entered, issued an order to Kiri, who scuttled off, and then, as she appraised Eliza, smiled.

'But how beautiful you are. Why do you hide your light, my child?'

'I . . .'

'I have embarrassed you. Forgive me. But you will need to cover your shoulders.'

'Oh! I almost forgot,' Eliza said, and dashed to the wardrobe where the shawl was hanging. She took it out and held it up for Laxmi to see.

The older woman ran her fingers over it. 'This is very fine indeed. Where did you get it?'

'Clifford Salter.'

'He's a good upstanding fellow. Isn't that what the British would say?'

'I suppose.'

'Perhaps not the most handsome among men.' Laxmi looked her up and down. 'But you could do worse.'

'I'm not in the market for a husband.'

'Isn't every woman in the market for a good husband?'

Eliza smiled. 'Is that what you really think?'

As Laxmi sighed, Eliza could sense her melancholy. 'I was lucky. I had a very happy marriage with a wonderful man. We were equals. That is not often the case here in the royal courts. But now, let us speak about you. What are your hopes and expectations? Even if you are not looking for a husband, there are many kinds of love. Without it your heart will be empty.'

'For now I love my work.'

The woman smiled. 'Indeed. Now come, let me show you the best place from which to watch the procession. We few modern-thinking women must stick together, especially these days.'

'Thank you.'

'You will need all the friends you can get, and don't forget what I said about Clifford Salter. A white married woman in India has more freedom than a single woman.'

'I'll remember that . . . I was hoping you might tell me about the bells I hear every day. I know they're temple bells.'

'They call us to our prayers, or *pujas* as we call them. You will find that here in Rajputana everything we do becomes a ritual or rite of some kind or other, and that in a way the gods we pray to symbolize various forces in our lives. We don't distinguish between the sacred and our ordinary lives. To us they are one.'

'I see. It's very different.'

'Yes, I imagine it is. Well, enjoy your night.' The woman turned to leave.

'Actually, Laxmi,' Eliza said. 'I'd like to go out to one of the villages to photograph the local people if I may.'

'Think of it as already done.'

The colonnaded archway lining the largest exterior gateway into the castle was illuminated by flaming torches fixed to marble urns, each one guarded by a single manservant wearing white. Once Laxmi had left her alone, Eliza looked down on the scene from a balcony and saw a long line of silver and gold *howdahs*, atop jewelled and painted elephants lumbering up the hill past a wall festooned with flowers. When they came to a standstill she gasped out loud, but not at the spangled spectacle laid out before her. In the space of one chilling moment she was ten years old again and leaning from a different balcony; the one where she had tried to wave at her father. Her eyes began to smart and she struggled to control her tears; she could not allow this to happen now. For years she had steeled herself against her weakness, taught herself discipline, made herself strong inside and out. She could not fail now.

'Eliza?'

She spun round and saw Jayant wearing a dark *angharki* or coat, deeply cut out in the front and threaded with gold. His teeth seemed very white against his dark lips and gleaming skin, and the fan of lines at the edges of his eyes grew deeper as he smiled. He was standing stock still and staring at her and the moment during which they held each other's eyes went on too long. As he blinked, she realized that there was something truly genuine about this man. And that something was affecting her deeply. She opened her mouth to speak but no words came. Then the moment was suddenly over as, ashamed of him seeing her weakness, she roughly brushed her tears away and took a step back, desperately trying to think of something to say to excuse her emotional reaction.

'It's very beautiful,' she managed to say. 'The procession.'

'As are you. Who would have thought it? I take back everything I said about your hair.'

She blinked rapidly. Please don't let him be kind to her.

'Will you allow me to escort you down?'

She nodded, feeling a mixture of relief that the moment of embarrassing shame was over, but also feeling uncertain about the consequences of making an entrance on the handsome Prince's arm.

As they headed towards the wide marble staircase curling down to the main *durbar* hall, she calmed herself and tried to relax. She felt very much on show and couldn't help feeling nervous being so close to him like this, and not only because of what other people might think. And her misgivings on that score were not in vain, because as they descended she caught Indira's eye. The girl wore a stunning scarlet outfit, but the way her eyes narrowed with sullen envy worried Eliza. That Indira was in love with Jay was clear, and though Eliza glanced sideways to see how he would react, he hardly seemed to have noticed Indi. Had he been at fault? Led the girl on? Or had Indira's adoration grown out of years of friendly proximity? Eliza hoped it was the latter.

Once the elephants had been unloaded of their cargo of aristocratic nobles and their retainers, all the guests were shepherded into the *durbar* hall by castle guards wearing formal livery. An orchestra was already playing western music on a stage at one end and, while everyone waited for the Maharajah and his wife, Eliza swayed to the music. When Anish appeared, sporting a dazzling array of jewels worn over a *kurta* of deep blue satin, the room fell silent and it seemed as if the entire assembly held its breath. Priya followed him, eyes cast down, wearing a pale pink skirt, bodice and matching scarf, with jewel-encrusted bangles all the way up her arms and around her ankles too.

The royals seated themselves on satin cushions topping thrones of ebony and silver, set on a dais at the opposite end from the orchestra. Once they were comfortable, Laxmi, Jay and the Maharajah's daughters joined them there. A roar went up from the crowd of about two hundred nobles and important families from around the state, as well as a scattering of local citizens, and the orchestra struck up a cheering tune.

A space was cleared and the Indian entertainment began with a *dholan*, a woman who played a drum and sang. Then came gypsy dancing girls, whirling and leaping with extraordinary grace. Eliza had been looking out for Dottie

75

but she and Julian didn't appear to have turned up. In any case, despite her earlier distress, Eliza was fully enjoying the evening; people had been friendly and she wasn't the fish out of water she'd expected to be. At one point she spotted Indira and Jayant talking, their heads bent close together, and when Indira turned on her heels and fled the room Eliza's heart ached for her. She decided to see if the girl might be outside.

She had hoped to find Indi on one of the tall swings made for women. They were typical of the region and much in evidence in the courtyards of the castle, but that part of the garden was empty, so she walked to a subtly lit corner where the scent of jasmine drifted across. The air was cooler than she expected and, wrapping the shawl around her shoulders, she gazed up at the stars. The same feeling of magic she'd experienced on the rooftop of the summer palace gusted on a light breeze, and she wished for something she couldn't define. She had closed her heart to the expectation of love and had placed all her energy into reaching outside herself and revealing the essence of a scene in just one brief moment. This was something divine when it worked.

As she turned to go back inside, she spotted Clifford walking towards her with a slightly uneven gait.

'Eliza. Eliza,' he said. 'My dear, dear girl. What are you up to out here?'

'I might ask you the same?'

'Looking for you.' He stood still for a moment, then came up close, gave her an enquiring look and spoke in a low voice. 'Noticed anything of interest lately?'

She stared at the ground for a moment before raising her head. 'Like what?'

76

'Chatur behaving himself?'

'I guess so, though he does seem a bit interfering.'

He laughed. 'That's Chatur all right . . . See much of Anish and that wife of his?'

She frowned. 'Not really. What's all this about?'

'Just making conversation, my dear. Shall we stroll?'

'Of course.'

As they wound their way beneath oil lamps that lit a narrow path, he was largely silent, though it wasn't an easy silence. She was just wondering what to say when he spoke, the tone of his voice deeper than before.

'Eliza, I have known you since you were a child in India.'

'Yes.'

'Though of course I didn't see much of you while you were growing up in England.'

'You came to the house once. I remember that.'

'Do you have any idea how fond of you I am becoming?'

'That's very flattering.' She drew in her breath and gave herself time to think. 'You have been very kind to me, Clifford. I know that, but I don't really know you all that well and you don't know me, at least not who I am now anyway.'

'Eliza, I'm not talking about kindness! I'd like us to get to know each other better. Do you see?'

This was exactly what she hadn't bargained for, but how perceptive Laxmi had been and how stupid she herself had been not to have seen it coming.

He leant towards her and, smelling the whisky and cigars on his breath, she took a step back, fearful that he might try to kiss her.

'You're a very handsome woman. I know it's not that long since you lost your husband but –'

She interrupted. 'I'm sorry, Clifford, I'm just not ready.'

He must have seen the look in her eyes, because he reached out and held her gently by the shoulders. 'I would never rush you. Just give yourself a chance to get to know me. That's all I ask.'

'Of course.'

'Is it because I'm older than you? Is that it? Because men can continue to father children and I'm not yet fifty and –'

Prompted by the need to curtail this, she interrupted. 'Clifford, I like you very much . . .' She paused, thinking of his white ankle and the red hairs, but then became aware of a look of sadness in his eyes.

'Wouldn't that be a good start? Liking, I mean?' he said.

Eliza didn't want to hurt or offend him but, for a moment or two, could not speak.

'Well, I wanted to declare myself. It would be kind if you'd consider what I've said. I can give you a beautiful home and I am an honourable man, not like . . .' He paused.

'Not like?'

'Never mind. It doesn't matter. Just think about what I've said. I am absolutely genuine in my intent.'

'As I said, I am very flattered.'

'Please take into account that there are not so many British to choose from over here. Have you thought about afterwards? What you'll do when the project is completed?'

'Not yet.'

'Maybe you should. In any case, I hope I can convince you that I have your best interests at heart.'

As he walked away, Eliza went to where there was a square pool that had been surrounded by candles. Small three-sided muslin tents circled the pool with the open side facing the water, each one just large enough for two people. She went over to the furthest one and sank into one of its thick silk cushions. There was a loud explosion and suddenly fireworks lit up the sky. At first Eliza tensed at the sound, but then she watched the spectacle and when it was over, close to tears for the second time that night, this time with no real understanding why, she gazed at the reflections of the candlelight dancing on the water and felt overcome by loneliness.

On the other side of the pool she saw that Jay was walking alone and seemingly deep in thought. He glanced across and caught her eye and she felt again the same connection that she'd felt just before they'd gone down the stairs to the *durbar* hall together. Now he walked around the pool towards her and, when he reached her, he smiled and asked if she was all right out there on her own. She nodded and he seemed to hesitate before bowing and walking away.

7

For a week or so everything seemed to go smoothly, and Eliza quickly dismissed the tears she had shed on the night of the *durbar* as fanciful. This was not the time to allow any kind of emotion to get in her way. This was a time to work. So far the staff allowed her free access to most of the castle, including the kitchens and store room, and even the women of the *zenana* were friendly. In fact, when she discovered Anish still kept concubines, Eliza found herself gravitating towards the women, many of whom were old and had been there since his father's time. Some of the women told stories of being brought as babies to be taken in by the castle. Many had never left the castle since. But they laughed and sewed and sang and, when she was with them, Eliza experienced a kind of camaraderie that was entirely new to her.

It bore no relation to the time she'd spent in a minor girls' boarding school, courtesy of a man her mother had called an 'uncle'. His name was James Langton and Eliza knew that he was not any kind of relation at all, though she and her mother were given a small lodge on his estate and all Anna had to do in return was check up on his staff whenever he went away.

Up until now the ease with which other people appeared to be rooted so securely in their world had escaped Eliza. But now, even if the women of the *zenana* might gossip about her when she wasn't there, Eliza didn't mind. She found them fun to be with. The girls at the boarding school had not been fun and she hadn't trusted any of them. But she only heard the women of the *zenana* being spiteful after one of those days when Priya had joined them, and Eliza could tell the women didn't trust their Maharani.

Just as Eliza was taking a photograph of one of the younger concubines, Indira entered the room carrying a bag and speaking in English so that none of the other women could understand.

'You want to see something?' she said, with a wide grin on her face, and, looking pleased with herself, she pulled up a chair and threw herself down.

'Depends.'

'A kind of funeral.'

As the words sank in, Eliza frowned. She'd had more than enough of funerals.

'You'll like it. I promise.'

Eliza hesitated. She hadn't seen much of Indi since the night of the ball, when the girl had so clearly revealed her jealousy.

'Kiri is coming.'

'Really? The handmaid?'

Indi nodded. 'We're meeting her in town.'

Eliza made a decision and began packing up. 'I've finished here, so why not. Can't be too long though, as I want to develop the plates as soon as I get back. Is it all right if I take my Rolleiflex?'

'If you carry it in a bag over your shoulder.'

She then jumped up and held something out. 'We won't be long but you will need to change. I've brought Indian clothes.'

'Where from?'

Indi tilted her head to one side and smiled mysteriously. 'I can get anything. Now change.'

81

'In front of these women?'

Indi laughed. 'Of course. We are all women together here. They have seen it all before. You can pick your own clothes up later.'

Eliza was not a prude but, as she changed, her cheeks burned with embarrassment as she attempted to cover different parts of herself. The women laughed and chattered, speaking so fast that Eliza couldn't follow. It seemed good-natured enough, though the excitement of seeing a semi-naked white woman turning raspberry pink was probably rivetingly new for them. By the time it was finished, Eliza, wearing the typical full skirt and figure-hugging blouse, felt quite different.

As they left the *zenana* Indi suddenly pushed Eliza into a recess in the corridor. Eliza frowned, but Indi had a finger to her lips. After a moment she spoke.

'Chatur! The *dewan* – the senior court official.'

Eliza remembered the man's shadowy dark eyes and bushy brows. 'So?'

'He has eyes in the back of his head. He's used to me, but the less he knows about you the better. He'll want to poke his nose into everything you do if you're not careful. Come on. He's gone.'

'Why do I have to be careful?'

'He hates change and is no friend of the British. I doubt he approves of you being here at all. He is very old-fashioned. He and Priya are close. Both best avoided.'

After that Indira chatted about this and that. Whatever the upset at the ball had been about, it seemed to have passed. Maybe Indi and Jay had managed to talk? Either way Eliza felt relieved that no more trouble beckoned. Enthralled by glimpses of castle life, she had been worrying that bad

82

feeling might spoil things. As for Clifford, she put him to the back of her mind.

This was Eliza's first real visit to the heart of the medieval town and it was where they met up with Kiri, who would be accompanying them. Excited by the vibrant colours inside the tangle of winding streets, Eliza's heart began to beat a little faster. The bazaars of the old city seemed to radiate in narrow ribbons from the main clock tower and, as Eliza followed Indi and Kiri, they passed everything from tie-dyers to puppet-makers; it crossed her mind that if she got lost here she'd never get out again. Would these bustling people help her, all with their own little lives, their own joys, their own fears, seeming so close yet possibly so far apart from one another?

In the spice markets the scents of incense drifted around them, as did the tangy aroma of charcoal-cooked goat. Then, as they went further and further through bazaars selling everything from sweets to sarees, the drone of a drum seemed to grow louder, just as the whiff of drains grew stronger.

'Is it a festival?' she asked, knowing that India's love of festivity ranged from celebrating the birth of a god, or a satisfactory harvest, to the many music festivals.

'Not quite.'

Eliza paused in the middle of the street. 'So?'

Indi beamed back at her as she walked on. 'Kiri's family are puppeteers. Today is a special day for them. Come on, or you'll be run over by a rickshaw.'

'But you said . . .'

'It was a funeral. And it is. In a way.'

'You're being very mysterious.'

Indi laughed, linking arms with Eliza and also with Kiri,

who was smiling broadly. 'You'll see. Do you believe in karma or destiny?'

'Destiny? I'm not really sure what it means.'

'I believe. We have something called *adit chukker*, the unseen wheel of fate. We are all about destiny here. And today is no exception.'

At that point Eliza heard an English voice calling her name. She spun round to see Dottie looking red-faced as she ran towards her. 'I thought it was you,' the woman said. 'Gosh, I'm out of puff. Rule number one, never run in this heat! But what are you up to, wearing that outfit?'

'It is a bit odd actually. I'm going to some kind of funeral.'

'Good grief, is it safe?' She glanced around as though looking for assailants hiding in the alleyways.

'I'm sure it is,' Eliza said. 'Anyway, how are you, Dottie? I was sorry not to see you at the *durbar*.'

'I had one of my ghastly headaches. Julian gives me something but it just knocks me out.' Dottie touched Eliza's forearm and paused for a moment. 'But seriously, traipsing about like this on your own . . .'

'I'm with those two.' She pointed at Indi and Kiri.

'But I meant . . .'

'I know what you meant, but I'm fine. Really.'

'Would Clifford approve?'

'Probably not. But look, why not come with us?'

Dottie smiled. 'You know, I rather think I'd like to, but actually I'm with Julian. He's looking for a chess set.'

'Pity.' Eliza took a step away and glanced across at Indi. 'Another time maybe?'

Eliza nodded. 'Sorry to dash, but I can't hold them up any longer.'

'Of course. See you soon?'

Eliza heard a pensive note in the woman's voice and realized Dottie might be a bit lonely too. She would make an effort to call on her soon.

Dottie moved off and Eliza went back to the waiting girls. When they finally arrived at the outskirts of the town they reached a river bank. It wasn't particularly wide and certainly didn't look very deep, but here it seemed less dusty than the main town had been and Eliza felt a certain freshness in the air. And then she saw that a small crowd had assembled to watch a puppet show.

'We're here for this?'

'Sort of.'

The impressive sight of three-foot marionettes on a miniature stage, their heads carved out of hardwood and wearing elaborately made costumes, was like nothing Eliza had seen before. The semi-concealed puppeteer made sounds through what looked like bamboo to disguise his normal voice, and he moved the jointed limbs of the puppets by manipulating the strings attached to them. A woman next to him played the drum Eliza had been hearing.

'It's a *dholak*, the drum,' Indi said. 'These stories are about destiny. And love, war and honour. You can ask Jay about that. He knows all about honour.'

Eliza wondered if there had been a hint of something in Indi's voice but shrugged. She was probably imagining it.

'These people are agricultural labourers from the Nagaur area, known by the name of the *kathputliwalas*. They usually perform the puppet shows during the late evenings, but this is different.'

Eliza listened as the puppeteer hooted and whistled and the story was narrated by a second woman while the first one continued to sing and beat on her drum.

'We're here for a funeral,' Indi continued.

'Whose?'

'He's lying over there.'

Though she had no desire to see a dead body, Eliza couldn't help turning her head to look. She saw only Kiri, sitting on the ground beside another three-foot puppet lying on a bed of silk.

'That puppet is old and too worn out to be used now.'

Eliza watched as the show came to an end. The puppeteer went across to Kiri and kissed the top of her head, then he picked up the old marionette and carried it lovingly to the water's edge, where he began to pray. Eliza caught the scene on her camera and then, as his prayers continued, he placed the puppet on the water with Kiri's help.

'The longer it floats the more pleased the gods will be,' Indi said.

'Why is Kiri helping?'

'The puppeteer is her father.'

'But she doesn't live with her family?'

'She cannot. To work at the castle she must live at the castle.'

After the scene by the river the three wandered through the bazaars dodging the bicycles, the cows lying asleep, and the wares laid out on the pavements, only stopping to wrap brightly coloured scarves around each other's throats and to try on necklaces, while posing and giggling.

'You suit the Indian style of dressing, Eliza.'

'But why did I need to dress like this? Surely I could have just covered my head?'

'Yes. But I thought it would be more fun and fewer people would stare at you this way.'

Eliza smiled. She was enjoying herself, if a bit conscious

of her pale skin; unusually light-hearted and full of admiration for Indi's knowledge of the town, she seemed to be discovering a different part of herself. Nobody bothered the girls and the streets throbbed with a mix of women still in purdah and those who had come out. They bought little cooked flour-balls or *golgappe* and also lentil fritters that Indira called *daalbaatichurma*, and went to one of the parks to eat them.

By the time they reached the beginning of the hill it was dusk, and Eliza looked up in amazement. The entire fortress was now brilliantly lit and seemed to have been brushed with gold. Every sparkling window beckoned, and it occurred to Eliza that if she didn't hold on she would drop into fairyland, never to return to the real world. It had been a lovely, happy day, a day to rejoice at how easy life could be when you didn't have to try to protect yourself. Eliza hoped that she and Indi might become real friends. It was a long time since she'd had a real friend.

8

Eliza had been dreaming of Oliver in the night, and when she woke old forgotten feelings and memories came unbidden from the depths of her heart. She couldn't stop thinking of the day she had met him. She'd caused him to drop the pile of books he'd been carrying when she'd accidentally bumped into him in a bookshop, or rather, walked backwards into him. When she'd bent down to help him gather them up, she'd seen they were all about art, including catalogues of exhibitions in London and Paris. She'd squatted on the floor gazing at the photographs and then he'd sat down beside her. At first she could only nod wordlessly but, after a few moments of talking about the weather, they'd both begun to laugh. It had been funny sitting on the floor with a complete stranger. And then he'd helped her up and invited her to join him at the tea shop next door.

The good times hadn't lasted and she thought of the day they had quarrelled so violently. All she'd said was that she wanted to become a photographer. He wasn't supposed to die, but he'd been so angry, slamming the door and marching out into the street without understanding her reasons. She'd been afraid, as if punched hard in the pit of her stomach, and she had been right to fear: Oliver had not seen the bus that killed him and she had learnt to swallow the agonizing guilt.

A knock at the door interrupted her memories and she was surprised to find the *dewan*, Chatur, waiting for her. He didn't smile, and with a look of disdain held out a sheet of paper with just the tips of his fingers.

'I have brought a list of the people you should photograph and the order in which it is to be done. You will see I have suggested suitable locations too.'

'I see.'

He gave her a cool smile. 'I'm sure I can afford the time to be present on some of these occasions, but if I'm not available one of the guards will accompany you.'

Resenting the intrusion, Eliza frowned. 'I do like to choose my subjects myself and I thought I was to have free access.'

'Up to a point, Miss Fraser. Up to a point. Well, I trust you will find the list useful. I have some guards waiting to be photographed now. You'll find them in the nearest courtyard.'

As he bowed and turned to go Eliza thought about what Laxmi had said. Surely she was to be allowed to do whatever she wished, not follow anybody's orders. She would simply ignore Chatur's list.

Out in the courtyard the three guards stood in a stiff formal line and nothing she could say made the slightest difference. She was racking her brain trying to work out how to get a more informal shot when Dev turned up and stared at her. She took in his hair, shorter than Jay's, his eyes, which were darker, and, with a larger nose, his face had a rougher look about it. There was also a slightly odd feel to him, as if he was balanced on a fine line, though his fixed smile gave nothing away. He looked back at her warily at first but then, after sizing up the situation, seemed to change.

'Need some help?' he said.

'Not really, though I can't seem to get them to relax. I really want to catch them in an unguarded moment.'

Dev glanced across at them and appeared to be thinking. Then he smiled. 'I have the very thing.'

He produced something from the bag he carried and also took out a small pouch. At the sight of it the guards came straight over to him. He spoke a few words and they nodded without a second glance at Eliza.

'It's a game,' he told Eliza. 'We call it *challas*.'

He unrolled a large canvas square that seemed to be covered in silk with squares and designs all over it. Then he squatted down on the ground and the men joined him. He emptied tokens and cowrie shells from the pouch and she noticed that the board itself was truly beautiful.

'You know your way around, don't you?' she said.

He had his back to her but she saw him nod and then seem to forget she was there. It was very clever of him, because now she could take the shots she really wanted. But she couldn't quite work Dev out. One minute he seemed to be almost suspicious of her and the next so very helpful. Why?

During a short break in the game he got to his feet and came across to her. 'It's a game we've played for centuries. We used it to teach young men war tactics and strategy.'

'Is that something you're good at? Tactics, I mean?'

He shrugged.

'So what are you doing here today?'

'I've just been doing a spot of hawking with Jay. Please don't make life harder for him, Miss Fraser. He doesn't have an easy time of it here as it is, and I'm not sure that his spending time with you will benefit his already troubled relationship with Chatur.'

'Is Chatur really so powerful?'

He nodded. 'I'm afraid he is. Anyway, on another note Jay tells me you once lived in India.'

'Just in Delhi when I was a child, but after my father died we went back to live in England.'

He was looking at his feet and stubbing his toe into some pebbles, and didn't speak.

'Well, thank you for helping me,' Eliza said. 'I appreciate it.' And she turned to pack up her things.

The next day she found herself alone with Jayant again. This time she was climbing into an open-top sidecar attached to a motorcycle. She hadn't known Jay would be the one to accompany her to the Indian village but apparently he had offered to do it, which surprised and delighted her. Today he wore a long Indian-style tunic shirt with European trousers, both in charcoal grey, and on his skin there was the faint scent of sandalwood, just like Laxmi, but with a tang of cedar too and maybe limes.

'I like the motorbike,' she said.

'I used to have a 1925 Brough Superior but it was stolen earlier this year. This is a Harley-Davidson.'

As they got going, sand rose in clouds from the wheels of the bike, but she focused on the road ahead and, only after she'd recovered from the strange feeling of self-consciousness, she decided to use it as an opportunity. There was so much she still didn't know about Jay and about his world. Sometimes a kind of darkness surrounded him, but there was joy and vigour in him too, though there was also an edge. Definitely an edge.

'I hope you're not going to tell me this is another journey of several days?' she shouted up at him.

He laughed. 'It's really not so far, there and back by tea time, but there's a great deal to see. It's a perfect rural village and you'll be able to see how life is lived and hopefully capture some interesting faces. It's also where Indi came from.'

As they rode through the Rajput countryside the air was still surprisingly moist. Eliza spotted goats grazing in the middle of the road, and they passed camels and buffaloes; it made her realize how quickly she was becoming acclimatized to this new world. She loved the smells of the desert sands and the wind blowing through her hair and the way it seemed to fill her up with the thing she had been missing for so long.

'The simple life continues here as it has for many centuries,' Jay shouted above the noise of the engine. 'Craftspeople weave rugs of camel hair, as they always have, and make water pots of local clay. I like to come this way for the birds.'

'You're a birdwatcher?'

'Not really, but we're on the migratory path of many species. If you keep your eyes peeled, you'll spot parakeets and peafowl.'

The whole time he was talking Eliza was thinking and appreciating a new kind of excitement about life that she'd never experienced before. Every time they met, something new about him surprised her.

'If we go out to Olvi lake there are waterfowl, herons, kingfishers, grebes and waders. Sometimes demoiselle cranes.'

'Stop,' she said with a laugh. 'I've got a head full of sand and heat. It's too much to take in and I can't hear properly over the noise of the bike.'

At that moment she spotted an animal she'd never seen before and he stilled the engine.

'It's the chinkara, an Asian gazelle, though you're likely to see more black buck here.' But he seemed distracted and paused as if thinking something through. 'While it's true that much of ordinary life is unchanged, for us – the rulers – you have to understand that the British have supplanted our powers with their own system of indirect rule.'

She frowned but felt encouraged enough to question him. 'But I don't understand why the Princes signed the treaties with the British. Why did they give so much away?'

'Rajputs originally came from beyond this region and needed to conquer lands that then became theirs. Everything came down to kinship and clan and the pursuit of territory. The different clans constantly fought each other in the hope of acquiring even more land and wealth. Our military strength increased through marriages arranged between different clans.'

'At home the aristocracy only marry each other too. Weak chins, you know!'

He laughed.

'The British offered to take on the responsibility of safeguarding our territories, but in exchange we had to act in subordination to them.'

'Strange that you agreed.'

'I think we were sick of fighting each other and of how much it cost us. Your people used to fear challenges from the princely states, so they kept us isolated from each other. It's a little better now that they are more sympathetic towards a co-operative relationship.'

'We're very different, aren't we?' she said. 'The British and the Rajputs, I mean.'

'Absolutely, though the British like the notion of nobility. But the differences are hard for some of us to assimilate. Educated in England, men lose their way when they come back to India and, with no real purpose, they turn to drink.'

'And you?'

He laughed. 'A foot in both worlds and no real place in either. My brother is happy to be a fancy-dress Prince. Not I.'

They were silent for a few moments, during which time Eliza turned it over in her mind and he lit a cigarette. She climbed out of the sidecar to stretch her legs, then watched him as he smoked sitting astride the bike. His hair was dishevelled from the wind and his left hand was smeared with oil. He wiped it carelessly on his trousers, then smiled at her. He was a complex man who had spoken light-heartedly about his life but she didn't believe he could be happy to live in such an aimless way. Though he was full of ease and charm, she guessed there was more to it.

'But you are not happy either,' he said, as if he had read her thoughts.

'I don't know what you mean,' she said, feeling suddenly irritable. This was too close to the bone. Also the fresh moistness had left the air and the increasing heat was making her cross.

'There's something about you that suggests detachment, though I am beginning not to believe it.'

'That's rather blunt,' she said, and made an effort not to sound upset. 'And hardly any of your business.'

There was a slight pause.

'I told you: I'm not British.'

'Clearly!'

'The British think we have mended our wicked ways,'

he said, 'but some of the old customs have simply gone underground.'

'How do you mean?'

'I'm thinking of Indi, I suppose. And what could so easily have happened to her.'

Eliza frowned.

'She came to the castle because her grandmother once helped save my life. My mother gave her grandmother a miniature painting as thanks, and told her if she ever needed help to bring the miniature to the castle and ask for the Maharani.'

'And?'

'Indi learnt to copy it.'

'With the help of a Thakur?'

'Yes.'

'But what might have happened to her?'

'I'll tell you later. We need to get going now.'

'Look,' she said, 'before we go I've been wondering if I should say anything, but Devdan warned me off spending time with you, said I could cause trouble with Chatur.'

'Did he?'

'The thing is, I saw something at the polo match where you got hurt. I haven't spoken of it before because I thought it might just have been my imagination, but I saw Chatur with another man seemingly laughing at your fall. I wondered if . . .'

He interrupted. 'You wondered if Chatur was behind it. That's what you think?'

'I thought it was just a prank, but could it really be more serious?'

His eyes darkened and he looked very thoughtful, then he muttered, 'The man is a menace but my brother does not see it. Chatur will stop at nothing. I've warned Anish.'

'But stop at nothing to do what?'

'To maintain control of my brother and his own power.'

She sighed. This really wasn't something to concern her.

Jay started the motorcycle up again and they continued on for a while, neither attempting to speak until he pulled up where a shroud of dust lay over a village of baked mud houses. Glad to stretch her legs, Eliza got out and gazed around her. The houses almost seemed as if they had risen from the earth like a tree or a bush might have done, and the simple beauty of the soft lines of the buildings drew her photographer's eye. This time she would only use her Rolleiflex.

'The *garh*, or fort, is the ancestral home of the landowner of the area,' Jay was saying. 'We will meet him first.'

'The locals too?'

'Yes, yes, but we must introduce ourselves to the Thakur first. He has an interest in art, and is something of an artist himself. He is the nobleman who took Indi under his wing. We have much to be thankful for.'

As they strolled through the village Eliza smiled as she watched the harmonious mix of craftspeople plying their trade, women walking like queens as they fetched water from the well, children running and shouting in the streets, and even animals grazing. Sleeping dogs lay everywhere and everyone they passed seemed friendly. Despite Jay's personal remarks earlier she felt a wave of gratitude that he'd brought her here, and followed as he walked through the village with easy long-legged strides.

'The family belongs to the same clan as we do,' Jay said. 'And my brother Anish is chief of the clan. See, there's the fort.'

Eliza gazed at a golden fort, small but very pretty, and as

they entered through a stone archway they were guided to an interior garden where the Thakur was painting at an easel. He was another of these tall dignified men Eliza was becoming used to meeting, except this man had grey in his moustache and was clearly much older than Jay. He rose from his seat, wiped his hands with a cloth and came towards them, arms outstretched.

'Welcome, welcome,' he was saying. 'Jayant. Wonderful to see you and your lovely companion. What can I get you?'

'A cool drink for both of us,' Jay said. 'All right with you, Eliza?'

She nodded and put her palms together in the usual way of welcome.

'So, please, take a seat, both of you.'

As they made themselves comfortable he carried on talking. 'This place was built some two hundred years ago, granted by the Maharajah for my ancestor's bravery. In return for the estate, he had to maintain eight horses for the Maharajah's cavalry and was expected to take part in any battles. Luckily that no longer applies to me.'

She smiled. 'I'm hoping to take photographs of the villagers. Will they be happy for me to do so?'

'No problem at all. I believe photography will be the new art.'

'I hope it won't replace painting but will live alongside it,' she said.

'Indeed. Jayant here tells me you speak our language.'

'A little.'

'She's being modest.'

'And how is Indira?' the Thakur asked Jay. He was smiling but his eyes looked tense. 'She rarely visits.'

'I know you understand why.'

The man's face fell. 'Yes indeed, though I miss her sunny presence, but let us not dwell on the past.'

Eliza longed to hear more, but something about the look on both men's faces stopped her asking. When they all got to their feet, Jay and the Thakur stepped away for a moment and Eliza couldn't hear what was said.

Then the Thakur led the way out of the fort. 'This place was once surrounded by mud walls. My grandfather built these stone walls but most of the *garh* stands as it originally was. The gate was enlarged so that a man sitting in a *howdah* on the back of an elephant could pass through.'

'It's very splendid,' Eliza said.

He nodded. 'Before you take photographs would you like to meet Indira's grandmother?'

'I'd love to.'

'I'll take you there and then leave you to it.'

Once into the village, they came to a halt outside a simple hut with a small courtyard and one scrawny rose bush. The Thakur called and a fierce-looking older woman with greying hair stepped out as if expecting them. She pulled her scarf over her hair and did not smile.

'She doesn't speak English. Will you understand enough?' Jay said.

'I'll let you know if I can't.'

Eliza concentrated as Jay and the Thakur spoke to the woman. She mainly wanted to know that Indira was well and happy and seemed pleased with their replies, visibly relaxing. But when Eliza heard her own name mentioned, the woman stared at her fixedly and asked Jay to repeat what he'd said.

'Eliza Fraser,' he said.

The woman's face closed up and she quickly took a few

98

steps back, then as suddenly as she had appeared she had gone again and the entire exchange was over. Jay and the Thakur exchanged glances.

'What was that about?' she asked, standing awkwardly and struggling to know how to feel.

'I'm sure it's nothing that need concern you,' Jay said.

She accepted what he'd said with no comment, but felt there had to be more to it. The Thakur stepped in to smooth things over. 'Let me tell you about the revenues. They come from the land as they have always done. The farmers culti-vate the fields for me and in return receive a part of the harvest. The shepherds are allowed to let their animals graze on the land in return for a share of their herd.'

'My friend Devdan would have something to say about that,' Jay said with a smile.

The Thakur raised his hands in an attitude of alarm. 'Remember I've met your friend. He's a revolutionary, is he not? Dangerous sort of a chap. A *badmash*.'

'He's not a bad character really. Just full of talk.'

'Well, I'd keep a careful watch on him. But now I must take my leave. Lovely to meet you, Miss Fraser.' And with that he again took Jay aside for a few private words.

Afterwards Jay and Eliza walked around the further reaches of the village. He was quieter than before and Eliza didn't know why, though she couldn't help but think it was something to do with her, and with that thought a prickle of alarm raised the hairs on the back of her neck. But because she had her hands full – a roll of film only allowed for six photographs, so Eliza kept having to duck into dark places to change the roll beneath a dark bag – she didn't ask what was wrong. Then, as they went deeper into the narrow alleyways and she saw the rudimentary ways in which the people lived in this barren place, she felt shock at the extreme poverty. How could it be right for the castle to become so wealthy while these people languished in utter penury? In these alleys some of the children were completely naked, and she could only just avoid walking in the stream of filthy water that ran in a ditch in the middle of the path. Here the people were thinner, with misery etched into the lines of their faces, and when she saw the difference between this part of the village and the other she fell rather quiet. There was nothing romantic about it, but she took photographs of it all: the poor, the lost and the seemingly forgotten. And it entered her head that by recording the plight of the poor she might be able to find a way to give voice to the voiceless.

As she climbed back into the sidecar, Jay asked if she'd like to go to a bazaar a few miles away where she'd be able to buy fabric printed with hand-carved wooden printing blocks. He had a bit of business to see to as well.

'It's a remote, little-visited place. For authentic Rajputana you can't do better.'

It was a friendly suggestion, though Jay's voice was solemn and there was a sharpness to it she hadn't noticed before. As he drove along the bumpiest road yet, Eliza thought about Indi's grandmother and decided to ask Jay to tell her more about Indi.

Jay pulled up the motorcycle for a moment, as if deciding on the way ahead.

'You said something earlier about the old ways having gone underground and you mentioned Indi. What was the connection?' She hoped he might be ready to say more now.

He sighed deeply. 'You must have noticed Indi is different. She is a little lighter-skinned than the rest of us and doesn't know who her father was. Added to that, her mother deserted her. Although she comes from a long line of Rajput warriors, on her mother's side that is, she suffers the disgrace of her lost parents. Blood ties are everything to us.'

'The poor girl,' she said, knowing it had been bad enough growing up without a father. Being without a father and a mother must have left Indi feeling terribly adrift, and the sense of isolation must have been awful. Hardly any wonder if the girl had become emotionally attached to Jay.

They had grown quiet, and when she glanced across at Jay he turned to look at her briefly.

'What?' he said.

'Are you so blind you don't realize she's in love with you?'

He looked blank, then drew his brows together and spoke almost as if she wasn't there. 'Nonsense. She's like a sister to me.'

Eliza made a gentle snorting sound.

There was a prickly silence for a moment.

'The Thakur's interest set her apart from the other villagers, and if it wasn't for his and her grandmother's protection, she would have been marked out as a *dakan*.'

'And that is?'

He gave her a look as if he was judging her reaction.

'A woman suspected of witchcraft.'

'In this day and age?'

He nodded slowly. 'When another woman thought to be a *dakan* was found dead with an axe in her back, Indi's grandmother acted quickly and sent Indi to the castle along with the original miniature, plus some pictures of her own. Indi told Laxmi she no longer had a safe home and, out of obligation to the grandmother, my mother had to take her in. They get rid of witches with an axe in the back.'

Eliza felt a shiver of alarm. 'You mean they might have

killed her too? That's what you meant when you said you worried about what might have happened to her.'

'Indi is talented, and very beautiful. Other women would have been jealous.'

Remembering Indi's looks, Eliza could understand why.

'So what happened when she came to the castle?'

'She started off as a handmaiden, but when her talent became fully known my mother gave her the task of painting each member of the royal household. She became my mother's eyes and ears. Remember Laxmi was Maharani then. I don't exactly know how, but Indi continues to have an ear for all the castle intrigue, gossip and plotting.'

'I imagine Laxmi was a wonderful queen.'

'She was. And a wonderful mother . . . though sometimes a bit too wonderful.'

The last part of his sentence had almost been an aside, and Eliza couldn't help comparing Laxmi, who almost certainly lived for her children, with Anna's lack of interest. So far Eliza had given little thought to motherhood and had scant regard for it.

Jay looked distracted for a moment, glancing at both possible tracks ahead, then picked up on Eliza's previous comment. 'Though of course the British disallowed the use of the words king and queen. A chief was what my father had to become. We were also banned from wearing crowns. They were the preserve of British royalty.'

Eliza grimaced. 'Honestly, that's almost funny, but I do feel a little guilty.'

He gave her a candid look. 'Don't. There's plenty of wrong on our side too. Had a son of my mother's not succeeded the throne, as a widow she would not be enjoying the high status she does.'

'I see.'

'We'd better get on.' He got back on the motorcycle. 'This way, I think.'

After a few more miles he cut the engine and they came to a halt. 'Please stay close,' he said, as they left the bike against a tree. He gave the appearance of walking nonchalantly but Eliza could tell something was up from the stiffness of his shoulders and the tight expression on his face. He found a local man and they spoke rapidly, Jay raising his voice but the man simply shaking his head.

Eliza heard a strange strangled bleating sound and, glancing down a side alley, saw a live goat hanging by the back feet. She shuddered as a village man drew a sword and with one strike decapitated the creature.

Jay turned to her. 'Quick, back into the sidecar.'

'But I just saw a –'

'Don't talk now, we have to hurry.' He put a hand on her back and almost pushed her.

'What's happening?'

As he started the bike up he turned towards her, a look of extreme anguish on his face. 'I told you the old customs had gone underground.'

'Yes.'

'Something terrible is about to happen.'

9

As Jay rode furiously along an increasingly rocky dirt track, Eliza gripped her seat. Fear locked itself behind her ribs. The not knowing made things worse and up until now she had not seen him look so worried. She sensed he lived within a world beyond her sight, an inner, protected realm – and, just like the Rajput kingdom she might never fully understand, there were layers within layers to this man. Hidden beneath the rituals and customs of his life lay something important, something that glued it all together. She wondered what it was and decided to make it her business to learn more about the Hindu gods. It might help her understand these people better, but for now this was nothing mystical or strange, merely the private workings of another human being who, at this moment, was excluding her.

'So tell me, please,' she shouted. 'What's going on?'

'It's a widow-burning. The Thakur had heard a rumour that there might be one tomorrow, but Indira's grandmother told me to come to the village we've just left and that's when I found out it is today.'

'Oh, dear God. But I thought you said suttee is illegal? We must stop it.'

'That's what I'm intending to do. It is illegal but that doesn't mean it is at an end. The people know the British will be reluctant to intervene if they choose remote locations.'

The sun, now directly overhead, beat down on a bleached landscape that had turned menacing in its emptiness. On the brink of tears, Eliza wished herself anywhere but there.

'Look, Eliza,' Jay was saying, 'I warned you the old rituals had gone underground. This is what we're up against.'

'But burning a woman alive!'

'Nothing changes overnight.'

As Jay rode on in silence Eliza gazed out at the stark beauty of the fringes of the desert, feeling sick inside. Then, a little later, the sound of drums alerted them to the fact that they were drawing closer.

As Jay climbed down, Eliza made a move too.

'No, stay. We may already be too late.'

'I'm coming.'

He paused for a fraction of a second only. 'Very well, but we'll have to run.'

Though December was considered the Rajputana winter, it could still become hotter than an English summer. This day was no exception, and Eliza's forehead was already beading with sweat.

'Cover your head with your scarf and as much of your face as you can.'

As they neared the gathering, the sound of the drums and a kind of chanting took over.

'What's happening now?'

He paused and stood still for a moment. 'See over there behind that building, by the scant river bed?'

Eliza twisted to see a large group of people partly obscured from view.

'I need to skirt around, but I want you to stay back here. There's nothing you can do, but if I tell them who I am I might be able to stop this.'

This time Eliza did hold back and she waited, at least for a short while; but after a few minutes, when Jay had disappeared from view and the chanting hadn't stopped, she began to shiver. She ran after him until she reached a spot just past the building, where she knew at once that the drumming had been an invocation of death.

At first she saw Jay shaking his head and, with voice raised, arguing with a group of men. Eliza couldn't see the girl but about twenty yards away a priest, standing beside the funeral pyre, was swinging a large object filled with incense. Another was ringing a bell that was audible even above the drumming, while two other men poured oil from earthenware jugs on to hardwood logs. When another man lit a torch, then touched it to the prepared wood, small flames struck out at the air instantly and then died down. When she heard a terrible high-pitched keening she finally saw the girl being dragged forward.

Eliza took a step forward and shouted, but no one even glanced her way. All eyes were on the slight figure being hauled on to the pyre. Everything seemed to go still, and Eliza was horrified that although the girl's hands were tied together, for a moment it seemed as if she had accepted her fate. But then everything changed, as Jay turned his back on the men and raced towards the girl, where, pushing and fighting his way, he broke through the cordon of men.

From a low crackle and spit, suddenly the fire was fully ablaze. Eliza's heart almost stopped as Jay caught hold of the girl's hands and began pulling her away from the flames. Seconds passed and Eliza smelt the girl's fear in her own nostrils, felt the terror on her own shivering skin. Jay struggled to drag the girl away and for a moment it looked as if he might be burned to death as well, but then three men grabbed hold of him and pulled him off the girl. He fought to escape their grip and launch himself at her again, but they held him tight. Now the flames sprang up around the edges, enclosing the girl in the centre, from where she was still trying to break through. She screamed repeatedly as a larger group of men and one older woman surrounded the pyre, again pushing her back, but this time with long sticks, on to a supine body wrapped in white.

And yet the girl managed to whip round and run to one side, where the flames were weakest. A man raised his sword to strike her so she was forced to shrink back into the flames. Beyond her a huge crowd stood silently watching. Eliza longed to run over to the fire and drag the girl away, but then Jay broke free and once again attempted to reach the girl. He was too late, as in that instant yellow flames licked at the young woman's feet; her skirt caught alight, then her scarf and finally her hair, the colour so bright and sharp Eliza could barely look. As an inferno engulfed the girl, Eliza couldn't see Jay but the screaming continued, sounding more and more desperate.

A pitiless cloud of black smoke rose into the air and with it a smell Eliza knew she would not forget as long as she lived. The wind got up and the flames leapt higher, swirling and dancing as they carried the girl's screams up into the blue, blue sky.

Eliza staggered backwards and then began to run wildly from the terrible scene. And when the girl stopped screaming, all Eliza could hear was the crackling of the fire. In deep shock she doubled over, and with tears blinding her she felt Jay's arms around her, pulling her further from the smell of burning flesh.

'You shouldn't have seen this,' he said.

She twisted away from him and began to beat him on the chest with her fists. 'Why did it have to happen? Why?'

He held her again, only tighter this time, and she saw that one of his hands was burnt.

'You're hurt.'

'It's nothing.'

'I saw what you tried to do.'

He shook his head. 'I was too late. I had hoped to talk them out of it. They had hidden the girl. I thought I had time.'

He put an arm around her shoulders and helped her back to the motorcycle.

As Eliza climbed up into her seat, her heart still pounding to the beat of a drum that had surely been calling the woman to her death, she wept. Then, as it passed a little, she gazed at Jay, whose arms were folded on the handlebars with his forehead resting on his hands. There was such a bursting pain in her chest that she knew her own voice might take over from where the frantic, screaming woman had left off.

'She was so young,' he said.

Eliza didn't reply, but gulped at air in an effort to breathe normally.

'We won't go home. I think I'll take you to my palace. It's only an hour from the Juraipore castle but there's more privacy. We'll be able to talk in a way we could not back at the castle.'

'There's nothing to talk about,' she managed to say through subdued sobs that very quickly began to erupt again.

'There's a great deal to say, but first you have to deal with the emotion of witnessing such a thing. I have seen it before.'

They didn't speak during the journey and, after about an hour, they arrived at what she immediately could see was a palace of faded beauty. He took her through a large gateway set into a long high wall, and into a beautiful area surrounded by buildings of golden stone on three sides, with doors on two sides facing into the courtyard.

'Servants' quarters, stables and store rooms,' he said.

On the side opposite the gateway a colonnaded veranda stretched the length of an ancient two-storey building. It was clear there was water here too, because, unlike everywhere else she had been, the courtyard was remarkably green and what looked like pink and red petunias spilled from tubs placed around the edges. A tall yellow flowering tree with long leaves stood in the middle, providing a vast amount of shade to the two benches beneath.

'It's Siamese cassia,' he said when he saw her looking. 'They can reach a height of sixty feet. This one is not quite that yet. We use this kind of tree for furniture and crafts. There are more in the gardens beyond,' he said, pointing at somewhere beyond the colonnade.

As they walked through the building and along an open gallery and terrace at the back to an exterior staircase, Eliza could see the extensive gardens and what looked like an orchard. The scent of grass drifted across and she breathed in the green freshness of the air. Though she still had no idea how she would ever process her disgust and horror, it had been a thoughtful choice to come to this quiet retreat. She stopped for a moment to gaze into the distance and saw that the land right at the back sloped gently downwards.

Jay showed her to a first-floor bedroom. 'When it is cooler and you are ready, join me on the terrace below.' He squeezed her hand. 'Until later.'

Eliza lay down on a bed that could not have been slept in for some time. She could smell mothballs, but also some kind of perfume that reminded her of Laxmi. Perhaps this had been Jay's mother's room at some point? There was a small drawing room attached too, which Jay called a *dari khana*, with a large rug on the floor and several cushions. Eliza tried to think of other things but all she could hear were the woman's screams, over and over in her head. A stranger in a strange land, she had hoped that coming here would help her find her feet but, in fact, she was sinking further out of her depth. This was not a comfortable world for her, for any woman, she thought, and couldn't help wondering if she was even safe? She was a widow too. How must it feel to be put to death in such an agonizing way: the searing pain, the dread, the raw cruelty more awful than she could ever have imagined?

As the brightness of the day faded and the sky turned lilac and then pink, she went in search of Jay, eventually finding him nursing a whisky and slumped in a wicker chair on the arched terrace or gallery at the back of the building, this one smaller and more intimate than the colonnaded walkway at the front. With a dejected air he ran his hand over his head to push the dishevelled hair from his face. When he rubbed his forehead she could see it was smeared with black from the fire.

'We used to live out here, most of the time,' he said, and waved a bandaged hand at the area beyond. 'Drink?'

While a butler fetched her a drink, she sat in a chair opposite Jay. As darkness descended, the moon was rising and casting a silvery light over the garden, from where night-time scents of earth and some kind of intensely aromatic stocks infused the air. She felt as if she could lose herself in its gentle warmth, but then Jay began to speak.

'A couple of weeks before my grandfather died, my

grandmother stopped eating and drinking. She looked after her husband and nursed him, but late one night I heard her chanting *"Ram-Ram"* repeatedly. He had just died and she had already announced that she was going to commit suttee when he was cremated the next morning. She believed it a dishonour for a wife to outlive her husband.'

He pocketed a box of matches that had been lying on the table, got to his feet, and picked out a taper from a metal box attached to the wall. He pulled out the matchbox, struck a match and lit the taper. As he touched the taper to a couple of lamps fixed to the exterior wall, the smell of burning oil filled the air. The light flickered and Eliza watched the trail of smoke for a minute or two.

'You were there?'

'I'd gone there with my mother because she knew her father didn't have long. After he died my grandmother washed herself and put on her wedding clothes, then sat with my grandfather's body for the rest of the night with only the howling of the city dogs for company. When the sun rose her *devar* arrived, her husband's brother, who was going to perform the last rites. When a *sati* goes to the pyre she is accompanied by crowds of people and they had already started gathering.'

'You saw all this?'

He had been gazing out into the darkness but now he turned back to look at her, his eyes sombre, the light gone, but with his lips twisted in a grim smile.

'She had sent for me, but my mother intercepted the message and ordered me locked in my room. My mother didn't approve, but I had to see so I climbed out of the window. I loved both my grandparents.' He paused and swallowed visibly before resuming. 'Sometimes they tie the women down. Not my grandmother. When I finally arrived the flames were raging and I couldn't even see her – but I could hear her. She was chanting *"Ram-Ram"*, right up until she died. People still worship her to this day.'

Eliza fell silent for a few moments. She gazed at the chiselled angular lines of his face, seeming more full of shadows in the lamplight, and could see the grief and shock still etched there. How had she not spotted it before? But then he hunched his shoulders and sank into some kind of internal silence, bending his head and gazing at his hands. She could see the muscle in his jaw working. What an awful thing for a child to witness; it must have broken him, just as her father's death had broken her.

'How old were you?'

'I was thirteen. It was a week before my fourteenth birthday. It happened during the school holidays or I'd have been in England.'

She watched him with tears moistening her eyes, full of pity for the child he had been. 'And I don't suppose you told anyone when you went back to school?'

He shook his head and looked back at her. She felt as if she was seeing right into him and he into her. Then he glanced away.

'They already thought of me as a savage or a pet. My grandmother adored her husband and was devastated by his death, but apart from my mother nobody tried to dissuade her. Her brother-in-law was only worried that if she did not go through with it she'd bring shame to the family.'

'Why do women allow it?'

He shrugged. 'A few still see it as the ultimate form of womanly devotion and sacrifice. She wanted to be with her husband in the next life, so for her it was the only way.'

'But it's a crime against women.'

He looked at her again, with such sadness in his eyes she longed to comfort him, but still she had to speak.

'What if there is no next life, Jay?'

He sighed deeply but held her gaze.

'Women are of so little value?' she said.

'Those who wish to become *sati* speak of it as a voluntary act of devotion. You and I might say they have been brainwashed. They have certainly internalized the old beliefs. The choice was to be burned or regarded as a failed wife.'

'With no coercion?'

He snorted and finally looked away, and for a moment she felt as if a spell had been broken. 'Oh yes. Priests who receive something of value from the women's possessions encourage them. The relatives of both families who want their jewellery encourage them, and in some cases the women have to be drugged with *bhang*, marijuana to you, or opium. Or tied to the husband's corpse with cords, or otherwise weighted down. However, even though life as a widow is hard, many did try to run away. And if they did they brought disgrace on their entire family.'

'The pull of life stronger than family ties or any promise of immortality?'

'Yes.'

'But some truly believe. Like your grandmother?'

'I think so. To some it is, and was, a deeply spiritual choice. Hard to understand, isn't it? But it happens for many reasons, not always coercion or religion, and sometimes a depressed or despairing woman uses it as a means of straightforward suicide, which of course is illegal.'

'It seems bound up with this idealized version of how a woman ought to be.'

'It's not so different in your culture, though less extreme of course.'

'We don't burn women.' Despite the misery stamped on his face, she gave him what she realized must be a sharp look. 'And female infanticide doesn't happen in England.'

'Not now maybe, but go back in time. Did you know that after the British outlawed suttee here there were more cases than before?'

She shook her head and there was an uncomfortable silence for a few moments.

'What will you do?'

'Tell Anish and then Chatur, both of whom will do nothing. And I'll speak to Clifford Salter too. The British might chase up the culprits but they'll get nowhere. The villagers will close ranks.'

'But you could identify them.'

'The British won't take it that far. They know it still goes on.'

'Why is it that all over the world women are, and have been, so badly mistreated?' she said, feeling such a sense of anguish she hardly knew how to deal with it.

He shrugged. 'It's the age-old question. I don't know the answer.'

Eliza became aware of how far out on the edge she could end up here, but, at the same time, if she was going to stay, she also felt a growing need not simply to judge India, but to better understand it.

Night lay over the garden like a blanket. She could see nothing, but listened to the creaking of branches and animals shifting in the undergrowth and hesitated for some minutes before she opened her mouth, scared that, if she made the wrong move or said the wrong thing, the foundations of her life might crack open. In Jay's sad eyes, she saw herself, and because of that she wanted to give him something of herself. She had always believed that if she didn't speak of her father she could protect herself, but she had been living behind glass that she realized might now be about to crack.

Eventually she broke the long silence and looked straight into his eyes. 'My father died when I was ten,' she said, as her heart began to hammer.

'I'm very sorry to hear that.'

She could see in his eyes that he meant it.

'I witnessed his death too.'

10

Eliza opened her eyes on a gilded morning, the air so sweet and fresh she could almost persuade herself it hadn't been real, that it had only been a nightmare mercifully dissolved by daylight. But for the smell. She had fallen into bed the night before, still dressed; now she tore off her clothes, where the smell of human sacrifice still clung, and found a robe in a tall dark wardrobe. Wrapping it around herself, she went to the terrace in search of Jay.

Out there the day was so still that not even a leaf was moving, but still the scent of aromatic herbs drifted across from where they seemed to be growing, and the scent of jasmine and something like honeysuckle infused the air. She noticed that the arched arcade that lined the terrace was the colour of sand and was shimmering in the sunlight. The evening before she hadn't noticed the colour.

'If only it could always be like this,' she said, as she saw Jay following the butler, who carried a tray of what looked like coffee.

'How?'

'Peaceful.'

He stared into the sky as if looking for an answer and then glanced at her.

'It's where my heart is,' he said, his eyes glowing with feeling. 'It's where I come when the world feels impossible. And, as it happens, where I was born.'

'Was the room I'm staying in your mother's?'

He nodded as they looked at each other. 'We all of us have broken hearts. You, me, Indi. It's what unites us.'

As he sank into thought she could believe what he'd said. With stubble on his chin, he was still dressed in yesterday's clothes, smelling of dirt, sand and smoke, and though his face was clear of black smears, he looked somehow lost.

'You need fresh clothes?' he asked. 'I certainly do.'

She nodded.

'I can sort that.'

'I need to wash my hair too.'

Eliza, unlike Clifford, increasingly did not think that the British in India had been sensitive to the customs of the native races. But up until now she had believed the British had right on their side, and yet if they were just going to turn their back on such horrors it made them culpable too. They had certainly overreacted when subduing rebellions, and really, what right did they have to be there at all? This awful thing made her feel sick to her soul. Misogyny had many faces in different parts of the world, but nobody deserved to be burned alive, cooked as if they were nothing but meat. Nobody.

She gazed out at the beautiful tangled garden and felt its calmness and tranquillity. It was wild and it was wonderful, with pathways still kept clear and flowers – climbing roses, jasmine, she knew not what – all tumbling in profusion. Though it wasn't hard to see how it could be made even more magnificent, with perhaps the vista opened up in places. It was clear there was water somewhere too, and perhaps the slope of the land had something to do with it.

She decided to ask.

'Some of it is rainwater, collected in small tanks. There are small rivers or *nallahs* which flow in the rains and we have wells here. But we need to do more by constructing dams, tanks and bunds. Basically we need irrigation works, but I'm not sure what I can do.'

'Don't you want to make a difference to people's lives?'

He frowned, but her last thought had struck her with force.

She carried on thinking about the water. There might not be anything she could do about the treatment of women, but it made her feel better to think of other ways to help people.

'There must be a way to help the people.'

'I do everything I can, employ only locals, allow them to come for well water in our courtyard, but it's up to my brother to make the taxation fairer and he will not.'

'But what about irrigation?'

'Well, as I've said –'

She interrupted. 'Surely you could build some kind of system,' she said.

'I have looked into it.'

'But here. It's the perfect place. On your own land, where it slopes you could dig out a lake and maybe others beyond.'

'You must think I'm made of money? I own this bike, but Eliza, the car is my mother's. I have this beautiful old place I can barely afford to restore and a fairly generous living allowance, but it would never stretch to funding an irrigation project.'

'Then raise the money. Where there's a will . . .' She paused for a moment but couldn't stop herself. 'Do you even see the poverty of the people?'

'Of course.'

'No, Jay. I don't think so. You see what you want to see, but I'm going to develop yesterday's photographs and you're going to look at them with your eyes wide open. You won't be able to ignore it so easily when you see things in black and white. It's time to take action. Do something.'

'You sound like my friend Devdan.'

'Well, if his aim is to do something about the inequalities here, then I'm with him. You have water here. So start here.'

'And the cash?'

'Raise it. I'll do whatever I can.'

Eliza appreciated that Jay's palace was a special place of retreat, refreshing to the mind and soul. Despite what she had witnessed, she still felt as if she'd taken a step into something she had lost and it was making her think differently. She couldn't have said what it was. Belonging, perhaps. Though that seemed a strange thing to say after seeing something that could only make her feel like an outsider.

After breakfasting on some kind of cake with milky curd and honey, she went back to her room, where a set of Indian clothes had been laid out, and at the small washstand she discovered a bowl of tepid water and a jug. She washed her hair to rid herself of the last of the smell, but couldn't prevent tears forming as she thought of the young woman again. No more hair-washing for her, no children, no life. She left her hair to hang down still wet, dressed, then found Jay sitting in a sparsely furnished but light and airy downstairs room with soft walls that shone like polished eggshells.

He smiled and stood up when he saw her. 'You have beautiful hair.'

'Like this?' She lifted the wet strands.

He laughed. 'When it's dry. There are so many different colours in it. Sometimes like gold, sometimes like fire.'

'So not camel after all.'

'I was rude. Forgive me.'

He looked into her eyes and just for a moment she felt she could forgive him anything.

'I thought you were yet another British person come to gape at us quaint natives.'

'I was never that.'

As they walked they talked. First he took her to the beautiful colonnaded walkway he had once described. It was in fact a loggia or large porch, as he'd said, and led away from the terrace down one side of the garden. The arches were pointed and the spandrels were sculpted with delicately carved flowers and leaves. Some were broken, but the stone was softly golden.

'We have abundant sandstone, slate, marble and other materials here in Rajputana. The Makrana quarries provided much of the marble for the Taj at Agra. But we also have limestone from Jaisalmer and red stone too, used to build the Red Fort in Delhi. Have you seen it?'

'Yes, and I'd like to go back to Delhi. As you know, we used to live there. In fact I might have to go at some point to pick up my finished prints.'

'Well, make sure you stay at the Imperial. All the British do.'

She nodded, and they went through a wide doorway to the most astonishing, double-height room, where the light flowed in from windows she couldn't even see.

'They are above the arches,' he said, seeing her looking.

The way the light lit the top half of the room made it seem as if the sun had been invented for just that purpose, and its height was such that their voices seemed to rise up and become changed.

'It's a reception hall, but look at the floor.'

She glanced down and saw that the marble floor was broken and crumbling in places.

He stood still for a moment. 'Do you want to talk about what happened to your father?'

She closed her eyes for a second or two, and when she opened them he was looking at her with such kindness that she had to blink away the heat at the back of her lids.

'It happened on December the twenty-third, 1912. I'll never forget the date because he was sitting on an elephant following immediately behind the Viceroy at the head of a procession. My mother and I were so proud. Delhi was going to take over from Calcutta as the centre of British Government, and this was the day the Viceroy made his ceremonial state entry into the city.'

Jay was looking at her very intently and his eyes had darkened. 'Go on.'

She prepared to answer calmly. 'Somebody threw a bomb. My mother and I were standing on our balcony watching. I saw my father slump over and when I ran down to the street, I found out that the bomb had killed him.' She paused and he reached out a hand to her.

'It was my fault. I'd asked him to stop and wave at me. If I hadn't done that . . . Anyway, I went to him and threw my arms around him. I told him I loved him. For many years I pretended to myself he had heard me. Somebody helped me up, but my new white dress was red with his blood.'

'Eliza, this may seem an odd question, but do you believe in destiny?'

'I'm not sure if I really know what it means,' she said.

'We believe you can alter your own destiny but there are some things that seem to be meant to be. That they have no option but to happen.'

'Like what?'

He looked as if he was judging whether to say something serious but in the end had decided not to.

He smiled, then waved his hand about dismissively. 'It means different things to different people, I suppose. I just wondered what it meant to you.'

A little later Jay led her through the garden to some stables at the rear of the palace. She wondered why they weren't setting off back home and asked him why not.

'Do you ride?' he asked with his face to the sun.

'I'm a bit rusty.'

He glanced down at her. 'I thought we might take a short trip off the beaten track.'

A stable boy greeted him and Jay returned the greeting affectionately, then the boy brought out two horses. Meanwhile Eliza was still fretting about destiny and why he had asked her about her beliefs. She resolved to question him later.

'Desert horses,' he said, unaware of her train of thought.

Eliza was astonished by the magnificent heads that rose from thick arched necks, and the beautiful curved ears rising inwards to a point, but what really caught her attention was the long lashes and gorgeous flaring nostrils.

'The desert horse was originally sired from Arab horses.'

'Actually, could we do this another time? I need to get back to the castle to get my film developed before it goes off. Do you mind?'

'Just a short ride? Don't worry, yours is very docile.'

She felt torn between wanting to spend more time with him and anxiety about her horse-riding skills. 'I'll hold you back.'

When he just smiled she could see refusal was pointless and nodded her nervous acceptance. The last time she'd ridden had been when she was a teenager, but as she was beginning to feel he might be somebody she could really trust in this alien world, she couldn't resist the chance to spend a little longer in his company.

'Shall we try bareback? If you haven't experienced it before you'll find it quite wonderful. It will help you get over the awful memory of what happened yesterday.'

She didn't say, but thought nothing could ever erase that.

'You form a much greater bond with the animal. Willing to give it a go? You won't be able to go side-saddle.'

Eliza just looked at him but didn't speak. He took her silence for acceptance and went on to help her up on to the horse, where she sat with her heart pounding.

'Watch me,' he said as he mounted. 'You need to sit a bit more forward on the horse and rest your legs more forward too, and don't squeeze your heels or lower legs into the horse's sides when slowing or stopping. Don't be nervous.'

But Eliza didn't want to put her life into the hands of the animal.

'It will be fine. Trust the horse. If you don't he will feel your fear. Just relax and enjoy the ride.'

Before they moved she glanced across at him. 'What do you mean by destiny?'

He shrugged. 'We think a lot of destiny here.'

His answer did not feel satisfactory, and something about the way he looked away meant she didn't fully believe that was really why he'd raised the subject earlier. There was something he was avoiding saying.

They started off gently, and even though the pace wasn't fast, Eliza's scalp and palms began sweating. They passed several poverty-stricken villages and she could see the misery of lives eked out in this parched landscape. It made her think again about how water would change these people's lives. Then gradually, as they left the villages behind, with the wind blowing in her hair, she began to enjoy the experience of riding the magical rough terrain of Rajputana. She even began to feel a closer connection with her horse.

Jay was true to his word. The ride was short, and before long she was back in the sidecar.

'Did you enjoy it?' he asked before revving the motorcycle.

'Do you know, I surprised myself.' It was true. Though the woman's screams still echoed inside her head, the ride had helped her feel less taut.

He laughed and she looked at him. 'You should have seen your face,' he said. 'Flushed and pink. I wanted to carry you off to my private kingdom and keep you prisoner.'

'You have a private kingdom?' was all she said, then she looked away, though whether from embarrassment or because her heart was pounding again she was, as yet, unwilling to consider.

II

Back at the castle the first person Eliza saw was Indira. Light spilled through the tall windows of the hallway, tracing patterns on the floor, and as Eliza gazed at them she was aware of feeling out of step with such brilliance.

'You were longer than expected,' Indi said, and smiled, though she seemed a little edgy as they walked through the downstairs rooms together.

'Yes.'

Indi paused while Eliza walked on. 'Why? It's only a day trip to my village and back.'

Thinking the girl was merely being inquisitive, Eliza turned back to look at her. 'Something happened.'

'With Jay?'

Eliza's heart sank. She had hoped maybe to talk about what had happened with Indi but, shocked by Indi's hard cold eyes as she stared back at her, Eliza knew she could not. 'I'd rather not talk about it.'

'Did you stay at his palace?'

'Yes, in Laxmi's old room I think.'

'That's Jay's bedroom now.'

'I didn't know that.'

'So where did he sleep?'

'I don't know. Look, I do have to get some developing done.' Eliza took a couple of steps away, but Indi came up to her and caught hold of her sleeve.

'These are not your clothes. What happened to your clothes?'

Indi's eyes had narrowed and that same look of jealousy and suspicion that Eliza had spotted during the ball was back again. Stunned by the open hostility, she responded in a clumsy way.

'I . . . I . . .'

'He gave you his bedroom. You are privileged. He's never given it to me.'

Eliza balked at Indi's tone of voice. She would not allow the girl to speak to her like this. 'I'm sorry, but that isn't my fault. Now please, I really have to go.' She shrugged her off and managed to get away, but the short interaction had left a bitter taste in her mouth. She really didn't want to make an enemy of Indira.

Although Eliza tried, she couldn't get the suttee out of her mind. It wasn't even the horror of seeing it that caught at her heart, it was the terrible smell that had crept into her nostrils and stayed there. She decided she really had to talk to someone; someone English who might fully understand how she felt. So she slipped out and, after acquiring a rickshaw to take her, fifteen minutes later she was sinking into a comfy sofa in Dottie's parlour and drinking tea from a bone china cup.

'Well, I must say this is a real treat,' Dottie was saying. 'I find it hard to fill the hours, though I don't suppose you have that problem.'

Eliza shook her head, only half listening. The normality of Dottie and everything that was English struck her: the little bowl of sweet peas on the coffee table, the piano in the corner, the paintings of sheep dogs and the pretty floral curtains. A Liberty fabric, she thought as she shook her head again and felt a wave of homesickness.

'I wanted to talk to you,' she said. 'My mind is running wild and I hardly know how to think or feel.' She felt a lump in her throat as she spoke and took a deep shuddering breath. Could she even speak of it? Words seemed an imperfect match against the reality of such a death.

'Of course.'

Eliza glanced at Dottie's kind face. 'If I tell you, I'm not sure who should actually know.'

Dottie looked puzzled.

'I . . .' Eliza paused. 'I saw something.'

'Yes?'

'A woman burned to death.'

Dottie bit her lip. 'How awful. An accident?'

'No. You don't . . .' She took a breath. 'It was . . . a widow-burning.'

Dottie's hand went straight to her mouth and the colour drained from her cheeks. 'Dear God! I don't know what to say. You must be in a terrible state of shock.'

'I think I must be. I thought I was all right but I keep smelling her burning flesh. I can't get it out of my mind. Dottie, it was the most heart-breaking thing I've ever seen.'

'Oh, darling.'

A sob burst from Eliza.

Dottie stood up and began to pace the room. 'Well, it's against the law, so first of all we must tell Clifford and then –'

'No,' Eliza interjected. 'No. Please let Jay do it. He says it still happens and the authorities do absolutely nothing. I'm wondering if he might just deal with it within the state and leave the British out of it.'

Now Dottie looked shocked and stood to stare at Eliza. 'He surely didn't take you to see it!'

'No. We were on our way somewhere and he tried to get it stopped.'

'And?'

'He was very brave, even burned his hand, but . . .' Another sob erupted. 'We were too late to stop it.'

Dottie walked over to the drinks cabinet and turned the key. 'I think you need something stronger than tea. I know I do.' She held up a bottle. 'Brandy do you?'

Eliza nodded, and Dottie brought over two tumblers of the amber liquid, downing hers in one as soon as she sat down on the sofa next to Eliza.

'Christ, these people,' she said. 'I don't care about their belief system; this is an absolute abomination. Utterly barbaric.' She shook her head. 'Just when you begin to feel at home, something like this happens.'

'But there really isn't anything *like* this, is there . . . I don't know what to do. It was the most awful thing I've ever seen.' Eliza hung her head and felt the tears burning her eyes.

'I'm sure it was.'

'I just feel so sickened.' Eliza bent forward and buried her face in her hands.

Dottie patted her on the back. 'You poor, poor girl.'

Eliza twisted her head to glance up at Dottie. 'Jay says suttee has gone underground and that for a while it happened even more frequently after we made it illegal. It must be Jay who reports. It's better coming from him.'

'Did he tell you to say that?'

Eliza glanced up. 'No! Of course not.'

'Because it's murder, Eliza. They can't be allowed to get away with it.'

'They already have and they already do. Look, I'd better go. Please keep it to yourself for now. I don't really want Clifford knowing I was there. He'll only blame Jay or try to restrict what I can do.'

Dottie touched her hand. 'Darling, I can't let you go in this state. You're actually shaking. Stay and have a bite to eat. Just a sandwich maybe?'

Later that afternoon Eliza busied herself in her darkroom, and when she wasn't in there she lost herself in remembering what she had seen and what Dottie had said. When she thought of Jay she found herself warming to him even more than before. She had wanted to ask him again about destiny and couldn't stop thinking about that either. Was it, like fate, something you had no control over? If it was, she could never agree with such a fatalistic view of life.

Her thoughts turned to Indira. She'd need to think of a way to encourage friendship with the girl rather than competition. After a while she undressed and lay on her bed, listening to the birds outside her window. At first the voices of the past wouldn't let her go. First her father promising her he would wave, then Oliver just before he stormed out, slamming the door on the marriage and on his own life. But eventually, exhausted by a mix of grief and shock, she fell asleep.

A knock at the door woke her and, thinking it must be Indi or Kiri, she wrapped a loose silk robe around herself and went to the door, her hair completely dishevelled. To her surprise Jay stood there. They stared at each other and, as her cheeks grew hot, she pulled the robe more tightly over her breasts.

'What do you want?' she managed to say.

'My mother wishes to speak with you.'

'Why did you come to tell me? Have I done something wrong?'

'No. She simply suggested it.'

Throughout this exchange she had held his gaze. Now he averted his eyes for a moment before looking back at her. 'Eliza, I . . .'

'Yes?'

He reached out and touched her hair. 'You have beautiful hair.'

She smiled. 'I think you may have told me before.'

There was something in his expression that made her feel more than she wanted to feel. But was he playing with her? She fingered the silver chain she always wore and the small gemstone that sat in the hollow of her throat, then touched the place where her pulse raced. In that moment England seemed very distant. In fact every time he looked at her, England felt more and more distant.

'Will you wait in the corridor? Actually, hang on, you might take a look at these while I get dressed.' She stepped back, picked up her contact sheets and handed them to him, her hands trembling. She mustn't let him affect her like this.

While dressing she heard someone speaking in Hindi out in the corridor and went over to the door to see if she could hear what it was about.

First she recognized Jay's low voice, but then a shrill female voice took over and, though she couldn't make out the words, it became clear that the voice was Indira's. Eliza did not consider herself beautiful but had experienced female envy before. When she was at boarding school a group of girls had held her down and chopped off her long hair. She'd lived in terror after that, and the last thing she needed now, where she was feeling so out of her depth, was to be the victim of another woman's malice.

Eventually the corridor went quiet and, as Eliza emerged, Jay was pacing up and down while glancing at her photos.

'Trouble?' she asked.

'Sorry, I didn't get much of a chance to look at these but I really do understand what you mean about the poverty. We become inured to it, you see. Can I keep them for a while?' He gave her half a smile and then shook his head. 'You were right about Indira too. I've been blind.'

'Always easier for an outsider to spot such things.'

He sighed. 'I never encouraged her. I have no feelings of that kind towards her. It would have been absolutely wrong and I always think of her as a kid sister.' He gave her a look she couldn't interpret. 'When I marry it will have to be with somebody of equal birth. If anything happens to my brother I have to take over.'

Well, that's pretty clear, Eliza thought.

'As I said, if Anish dies, I succeed to the throne, though Chatur will do everything in his power to prevent that. There is a great deal I'd want to change, and right at the top of the list would be reducing Chatur's role. But to do it I would have to conform to tradition.'

'Of course. It's nothing to do with me either way.' She steeled herself not to show any emotion at his tone of voice or the content of his words, but what he'd said had taken her aback and she wondered if it had been a warning message for her too.

'Now let's go and talk to Laxmi. By the way, I have already spoken to Clifford Salter about the *sati*. He was shocked, as you would expect, and promises to look into it.'

He paused. 'I didn't mention you had seen it too. Should I have?'

'No. I'd rather he didn't know. I don't want him to over-protect me.'

'The fact is he will be able to do very little.'

Jay led her through the endless corridors and rooms to the blue vestibule she'd waited in when she'd first arrived.

'Indi painted this room for my mother.'

Eliza looked at the blue flowers, leaves and filigree scrolls picked out in gold, rising up the walls and trailing across the ceiling.

'She is amazingly talented.'

Laxmi came out at that moment and held out a hand to Eliza. 'I'm pleased to see you. My son has been telling me about your trip.'

Unsure which bit of the trip she was referring to, and listening to the unsteady rhythm of her own heart, Eliza nodded.

Once within the inner principal reception room she saw that it was beautiful. Like a gleaming mirrored palace or *sheesh mahal*, all the walls were adorned with inlaid col-oured glass mosaic, with winged angels painted on the ceiling and gilded plasterwork. She gazed in amazement. It was like nothing she'd ever seen, and the floor was piled high with silk cushions, though Laxmi indicated that they were to sit on chairs. Eliza perched on the edge of a red vel-vet upright affair, while Jay sprawled on a chaise longue.

'I understand you have an idea about irrigation,' Laxmi said.

'It was just a thought.'

'And a good one, though my eldest son, Anish, might not agree, but since Jayant spoke to me about it this morning I have thought of little else. It seems to me that if we are to keep the people on our side we have to make their lives easier; if not, the British, or the rebels, will easily persuade them to turn against us. As you know, it is already happening in some parts of the state, and this kind of unrest can only increase. I fear for our kingdom and I have been waiting for Anish to take action but, as he has not, I feel I must take matters into my own hands. So now I have come up with a plan and wish to unburden myself.'

Jay raised his brows. 'Prepare to be shocked.'

'My idea is this. We have considerable family jewels in our vaults. If we are able to obtain a promise of British funding, I would happily cover the initial costs of an engineer to develop a plan for the project.'

'We should be honest, Mother.'

Prompted by Jay, Laxmi shrugged. 'Very well.'

'Eliza, my mother's idea is that once the engineer had worked up a plan, we would mortgage some of the family jewels on the understanding that the British loans will materialize at a later date.'

'But this would have to remain between the three of us,' Laxmi added. 'My elder son can know nothing of the mortgage. Jayant assures me we can rely on your discretion.'

'Of course.' Eliza thought for a moment. 'You'll need to know that the project will be approved and that there will be money available before you begin.'

'Exactly, and that's where you come in. If you are able to discuss the project with your Mr Salter and persuade him to organize the rubber-stamping of the necessary permissions, that would go a long way towards securing those loans. He might even help with finding the financiers who will back the project.'

Eliza hadn't expected Jay to take her off-the-cuff remarks so seriously, but felt delighted that he had. 'I don't know how much influence I have, but I'll try.'

They discussed the idea for another half hour and then, when Jay left for a polo match, Eliza got to her feet.

'Stay, Eliza. Now that you've got to know us a little, are there questions you need answering?' Laxmi asked, indicating that Eliza should sit again. 'Is there anything you'd like to know?'

Eliza was pleased. What had happened had left her feeling anxious about her own safety at the castle, but at the same time she couldn't rid herself of the thought that she needed to know more if she was ever to feel at home here.

'I'd like to understand more about your culture,' she said, though at the back of her mind the image of the flaming funeral pyre would not fade.

'The castle culture? Or the strict etiquette that governs our relationships?'

Eliza thought about it and decided to say nothing about the *sati*. 'Well, both, but I meant the rituals, the prayers. The gods. What are they for? There seem to be so many.'

'We are a custom-bound society, but our *pujas* or prayers give us meaning in what might otherwise be a meaningless world. We are Hindus. It is not a religion, though some people think it is. It is what we are born to, a way of life.'

'But if these gods don't really exist?'

'What is real is a matter of interpretation. They exist in our minds and hearts. That's where they matter. They give us the structure within which we live our lives. Not all of it is good, but we know where we are. We know our place in the world. Can you say the same?'

Eliza thought of the villages, where narrow dusty lanes

twisted and turned with just a drainage channel dug out daily along the middle of the street. Despite the poverty she'd loved the baked clay houses, the sleeping cows and dogs and the tiny black-eyed children who'd watched as she'd wandered. She'd admired the incredibly graceful women: tall, straight-backed, heads and faces covered in the lightest muslin shawls. They were all as far from England as they could be, far in time and space but further still in dignity and tradition.

'I haven't really thought about it,' she said, returning to Laxmi's question, though it wasn't strictly true. In some ways she had no idea where her place in the world really was, and she longed to tell Laxmi how terrible it had been to see the widow-burning and that it made her feel vulnerable because she too was a widow. She so wanted to be honest with this generous woman. Tell her the truth.

'Now what can I do to help you settle in here even more?' Laxmi was saying. 'You still have a look of anxiety in your eyes, and you still have many months if you are to complete a year of our lives here in Juraipore.'

'I'd like to be shown around the entire castle. The fortress too. I have no idea how to get from one place to another and I don't really want to have to rely on other people all the time.'

PART TWO

'If you cry because the sun has gone out of your life,
your tears will prevent you from seeing the stars.'

– Rabindranath Tagore

12

Eliza had fallen asleep to the sensuous ringing of prayer bells, and in the morning woke with a stronger feeling of hope than she could ever have dared imagine. She gazed at the unbroken blue sky, watching as a dozen bright green parakeets took off from one tree for another, their fluttering wings revealing flashes of yellow under-feathers. Then, finding a staircase that led straight down to it, she went to walk under the scalloped archways and delicate columns in the courtyard below.

A little later Jay arrived to help familiarize her more fully with the castle.

'I didn't expect it to be you,' she said.

He bowed. 'I especially asked to be allowed the pleasure.'

He kept it on a formal basis and she was shown everything: the *durbar* halls, the rooms for weaponry, all manner of sitting rooms, the men's living quarters, banqueting halls, interconnecting offices, vast libraries, endless workrooms, stables, store rooms, kitchens, even more walled gardens, and then back to the *zenana*. Eliza tried to map as much of it as she could in her memory, as he explained each part, though it was so monstrously vast she could only hope to retain a fraction. But if she could now walk unaccompanied, and with some sense of knowing where she was going, it might minimize the feeling of not belonging.

'So,' he said, when they had finished. 'How are you now? Honestly?'

'You mean after seeing . . .'

'Yes.'

'I'm getting over it, I suppose.'

'A thing so terrible does not fade quickly. Don't hesitate if you ever need to talk about it.'

'Thank you.'

He smiled. 'And now I have a little rooftop escape planned for us. A little distraction.'

She took a step back. 'Really? Where?'

He tapped his nose. 'Follow me.'

Jay led her through a doorway and into what seemed to be a dark, unused part of the fortress. Eliza shivered as they passed cracked plaster walls and climbed dingy narrow staircases. The windows were small and the maze of inter-connecting corridors and dank rooms reeked with an air of desolation. Even the workrooms were more claustrophobic than the rest of the castle.

'This is the oldest part of the fort and castle and, as you can see, we have abandoned it. Watch your feet, there are cracks in the floor just ahead.'

After climbing several more winding staircases, he even-tually took out a key from his pocket and unlocked a large studded door. After the darkness the light hit Eliza with force and she gasped in surprise, stumbling for a moment. He reached out a hand to steady her and then led her on to the roof.

'This is my private escape,' he said. 'Nobody comes here.'

Eliza gazed around her at the view, staggered by the opalescence of the endless pale blue sky. It felt glorious, like being on top of the world, with the wind blowing in her hair and the air so fresh she felt light-headed. 'It's truly beautiful.'

The town below glowed golden, and the wide plains with their hilly outcrops seemed misty and grey. Between these low hills and the town, huge flocks of sheep wandered freely. She glanced up at the sky and watched a buzzard fly across from one side of the ramparts to the other. They were at the very back of the castle, and when she went to the edge to look down she could see the layout of the building below, with its many walkways and courtyards. But the people seemed tiny, and that made her realize how high up they actually were. She stepped back, feeling giddy.

'All right?' he said.

'Yes. It's just the air. It feels so pure.'

'Like the very best champagne.'

'Better.'

'Now I have something to show you.'

He walked over to a small round brick-built structure and opened the door. The next thing she knew, he was carrying an enormous kite across to her. Diamond-shaped, with simple cross-bars, the silk stretched over the frame was bright red and orange and painted with intricate patterns on the surface. Dozens of long yellow ribbons fluttered from the point at the base.

'Want to learn how to fly it? It's a perfect day for it, with just this light wind.'

'Let me watch you first.'

'Why not help me launch it? We actually fly kites all year round, but mainly from early December up to the festival of Sankrat, when you not only display your fabulous kite and your flying skill, but also use your line to strangle a competitor's line so his kite crashes and yours stays up.'

'I'm not going to compete with you, I hope.'

He laughed. 'Well, certainly not at flying a kite.'

She watched as he held the ball of string and asked her to hold the kite. He unwound about sixty feet of string and then waited, as if paying attention to the wind direction. Then he asked her to walk sixty feet away, far enough so that the string stretched between them, and told her to stand with her back to the wind and the kite facing her.

'Now just let it go,' he said.

She did so and watched as it tilted and then soared.

'When wind travels over the surface of the kite, it divides into two streams of air. One flows over the kite while the second stream goes beneath. That's basically what gets it up.'

He unwound more string to allow the kite to go higher. She watched it whirling and swooping as if it was actually a living thing, its ribbons trailing and carving patterns through the air.

'Come and hold it,' he called.

She went to him as he passed the ball of string. She hadn't expected to feel such a strong vibration and almost let go in surprise. So he stood behind her and put his arms around her, then covered her hands with his own so that they were both holding the kite in the air together. With Jay so close and feeling the vibration in his hands, and in her own too, her mouth dried and she found it hard to swallow. She gazed out at the green speckled landscape and the sandy area beyond, where tiny smallholdings and villages were now mere dots. She spotted a thin ribbon of blue. Maybe it was the same river the puppet had been laid to rest in. And while she was seeing all this she was really only aware of her heart thumping. Time didn't just stand still, it seemed suspended and shivering as if waiting for one of them to move.

There was a sudden gust of wind and he pulled the kite

closer, then let it out again. She stood still with his arms around her, feeling breathless.

'I'll take over now,' he said.

She moved away.

'Thank you.'

'I wanted to do something to make you feel better.'

'It worked.'

'Look, I may be away for a while now. I need to chase up contacts, maybe even in England, see if I can attract sponsorship or backers for my irrigation. Will you be all right?'

'Yes, of course. And I always have my friend Dottie.'

It was with Jayant Singh in her mind that Eliza set out for the Residency, Clifford Salter's grand town house, accompanied by one liveried guard and a rickshaw driver, who would show her the way and wait to accompany her back. She would deliver her contact prints and plates and also ask him about helping Jay to access permissions and loans for the water project.

The room she was shown into looked as if it belonged in an English country house, with just the faintest touch of the oriental. She seated herself, back to the window, and carefully put down her envelope of prints and her package of plates.

When Clifford entered the room, dressed in a pale linen suit and shirt and tie, she rose from her seat and stretched out a hand. He ignored the hand and came across to kiss her on the cheek. His eyes shone with pleasure and she could see how genuinely delighted he was to see her.

'How lovely. I'll order tea.'

Then, drawing up a chair, he seated himself opposite her

and shook a small bell. He ran a finger inside his collar. 'So? Spill the beans.'

She smiled. 'Not much to spill. I've been able to take rather more informal pictures lately.'

'Capital. We want the true flavour of Rajputana, not just the stiff set photographs these so-called royals are so fond of. Now tell me, does Jayant Singh have many visitors?'

'I really have no idea.'

'But you must have seen something? Maybe somebody who appears a little out of place. Maybe rather rough. You never know who is influencing these people.'

'He has a friend called Devdan who does seem a bit different, but that's all I know.'

'Very well. What about Laxmi?'

'Laxmi? I've never seen her visitors, though I expect she does have them.'

'And Chatur? Does he have any unusual visitors?'

'All I know about Chatur is that he's haughty and condescending. How would I know if he has unusual visitors? It's a very large castle, Clifford.'

'Of course it is. Of course. But you haven't told me why you're here. Unless it's . . .' He paused. 'Can I hope?'

She shook her head. 'I'm sorry.'

'So . . . ?'

'Jayant Singh has decided to employ an engineer to draw up plans to capture water to irrigate his lands and also the villages local to him. He wants to bring prosperity to the area and believes water is the solution.'

'I see . . . water. Well, it does bring prosperity. He intends to drill?'

'Don't think so. It's just in the early stages, but Clifford, the people are poor and there has been little rain. When I look at their ravaged faces I feel so guilty. The thing is, we need your help.'

He twisted his mouth to one side. 'We?'

'Well, not me, but Laxmi and Jay, though I have offered to do what I can. You only have to see the poverty to want to help.'

'Jay? You call him that?' There was an uncomfortable pause before Clifford continued, during which he studied her. 'Not more going on than meets the eye, I hope?'

'Of course not.'

He looked as if he was considering. 'And this help?'

'Involves raising money and rubber-stamping the idea. Jay needs British approval to go ahead. And he needs permission to dam a small river.'

'And British cash?'

'Exactly.'

He snorted. 'They have wealth hidden away and yet here they come cap in hand as usual!'

He got to his feet and with his hands in his pockets seemed to be thinking. 'Would you stay to lunch, Eliza? It will give me time to give it some thought and maybe get some messages to key individuals. What do you say?'

Eliza inclined her head. 'I'd be delighted.'

'Let's go out to the garden. There's shade.'

In the garden they sat on a bench together – a little too close for comfort, but Eliza thought it a small price to pay if Clifford agreed, and so, despite her inclination, she didn't shift away. Instead she sat calmly with her hands in her lap and waited, just as Laxmi would have done. She smiled at the thought that she was being influenced in that way and remained looking at the pretty gazebo, the dainty splashing fountain, and the climbing plants spilling over the garden walls.

'Penny for them?' he said.

'Just what a lovely garden,' she said, and was rewarded with a smile.

'My pride and joy. By the way,' he said as he adjusted his tie, 'I've a letter . . . judging by the postmark it's from your mother. I'll let you have it before you go.'

Eliza thanked him, though a letter from her mother – likely to be full of complaints – wasn't something she relished.

'So how are you really getting on?' he asked.

A butler in white came out with pre-luncheon drinks on a silver tray and Eliza watched as Clifford picked up his glass and sipped. He was clearly a fastidious man, finger-nails clipped short and always immaculately dressed, whatever the weather.

'Well, it is strange, of course,' she said.

'Strange? Is that all?' He frowned. 'You don't mind the polygamy? The concubines? As a woman I would have thought you'd find it abhorrent.'

'I try not to think of it, and the concubines are friendly.'

'What about the idolatry?' he continued doggedly.

'Laxmi explained it to me. It all sounded quite sensible.' She knew she could never bear to speak to him about the widow-burning.

He raised his brows. 'Not turning native, I hope? You really would have trouble on your hands then.'

If only he knew how far from that she was. 'Really, Clifford, hardly,' was all she said.

He squinted at her behind his spectacles. 'Be careful, Eliza.'

'As I said, I'm fine.' She looked up and held his gaze, hoping that it was true.

'Well, Anish isn't fit to rule. We're constantly crushing

146

civil disobedience and potential rebellions he barely seems to notice. The British Crown is supreme in India and this fellow sometimes forgets it. We'd like to get him out, if I'm honest, and you may be able to help.'

'How?'

'Not sure yet. Just a thought. His old man was a good fellow, open to making the changes we suggested, but this one wants only to dress up in his finery or play polo, though now he's getting too fat to even do that. If we can't keep the princely states on board, the rebels will have rich pickings.'

'The rebels?'

'Those who favour an independent India. We can't have any further mutinies. As it is, civil disobedience is on the increase.'

There was a short silence.

'Clifford, are you religious? Do you believe in fate?'

'Fate as a predetermined course of events beyond human control?'

'I suppose.'

He shook his head. 'That's just fatalism. If we can't change destiny, then why even try?'

'Quite.'

'In any case, I'm not a religious man.'

'I don't think the Hindus quite see destiny as we do,' Eliza said.

'No. You'd have to ask one of them, but I believe it's all connected with their idea of karma. Destiny as we define it simply means something that was meant to happen. They think it can be affected by past and present deeds. I sometimes wonder if the misunderstandings between our cultures are down to the interpretation of language.'

★

Back at the castle Eliza went straight to her rooms, where she was horrified to see that the padlock on her darkroom wasn't properly locked. She could have sworn she'd locked it after picking up the contact prints and the plates for Clifford, but perhaps in her haste she had not done so fully. She rang the bell for some masala chai, then sat at the desk to read her mother's letter.

When she had finished she let it fall to the floor and buried her head in her hands. It simply could not be true. Her mother was lying. She had to be lying. A long-repressed memory came back. She must have been about eight and it had been a lovely sunny day. Eliza had been delighted to accompany her ayah, who needed to buy some lace in Chandni Chowk. While the ayah was paying, Eliza had glanced out of the shop window and spotted her father in the street, holding a huge bouquet of flowers. When she'd got home she'd excitedly asked her mother where the flowers were that he'd brought home. There were no flowers. In fact her mother hadn't seen him for two days. Eliza had been so little but, despite that, something about it had chilled her.

She picked the letter up and read it again, her heart sinking further with every word.

My dear Eliza

This is a letter I have been intending to write for many years. I wanted to tell you when you married Oliver, but the words just would not come and I could never bear to speak of your father's despicable behaviour face to face. I know you idolized him, but everything I am about to tell is, I swear, God's honest truth. Now that my health is beginning to suffer I must speak while I still can. Don't worry, I'm not asking you to come home, at least not yet.

It all began when I was carrying you, some months before you were born. I hadn't suspected a thing until one of my friends told me she had seen David kissing a dancing girl in one of Delhi's gardens. I loved him and refused to believe her, then I put it to the back of my mind. After that I preferred not to consider her a friend. I trusted David. We were happy and I could only suppose she was jealous. I had a dashing young husband, while she was a spinster reliant on her brother's largesse.

But the damage had been done and gradually I noticed little things. The way your father came home smelling faintly of jasmine, his collar a little awry. The occasional unexplained late nights that gradually turned into days. When I found out he had hefty gambling debts I actually felt relieved. Imagine that. At least he hadn't taken a mistress, that's what I thought, that's what I told myself over and over. But I'm afraid I was wrong. Soon I was to understand the full extent of his betrayal, not only of me but of you too.

It all came out even before his death. Not only had he ruined us financially with his incessant gambling, he had also squandered almost everything we had and incurred other debts, because for years he had been keeping a dancing girl in a small apartment near Chandni Chowk. Debts which, after his death, I was somehow expected to make good. There is more, much more, but I can't bring myself to speak of it.

I never wanted to ruin your idolized view of your father but I don't feel I can keep these secrets any longer. I'm sorry.

I hope this letter finds you well. Please give my regards to Clifford. If he is showing an interest I hope you'll be compliant. As you now know, no man is perfect, even your beloved father.

Your loving mother

The ground tilted but Eliza got to her feet and paced back and forth, distraught at the bitterness that spilled from the pages. What could her mother's purpose be in telling her these dreadful lies? Anna had struck a blow to the very heart of who Eliza believed she was and who she believed her father had been. She thought of his bear hugs and his warm smile and then she remembered his absences. Oh God! What if this was all true? But no. This was another of her mother's attempts to undermine her love for her father. She could hear the tone of her mother's voice as she penned it. Yet whether it was true or not, Eliza felt devastated; the fact that Anna had even written of these things made her feel sick at heart and she had mentioned *more*. What *more* could there possibly be? And was her mother's health seriously deteriorating or was this a less than subtle touch of emotional blackmail?

She went in search of Jayant but was told that he had gone and would be away for some time, meeting with British engineers. She was surprised he hadn't even waited to hear how she'd got on with Clifford.

On her way back to her rooms she heard footsteps that seemed to be coming from behind her. She felt the hairs on the back of her neck rise and she spun round. Nobody. Just the old castle creaking and groaning. But a chill ran through her at the possibility that somebody might be silently watching and listening. She told herself it was just her imagination, but something prowled these corridors, she was sure of it. Maybe a padding servant girl? Maybe a stealthy guard? Either that or the castle was full of ghosts, which wouldn't have surprised her. This presence she couldn't identify, and the way she felt she was accompanied by shadows through the half-light of the corridors, left her with a nagging undercurrent of fear.

She hurried out into the relief of a sunlit courtyard, where Indi appeared to be starting a new drawing at a small easel. The scent of rose and jasmine drifted in the air and, longing to feel a proper part of life at the castle, Eliza watched her for a few moments. Then, desperately in need of a friend while feeling so low, she decided to reach out to the girl once again.

'Is it a sketch for a new painting?' she asked in a friendly voice, while taking a few steps forward.

Indi spun round, but with no smile on her face. 'Just a sketch.'

'It's good.'

Indi didn't reply, and Eliza felt as if she might be wasting her breath. 'I wondered if you might like to learn more about photography? I'd love to show you how I go about catching a particular moment.'

Indi stared at her. '*Nahin dhanyavaad.*'

Then she studiously turned her back and ignored Eliza. It had been a very determined 'No thank you.'

13

After that Eliza gave herself over to the only thing she knew to do when life upset her. Engrossed in work, she did not feel the hurt of her mother's accusations. Up before dawn, when a soft blue mist hung its veil over the town below, and before the temple bells began to ring, she explored the castle, seeking out unusual shots of external architecture, little corners of exquisite, detailed decoration, or sharp contrasts between light and shade. These were strange, sublime moments of almost enjoyable loneliness. She went to the town, accompanied of course, and managed to capture images of craftsmen at work; she even spotted a musician playing an instrument that seemed to have been made from a coconut.

Back at the castle, the one positive was a short note from Clifford telling her that he'd set the wheels in motion and it was probably safe for Jay to go ahead with the irrigation project. After that she photographed the servants with a lighter heart. Everyone seemed willing, and she was invited to spend time with the concubines, the swirling pinks and oranges of their long scarves shimmering against the emerald of their skirts and tunics. They began to trust her and, as they chattered and giggled, allowed her to take the relaxed shots she desired. When she revealed the contact prints later on, they exclaimed and excitedly pointed out the images of themselves and in return offered to initiate her in the sixteen arts of being a woman. Afraid of what that might involve, she declined at first but, as they were utterly insistent, she was left with no choice.

The room they led her to was on the ground floor and enormous, its walls and floor tiled in pale pink marble. The windows, covered by carved *jali* screens through which the sun filtered golden geometric patterns on the floor, seemed more beautiful than secretive. Brighter. Less made of shadows. And when the maids carried in huge bowls of steaming water which they poured into a deep copper *ghangal*, a sort of tub, Eliza felt expectant and happy.

As she sat on a wooden bench, the concubines washed her hair in coconut water and bathed her in jasmine-scented water. But, acutely shy to be naked before them, and with so many pairs of eyes appraising her, and so many fingers touching her pale skin, her smiles turned to embarrassment. They made personal remarks about her breasts and thighs, but gradually she relaxed, and as she surrendered she became more languid with each moment. When they had dried her and while they were massaging her body with rose-scented oils they told her their stories. One said she was the third daughter born to a poor family, far away in a barren land, with no sons.

'So you have sisters?' Eliza said. 'I always wanted a sister.'

The girl shook her head and began to scrape Eliza's feet with something sharp. 'They were taken by wolves and I was brought here.'

'As a baby?'

'My parents could not afford to keep me. What use is a girl?'

The girl then rubbed Eliza's feet with what looked like butter and sang softly as she worked.

Another girl pointed out that Eliza must wear more jewellery or she'd be taken for a widow. Eliza protested, but they told her to visit the *sonar* or goldsmith as soon as she could and buy plenty. Eliza laughed but took note. All the time she was there the women cuddled each other and dissolved into laughter at jokes Eliza didn't understand, but a kind of chaotic reverie developed and she enjoyed feeling as if she understood a little more of this land of diverse traditions.

One of the women had made what she called *kaajal*. It was the dark black stuff they ringed their eyes with, and she offered to show Eliza how to use it. After it was finished Eliza glanced in a mirror and was astonished by the drama it added to her eyes. They looked greener, brighter, and when she smiled at the result the woman gave her a little pot of the stuff in a tiny silver box, with a little wooden stick with which to apply it.

She'd been at the castle since the middle of November, and had passed a quiet Christmas at Dottie's. Now it grew quite cold at night, so she had to seek out an extra blanket or two. She was given a *razai*, a quilt filled with cotton and smelling quite strongly of musk. It was thought to help retain heat in the body. And so, like the rest of the household, Eliza became used to wrapping a large cashmere shawl around herself in the early morning, only shedding it as the heat of the day took over. She still felt as if she was being followed, though nobody had been there each time she'd turned to look. The castle seemed shrouded in mystery. Sometimes she felt as if she was waiting for something awful to happen, and the uncomfortable sensation of being under observation left her feeling strained and tense. Other times she put it down to sounds coming from elsewhere.

She was surprised how much she missed Jay and, wishing it was his footsteps she heard echoing down the long corridors, she couldn't rid herself of the feeling that something was wrong.

Early one morning she heard a knock at her door, and when she opened up she found one of the maids indicating that she should follow. At first she had no sense of foreboding, but as they descended into the bowels of the building her skin prickled with apprehension. In a place as vast as this it wasn't easy to keep things in perspective; it wasn't just that these lower corridors were cold, windowless spaces, lit only by oil lamps, there was something odd going on.

When the girl stopped outside a dark wooden door, Eliza was surprised when the *dewan*, Chatur, opened the door and signalled that she should enter. She hesitated and twisted to glance back at the handmaiden, but the armed guards who had suddenly appeared in the corridor blocked her path. She did not like, nor trust, Chatur. Everything, from his upright bearing to the curl of his lip, not only implied disdain but actively expressed it.

As she entered the dark suffocating room his smile was intimidating and completely lacking in warmth. 'This photography project means a great deal to you?' he said.

'It does,' she replied in an even tone of voice and with as much dignity as she could muster.

'That is a pity.' Another of those smiles that never reached the eyes, giving her the impression that he was mocking her. 'You may have heard that a widow is deemed a guilty woman. We consider it dishonourable for a woman to outlive her husband.'

He was playing cat and mouse and she swallowed

rapidly. 'A belief that is utterly ridiculous to my way of thinking.'

He ignored her comment. 'It has come to my attention that *you* are a widow, Mrs Cavendish. These rumours do rather spread in our enclosed world.'

Her heart began to gallop, but as she opened her mouth to ask, he interrupted.

'How I know is no concern of yours.'

'I disagree.'

'Well, be that as it may, the end result is that a woman like you cannot be allowed to move freely around. We believe contact with a widow to be extremely unlucky and few will wish to be in your company. To that end I, or one of my men, will accompany you everywhere and oversee all the pictures you intend to take, including the scrutiny of your contact prints. Anything I deem to be unsuitable will be destroyed. Is that clear?'

Fired by indignation she stood her ground. 'Perfectly clear, though I think the British Resident may have something to say about it.'

'I believe Mr Salter is currently in Calcutta and likely to be away for some weeks.'

'Well, Prince Jay –'

'Do not be misled. The Prince will have no option but to do as I say. It is the Maharajah's order.'

'You told him I was a widow.'

'I know my duty. We believe in duty here, and the first duty of a wife is to keep her husband alive.' He laughed a bitter laugh. 'So there you have it.'

She turned away, but then twisted back and, sick of constantly wondering if she was imagining things, just came out with it. 'Why are you having me followed?'

He smiled. 'It is your imagination. You are not being followed, but, if you were, would it not be in your own interests to leave the castle now, before, shall we say, something worse were to unexpectedly occur? To you, or even to somebody else. These castles can be dangerous places.'

She shrank from the menace in his tone. 'Why would anything happen?'

'Just a figure of speech, Miss Fraser. But you saw what took place at the polo.' He spread his hands and, with a look of mock desolation, shrugged.

This made Eliza feel certain Chatur had been the one behind Jay's fall, and now the worry was not only for herself but for Jay too. Although defenceless, she could not allow Chatur the pleasure of seeing how much she was affected, so she did her best to swallow her fear. The veiled threat was bad, but also her movements would now be terribly restricted. Things couldn't be any worse.

She wished Jayant would come home, and now that Chatur knew the truth, Laxmi would also know. Ashamed at concealing her true status, she fought to control her distress. What would Laxmi say? And with her every move under the scrutiny of Chatur, how safe would she be at the castle? Eyes smarting, hands sweating, she told herself not to be silly. Nothing worse would happen to her. He was just a bully, wasn't he?

14

When Jay still did not return, Eliza knew her only ally was gone; the chattering concubines no longer called for her, and her access to the castle was severely restricted. She occasionally spotted Anish's daughters roller-skating, but as she was always accompanied by a guard she dared not call out to them. It was clear the guards had been given orders to disrupt her plans and, feeling trapped and frustrated, time hung heavily. At times she felt she might drown in silence that was never truly silent.

As the images she was able to capture grew fewer and more formal, she began to feel she was destined to fail her brief. Her nightmares returned too, only now it was not only the terrible noise of a bomb exploding, the blast thundering over and over in her head, but also the smell of burning flesh in her face and in her hair. She woke scraping and scratching her skin. If not that, she would see her father's face disintegrate before her eyes, to be replaced by the image of a funeral pyre, and then she would wake trembling, her nightdress sticking to her skin and her hair soaking wet.

Most of the time she was still aware of being followed, and frequently expected to come across someone lying in wait. But was she more afraid of actually being followed or of what was going on in her head at the thought of worse? She had to hope Chatur was all talk and that she wasn't in any danger, but it was only human to consider packing up and leaving. And yet, if she were to leave, what would there be for her in England? She'd spent a great deal of her money on her equipment, relying on this project to lead to greater things. While she was being paid on a monthly basis, an unfinished project meant no lump sum at the end and a damaged reputation as a photographer.

She was walking along the corridor to her room planning her next batch of photographs when she froze and then quickly slipped into an alcove. She had spotted a man backing out of her bedroom surreptitiously and locking the door after him. When she was certain he had gone, she ran to her room, her hands shaking as she turned the key in the lock. Inside he'd done well to cover up his presence but, while everything was more or less in place, she could see that her belongings on the dressing table had been moved around. Now, faced with the evidence that she really was under observation, she felt scared and very angry. How dare they enter her room without permission? She was certain she had recognized the man as one of Chatur's guards, so Chatur had to be behind it. She dragged a chair and leant it against the door. It wasn't much of a deterrent.

The next morning, after a fearfully sleepless night, the guard left her alone outside. She sat on one of the giant swings, capable of accommodating four women at a time, and as she dragged her toes on the ground she heard a voice and looked up to see Indi walking towards her.

'Did you tell them?' she asked straight away. It stung to think Indi had given her secret away, and she couldn't mask her annoyance.

Indi frowned.

Eliza raised her voice. 'Did you tell them I'm a widow?'

'Of course not.'

'Then who?' Eliza prompted. This was a closed society, rife with whispers and rumours, and secrets would find a way of slipping out. She knew that.

'I don't know,' the girl finally said.

'Well, the truth is out and I'm constantly under observation. I don't know what they think I'll do.'

Indi sighed. 'Contaminate the other women, probably. Look, let me help you. I know all the hidden places in this castle, better even than the guards. I can get you out without them knowing.'

'They want to veto the contact prints.'

'I can smuggle them out too.'

'You'd really help?'

Indi nodded, and Eliza hoped she was being genuine. 'And I can also show you the secret passage between the *zenana* and the *mardana* or men's quarters. It's great for overhearing what's going on.'

'What can I do for you in exchange?'

Indi smiled. 'I've been thinking about that. I'm sorry I was mean. You offered to show me how photography works. Not just the technical detail but the artistry. Would you still be prepared to do that?'

This glimmer of hope delighted Eliza and, coaxed into believing all was well, she took the girl's hand. 'I'd be happy to. Truly. We can learn to see the world together. Let's help each other.'

In the darkest of times just one friend might be enough, Eliza thought as she got to her feet. And as they walked up the narrow staircase to her rooms, she questioned Indi about her early life.

The girl paused and stood still. 'I loved my grandmother.'

'I met her. Did you know that?'

Indira nodded. 'I heard.'

'Jay told me a little about what happened. Your grandmother thought you might be in danger.'

'I wore a necklace round my neck all the time. Most children did. Then one day it was missing. I swore I hadn't lost it myself and when a suspected witch was found dead with an axe in her back, my grandmother knew my necklace had been taken while I slept and I would be in danger too. It is a backward sort of a place and the villagers are peasants. I had no mother, no father, and ideas above my station.'

Eliza recalled the softly rounded lines of the ochre-painted huts and their surrounding wall. 'It seemed peaceful.'

'Peaceful enough, but I was not submissive and they thought I should have been buried in an earthenware pot.'

'What?'

'It's what they used to do with unwanted girl babies. Many newborn girls were put in clay pots and buried in the desert. Ask your Resident. The British dug up some of them.'

Horrified, Eliza gasped. 'You mean buried alive?'

'I don't know. Probably, yes, so they didn't have to actually kill them. In a way it's understandable. The people are poor and girls are costly. The parents get no return on their investment and then, when the girls have to leave to live with their husband's family, there is nobody to look after them in their old age. They are left with broken hearts, because of course they grow to love their daughters. It is said a mother cries when a girl is born but weeps when she must leave. Boys stay, you see.'

'It doesn't still go on? The infanticide?'

Indi shrugged. 'It's surprising how many girl babies are said to have been taken by wolves.'

15

February

Eliza felt a moment of dread when she came face to face with Chatur the very next day, but she knew that no matter how frightened she was, she had to stand up to the man and, as she drew back her shoulders, she resolved to give voice to her anger and frustration.

'Why are you having me followed?' she demanded, fighting to control the tremor in her voice but feeling the flush in her cheeks. 'The truth. I know it is one of your guards.'

He frowned and drew himself up tall, then took a step towards her. 'I warned you that you would be accompanied at all times.'

'Oh, no. I'm not letting you get away with that. This is different. Stealthy. And I saw somebody leaving my rooms.'

He smiled coldly. 'One of the cleaning maids, no doubt.'

She held his gaze. 'It was a man.'

'You have a fertile imagination, Miss Fraser. If I were you I'd keep that in check. And remember, whatever you may think of me I am not a stupid man. Wild accusations won't go down well with Anish, and if you go running with tittle-tattle you will not be believed. I shall make quite sure of that.'

'Tittle-tattle!'

'You don't fool me. I know you have been placed here to watch us. Who are you really working for?'

Eliza almost laughed. 'That is utterly ridiculous.'

'Is it?'

'Of course.'

'Then ask yourself this: does your Mr Salter ask you detailed questions about our life here?'

She glanced at her feet but didn't reply.

He raised his brows. 'I think that rather proves my point. I hardly need to say we don't take kindly to interlopers here. I advise you to watch your step. Good day, Miss Fraser.'

Eliza was fully aware that Chatur could be a danger, but as for his claim that he believed her to be a spy, it seemed like a nonsense concocted to undermine her. Should she speak to Laxmi about this? Maybe, but what if she wasn't believed? What if Chatur was already spreading lies to undermine her? No. Better to hold her nerve and keep her suspicions to herself until she got the chance to speak to Clifford. In any case, she still needed to ask him to persuade Anish to allow her full access again, and as both he and Jay had been absent for some time it had left her feeling adrift. The trouble was, the thing that now stuck in her mind was that from the start Clifford really had asked detailed questions about what she'd seen at the castle.

As it turned out, it was Jay she told when he turned up unexpectedly later that day. He knocked on her door and when she opened up he was standing there, with a burgundy blanket loosely thrown over his shoulders and a friendly look in his eyes.

'Pleased to see me?' he said, and beamed at her.

She breathed a sigh of relief and had to hold on to the

doorframe to stop her legs from trembling. 'You have no idea.'

'I'm not here for long. Shall we walk? In the town, I mean.'

'I'd love to get out,' she said. Anything would be preferable to staying at the castle at the moment. 'Is it all right to just go?'

'Absolutely, why wouldn't it be? Just make sure you wrap up. There's a real chill in the air.' He laughed. 'Though after Yorkshire it's nothing.'

'So you did go to England?'

He nodded, and held out an arm for her to pass on ahead.

In the town, winter, for what it was worth, had changed nothing. Stalls were still wide open on to the street and people milled about as usual, though now wrapped in blankets. Nobody appeared to be wearing a coat – mainly, she assumed, because there was no rain during this bright blue chilly time.

'Chai?' he offered, and brought two cups of the hot sweet drink over to her. 'It always tastes better in the cold, I think.'

They drank their tea, then she stopped to examine some exquisite silk shawls in gorgeous reds, blues and golds. A deep peacock blue-green one caught her eye and she fingered its silky smooth texture. Out of the corner of her eye she saw Jay approach the trader and after a brief negotiation he came over to her. 'It's yours. Silk and cashmere, he said.'

'Really, I can't.'

'Of course you can. Regard it as a token of my esteem.' He gently wrapped it around her head and then touched her cheek. 'Beautiful. Brings out the colour of your eyes.'

She felt her skin reddening but smiled up at him. 'Thank you.'

'So how have you been?'

She hesitated for a moment. 'A lot has happened. Chatur has convinced Anish to restrict my movements, but the thing that has really worried me is that I saw a man leaving my rooms. I challenged Chatur, but he denied it and accused me of being some kind of spy. I ask you? How crazy is that?'

'It is actually insufferable. But what triggered these restrictions?'

'Chatur found out that I am a widow. It seems to have given him carte blanche to do whatever he wants. They think I'll contaminate other women.'

His face clouded and he glanced away. 'Doesn't sound good. I'll talk to Anish.'

'Well, I'm not sure if it will help. If you speak to Anish, and he ticks off Chatur, the man will hate me even more than he does now. They've been following my every move. I thought at first it was my imagination but now I'm certain.'

'I'll get a locksmith to change the locks on your room. Chatur doesn't have to know, and only you will have the key. Or if you feel that's not enough, maybe you could stay at your friend Dottie's house.'

Eliza pulled a face. 'Dottie's lovely, though I'm not sure I'd want to be so close to Clifford.'

'Maybe a case of the devil you know?'

'Maybe.'

'We need to keep you safe. I'll sort out the locks, but then I'll be off to Jaipore later today. Only for a few days this time. If you feel in any danger while I'm gone, go to your friend. And see Clifford to get your restrictions reversed. He's back now.'

That night, after she was satisfied that her new lock was in good working order, she waited for Indi. When the girl turned up with Indian clothing, Eliza changed and followed her to the lower corridors. She had decided to put her faith in Indi and hoped that she'd be able to slip around at least some parts of the castle undetected. While she would initiate the girl into the arts of photography, Indi was going to ensure she could exit the castle, either very early to take photographs or, as now, at dusk to deliver the prints.

When they heard someone cough further down the corridor, Eliza hung back, glancing around for an alcove while Indi walked on. If it was Chatur, or one of his loyal guards, she'd never get the prints to Clifford. Chatur would impound them and that would be that. Eliza suspected that, not far from the main store rooms, with the aroma of cardamom, chilli and coriander spicing the air, this long sloping corridor ran parallel to the kitchens. There was something else too; even down here the cloying scent of incense from evening prayers drifted through the dark spaces, which, along with the smell from the occasional oil lamps, made it hard to breathe freely.

She heard a laugh. Indi, she thought, and waited a little longer before deciding to risk moving. When she did, Indi was waiting for her.

'Almost there,' the girl whispered, and beckoned her on. 'No problem.'

'We seem to be going further down?'

'I want to show you something before we leave the

castle. It is not quite dark yet, so a few minutes longer won't hurt.'

After a few more minutes Indi paused again. There was no oil lamp here, but in the gloom Eliza could make out a framed drawing of the castle hanging on the rough stone wall. Indi lifted it off and carefully placed it on the ground. Then, with the aid of a file she took from a pocket, she dislodged a small stone and put her ear to the hole in the wall.

'Your turn. Listen.'

Eliza hesitated.

A broad grin spread across Indi's face and Eliza couldn't help liking the younger woman's enthusiasm – the way she grasped at everything life offered and to hell with authority.

'Go on.'

Eliza did as she was told. As she laid the side of her face against the icy cold stone wall, it wasn't the cold that shocked her; it was the voices she could hear. She appeared to be listening to Jay's friend, Devdan.

'Don't you see, we have to decide?' he was saying.

'I don't see that it's necessary,' another man replied, though *his* voice wasn't as loud or as clear. 'Why should anything have to change?'

'We will have to choose.'

'You mean throw our lot in with a bunch of rebels?' The voice was muffled, but Eliza was almost sure that was what he'd said and that it was Jay speaking. And yet she thought he had already left Juraipore.

'It's either that or put your faith in a crumbling Empire. Your treaties will be worth nothing when the British fail.'

'Will they fail? Do you believe that?'

'You have seen the widespread civil disobedience. The British Crown is finished.'

There was silence, then the sound of chairs being scraped back. Eliza shook her head and turned to Indira. 'How many people know about this?'

'It's a listening shaft. A narrow tunnel or tube. I unblocked it one day when I was younger. It's mentioned in an old book of castle records and I worked out where it might roughly be.'

'Nobody else knows?'

'I can't be sure, there might be others. These fortresses were terribly perilous in the old days. Riddled with intrigue and murder because everyone was after the throne for themselves. I made it my business to learn the secrets of the castle while I was still a child. Everyone ignored me and I could hide easily, so it wasn't too hard. When Laxmi realized what I was up to she asked me to keep an eye on Chatur. She doesn't trust him.'

'Where was Devdan talking just now?'

'Jay has a small study just off the corridor leading to the men's quarters.'

'You should have told him about this.'

'Why give away what little power I have?'

'But you like him?'

Indi snorted. 'I have to look out for myself.'

And as they walked to a low archway that led to one of several tunnels connecting to an exterior courtyard, Eliza could well believe that someone with Indi's background would need to find ways to protect herself, whatever it took and whoever she might have to betray. Maybe Laxmi's support alone just hadn't been enough for Indi.

'Have you thought any more about who told Chatur you were a widow?' the girl said.

'A little, but I don't know yet.'

'It might have been Dev, I suppose. Did he know?'

Eliza nodded and turned the idea over in her mind. Maybe it had been Dev who'd told Chatur or, far worse, might it even have been Jay? Had he let the truth slip? It was an awful thought that made her feel terribly at sea. Surely it couldn't have been Jay? She had trusted him and he would not have gained anything by it. But the thought would not let her go as she followed Indi out to the courtyard, where water, tumbling from fountains in the shape of peacocks, glittered in the light from the windows beyond, and lamps of clay dotted along the pathways guided their feet.

'So pretty,' Indi said, 'yet nobody comes here. Laxmi always has it kept perfectly. It's where her youngest child and only daughter died.'

'I didn't know.'

'Never speaks of it, but people whisper that it was Anish who pushed her when he was a boy. She cracked her head on one of the peacock fountains and never regained consciousness.'

'How sad.'

'She wanted a daughter so badly and then, long after the boys were born, she had her little girl. Sometimes I think she wishes I were the daughter she lost.'

As the night drew in they escaped the castle and melted into the streets, where the dark side of Indian life went on completely unaffected by the British. A world where mystical drumming sat cheek by jowl with opium dens in gullies just a couple of feet wide. When Eliza saw the half-lit nocturnal life in this hidden part of the city she was terrified for her life, but she kept her head down and followed Indi. The maze of streets was a necessary short cut that led to the British Residency on the other side of town. The other way round, avoiding these streets, would have taken them too long on foot.

As they approached the Residency a car drew up and Eliza stepped back when she saw Clifford get out, but he'd seen her through the window and frowned. Although she needed to speak to him she'd wanted to knock at his door, not be discovered lurking in the dark like a thief.

Someone else climbed out as the liveried driver held the door open, and Eliza saw the face of a well-known British woman. For a moment Eliza couldn't place her, but then she realized it was the current Viceroy's wife. She was followed by an important-looking silver-haired man. Of course Clifford would have connections at the maximum level and speak with the backing of a higher authority. And there would be many parties and social events just like this.

The woman's voice was crisp and sharp as she spoke to Clifford. A butler came out and escorted her and the man indoors, while Clifford signalled to Eliza.

Eliza walked over to him but he was clearly not impressed.

'Good grief, Eliza! What the devil do you think you're doing, scampering about at night dressed like that?'

'Indira helps me get out of the castle. I've brought you some prints and plates. They've restricted my movement, you see.'

'Have they? We shall see about that. No doubt Anish's doing or, more likely, that darn interfering wife of his. Washes her hands after touching an Englishman. Can you imagine! Damned effrontery. Anish will be doing it too if she has her way.' He paused. 'Actually, coming across you like this gives me an idea. I can't talk now.' He indicated the door through which the Viceroy's wife had just vanished. 'But you remember I suggested you might be able to help us?'

'Yes.'

'Well, I'll pop up to have a word with the Maharajah, and we can discuss it then.'

16

The next day, soon after Eliza heard the morning temple bells, she was summoned to Jay's study. Too nervous to attempt the secret passage alone, she threw her new cashmere shawl around her shoulders and took the normal corridors to find her way there. He smiled broadly when he opened the door and saw her standing there, but she took a step back.

'What is it?' he said. 'Has something happened?'

She stared at him, not really knowing how to feel. He had stubble on his chin, but his amber eyes sparkled and his skin glowed with health and vitality. Her fears over who might have told Chatur had continued to prey on her mind, and now she had no option but to question Jay.

'Eliza, come in. Let us not talk in the corridor.'

She shook her head.

'Tell me what the matter is?'

She opened her mouth but her voice caught, and she couldn't bring herself to meet his gaze for a moment or two.

He frowned. 'So?'

She hesitated, but then the words tumbled out. 'I need to ask you something.'

He smiled. 'Fire away.'

'Was it you who told Chatur I'm a widow?' she said, feeling sick inside, and now fully returning his gaze.

'Of course not. Why would you think that?'

'Indi swore it wasn't her. She suggested it might be your

friend Dev. He did know about me, but the thing is he hasn't even been here, until yesterday that is.'

He frowned. 'Devdan was here yesterday?'

'You know he was.'

'This is sounding most odd. To my knowledge Dev hasn't been here during my absence.'

'What time did you arrive yesterday?'

'About midnight.'

She lowered her voice. 'I thought I heard you talking to him.'

'When?'

'Just before nightfall.'

He shook his head. 'Not guilty.'

She thought quickly. If it hadn't been Jay talking to Devdan, then who? The voice had been a little indistinct and so maybe she had jumped to the wrong conclusion. Perhaps it had been Anish?

'Where did you hear this?'

'We can't talk here. Can we go out to one of the court-yards?'

'Of course. But you must admit this is sounding a little bizarre.'

In the courtyard they sat together on a bench beside one of the fountains. She gazed up at the luminous blue sky and watched the parakeets as they fluttered away from one dusty silvery tree to alight on another. The sight of flashes of yellow under-feathers usually filled her with joy. Today it did not.

'It'll be getting warmer soon, almost spring,' he said. 'And after that it'll be unbearably hot.'

Eliza didn't feel a bit warm, and that same self-consciousness once again rose in his presence, especially now that they were completely overlooked by the *zenana*.

'Just act naturally,' he said, as if he understood the reason for her reluctance. 'Smile, and don't twist your hands in your lap.'

She felt herself redden. 'I didn't realize I was.'

He paused and looked at the ground for a few seconds before turning to her.

'I do admit I told my mother about you.'

She turned to look at him. 'You knew how much it mattered. I trusted you.'

'I'm sorry.'

'I went to Clifford for you.'

'And that was terrific. The engineer is coming tomorrow with the first plans. You'll be impressed. Though the permission for the damming of the river might have to wait.'

'Don't you see what you've done?'

He frowned. 'Look, it just slipped out. My mother is a great admirer of yours and she understands, Eliza, truly. She has not judged you and would never tell anybody else, and I certainly have not.'

A surge of anger swept through her: that he could have thought it was acceptable to tell Laxmi! She'd so wanted to be honest with Laxmi herself and now that could never happen. His mother would consider her deceitful at best and a liar at worst. She bent her head and covered her face with her hands.

'Take your hands from your face. We are being watched.' He was behaving as if everything was normal, but Eliza had seen the worry in his eyes.

She rose to her feet, ignoring the fixed smile on his face. 'No, you may be able to dissemble but I cannot.'

'Please stay.'

She turned her back on him. He'd known Chatur would

174

object if the truth about her came out. It was Jay who'd said things had a way of getting out. Now he'd spoiled everything for her, so why should she help him by telling him about the listening shaft? He deserved to be overheard.

She marched back to her room, where she lay on her bed feeling fragmented. Although she was fuming, worse was the crushing pain of having been foolish enough to trust Jay. She scolded herself for caring about another man who had managed to let her down, but she couldn't prevent herself hearing his voice and couldn't stop seeing the worry in his eyes.

Alone with her anxiety, Eliza watched the gold of the morning sun painting the town a pale rosy pink. Then, a little later, she heard the sound of a car's horn and hurried to the large hall overlooking the main entrance, from where she saw Clifford climbing out of a large black vehicle. A smaller car pulled up behind him. A youngish man carefully slid out feet first, then, as he straightened up, she saw he was carrying a large roll of papers under his arm. He was dressed in western clothing but looked as if he might have some Indian blood. An Anglo-Indian perhaps? Eliza reckoned he must be the engineer Jay had hired. Really she longed to see the plans, but although a messenger had been sent to request her presence in Jay's study, she couldn't allow herself to go. Still smarting over his thoughtless betrayal, she sent a message saying she was indisposed, then marched back and forth in her room, righteous indignation stiffening her jaw and leaving her hot and feeling ruffled. It was only when she remembered that his plans might be overheard that she knew she could not let that happen. Despite his indiscretion, the irrigation project would improve so many people's lives and she could not be the one to ruin that possibility if the plans were to get into the wrong person's hands. Once she had decided to go, she plucked up courage and ran along the secret passage Indi had shown her, past the astonished guards, and, arriving out of breath, tapped on Jay's door.

Her insides were somersaulting as he opened it and she saw several pairs of staring eyes.

'I thought you were ill,' he said, giving her just the ghost of a smile.

'I have to speak to you. But first tell them to take the plans to Laxmi's rooms. It's really important.'

'Very well.' He went back into the room.

She heard the murmur of voices but then he came out to her again. 'They've agreed, though my brother looks furious.'

'It's your project. You need to safeguard it. Your study isn't safe.'

'Eliza –'

She interrupted as they walked out of earshot of the room and kept her voice low. 'Where did you tell your mother I was a widow? In which room?'

'Where? What difference does that make?'

'Tell me.'

'She came to my study one afternoon.'

Eliza shook her head. 'Jay, I promise you that room isn't safe.'

She explained about the secret listening tube and told him that when she'd put her ear to the hole in the wall she had heard voices coming from his study.

'Good grief. So that's why you didn't want me to reveal the plans in there?'

'I didn't know if the plans needed to be kept private at

this early stage . . .' She paused. 'So who do you think Devdan could have been talking to?'

'It was definitely a man?'

She nodded.

'Perhaps my brother, then?'

'It sounded a bit as if they were planning something against the British.'

'Sounds like Dev. Though I thought he'd given up pushing.'

'Pushing?'

'For a way to change the minds of the people.'

'I sometimes think it would be better if the people did rise up against the British.'

He smiled. 'Well! That's rather unpatriotic, isn't it?'

She shrugged. 'I just don't like the way Clifford and his kind talk.'

Eliza followed Jay to Laxmi's apartment and, as they passed through the sandalwood doors and entered the jasmine-scented room, the gleaming mirrored space took her breath away, as it had before. She saw Anish, Priya, Laxmi, Clifford and another man, the one she'd spotted earlier with the roll of papers. These were now spread out on a large table.

Laxmi smiled. 'I'm so glad you could join us, Eliza.'

Eliza smiled back, though she did not enjoy feeling so exposed now that Laxmi and the others knew about her, but she was glad Chatur had not been included.

'So why the sudden move?' Anish demanded, clearly irritated by the change of room. 'What is the mystery?'

'No mystery,' Jay said. 'I spotted that the table in my study wasn't wide enough for all the drawings.'

'And why is the Englishwoman here?' Priya asked, displaying her usual arrogant attitude.

'It was her idea in the first place,' Laxmi said, smiling warmly at Eliza.

'You're allowing an English widow to dictate what we do?' Priya snorted dismissively, and then a stream of words followed, far too rapidly for Eliza to follow, though she managed to pick up the gist of Priya's disapproval.

'As I recall, you are capable of a vigorous amount of dictating yourself,' Laxmi replied. And this Eliza did understand.

She smiled inwardly, sensing that there were unsettled scores between the two women, but that Laxmi would always have the upper hand. She wondered about the source of the woman's inner strength.

'Mother. Priya,' Anish said. 'Let us put our personal differences aside and discuss the plans.'

The engineer stepped forward. 'My name is Andrew Sharma. I was trained in London and have worked on several irrigation projects across the Indian Empire.'

'Rajputana isn't like anywhere else,' Anish said, his voice expressionless.

The young man bowed. 'Indeed it is not, sir, but I've taken everything into account.'

Anish smiled indulgently. 'As you know, many projects have already failed. Why should yours be any different?'

As a gust of wind blew in the fragrance from the gardens and something more, Eliza thought she caught the scents from the desert and tried smiling at Priya. The woman only raised her brow and smirked before turning away.

The young man glanced at Clifford, who nodded. 'With respect, they failed mainly through ignoring the knowledge of local people. In sounding out the locals I've discovered exactly where the lakes should be dug, how deep they should be and how to deal with the slope of the Prince's land. Eventually we'll be able to move on to the damming of a river, but for now we're keeping it simple. These people know so much about the weaknesses in the land and where there need to be walls to prevent seepage. My plans take all of that into account.'

'Why waste all this time and money on a few peasants?' Priya said. 'I don't see the point.'

Eliza laced her fingers behind her back as Anish turned to Jay. 'And you are prepared to assume total responsibility for the project?'

Jay nodded. 'I am.'

'And if it fails?'

'I don't believe it will.'

'And the British are willing to back this with their money?' Anish asked Clifford.

'To some extent.'

When they had all examined the detailed plans, Clifford wanted to speak with the Maharajah privately and Eliza hoped it was to insist that Anish's orders about her must be overturned. Then the others left and only Jay and Eliza remained with Laxmi. Jay told her that even though Anish had not seen the plans until today, he had gambled on his brother's agreement.

'At the moment I'm using old steam-powered shovels, great for excavating and moving rock and earth. But they are heavy, complex machines needing three men to operate them, so I plan to get hold of some cheaper, simpler, diesel-powered shovels as soon as I can afford them. At least the men have arrived and the digging is already well under way.'

'I tried to convince him to wait,' Laxmi said, 'but he needs the first lake finished before the rains come in July.'

'There should be time as long as there are no unforeseen problems,' Jay added.

Laxmi immediately held out her hands to Eliza. 'Come here, my dear.'

Eliza took a step forward but hung her head, feeling terribly embarrassed. 'I'm sorry . . .'

'No need for apologies. I understand.'

Eliza glanced up and tried for a smile. 'Really?'

'Let us forget it. I will do what I can to persuade people to allow you to photograph them. Many of them are simple souls with little or no education beyond these walls, but if I explain that it is quite a different thing to be a widow in your culture they may understand. I heard you were enjoying taking pictures of the concubines?'

'I was. They are so warm and funny.'

'I'll see what I can do.'

Jay looked at her appraisingly and with slightly flaring nostrils. 'So am I forgiven?'

'I suppose. Though I still don't know who told Chatur.'

He held out a hand. 'He must have heard through the listening tube. Now it's time to leave my mother, for she must go to her *pujas*.'

As Jay and Eliza left his mother's room they took one of the main staircases down to the large hall where the huge *durbar* had taken place. She asked him about the relationship between Priya and Laxmi.

'Indian mothers-in-law can be very cruel,' he said.

'Surely Laxmi isn't?'

'No, but she was treated badly by my grandmother, her mother-in-law. My grandmother would lock her alone in a room for days to keep her from my father.'

'But why?'

180

'So that my mother couldn't influence my father. My mother was always ahead of her time. But in our culture the parents' will must always be obeyed.'

'Even when they are wrong?'

'Indeed,' he said, somewhat gravely.

'And your father could do nothing?'

'Our etiquette expects a husband's silence. Laxmi tried to please her mother-in-law, but it was hopeless. Luckily the old crow died young and my mother was able to blossom.'

'But that doesn't explain how things are between Laxmi and Priya.'

'No, it doesn't. I think my mother simply doesn't like my brother's wife.'

'And maybe doesn't trust her.'

'Maybe.'

They walked slowly, and Eliza felt uncertain about what to say. 'The new lock works well,' was all she managed.

He smiled. 'I'm sure it does . . . Look, by way of an apology will you allow me to take you to the second night of the Holi celebrations in the oldest part of the town early next month?'

He'd dropped the invitation in quite casually and Eliza was surprised. 'You're allowed to go into the town for that? I thought you'd have to celebrate Holi at the castle.'

'I usually slip away from the celebrations here, already covered in coloured powder. It's a great disguise. If you also dress in Indian clothes and have some colour on your face and hair we won't be noticed.'

She thought about it for a moment. 'It sounds like fun.'

'I promise it's like nothing you'll ever have seen. It will touch your heart – a festival of letting go of what has already passed.'

Just what she needed, then, she thought wryly.

'A celebration of spring. Time to awaken hope,' he added.

'Don't you get recognized?'

'It doesn't matter if I am. But I wear old clothes and nobody is expecting to see me, so they don't. It's so often about expectations, don't you agree?'

17

Eliza loved the early morning and thus far there had been no further sign of shadows slipping just out of her sight, no fear of whispers, no silent tread. She was not being followed and felt more hopeful. As she rose early to catch the best light and went outside with her Rolleiflex, she thought of Jay's offer to take her to the Holi celebrations. She had to admit that the thought thrilled her. She breathed in the cool morning air and began photographing the giant swings in the courtyard. When something startled her, she glanced round and heard light footsteps. Not again, she thought, and put her camera down. She walked over to the archway where the footsteps seemed to have been coming from, then carried on down the passage a short way. Silence. But there had been someone. Someone light-footed. Of that she was certain. Maybe one of the concubines had wanted to speak to her but had been too frightened? The silence seemed to grow even louder, so, panicking a little, she listened out for whispers. Still nothing. Eliza turned back and returned to the courtyard to finish her task, but when she picked up her camera she experienced a moment of panic. The lens was cracked, although it had been fine before. Had she put it down too suddenly and knocked the lens? She was sure she would have noticed, so that seemed highly unlikely. Who had been in the courtyard? She went back to her rooms, muttering to herself.

It was now a little warmer, but still hadn't reached

anything like the scorching temperatures of summer. She knew that escaping into the town might be impossible when the extreme heat came, and as she wanted to get to the bottom of what had happened to her camera, she decided to make the most of a lunch party Clifford had invited her to. She would pick his brains about where to have the camera repaired.

She dressed in a pretty pale pink summer skirt made of silk crêpe de chine, and added a blouse with a slight puff to the sleeves. The skirt fitted at the waist and, clinging at the hips, showed off her figure more than anything else she owned. It was the outfit she wore when she needed to impress. She clipped a string of real pearls around her neck and then, as she hooked through the matching earrings, she decided, now that her lock had been changed, not to tell Clifford about the man in her room. He'd probably only insist she move to Dottie's.

On her way out, just at the point where a sprinkle of sunlight danced patterns on the marble floor, she passed Jay.

'You look very lovely today,' he said with a broad smile. 'The colour suits you.'

'It's a lunch party,' she muttered, feeling a bit too much on show.

'How very British.' He bowed. 'Enjoy yourself. By the way, progress on the irrigation project is terrific, but we do still have to get the funds finalized so that this first lake can be finished, or our current work will be spoiled.'

'And will you?'

He inclined his head in that way that you never quite knew if it was yes or no. 'You must see it before then.'

She couldn't say that she would far rather be spending time with him than with Clifford, and that she would willingly go right now. As she thought that, the burn of a flush spread up her neck and the moment passed.

'And you look even more lovely when you blush,' he added.

'Oh, do shut up! It'll probably be terribly boring.'

'Perhaps you might have another word with Clifford about his progress with the backers and the permission to dam the river? Negotiations seemed quite positive when I was in Calcutta but I haven't heard anything definite since I returned.'

A little later, as she gazed out of the car window, the poverty continued to shock her and she was still trying to make sense of what she saw here. Children, little more than waifs with huge dark eyes, followed the car greedily, hoping no doubt to be given something when the vehicle reached its destination. Judging by the shacks at the side of the road, it was clear many people had no homes. She searched her bag for a few rupees and held them in her hand ready for when she got out. She noticed details, always had. It had been her escape, a way of coping after her father died. She'd notice things and then, in her mind, tell him about them. Once her mother had come across her in the garden holding up a daisy and talking to her imaginary father aloud. Her mother had slapped her hand and the daisy had fallen to the ground. After that Eliza had kept her conversations with her father secret.

As the car neared Clifford's house, Eliza still thought it was to be a lunch party but, once again, it turned out she was on her own with Clifford. After a delicious meal of roast chicken with steamed potatoes and vegetables, Eliza sat back replete. Though she enjoyed the Indian food she'd been eating, she was beginning to tire of rice and dahl.

'So,' he said. 'Room for apple pie?'

'You trying to fatten me up?'

'Not at all. I think you're perfect just the way you are.'

She laughed. 'You didn't ask me here to tell me that.'

He smiled. 'No. I wanted to let you know that your freedom has been restored.'

'Thank you. It means such a lot. But I need your help with something else now.'

'Oh?'

'Something odd happened this morning. I turned my back for just a few minutes and when I turned around I found my camera lens was broken. A crack right down the centre. It's the one I need to use when I'm out and about.'

'You must have knocked it without realizing.'

'I really don't think so, but where can I get a new lens? And I'm worried that the body of the Rolleiflex might have been damaged too.'

'Do you have the camera with you?'

'I left it on the hall table.'

'I'll get it sent to Delhi, but I have to warn you it won't be speedy.' He paused. 'Now I want to explain my idea. Run it past you, if you like.'

'Go on.'

He nodded. 'Well, as you know I'm doing my best to ferret out funding for your Prince's irrigation project.'

'He isn't *my* Prince, Clifford.'

'Just a figure of speech. What I mean is that if you could do a little something for me in return that would be absolutely spot on.'

'Of course. Anything.'

'We'd like you to keep your eyes peeled and report back to me if anything out of the ordinary happens. I think I told you that we believe Anish to be a weak, self-indulgent ruler, and we wouldn't mind making a few changes, if you get my meaning.'

'Are you asking me to spy for you?' she said, unsure how to respond to his astonishing request and worrying that Chatur's accusations might well have some basis in truth.

'Of course not. Just keep your eyes open. If anything happens that you're uncertain about, or that seems odd, let me know. You can always say you need to see me on the pretext of delivering your plates and marked-up prints.'

18

March

The second day of the Holi celebrations came round. Excited, but also nervous about going into the town at night with Jay, Eliza recalled her first journey with him. Part of her longed to be out in the wild forests of the Aravalli hills, watching the demoiselle cranes flying low over the desert, and the great white pelicans taking off from the water's edge. Clifford's request had unsettled her, and Jay remained the one person she did tentatively feel she could put her faith in.

That evening, when she joined the celebration taking place in one of the courtyards, she kept an eye out for him and soon spotted him with a young boy. She assumed the boy must be Jay's younger brother, whom she'd heard about but had never seen. After an hour or so Jay came over, wrapped in a striped woollen blanket. He whispered in her ear, and they slipped out of the courtyard and through to another unfamiliar passageway. Immensely relieved to be leaving the cloying atmosphere of the castle behind, Eliza breathed more freely.

'Was that your brother?' she asked.

'Yes. He's at boarding school in England but he's back for a short visit. It's important he doesn't become too English, but it's a long journey here and back so he doesn't come back as often as he should.' He paused. 'Now, nobody except the family knows of this exit. Take my hand. I'm afraid you'll have to hold tight. It's very dark.'

She laughed. 'I feel honoured.'

They walked slowly, and something about being in the dark with him loosened her tongue. 'You asked me once if I believed in destiny. Why?'

'It's a long story. I'll tell you one day.'

'Tell me now. Please.'

Where the tunnel was so narrow it allowed for only one person at a time, she smelt damp earth and foliage and heard the faint drip of water. 'An underground stream,' he said, and reached back for her other hand too, his fingers closing tightly around hers. They stopped walking.

'You told me about your father and the bomb that was thrown that day in Delhi.'

'Yes,' she said, hearing the buzz of flying insects and wondering what he was about to say.

'Do you recall a young Indian boy at the scene?'

She thought about it. 'I think I do. Do you mean down on the street?'

'He helped you up when you had been kneeling at your father's side.'

'Yes.'

'It was a terrible thing to have happened, but I never forgot the young English girl. I never forgot you. It was me. I was the young Indian boy.'

It felt unbelievable that this could be true, but Eliza was glad he couldn't witness the tears that burned her eyelids. She squeezed his hands very tightly and, even though it was dark, something inexplicable passed between them. They stayed like that for a few minutes and an extraordinary feeling of peace washed over her. Because he had been there, had shared the very moment she had lost her father, it seemed to release something inside her. She couldn't explain it, but because she had not been so alone in those awful moments after all – he had been there too – she felt she might be able to come out from living in the shadow of her father's death. She held her breath and let this new thing wash over her, whatever it was, not wanting to move, ever, but the tunnel was cold and when she shivered they began to walk on.

'I was in the procession,' he said, 'with my mother in a *howdah* on one of the elephants. I climbed down when the explosion happened.'

'Did you know who I was straight away – when I first arrived here, I mean?'

'Not immediately, but you told me you had lived in Delhi and I recalled that the name of the man who had been killed was Fraser. After a few enquiries I wondered if that might be who you were.'

'Why didn't you say when I told you about the bomb?' she asked.

'I didn't feel I knew you well enough. I was worried about how it might affect you.'

'I'm glad you've told me now. It means such a lot and I'm very grateful.'

The exit from the castle was concealed behind a heavy wooden door that creaked as he unlocked it. 'Mind the thorn bushes,' he said as they went out. Then, as they made their way into the old city, he gave her the blanket and told her to cover her head and as much of her face as she could, though by now she was so coated in the coloured powder that had been all around them, nobody would know she was not one of them. Nothing about the celebration at the castle had prepared her for what was to come here in the town.

It was the night before full moon: everywhere bonfires were burning all the dried leaves and twigs of winter, and huge crowds of people had filled the streets and squares. But it was the mesmerizing drumming that thumped in her blood, the rhythm weaving through the dancing people who continued to throw coloured powders. Clouds of it brightened the air: red, blue, green and yellow swirling, flying in great puffs and then drifting over everyone. It was as if heaven had opened its paintbox and emptied the colours on to the world below. The noise of it all made speech impossible, but Jay held her hand tightly and she knew not to let go. Eliza touched her face and when she glanced at her fingers she saw they were blue. The powder was in her hair, in her eyelashes and in her mouth, and she was relieved when people in the upper balconies of houses lining the street began spraying water from long hosepipes. But with the addition of water the colour simply congealed and didn't run off. If Eliza had not been with Jay, the exotic, crazy night would have been too much. As it was, there were only moments of anxiety when the chaos and noise threatened to crush her English sensibilities. The whole town seemed to be spinning out of control, yet it was the most perfect celebration of life she'd ever experienced and eventually she allowed herself to surrender to it. Jay was in his element, laughing as he dodged the water and the powder, and she, helpless, threw back her head and laughed too.

A little after that Jay caught hold of her and pulled her into an alleyway out of the way. She was shocked to see people scattering in all directions as Rajput men pounded by at speed, riding horses through the red and pink clouds of colour, and throwing even more powder on the crowd as they passed. She was deeply aware of Jay's proximity and when he didn't move she was conscious that her heart was beating too fast. When he wrapped both arms around her she didn't think about it but simply sank into him. He continued to hold her tightly, the heat from his body so alarming and yet so exhilarating that she wanted never to be released. When he drew back a little he tilted her chin and she gazed right into his amber eyes.

'Eliza. I have been waiting for you to realize how I feel.'

She could hardly draw breath, her heart feeling as if it was actually pounding in her throat instead of her chest. And then, when he kissed her gently, she hardly knew how to think. He didn't stop, the kiss growing fiercer, his left hand holding the back of her neck. Dizzy from the Holi celebration, she felt the whole world tilt. Any further and she'd go sailing over the edge. When it was over she struggled to find words and then gave up. It didn't matter. Words didn't matter now. Tonight was entirely about sensation. Under the light from an oil lamp she gazed at the curve of his lips and his burnished skin, then reached out to touch his cheek. The skin was softer than she'd imagined, with a suggestion of sandalwood and cedar, but it was the pallor of her hand against his darkness that shook her.

A great cheer rose up and Eliza realized a change was going on around them. He grinned as he removed her hand from his face.

'You have to see this.'

They stood with their backs to the building on one side of the street as brightly painted elephants with embroidered head-plates lumbered along the centre of the street, the bells at their legs tinkling as they raised one enormous foot after another. The mahouts all held bright parasols and sat on golden embroidered rugs.

'So,' Jay said when they had passed, 'I don't believe it's possible to have no regrets at all, but are you ready to wave goodbye to the past?'

As Eliza lay in bed watching dawn approach, she went over every detail of the night. She focused on Jay's fine amber eyes, and the way the intoxication of Holi had made her feel light-headed. She had never felt that way when she had been with Oliver. In fact, now she thought about it, she could hardly remember how it had been with Oliver. Instead she imagined Jay's arms wrapped around her and, as the sensation fizzed through her, she felt as if her entire body was awakening. She rolled on to her stomach, longing to feel his hands on her skin, and pressed herself into the mattress. The arousal was almost unbearable. Then she thought about what he'd asked. Was she ready to leave the past behind? A part of her genuinely longed to, but then she remembered what Jay had said about the day her father had died. Did she believe in destiny as a prearranged formula for life? No. But she had to admit it was extraordinary that he should have been present all those years ago, at the most shocking moments of her entire life, and, now that he was here again, she tried very hard not to think of the future. Yet her mind still swelled with images, leaping into one scenario after another, and she couldn't stop projecting herself into some kind of idealistic future. With him. Of course it was impossible. She knew that, and yet she couldn't help falling into a dreamy state of hopefulness.

She tried to talk herself out of her feelings, blaming it on the night, the enchantment of Holi. But he had touched her soul and no amount of talking could diminish the feeling of connection she had experienced when she had been with him. It was a bit like coming home, only home wasn't a place, it was a person . . .

The next day a servant came with an envelope and as soon as she opened it she saw it was a note from Jay. He said that he had enjoyed her company very much and would hope to see her very soon. He also said that she'd never been as beautiful as when she had been dusted with coloured powder. When Laxmi asked to see her later on, Eliza worried that somehow the events of the night had leaked out. Maybe Chatur had spied, or he might have sent somebody to spy: someone who had been watching and had seen everything. Someone who had observed them leave the castle and who had followed. Eliza hated the thought of her every move being scrutinized and that crippling sensation of there being nowhere to hide. Laxmi would not be happy about her going out into the town with Jay, and she certainly would not be happy about the kiss. Eliza knew that his mother had been trying to arrange a marriage for Jay for the last few years and was hoping for a strong alliance with another royal family – not a Rajput, apparently that wasn't allowed, but from somewhere else in the Indian Empire.

Eliza steeled herself as she slowly walked to Laxmi's rooms. To reach the older woman's apartments she had to pass through four different corridors, usually patrolled by eunuchs. Eliza knew that the eunuchs were traditionally the guardians of women's chastity and they helped maintain a barrier around the Maharani. But the inner apartments were always guarded by two women. Eliza nodded at these two and tapped gently on the door. Laxmi opened it herself and Eliza was relieved to see the older woman smiling warmly. Perhaps she didn't know after all.

'Would you like some refreshment?' Laxmi asked. Dignified, proud and yet kind and generous too, she was gracious as always. Warm, friendly eyes, wrinkling at the corners, in an otherwise smooth-skinned face, were the only sign of ageing.

Eliza asked for water.

Today Laxmi was looking every inch a queen, in a mixture of blues and greens with trimmings of silver. Whenever Eliza was with her she always found herself sitting up straighter. Or maybe it was the grandeur of walls adorned with inlaid coloured glass mosaic and winged angels painted on the ceiling.

'I hear you went into the old town for the Holi celebration.'

Eliza gulped her water then put the glass down, spilling it on a beautiful mother-of-pearl table. 'Oh, I'm so sorry, I'll –'

Laxmi waved her apology away and rang a little silver bell. 'The handmaiden Sahili will see to it. She is very skilled. Do you know she came with me when I was a girl?'

'Really?'

'She was part of my dowry. Now look, my dear, I do not object to you spending time with my son. I hope you understand that. Indeed, it was I who suggested he take you to the camel fair and to the village.'

It was true. Laxmi had definitely brought them together, though of course not fully realizing what might happen. Was she now about to pull them apart?

'He had spent so long at school in England. He seemed bored and I assumed he would relish some English company.'

She had spoken in a consoling tone of voice but Eliza held her breath.

'But he will never be able to offer you anything more than friendship. Do you understand that, Eliza?'

Eliza took a quick breath at the certainty behind Laxmi's gentle probing. 'Yes, of course.'

'It really isn't just that you're English. There once were many marriages between Indian royals and European aristocrats, sometimes not even aristocrats. They used to be recognized as legitimate wives and their children as legitimate heirs. Then Lord Curzon passed a law that meant that no child of an Indian ruler from his European wife could succeed to the throne.'

'I didn't know.'

'Although Jay isn't on the throne, he would be if anything happened to Anish. Anish has no sons. A kingdom with no heir is wide open for the British to take over. But there is also a bigger issue. It is not that you are English, nor is it even that no child of yours could succeed to the title.'

Eliza frowned. 'I'm not sure what you mean.'

'He cannot marry a widow. Other than the wife of his predecessor.'

So that was it. She struggled to know what to say for a moment, but then managed to speak. 'But I'm not looking for a husband, Laxmi. I promise you.' She tried to push Jay to the back of her mind.

'Then that is good. I just don't want you to raise your hopes or see you hurt, or end up little more than a concubine, or maybe a second or third wife, hidden from the world. I hope you understand. Marriage here is not a romantic matter. It is a complicated case of working out a strategy that will improve the fortunes and status of both families.'

There was a brief silence.

'I daresay you will be happy to leave after the trouble with Chatur. Yes, I do know about it . . . so maybe it will be a good thing that you are gone before the rains, and not stay the full year,' Laxmi added.

This last comment struck Eliza with force and she was stunned by the implications. She stared at Laxmi's intelligent face and wondered what the older woman was up to. She had always planned to be here for the start of the rains, and beyond. Not only did she want to photograph the finished initial stage of Jay's project, she really wanted to capture something of the rains themselves. Everyone spoke of them in such reverent tones that she wanted to see for herself. Jay had said she should see the clouds rolling in above Udaipore, the city of lakes.

Eliza nodded, but did not speak at first. Before the rains was too soon, and leaving was not in her plan. Clifford had arranged for a year.

'I admit I like Jay,' she said after a few moments, 'but I need to be here for the rains and then the start of autumn. You need have no fear about my expectations.'

'Be that as it may, let me explain a little more so that you truly understand. I'm thinking of you, my dear. It is pre-arranged that a Maharani is allotted higher status than a Rani, or second wife. A Maharani has a gorgeous apartment, eats off golden plates, wears beautiful clothes and is showered with gifts of jewellery. A Rani, whether she is second, third, fourth, or no matter what, will only have one room to call her own, maybe with her own small court, maybe not. A concubine is unlikely to even have a room of her own. So you see, status is everything.'

'Like I say, I have no expectations regarding your son,' Eliza said rather hastily.

Laxmi nodded approvingly. 'Women from European cultures are never truly accepted by our people. Our relationships with those we govern are specific and very special. The ordinary people would never accept a widow, you see.'

There was a brief silence. Eliza didn't know what more she could say to convince Laxmi that Jay was safe from her.

'Anyway, I'm delighted to say that I have consulted horologists and several priests and it looks as if I have found an auspicious match for my son. A wonderful girl from a royal family who has an important dowry. I hope they will be married before long.'

Laxmi had spoken with animation and was now smiling broadly, but Eliza struggled to conceal her shock. Did Jay already know? Had he already agreed to this? It was as if fate stood motionless above her, poised to mete out its punishment for that kiss, and she felt like crawling away to lick her wounds.

'So I think we understand each other now. There is a strong practice of spying in all palaces and castles. Nothing goes unnoticed, my dear. Nothing. I would have said something before, only I didn't want to interfere if there wasn't anything to worry about.'

'And you think there is now, even though he is to be engaged?'

'I understand my own son.' Laxmi paused and, in the pause, there seemed to remain a worry.

Meanwhile, Eliza wanted to be somewhere else. It didn't matter where, as long as she could find some comfort and the chance to still her chaotic thoughts.

'It can be hard for a woman. You know, in the past, if a Rani or concubine was discovered to be having a liaison with another man, a death sentence was imposed. We used to rule with fear and awe. No woman of the palace would dare show her face to a man who wasn't her husband.'

'And you approve of all that?'

'I wouldn't say that. I do, however, believe in a wife's duty to hold the marriage and her family together.'

'Even if the husband strays?'

'The husband?' She laughed. 'The husbands had so many wives and concubines. My father had three hundred. *Straying*, as you put it, was built into the system.'

'And you don't think the inequality was wrong?'

'I only think that if a woman isn't holding the marriage and the family together, who will? We are not men. It is different for us.'

'I learnt recently that my father had a mistress. It destroyed my mother.' It was the first time Eliza had spoken of it. In fact it was the first time she had allowed herself to even consider that her mother's accusation might be true, but something about Laxmi seemed to elicit confession.

'Men will be men, my dear, so far better to build a way to accommodate them into the system, don't you think? Then there can be no nasty shocks.'

'You don't have a very high opinion of men.'

'On the contrary.'

'And what of jealousy? Surely it's human nature.'

'Many of the Rani and concubines were, and are, good friends, but of course there is and was jealousy.'

'And what happened then?'

'Poisonings, more often than not.'

19

Eliza's mood had altered drastically since her talk with Laxmi. What a fool she had been to indulge in such hopeless romanticism. From now on her relationship with Jay must remain on strictly formal grounds and, when she passed him leaving the entrance to her part of the building, she merely gave him a curt nod and then hurried past and up her staircase. She hadn't paused to see what his reaction might have been and, once in her own room, she locked the door, her heart pounding against her ribs. She felt out of breath, even though she hadn't been running, but, thinking about what had happened, realized that beneath the dignity Laxmi embodied there lay a will of steel.

Perhaps Laxmi was right? Maybe the best thing she could do was to wind up this entire project as quickly as possible. Call it six months in Juraipore and then get out of this godforsaken castle once and for all. Dottie would agree with that, she felt sure. She would just take a few more shots of the royal family and some more in the old city, though of course she'd have to use her Sanderson.

In fact Clifford had organized a picnic beside the lake just outside the town, and there she would tell him that she wanted to speed things up. As for Jay's irrigation plans? He'd have to continue without her help.

Nothing truly good lasts, she whispered, thinking of when she and her mother had left India to live at James Langton's place in Gloucestershire. She'd thought he had wanted her there, that he'd welcomed having a child about the place, but then she'd been sent away to a third-class boarding school and she'd always believed it had been because he'd wanted her out of the way.

Thinking of Clifford's picnic brought back another memory. She recalled that it had happened just before she'd been sent away.

The only time James Langton had accompanied Eliza and Anna on a little outing, they'd walked through sun-drenched fields with him carrying a picnic basket. It was early spring, and Eliza had felt so happy that he was so unusually joining them. But he hadn't liked the chicken pies her mother had made, and when he accidentally sat on a cowpat, Eliza had laughed. He'd taken hold of her by the elbow, pulled her from the rug she was sitting on, and smacked her hard. She must have been almost thirteen and had found the episode utterly humiliating. She had run back home, crying all the way, and Anna had eventually returned home over an hour later, hair dishevelled and with the buttons on her dress awry. Just when she'd needed her mother's love and consolation, Anna had taken Langton's side; it had been a bitter betrayal.

Eliza wasn't in the mood for a picnic, but had dressed in a full-skirted fine lawn dress in palest green with a wide-brimmed straw hat. Several of Clifford's acquaintances were to join them, and Eliza mentally prepared herself for an afternoon of small talk. Whatever might be wrong with the palace, you could never accuse its inhabitants of small talk.

She was surprised when it didn't turn out quite like that.

The location of the picnic couldn't have been more stunning. Servants carried armchairs, a table, fans and several enormous sunshades from the wagons and horse-carts. Everything was laid out overlooking a lake shimmering in the afternoon sunshine. Cranes, pelicans and storks gathered at the banks; there were even ducks on the water, and the trees lining its edges were bursting with the sound of birdsong. With the surrounding hills rising to blue in the distance, it seemed that Clifford had spared no expense and had thought of everything. Julian Hopkins, the doctor, and Dottie were always friendly, though Eliza felt a little guilty as she gave the woman a hug. She had promised herself that she'd visit Dottie but hadn't done so recently.

'Not too hot for you?' Clifford asked as he pointed out a seat beneath one of the shades. 'We could have gone down to the lakeside but the air is fresher up here. I hope you like it, Eliza.'

'It's lovely,' she said, and watched the birds gathering at the water's edge. 'I want to take a few shots after lunch, later in the afternoon when the sun is a bit lower. I love to catch low-level light.'

The others were talking amiably as the table was laid with a crisp linen cloth and the silver cutlery was set. There were even two tented enclosures that appeared to be made of silk with muslin roofs, and with no curtain on the side facing the lake.

'They are *kanats*,' Clifford said, seeing her looking. 'Perfect for a rest after a long lunch.'

She got to her feet and went over to glance into one. Inside it was heaped high with satin cushions, and three musicians had now set up beside it. The air smelt fresh and surprisingly cool and Eliza longed to relax a little, and yet all she could think about was Jay. What had happened the night of Holi had shaken her and left her feeling taut. She had not come looking for love, and of course it had not been love. But what had it been? Lust? Surely there had been something deeper that connected the two of them? She stood immobile, thinking this and facing the lake, staring but not seeing. Hadn't he once said that heartbreak united them, though when he'd said it he'd included Indi too.

'So,' Clifford was saying, 'what do you think?'

'Pardon?'

'Haven't you been listening?'

'Sorry, miles away.' She waved vaguely at the view. 'It's all so beautiful.'

'I was saying we should visit the palace on the lake at Udaipore. It's the most romantic place in the entire world, especially in the rainy season.'

'A place to fall in love, eh, Clifford,' one of the men joked, and nudged the other.

The other two men who were part of the small gathering were army, stationed down south, but the wife of one of them, who had accompanied them today, had known Clifford when she was a girl, so they'd come to visit on their way to her sister's wedding in the Punjab.

'Must be nice for you to be with your own kind again, Miss Fraser,' the younger of the two men said.

Annoyed at the assumption, Eliza just nodded.

The woman, who was called Gloria Whitstable, spoke up. 'I don't know how you stand it. I couldn't sleep a single night in one of those ghastly castles. I'm sure I'd be murdered in my bed.'

'Actually,' Eliza said, feeling a growing prickle of irritation, 'I've rather enjoyed it. And I've not finished my year yet.'

'I'm sure it's fascinating,' Dottie interjected, and Eliza shot her a smile.

'I have news,' Clifford suddenly said.

'Oh?'

'I've been asked if you'd consider going up to Shimla to undertake a short project. It's a good offer and you wouldn't survive in the heat out here. To be honest, Shimla is the only place to be. You wouldn't have to live with the Indians either. It's to be a visual record of the British at play. You know – the summer parties, the amateur dramatics, the club, all that sort of thing.'

Even though she had been considering asking Clifford if she could wind up her current project a little early, now it had come to this Eliza's heart plummeted.

'Oh, we'll miss you,' Dottie was saying. 'Though of course Shimla is wonderful. I'm rather envious.'

Eliza felt even more guilt as she recalled how lonely Dottie had seemed. When she didn't speak, Clifford looked a little hurt. 'A thank you will do, Eliza. You wouldn't be so alone and I'd get up if I could spare the time.'

She still didn't know what to say. Of course it would be a means to escape her current predicament, but she wouldn't see Jay, and the depth of her feeling shook her. It was easy to think of leaving in a casual kind of way; much harder to face a concrete prospect.

'Eliza?'

'Sorry. I was just thinking.'

'Wouldn't have thought there was much to think about. It's a terrific opportunity.'

'But I haven't finished my year here.'

He shrugged.

'Did you ever intend it to be a year, Clifford?'

'Of course. It's just that this came up.'

'Well, do you mind terribly if I sleep on it? You know, my

camera isn't back from Delhi and I wouldn't want to miss out on something crucial for the archive.'

'I'm sure you won't, but be aware they want an answer by the end of the week, or they'll go elsewhere. You can always come back here in September.'

'You'll have your answer. Sorry to be difficult.'

'You're not being difficult. I understand.'

But it was clear from the marginally aggrieved look on his face that he did not understand. Eliza kept her thoughts to herself and was not about to enlighten him, but she continued to follow her own train of thought, ignoring the look on his face. As a sumptuous meal was set before them she already knew she had no appetite and, while she played with her food, she hoped Clifford wasn't expecting her to lie down in a tent with him.

'By the way,' he said and gave a small cough, 'there are a few problems with funding the irrigation project.'

'I thought you said the money would be there.'

He shook his head. 'I hoped, Eliza, never promised.'

'But Jay has to get the first stage finished by July, when the rains come, or all the work will have been for nothing. The rains will wash the banks away if the supports are not completed.'

'I'm sorry. I did my best.'

'So you're saying there is no money.'

He shrugged again.

'Clifford, that's awful. It would mean so much to the village people.'

'So much for the village people, or for you, Eliza?' He was looking at her intently and she found it almost impossible to disguise her real feelings.

He leant towards her and spoke in a low voice. 'Have you

got yourself into trouble, Eliza? Developed feelings for a chap like him? It would be most irregular.'

She balked at his peremptory tone. 'Of course not,' she said, and drew back, trying for an affronted look.

'Good. He'll do you no favours, you know, and my offer still stands.'

'Shimla or . . .'

'Both, my dear. Both. You'll find I don't give up easily,' he added in a persistent tone. 'But if you make me happy, I'll make you happy, if you get my drift, and, you never know,' he paused as if thinking, 'the funds for the irrigation project might yet come good after all.'

20

When Eliza arrived back at the castle it was almost night and she was in a furious mood. She had not failed to grasp the hints beneath Clifford's words, and fumed at what he had said, but soon forgot that when she saw that the castle was in uproar. She let thoughts of Clifford go, at least for the time being, and watched as people bustled about, marching back and forth across the courtyards with grave expressions on their faces. Nobody paid her any attention. She was about to escape to her room to think about Shimla, but then spotted Indi standing under one of the colonnaded archways. The girl beckoned her across and Eliza went over.

'What's going on?' she said.

'Anish is sick.'

'Is it serious?'

'I think so. There are physicians and astrologers in attendance.'

'Do you know what it is?'

The girl shook her head, but Eliza had the distinct impression something was troubling her.

'But he'll be all right?'

Indi again shook her head. 'Nobody knows. The trouble is if anything happens to Anish, Jay will have to take over and Chatur will stop at nothing to prevent that.'

'But why?'

'Jay is a modernizer. Chatur is the exact opposite and will

accept no other viewpoint. He can manipulate Anish to his own ends. He would not be able to manipulate Jay. I think Chatur has been worried about Anish's health for some time now and has been hiding it from us.'

As Eliza turned away she felt a little unnerved by what Indi had said. But maybe this was just Laxmi's talk of poisoning upsetting her and, while Anish's illness could have nothing to do with her, she decided to keep out of the way for the rest of the evening and get on in her darkroom.

While working she couldn't stop her thoughts revolving. She had tried to live up to expectations, first as a daughter and then as a wife, but she'd failed at both. She had done her best to love Oliver: cooked for him, kept their little apartment immaculate, and tried to respond to his advances, though it had usually ended in frustration for both of them. He was the only man Eliza had ever been with and, at first, inexperienced in the ways of lovemaking, she'd blamed herself, but she'd had one important ally. Books. She was a great reader and had spent much of her childhood with her nose in a book, so gradually, after reading about sex and growing more and more red-faced, she had realized that Oliver was not at all a tender lover or a tender person. He seemed to expect her to open her legs whenever he demanded and, with little input from him, to accept his body into hers. And when she didn't, all the worse for her. She had hated it. It was as simple as that, and she had fought not to hate him too. It was on one of these occasions that he, in anger, had told her she was cold and asexual. In retaliation she had flung her wedding ring out of the window and told him she wanted a career. The next day she had tried to make it up to him, arranged flowers on their dining-room table, put on her prettiest dress, sprayed perfume behind her ears. It hadn't worked, and her words had spilled out as she had told him she would be a photographer whatever he thought of it. He had slammed the door on his way out and that was the last time she'd seen him alive. And, although she realized now that she had never loved him, it saddened her that he had died in that senseless manner.

Gradually she grew calmer. The blank silence of her darkroom gave her space and time to think; it soothed her too, as if the mechanical pouring of chemicals smoothed out the creases in her mind. But, apart from her photography, she had to face the fact that she had nothing to offer a man. What good was knowing how to make a picture of who someone truly was? What good was her ability to put people at their ease so she could take a natural shot? She had been a hopeless wife before, and certainly had no desire to marry again if it meant wasting her life looking after somebody who should be capable of looking after himself. Of course Jay would want a subservient wife and could never be interested in her; he was destined for a vastly different kind of life. It had only been a kiss, after all, and he must have kissed countless women. She had been dazzled by him, nothing more, and so she tried to convince herself it didn't matter.

But Clifford had let her down. He had promised to help with the funding for the irrigation project and now Jay would be left high and dry. Laxmi had already mortgaged some of the family jewels to pay for the engineer and to hire the machinery and start the construction. It would be disastrous if everything were to be held up now. They had all been relying on Clifford coming through, and though she could never do it, it did sound as if he still might come up with the funds if she gave him what he wanted.

When Jay came to her room late that night, she opened the door and after glancing up and down the corridor allowed him in. He was waving a newspaper as he came in.

'Have you seen this?' He thumped the paper. 'Your Winston Churchill has called Gandhi a "half-naked fakir".'

Eliza was puzzled.

'Gandhi walked right up to Viceroy House wearing only a loincloth. The British didn't like that one bit.' He had spoken in anger but now he paused. 'Actually, it's almost funny when you think about it. Pity you couldn't have been there to take a photograph. You'd have made a fortune.'

'I see.'

He frowned and scratched his head. 'Is something wrong? I'm sorry this is the first chance I've had to come to you.'

'How's your brother?' she asked, but her throat was dry and she battled to find her way through a knot of contradictory emotions, longing to savour every moment with him, and yet knowing she could not. Even her own voice sounded strange. The ease between them had vanished, and now it was worse than if that one night of sharing his secret world had never happened.

He pulled a face, and she found it impossible to gauge what he was thinking or feeling.

'He's fine, or he will be. A spot of indigestion, probably.'

'But Indi looked worried.'

'Did she?' He paused and, as he walked across to sit in the armchair, she wished she could be more courageous. And yet always the fear of rejection, of saying too much, of being hurt. Better to keep her guard up.

'I haven't come to talk about Indi or my brother.'

She looked at his hands and imagined them on the back of her neck again when he had kissed her. 'Then what?' She had struggled to keep the vulnerable sound out of her voice but worried that he'd heard it anyway.

'I've been thinking about what happened on the night of Holi.'

'Me too,' she said, ashamed of her own lack of mettle, but glad that he had been the one to speak.

He sighed. 'Tell me about you.'

She was surprised. 'Tell you what?'

'There's always something holding you back, isn't there? I've known it from the first. You don't belong here, but I wonder if there's anywhere you do belong.'

He had spoken in a soft voice, the one he had used when telling her he'd been there when her father died. She threw herself on to the sofa, then sat hunched up and gazing at her feet.

'Sometimes you really need to take a risk in life.'

She glanced at him and then away again. 'I've taken a risk by coming here.'

'I mean with your heart.' He paused. 'Eliza, look at me.'

She shook her head. 'Clifford has offered me another job.'

'Well, that's good, isn't it?'

'It's in Shimla. I have to let him know by the end of the week.' She didn't dare look to see if his face revealed his feelings, but when he spoke his voice was entirely expressionless.

'When would you need to leave?'

'Immediately.'

She heard him draw in his breath. 'Eliza, I don't know what your expectations are.'

She looked up at him. 'You can relax. I have none.'

'It's important you understand that your life is in your own hands.'

'And what of destiny?'

'You make your destiny.'

'Is that what you really think?'

'It's what I believe. You know we believe in karma here. What you do now affects the future, whether in this life, or the next.'

'So if I'm a good girl I might come back as an Indian Princess. Somebody a Prince could be with. Is that what you mean?'

'Of course not.' He gave her a broad smile. 'You'd hate it anyway. Being an Indian wife, I mean.'

She didn't smile and wanted to glare at him. But whatever either of them were to say now, it would make no difference. She'd always be a widow from a dubious background and he'd always be the glamorous, inaccessible Prince Jayant Singh Rathore. A man whom countless women would adore. She'd never get below the surface of the palace, of India, or of him. Beads of sweat broke out on her brow and she swiped her fingers across to wipe them away. The back of her neck felt hot too.

'Eliza, what's wrong? Tell me.'

She drew in her breath. 'Actually I do have something to tell you. Clifford has failed to obtain funding for your water project.'

She steeled herself, longing for him to beg her to turn down the offer of Shimla, and tried not to falter under his gaze.

There was only silence and the air seemed to chill.

'Why are you staring at me?' she asked eventually, still hoping, though in her heart she already knew.

Her heart sank as he sprang to his feet.

'So that I can remember everything about you after you're gone,' he said.

She struggled not to crumple beneath a bewildering feeling of disappointment, strangely tempered by something almost resembling relief. That was it. All over before it had begun.

He made for the door. 'If you forgive me, I have some thinking to do. Don't trouble yourself about it. Now that I have the bit between my teeth I shan't stop. I have to finish before the rains and I still have a few months. Thank you for your help. Goodnight.'

He bowed and left the room.

21

Eliza slept badly and woke with her gut churning. But one thing became clear; she couldn't just leave it like that. She ached to see Jay, needed to talk with him again, though how much of this was genuine and how much the attraction of forbidden love she couldn't be sure. She washed and dressed quickly and then with a racing heart and sweating palms went to find him. After repeatedly knocking at the door of his apartment and getting no reply there was really only one place left, and that was his study.

She marched back along the main corridor, feeling increasingly that she was making a mistake, but as she approached the study she saw that the door had been left slightly ajar. No going back now! So she gathered her courage and pushed it open, expecting of course to see Jay. Inside the room a startled-looking Dev seemed to have risen hastily from where – judging by the angle of the chair – he'd been sitting at Jay's desk and typing. Eliza took the scene in and assumed he was waiting for Jay, though something about it niggled.

'How did you get in?' she asked.

'The door was unlocked. Jay lets me use his typewriter sometimes.'

'When did you arrive?' she asked, but now noticed that he looked genuinely ill at ease, as if he'd been wrong-footed by her arrival.

'Last night,' he said, with a quick smile, and, recovering

his composure, he folded the papers he'd pulled from the typewriter.

'Where's Jay?'

'Who knows? He went off on his motorbike at the crack of dawn.'

'Really? Where to?'

Dev shrugged. 'Didn't say. He does this from time to time, usually when he has something on his mind. Or if he's out of sorts. He might have gone to see how the irrigation project is coming on.'

'Well, I'd better get along,' Eliza said, as she took a step back towards the door. 'Lots to do.'

'Are you packing? Jay told me you were leaving.'

Eliza paused, not wanting her departure to be a subject of gossip, nor to make it real either. 'Nothing is settled.'

'Look, I have a bike of my own. Rode it here in fact. A bumpier ride than Jay's and no sidecar, but if you're willing to hang on, you could come with me to Jay's palace. See if he's there. Take some photographs of the progress.'

'I'm not sure,' Eliza said, hesitating, not wanting Jay to think she was chasing after him, but then she caught the memory of the scent of a desert morning and an irrational impulse took over – with nothing to lose, she found herself agreeing.

'I'll have to take the heavier Sanderson camera, plates and a tripod. It's cumbersome and harder to use, but it might be best. Will there be room on the bike?'

'We'll strap it on.'

A couple of hours later, under a glittering sky, Eliza was clinging on as Dev rode far too fast along the dusty desert tracks and bumped over tussocks of grass amid the many thorn trees. After a mile or two she wrapped her scarf around her head, covering her mouth, and hoped to avoid the clouds of sand and dust. The bike was smaller than Jay's and much noisier, and by the time they arrived at Jay's palace, the sun was directly overhead and every bone in her body had been jolted. The building lay somnolent beneath the haze, silent and seemingly empty. She attempted to smooth down her tousled hair, aware that she must look a fright, and it made her think, once again, that this mightn't have been such a good idea. She wondered at the dull thud of her heart, for her an obvious sign of unease – she had wanted to come and did not regret the impulse, but really, what would Jay think of her turning up like this?

'Is it all right to have come here without asking first?' she asked, trying not to sound pathetic.

He just laughed. 'Come on. Let's take a peek at the work in progress.'

'Shouldn't we find Jay first? Let him know?'

'If Jay is here he'll soon realize we've arrived.'

They walked round to where Eliza had sat with Jay all those months ago and, almost expecting to see him sitting there, she hardly knew how to cope. Was he really engaged or about to be? It made her feel a little sick that she had let him kiss her, had encouraged it even.

She followed Dev through the tangled gardens and then a small orchard, finally arriving at the place where a massive amount of work was already under way. Hundreds and hundreds of yards wide, an oblong pit had been partially dug out, although the rest remained clearly unfinished. Eliza looked at the rock-hard earth and was shocked by the enormity of the task. There was still masses of digging to complete and, soon enough, time would run out. She spotted that building work had been started close by: presumably one of the walls to keep the water from leaking. The pit was empty, of course, but with scant rain the previous two years Jay had to get this first lake finished.

'He'll need to get a move on if the reinforced banks are to be ready,' Dev said. 'Have you been here during a monsoon?'

'When I was a child. I hardly remember.'

'It's wonderful. When the heavens open, there is wild laughter and joy. The end of suffocating heat.'

'And water.' She pointed at Jay's dug-out lake. 'He hopes to dam a small river and build a massive embankment with marble steps down to the water. But I know when that's done there's a much larger lake that he's planning, half a mile wide and half a mile long.'

'But nobody is working now?' Dev said.

Eliza shook her head and, with a heavy heart, glanced at the steam-powered shovels lying abandoned. She struggled not to show how much she ached over what must be Jay's bitter disappointment.

'There's been a funding delay,' she said, once she had controlled her distress.

'Just a minor delay?'

'I don't know. Shall we walk round?'

As they began to walk around the edge of the newly dug area, Dev appeared to be lost in thought. Eliza didn't mind. She was thinking too, and wondering how it must feel for Jay to see the work lying abandoned like this. She longed to comfort him, but had a hollow sensation in the pit of her stomach when she thought she might bump into him at any turn.

'Is it British funding that has dried up?' Dev eventually said.

She nodded.

Dev stopped walking. 'So who has been organizing it?'

'Clifford Salter.'

Dev snorted and then gazed out at the empty pit. Eliza could feel that he was holding back whatever was going on inside him, perhaps in deference to her, but then the truth hit her.

'You don't like me, do you?' she said.

'With good cause, wouldn't you say?'

She raised her brows.

He shrugged and they carried on walking. 'The truth is I have nothing against you personally, but the British are no longer welcome. In the twelve years since Amritsar there has been bitter resentment. There are disturbances every-where now.'

'I know what happened at Amritsar was awful.'

He almost seemed to groan aloud. 'Awful? Is that what you call it?'

'What else?'

'The British fired at thousands of Indians during a peace-ful demonstration over a deeply unfair law that decreed that no more than five Indians could gather together. When the meeting took place to protest, the British troops opened fire. They left 379 Indians dead and 1,500 wounded. They were sitting targets, trapped within a walled park.' He paused. 'I think that was a little more than awful.'

She tried to imagine the terrible scene and felt sick at the loss of so many lives.

'All this in retaliation for the murder of three Europeans and one British woman who had been molested. They ordered Indians to crawl on the ground in the street where the English woman had been attacked.'

She looked up at him and saw how fired up he had become.

'Humiliation never goes down well.' He gave a bitter laugh. 'Above all else the British hate the thought of our dark lascivious hands touching the flesh of a white woman. To them it is an abomination.'

'I understand how angry you are, I really do,' she said, but thought of Jay kissing her.

'How could you possibly understand?'

She hadn't known what to say and knew it had been a weak response. But she didn't want to be seen as a representative of British domination and had felt compelled to say something.

'Back in the day the Brits would choose the prettiest girls from the villages to use as their whores. Then later the girls were thrown out. The families couldn't take them back after they had been so defiled. What do you think that did to people? So yes, people are resentful.'

'I'm sorry.'

'You think that helps?'

Eliza shook her head.

'I think Indira's mother might have been one of those women taken by the Brits and then thrown out when she became pregnant.'

'You think Indi's father was a British man? Is that what everyone thinks?'

He shrugged. 'She's paler and we know nothing about her. Indi's grandmother has never spoken about her granddaughter's origins. Shame would do that.'

They started to walk along the edge of the pit again and Eliza was glad. She wanted to see Jay but at the same time she didn't want to hear the truth about his engagement. So far there had been no sign of him, but her head was still ringing with Laxmi's words.

'Her mother might have been one of the used and abused. I'd marry Indi myself, but my mother would have a dozen fits at the thought.'

'And your father?'

'Long gone.'

'I'm sorry.'

He stared at her and a shadow passed over his face. 'Me too. The Indian relationship with the British has gone through many phases. But now it's time for us to claim our birthright.'

'You believe that?'

'I do, and many of the British do too. Even back in 1920 Montagu said that you couldn't remain in a country where you were not wanted.'

'And what are you personally doing to speed our withdrawal?'

'I'm not active these days. I tried to get Anish to give permission for a protest march but he wasn't keen. Anyway, didn't Jay tell you? I'm all talk.'

'That's not what I heard.'

'And your meaning?'

'Just rumour. You know.'

'I wouldn't be surprised if the British have pulled out of this –' he grimaced as he waved in the direction of the lake – 'by design.'

'Why would they?'

'Has Jay already incurred debts?'

She bit her lip but didn't reply.

'That could discredit Jay and cause trouble at the palace. It's no secret they want to get rid of Anish, and if Jay is discredited there'd be good reason for him not to take the throne either.'

Eliza thought about what Clifford had said. The British did want to depose Anish, so it was conceivable that financial trouble for Jay and ensuing trouble at the castle could work in their favour.

'So what now?' she said, lifting her upturned palms.

'You tell me.'

Jay had not been at his palace after all, and once they had returned to the main castle of Juraipore Eliza decided to slip down to the listening tube on the lowest corridor. She knew Jay had taken to listening in from time to time, but it was awkward for him to be seen down in the bowels of the palace. She'd gone on her own a few times but the room had always remained in silence. Until today, and today something was going on. She heard a deep sigh and then heavy breathing. Then she heard a man's voice. Perhaps Jay had come home, wherever he had been?

'You don't seem happy today. Have you grown bored with me?'

There was the murmur of a woman's voice and then it sounded as if something crashed to the ground. The man was cursing and the woman was laughing. Eliza recognized that laugh.

'The door is locked and I have left the key in the lock. Nobody will know.'

'Not in here. I told you, not in here.'

'Don't you want to imagine I'm your adored Prince Jay? I thought it would excite you to be in here.'

Eliza realized the man was Chatur, and she was certain he was in there with Indira.

She replaced the picture on the wall and ran to Jay's quarters, hoping that he had actually come home. But the castle was huge, and even using the secret passage it was easy to take a wrong turn. It took nearly ten minutes, and when she did arrive there was no one there. She dashed to his study without stopping to consider if her haste was strictly necessary. It hadn't sounded as if Indi was actually in danger, but Eliza couldn't imagine any woman choosing to be alone with a ruthless man like Chatur. The study door was locked, so she thumped hard, hurting her hand in the process.

'Who is in there?' she called out.

No reply. She waited for five minutes, and when she spotted Jay coming along the corridor she blinked rapidly and a lump developed in her throat.

'I thought you were leaving,' he said.

She shook her head. 'I'm not going.' Then she put a finger to her lips and moved a few paces from the door.

'I overheard Indira with Chatur,' she whispered. 'He was in there trying to have sex with her, I think. Certainly trying to do something.'

'Against her will?'

'It didn't sound like she was trying to stop him. I think she just wanted to go somewhere else.'

'She wouldn't want to be overheard in there.'

Jay walked up to the door and turned his key in the lock. He opened the door but they could both see that the room was empty. He went in, followed by Eliza, who was now beginning to wonder if she'd imagined the entire episode. Jay glanced around.

When he spoke he kept his voice low. 'Everything seems to be in place.'

After taking a few steps behind the desk he bent down, then held up a shard of broken glass.

'My clock had a glass face.' He glanced at his desk. 'It's missing.'

Eliza also spoke in a whisper. 'I thought I heard something crash.'

'Dear God, what has she got herself into now? Better come into the corridor,' he said and opened the door.

Once out in the corridor he looked around and continued to speak in hushed tones.

'What will you do?' she asked.

'Inform Chatur that I know what's been going on. That should put a stop to it.'

'Can't you get rid of Chatur?'

'I wish. Only Anish can do that.'

'So tell him?'

'He won't take my word for it, and it might only make trouble for Indi. I'll think of something.'

'You are very protective of her.'

'Apart from her ageing grandmother, she is alone in the world.'

'That's all?'

'I'm very fond of Indira, though not in the way you once thought. I blame myself for that. I'd become accustomed to thinking of her as a sister. I've been trying to distance myself a little, but I don't want to hurt her.'

Aware that her face was reddening, she turned away. 'Especially now that you're about to be engaged,' she managed to say, despite being blown about by confused emotions: fear, disappointment, embarrassment, but, worst of all, longing.

He threw back his head and laughed. 'You, my dear friend, have been listening to my mother. Let's get away from here.'

They went to her rooms, where he sat on the small sofa.

'Sit with me, Eliza. I promise I am not engaged, nor do I wish to be. Now tell me that you're really not leaving us? Leaving me?'

Her heart somersaulted with relief and she smiled. 'I'm staying.'

Even though she knew there could be nothing permanent with Jay, at least he cared that she might be leaving and, as she sat down next to him, she took a very deep breath. He picked up her hand and turned it over, then traced the lines on her palm.

'Can you see my future?' she said.

'Not yet,' he said, 'but maybe soon.'

She felt a strange humming in her head and lifted her other hand to smooth the hair from his temples. Watching his beautiful amber eyes, she marvelled at the intensity she saw boring into her. He let her palm go and took hold of her other hand, then he lifted it to his lips and gently kissed her fingertips. She loved it when he touched her, though he had never touched her like this before. The closer he was to her the more alive she felt, the love, the hope and the heat chewing up her mind until she felt empty of fear.

22

Later that day Eliza was summoned to Anish's outer sitting room, a place so ornate it was hard to know where to rest her gaze. He sat on a huge cushion, legs spread wide to accommodate his ever-increasing paunch, and Jay sat in a chair opposite. The floor was piled with more satin cushions, placed around a large low table. Eliza glanced at the slim *punkawallah* who was pulling a heavy rope that operated a large fan made of cloth stretched over a wooden frame. Back and forth it floated, as it hung from the ceiling directly above Anish. And little gusts of air reached as far as where Eliza stood, feeling increasingly uncomfortable.

'Do not hover, girl! Sit.'

She glanced around and chose a hardback chair, where she sat stiffly and with her hands folded in her lap. 'Are you well now?' she asked. 'I remember you were ill soon after Holi.'

He inclined his head. 'It started some while before, in fact. But at Holi, Chatur came to me with a bottle of some kind of chemical he had discovered hidden away somewhere. You are the only person with access to such things.'

'Which chemical was it?'

'Pyrogallol, I think. Something like that was on the label. I wondered if it was poisonous.'

Eliza could feel the blood draining from her face. The silver pyro crystals were terribly dangerous and could have long-term degenerative effects on the nervous system. It was a poison that could be ingested or could get into the system via the skin, which was why she kept the bottles under lock and key in her darkroom. Although Indi had also worked in there, she had always been supervised and didn't have a key of her own, so it couldn't have been her. Then, with a feeling of horror, Eliza recalled the day she'd come back and found her darkroom door unlocked. She had thought she'd accidentally left the padlock open, but perhaps she hadn't after all, and if she hadn't left it unlocked herself, then somebody else must have a key.

After she had told the two brothers about it, Jay got to his feet and swung his arms. 'So there you are, problem solved. Anish only wanted to know how the pyro had got out of your darkroom and whether you'd given it to anybody.'

'No. Of course I didn't. But why would anyone steal it?'

'Need you ask?'

'But surely nobody would hurt the Maharajah?'

Anish laughed, but it was a short, sharp, mirthless sound. 'I constantly fear for my life. This may be the twentieth century, but old habits die hard. I have a stream of poisoned ancestors stretching back in time. If I didn't know my brother has no designs on the throne I would be suspecting him.'

Jay rolled his eyes.

'Where is the bottle now?'

'I had it disposed of.'

'And was it full?'

'To the brim.'

She let out a sigh of relief. 'Well, I hope you are feeling better now, sir?'

'Better, though something still is not quite right. This is just between us, you understand, but I shall ask Mr Salter to recommend a good chest doctor. I don't want the castle unduly concerned.'

She got to her feet. 'There's a doctor living right next door to Clifford Salter. He will know.'

'Indeed. Now, just in case somebody else does have a key,' Anish added, 'count the bottles and make sure you change the padlock on your door. Do it today. Jay will help you.'

As she and Jay left Anish's chambers and walked down the corridor, Jay paused and looked into her eyes.

She smiled up at him. 'Did you know I went to see the project with Dev?'

'Yes.' He took hold of her hand. 'I can't tell you how glad I am that you're staying.'

How this man touched her soul. He made her feel more real, as if she had a place where she fitted in. She thought but didn't say that she had grown tired of running away: from school, from her mother – by marrying Oliver at just seventeen – and, if she was honest, from her mother again by coming to Rajputana. Her mother's pale pinched features came to mind.

'Penny for them,' Jay said.

She shook her head. 'It's nothing.'

'So,' he said, 'tell me more about this poison. Are you safe using it?'

'Pyro can cause convulsions and terrible gastro-intestinal effects over the long term. It can even kill.'

'In the short term?'

'Irritating to the skin and eyes. I always use gloves or it turns my fingers black. And I use a face mask too. I dread to think of what might have happened.'

'Show me your fingers.'

She held up her hands and wiggled her fingers.

227

He smiled. 'I don't know who might have taken it, but let's get a new padlock from the castle stores.'

'Have you had any success?' she said, in an effort to dismiss the lingering worry about pyro, and smiled at him.

'Searching for backers? Not yet.'

'I could speak to Clifford again, though much good it may do.'

'I don't want you to have to go begging to him.'

She sighed. 'He may be our only bet.'

'I have one or two contacts. People I was at school with in England. I'm trying them. Time isn't on my side, but look, when I've had a chance to sort something out, why not come to my palace with me?' He gave her a warm smile. 'Stay a few days. Once we get the project going again and the temperature starts rising it'll be cooler there. Come. Take photographs. And we'll have a chance to talk properly.'

'I'd love to.'

'And actually I might need a hand with the administration if you wouldn't mind.'

'Of course, but I've been meaning to ask if you've spoken to Indi about Chatur?'

'She admitted Chatur asked her to obtain information for him.'

'What about the other thing?'

'She looked affronted and wouldn't discuss it, but I have spoken to Chatur.' He paused. 'Do you know, it strikes me that he might be the one who stole the pyro, or more likely one of his men. I doubt he came across it hidden somewhere.'

'But why then give it to Anish?'

'To undermine you.'

★

When Eliza called at Clifford's residence a few days later, she found him sitting in a shady part of the garden under the veranda. He rose to his feet, but was less welcoming than previously.

'So what can I do for you?' he said, sipping what looked like a gin and tonic. 'Would you like one?' he added when he saw her looking.

'Just a lime soda for me, please.'

'With salt or sugar?'

'Actually I like both together.' She paused. 'Clifford, I won't beat about the bush.'

'It would be nice if you came to see me without wanting something.'

Eliza thought rapidly. 'Actually I've been trying to help you out with obtaining information about Anish.'

He perked up a bit.

'He's not well.'

'Well, I knew he'd had a little turn after Holi. Indigestion, wasn't it?'

'Not just that. He has a problem with his chest. He's going to ask if you could recommend a good western doctor. He wants to keep the problem he's having away from castle eyes, I think.'

'How interesting. I'll ask Julian Hopkins next door for a recommendation. If I can put one of our men in there it will help a great deal. Thank you. Let me know if you hear anything else.'

Eliza smiled. 'Look, I am glad to have been of help, but you're right, there is something.'

'The irrigation funding?'

She nodded.

'Well, as it happens I have found a new lead. Though its success rather depends on you.'

'Me?'

'I want you to reconsider my proposal of marriage. I am very fond of you, Eliza.'

Eliza examined her nails, wishing she were somewhere else, but Clifford was looking at her steadily, expecting an answer. She wondered if it might be best to pretend a little interest.

'And if I agree, this potential investor –'

'Will definitely be on the cards. But he not only wants to see detailed evidence of how his investment will be repaid, but also how he will make money.'

'Then I agree to reconsider. But that's all.'

Clifford sprang to his feet and held out both hands to her. She got up and let him take her hands, and then he kissed her.

23

April

Shubharambh Bagh

Jay and Eliza were now staying at his palace. He had been working solidly from the moment he arrived, ensconced behind a huge desk in his office from seven in the morning until late at night. Various files and drafts of letters were spread out around him and he had been sifting through the irrigation plans. The second stage was drawn out now, along with the plans for damming the river, but still no permission had come through to be able to do it. It seemed as if the British were prevaricating.

People frequently called on him: ragged petitioners from the villages, but stiff-looking Englishmen too, and also wealthy Indian merchants from other states and from British India. He treated them all with the same effortless good manners, and Eliza saw a determination in him she hadn't witnessed before. It endeared him to her. Not wanting to intrude, she was happy helping with the paperwork, and sometimes caught him gazing at her with burning eyes that said so much, even though no words were exchanged. Then he would see her looking and lower his head. When she passed him papers he would accidentally brush her hand, and a jolt ran through her every time. She longed for him to kiss her again and could have sworn he longed for it too, especially when he caught her staring and gave her one of his slow, beguiling smiles. Each day that passed was a torment, and she felt nervous that he might be regretting what had happened between them. Helpless with desire, she floundered in the near-unbearable pleasure of being near him and waited for something more.

One early evening, when it was cooler, and as the temple bells began to ring, they walked out to look at the project. He put an arm around her, holding her close as they gazed at the pit, and she knew this was the moment. He turned her towards him and kissed her very gently.

'I've been wanting to do that again,' he said, as he pulled away and put a palm against his heart. 'I'm so happy that you're here. I hope to have a little more time now.'

'It's all right.'

'No, it isn't. You deserve more.'

He held her close and ran his fingers through her hair. 'Sorry I've been distracted. Sometimes I feel as if all this is in the lap of the gods.'

'You don't pray though, do you?' she said, catching hold of his hand and bringing it to her lips. She kissed his fingertips and then let his hand fall.

'I leave praying to the women. The strength of our society has always been in our courage and resilience.'

'And your beliefs? Karma, for instance?'

They walked on a little further, arm in arm now.

'Karma plays a central role in life for every living being. We believe we are born not just once, but have been here for eternity. Lord Krishna says in the sacred books – there was never a time when I wasn't here and there will never be a time when I will cease to be!'

'I think I understand.'

'But karma has a past and a future. We can affect what happens. And now it's time to change things in India,' he said.

'You're helping them to change.'

'I don't just mean improving the lot of the farmers and peasants. I mean with regard to the British. Even in our own palaces and *havelis* we are separated from the very Europeans who are our guests. They take the best chairs and the highest placements at table and we are relegated to the side-lines. It's a game of one-upmanship. But have you any idea how that feels?'

He stopped walking and his penetrating stare unsettled her. And while she wanted him to kiss her again, she could feel the pent-up energy inside him and had the distinct feeling he really needed to talk.

'It must be very demeaning,' she eventually said.

'We feel like puppets in the hands of the government representatives. We're just a small part of the theatre that is the British Empire. The British accepted our demand for dominion status in 1929, but that only raised the thorny issue of giving equal rights to both Hindus and Muslims, so there's been no progress.'

'What needs to happen?'

'We need freedom untainted by religious difference. And we really need British withdrawal, irrevocable and complete, and then let us be judged by what we do.'

She stood very still. 'I do understand that. Really.'

He looked at her with sadness in his eyes. 'Do you? I hate having to go to people like Clifford Salter, cap in hand. I know the British are already devolving power, but it isn't enough. We want to see a day when we Indians rule our own free nation.'

'It will happen, Jay, because it must. Even I see that now.'

He stroked her cheek with the palm of his hand. 'I'm glad

you understand. I used to attend the Chamber of Princes, hoping to make a difference, even took a leading role for a while at the meetings in Delhi. Since 1920 we've been represented by the Chamber.'

'So why did you pull out?'

'Disillusionment mostly. There is no equality between us and the British. Whatever we do, we're banned from publicizing our meetings and threatened without impunity. The hands of the Chamber of Princes are tied.'

He had only invited her to stay for just a few days and she didn't want to outstay her welcome, so a little later, just as the light was fading and the sky was still pink, she asked if perhaps it was time she left.

He looked at her as if surprised. 'You want to go?'

She glanced away, then shook her head, the words sticking in her throat.

'Stay. I have something else to tell you. You've seen the men coming and going?'

'Of course.'

'I have borrowed money from the merchant classes and I have extended the project.'

She laughed. 'And I thought you were looking for ways to cut costs.'

'I was at first, but I am spurred on by Bikaner. He undertook to build nine irrigation projects, plus railway lines and hospitals. I will employ as many of the local people as I can. Some of these new men will start tomorrow by carrying on the digging. Some will work on building the walls and will then dig irrigation channels out to the villages.'

Eliza responded to his unfailing enthusiasm with such a feeling of hope, she feared her heart might burst.

'Of course Bikaner built the Ganga canal. It carries water

from the Punjab. We're too far from the Punjab for that, but there is that small river not far from my land. We just need the permission to dam it.'

'Have you fine-tuned the details with the investor Clifford told me about?'

'Indeed. I believe we will create fifty new villages within five years, and that the work they will do will not only pay back the loan but also provide a steady income.'

Eliza was pleased, though she hadn't confided in Jay about the string that came oh so neatly attached. 'Well,' she said instead, 'less than four months before the rains come.'

'Yes.'

'I wonder how Indi is?'

'She's gone back to her village now.'

Eliza was surprised. 'For good?'

'No. Her grandmother is very ill. Indi has gone to care for her. The Thakur will watch out for her and she will always have a place at the castle.'

'But as what? To fall prey to a man like Chatur? She needs her own life, a husband, a family.'

'You are a fine one to talk of family.'

'What do you mean?'

'You did leave your mother on her own. You said so yourself.'

'I couldn't help her. I tried. If I'd have stayed, my own life would have been wrecked too. She's an alcoholic.'

He stared at his feet for a moment and then glanced at her. 'Here we believe that it is the duty of the children to look after the parents.'

She stiffened. 'No matter what?'

He nodded. 'Does that distress you?'

She remained silently thinking and didn't reply. He had

no idea what Anna Fraser was like nor how it felt to watch her mother commit slow suicide.

'I tried and I failed,' was what she eventually said.

He reached out to her with both hands. 'I'm not judging you.'

'It sounds like you are.' Angry and upset, she refused to take his hands.

'Eliza, come on. I'm only saying it's different here.'

She turned on her heels and walked away. A minute later he came up behind and wrapped his arms around her. 'Eliza. Eliza.'

He turned her round and then his lips were on her neck. She shuddered, responding immediately to a hand on her shoulder, her breath shortening and her lips parting. When they kissed it seemed to have always been their fate. Then as they walked back to the palace, hand in hand, she banished the doubts to the back of her mind. He had given her his own rooms, and when they arrived at the *dari khana*, where a large rug on the floor was piled with several cushions, he ordered her to stand still while he undressed her, kissing the underside of her arms and her belly as he did. He was incredibly slow, and even though she was desperate to be lying on the cushions with him she understood what he was doing.

When at last she stood naked before him, he kissed her breasts. Then he held her away from him. 'How are you feeling?'

'Crazy. Uncertain. Terrified.'

'Good,' he said.

Then she lay back against the cushioned rug. The light in the room had faded and it was almost dark. Wanting to see his face, she wished the lamp had been lit. But now he was on top of her and their bodies were moving rhythmically. She forgot about the lamp. He held back for a moment and explored her face with his fingertips. 'I can still see your beautiful eyes,' he said, 'even in the dark.'

When his fingers slipped inside her she gasped. And then they were making love, in a way that she had never known could be possible: the feeling of connection so strong that it took the breath from her lungs. She tried to speak but could not, and then, when it was over, they lay on the bed, both of them dripping with sweat, their legs interwoven. She had lost the power of thought. She wanted this man, that's all there was. More than she had ever wanted anything or anyone, she wanted him with every part of her and she was not going to let him go.

'My beautiful Englishwoman,' he was saying, as he traced the outline of her jaw. 'Still uncertain?'

She laughed. 'You really want to know?'

'Shall I light the lamp?'

'Not yet,' she said. 'I want to feel you beside me.'

He appeared to be thinking and then he spoke. 'You're brave, my girl. Not sure if I can equal you.'

'Don't be silly. Of course you can. I'm not brave at all.'

Before Eliza fell asleep she lay absolutely still, listening to his breath and the silence of the desert night.

When she woke she saw that he was still there. Her heart leapt with pleasure as she took that in and she watched him lying asleep. As she gazed at his immensely long eyelashes, and the beautiful burnished quality of his skin, he looked the same. Everything about him and about her looked the same, and yet everything about them both had changed.

She touched his face, gently so as not to wake him, but

just to feel his softness. She moved closer and kissed his earlobe. He stirred. She ran a fingernail down his neck and then to his stomach. He groaned. Her hand went further down and he hardened beneath her grasp. She had never done this with Oliver, but wanting to now, she moved her hand. He groaned some more and she liked the feeling it gave her. That she could do this to him. Maybe there was something to the sixteen arts of being a woman after all, she thought with a wry smile.

Suddenly he pulled her on top of him. 'What are you doing to me?' he said.

'Isn't it obvious?'

'Who knew that behind all that English reserve lay such a wanton hussy?'

'And who knew that you are neither an officer nor a gentleman!'

Their days at his palace changed after that. Day after day they worked and made love; ate and made love; walked and made love. And sometimes they spent a day just making love. While they remained at his palace, the rest of the world did not exist. There was just the project and Jay. Eliza had never known such joy. She woke happy and went to sleep with a smile on her face. Why had nobody ever hinted that anything like this was possible? And that thought made her wonder how her parents had been together. Surely if you'd experienced this, even once, you'd be in love with life for ever.

When they weren't talking of water or their past lives, they read and talked about books. He said that he'd never read any of the Russians and she told him he had to read *War and Peace* and *The Hunting Sketches* by Turgenev. She said that she loved Thomas Hardy and Henry James, but couldn't get on with Dickens. His favourite poet was John Donne, whom she loved too, and hers was Emily Dickinson, whom he'd never heard of. He asked if she'd read Tagore, and when she shook her head he offered to lend her a book. They both liked the movies. They talked of food too, and their favourite places. He loved the squares of London. Had a friend who lived in Orme Square. She laughed and said she'd never had such grand friends. He said he wouldn't tell her about his teenage sexual exploits, and she said she didn't want to know anyway.

He never said that he loved her and she didn't say it either. And yet Eliza knew the connection between them went far beyond sex or books or films. And for the first time in her life she actually believed there was such a thing as a soul connection; that there were definitely people you'd meet on a soul level. Some you might only know for an hour or two, some might be friends for ever. And with that thought she recognized that India was changing her. Before, she'd never have thought of souls. Relationships for her had been tricky things, best avoided: not this triumphant process of unwrapping another human being while at the same time they unwrapped you. The space between them was present but it dissolved easily, like living with no walls or boundaries, and she couldn't tell where he left off and she began. And the closer they became, the more the thought grew that without his beautiful eyes to gaze at as they made love, it would be like parting from herself.

One evening, when she eventually felt safe enough to allow Jay into the deepest parts of herself, the pain of her father's death wrapped itself around her until something like panic rose from the pit of her stomach. All her attempts at controlling it failed, and now she knew the only thing left was to let the feeling swallow her. She'd either survive or drown. With each burst of emotion the pain increased, crushing her chest and squeezing the breath out. All she could feel was her mind collapsing as the long-held grief consumed her and she finally responded to her deeper needs. Then Jay held her and rocked her as she wept. It was as if she'd never truly cried for her father before and Jay's presence was the only thing that had made it possible.

After he had dried her tears with his fingers he held her away from him and looked at her. 'The only thing that can heal such grief is to release the tears you can no longer hide. You have to be ravaged by love to truly know it.'

'Are we ravaged?' she said.

He smiled. 'Not yet.'

'You know something about being ravaged?'

He shook his head. 'Maybe we'll learn together.'

When Jay needed to convince villagers that the scheme would benefit the ordinary people, they rode out to the villages on horseback, and though, at first, the people hung back, after a few visits they smiled broadly whenever they saw him arrive. The severe drought had meant they had been unable to grow crops for two years and their livestock had died. How some survived Eliza didn't know, but then she overheard Jay giving the farmers small loans. She couldn't help thinking what a wonderful ruler he would make. No sitting at home stuffing Turkish delight for him. He was fit and strong, and the more she got to know him the more she realized she had truly fallen in love with him. She put Laxmi's warning to the back of her mind. So long as Anish remained alive, she would not think of the future.

They went alone on these trips but for one of Jay's faithful servants, and they camped in small tents, usually set beside a small fire. On one of the return trips they had dismounted and Jay had gone off to collect wood to make a fire. Beyond their tents were some stumpy trees where small green birds fluttered and shifted in the branches and, in the distance, the sands of the desert could just be seen. After Jay came back with a bundle under his arm she watched the concentration on his face as he built the fire and then lit it, and she couldn't help smiling. By the time the fire was fully alight, it was evening but not completely dark, and as the flames of the fire flickered on his face, she sat gazing at him.

'What is it?'

'I was wondering about *your* father. I know so little about him.'

'He was a giant of a man. A reformer, unlike his father before him who almost lost us the state. I would like to be like my father and, with your help, I think I can do it.'

'With my help?'

'We make a good team, don't you think?'

She smiled. 'I hope so.'

'Whereas my paternal grandfather! The British accused him of misrule and he acquired a reputation for corruption and cruelty.'

'What did he do?'

'One of his wives committed suicide in the most horrible way but the story was that really he had killed her. Had he not died suddenly he would have been deposed by the British and we could have lost the kingdom. Luckily my father was an honourable man and became a reforming ruler. He served with the British Army and was able to cross the divide between our two cultures with ease and grace. I remember him, when I was very young, dressed in brocaded silk with a long plume in his turban.'

'Do you look like him?'

'A little. He had magnificent-looking escorts wherever he went, and when we had noble visitors they arrived in silver bullock carts.'

'Not as free in his ways as you are?'

'Times have changed, and he wasn't educated in England.'

'I like you best out in the wilds.'

'But, like me, he loved sport and he raised our state to greater heights by marrying my mother. She came from a very grand royal family. That's how it's always been done, you see. Marriage here is about the marriage of families, not just two individuals. And the entire reputation of the family is at stake.'

He stopped speaking and stared into the fire, seeming lost in thought.

Although he had dismissed the question of an engagement having already happened, it didn't mean it would not, and the thought played on Eliza's mind.

'Can I ask you something?' she said.

'I'm listening.'

'What about your arranged marriage?' she finally said.

He turned to look at her and she saw such sadness in his eyes that it hurt her too.

'This is so new between us. Let's not think about that now.'

And although Eliza was happy not to talk about it, she couldn't help thinking.

'Tell me more about your mother,' he said.

She sighed. 'My mother has had problems with drink for

years. I think my father's death broke her. She was proud but never a strong woman, and there was no money, you see. She had to rely on the charity of James Langton. Although she called him my uncle we were not related. She had known him before she married my father, and then when we returned to England he became my mother's lover.'

'That must have been hard on you too?'

'I only had her. No relatives, or at least no relatives who would see us. I loved my father, but my relationship with my mother has always been difficult. She sent a letter while I was here saying such terrible things about my father, accusing him of ruining us with his gambling and of having had a mistress for years.'

'Perhaps there's some advantage to having more than one wife.' He paused to gauge her expression. 'No mistresses necessary.'

She knew he was joking or at least half joking, but couldn't help her angry retort. 'Except that it doesn't work the other way round. Nobody stops to think that we might rather like to have more than one husband.'

He put on a severe expression and a mock-affronted heavily accented voice. 'That is deeply shocking thing to say, madam. What good woman is wanting with two men when she has one? One man: many women. It is the correct way.'

Even though she wanted to be annoyed she couldn't help but smile. 'Oh, shut up, you idiot!'

'You are telling a Raja to shut up? There is only one punishment for that. Come here.'

'And if I refuse?'

'I will keep you tied to the bed for many moons.'

'You have to catch me first.' She leapt to her feet and ran into the darkness beyond the fire. Then she hid behind a thorn bush while keeping an eye out for him and keeping her breath quiet. She could hear him moving about but could see almost nothing. From up above the powder of silver stars was the only light.

She heard the mournful cry of a distant jackal, then felt the sensation of a pinprick in her leg and shouted out.

Not knowing exactly where she was, he could only run towards the direction of her voice. 'Are you all right? You shouldn't escape into the darkness at night. All kinds of creatures are out there.'

'I think I was bitten, but it didn't really hurt.'

'You shouted out.'

'In surprise, that's all.'

'But did it hurt?'

'Honestly, it was just a pinprick, perhaps an ant?'

He had his arm round her now. 'You're certain it wasn't a snake?'

'I've no idea. It was pitch black.'

'A snake bite would hurt. I think we should pack up and get you back, just in case.'

'It's too dark. Honestly, I'll be fine. I just want to go to bed.'

They turned in for the night immediately after that, but after only about an hour Eliza woke with cramps in her stomach. She sat up in bed and doubled over, trying not to wake Jay and listening to the silence that, frighteningly, was not silent at all. During the rest of the cold desert night she lay shivering in the makeshift bed, as close to Jay as she could be without disturbing him. She felt nauseous and wanted to move, but, too nervous to leave the tent, remained where she was until the first pale light of dawn. When Jay eventually woke he took one look at her and his face fell.

'Tell me what you're feeling.'

'Sick. And I have a bad stomach ache. Maybe something I ate?'

But he looked at her so gravely she began to feel a prickle of anxiety.

'I want to look for that bite again.'

He had tried to find it using the light of an oil lamp the night before and had appeared very relieved when nothing showed up.

'Really?'

She showed him the place on her ankle.

'I don't think it's a snake bite. But the area around the bite has reddened and it's a little bit swollen too.'

'What do you think?'

He shook his head. 'Not sure. Any other symptoms?'

'My chest is painful.'

'It hurts to breathe?'

'A little.'

Jay held open the door flap and called the servant over, then spoke in a hushed tone and far too rapidly for Eliza to get the drift.

'What did you tell him?' she asked when he came back to her.

'I've sent for Indi's grandmother. It may take an hour or two but there's nobody better. He's taken my motorbike. Quicker than his camel.'

'Do you think it's serious?' Eliza tried to smile but couldn't quite manage it.

He held her hands in his, rubbing and warming them, but he didn't say anything.

'I thought Indi's *daadee ma* was ill.'

'We have to hope she's well enough to come.'

'How will we get her back home? How will we get home?'

'I don't want to move you, and certainly not on the back of a camel or a bike. I don't want you to worry about anything and I don't want you to overheat, but it's still very early so it's quite cool. You will need to drink. Could you manage some water?'

She tried to lift her head but fell back against the pillow. 'Everything hurts.'

He put an arm around her shoulders. 'Lean against me and just sip.'

With his other hand he held the cup of water to her lips.

'I feel dizzy,' she said, and slipped back down on to the bed but then didn't feel as if she could keep still.

'Lie still,' he said, and held her arms.

She was aware that he stayed with her all the time, except when he went out to check if there was any sight of Indi's grandmother. And even though she felt so ill, she could only wonder that they were together like this. How strange it felt. Yet how right.

'You didn't say if you thought it was serious?'

He smiled. 'I'm not a doctor, but I am sure it's not. So relax and rest.'

She attempted to sit up. 'I feel as if the room is going round.'

'All that gin you drank last night.'

'I didn't –' And then the room spun. She was aware of travelling down a dark tunnel at enormous speed and then him holding her as she fell forward. Then nothing.

When she came to, Jay was lying next to her on the bed. First she was only conscious of his palm gently stroking her hair, and then she became aware of his slow steady breathing. In that delicious moment she had forgotten about being ill, but then she sat up and was sick all over the bedcover. He jumped up, pulled the cover off, rolled it up and threw it outside the tent. Then from under the bed he pulled out an animal skin of some kind.

'This is all I have. Until the day warms up a bit more. How are you feeling?'

'Not sure. What if I'm sick again?'

'Let's hope you're not. But you must drink. I don't want you to dehydrate.'

He touched her skin, her forehead and the back of her neck. 'You're sweating a lot.'

'My head hurts.'

'Let's hope she gets here soon.'

'But what can she do?'

'She knows everything there is to know about the desert and what it can do to us.'

'Will she be able to fix me?'

'Don't worry. Everything will be fine. Now lie still.' Although he had spoken in soothing tones, Eliza could see the worry in his eyes. She let out her breath slowly and lay still.

She was only vaguely aware of the passage of time. Minutes seemed like hours, and hours went by in a flash.

Sometimes he asked her how she was and sometimes she asked him what he was thinking. But neither of them were telling the truth, she thought. He said everything would be fine but his eyes gave him away. She said she was feeling better even though she was not. When she was completely lucid she remembered they had not spoken of what would happen after the rains.

While she muttered about rain, Jay looked increasingly worried, pacing around the tent when he wasn't sitting by her side, but eventually she heard the sound of a motorbike and raised voices. Soon after that the old lady came in, walking with the aid of a stick. The first thing she did was to look at the site of the bite and frown.

'Two small red dots,' she said clearly so that Eliza might understand. 'Black widow spider.'

Jay visibly relaxed, letting out a long slow breath. 'I thought it might be.'

'You did well to keep her still. We do not wish the venom to flow further into her blood.'

'So I can't move her?'

'Not today. But you need to keep her cool. Only young children and the very old die from this.'

'But she has had a severe reaction?'

'Yes, just like you, my boy. Only when you were very small I gave you a herbal remedy. A remedy that I do not have here today. It may not be pleasant for her but she will survive.'

He nodded.

'Fan her, apply cool wet cloths to her skin – back of her neck, chest and face – and add a little salt to her water.'

'Strange that it should have happened to her too,' he said, as he accompanied the old lady to the door.

'You love this woman?' Eliza heard her ask, but she didn't hear Jay's reply.

A few minutes later Jay came back in, smiling broadly. 'So we stay put for today and if you feel better we'll go back in the morning.'

'How was she?'

'Much thinner and a lot frailer.'

'I feel awful making her come all this way.'

'Don't worry. She was happy to come. Now please drink. We have to avoid heat exhaustion.'

Eliza nodded. She could feel the day heating up and knew the temperatures could be stifling.

'I feel like there's an axe in the back of my skull. I must look an awful mess.'

'My poor Englishwoman. The axe doesn't help but you could never look a mess.'

'That's not what you thought when we first met.'

She didn't have the energy to laugh but he smiled. 'Now listen. Just before the rains come I'm taking you to Udaipore to see the monsoon arrive. Think of the rain falling. Think of being cool. That will help.'

'Why are they called black widows?'

'Because they are black and they eat their husbands.'

Now she smiled at him despite the pain.

Two days later and back at Jay's palace, they stood facing each other in her bedroom, not speaking for a moment or two. Then she slowly undid the buttons of his shirt, and he closed his eyes. Who was in charge? Who was leading? Who was setting the pace? She thought she had wanted it to be him, but somehow things were becoming more equal and she liked that too, loving the feeling of power in her fingertips.

'Are you sure you're well enough?' he said.

She laughed.

'What's so funny?' he said and opened his eyes.

'I'm well enough.'

Moments passed as they let each other in, or so it seemed to Eliza. This felt like entering a new world, one that was neither his nor hers, but one the two of them had made with no room for anything else. It was a world that once made could never be lost; a world that would exist even after they had gone. It made her want to reach deep inside him until she found what it was that made him, him.

Later, when they had made love, arms and legs tangled, he ran his fingers down her spine.

'Look at me,' he said. 'Open your eyes.'

She opened her eyes, then smiled and held his hand.

'Why are you smiling?' he asked.

'I don't know. Happy, I guess.'

He grinned. 'I love seeing you smile and hearing you laugh.'

'*You* make me laugh,' she said.

'Not sure if that's a good thing.'

'It's good. It's so good.'

He kissed her and she gazed right into his eyes and then she ran her fingers through his hair. He shivered and held her close. Sometimes she worried where they would go from here, but then, face to face with him, she didn't care. She slowly twisted round in his arms, her mouth against his cheek.

'Thank you,' she whispered.

'For?'

'For being you. For being here. For . . .' She paused.

'For?'

'For something I never expected to feel.' She stretched lazily. 'I wish this could last for ever. That we could stay just like this.'

He didn't reply, but stroked the inside of her thigh.

'Though I suppose we'd get hungry,' she added.

'I'm hungry already. Aren't you?'

'Yes, but I can't be bothered to move. Eating seems rather too basic after all this.'

'Basic is good, woman.'

'But not as good as love.'

He pulled a face. 'Mmmm. Now let me think. Food? Or love?'

She dug him in the ribs.

'Oi,' he said and, laughing, gathered her to him and hugged her.

She liked it when he held her, liked it when he smiled, laughed, or even scowled. Was there nothing about him to dislike?

'Do you want me?' she said, plucking up courage to ask. 'I mean really?'

'Haven't I already made that clear?'

PART THREE

'It is not light that we need, but fire; it is not the gentle shower, but thunder. We need the storm, the whirlwind, and the earthquake.'

– Frederick Douglass

24

With no further ill-effects from the spider bite and full of her love for Jay, Eliza was soon back at the Juraipore castle. Dottie had heard that she had been unwell and eventually plucked up courage to call at the castle, entering Eliza's rooms carrying a bouquet of flowers.

'I must say you look wonderful. I'd expected you to look pale and peaky.'

Eliza grinned and leant back against the sofa, feeling blissful.

Dottie stared at her. 'Oh Lor'! Has Clifford proposed?'

'Clifford?'

Dottie laid the flowers down on a side table. 'You have the look of a woman who has just said yes.'

'No.'

'Then what?' She lowered her voice. 'Or should I say who?' There was a brief pause, then her hand flew to her mouth. 'You haven't, have you?'

Eliza didn't reply.

'You've fallen for one of them. That's it, isn't it?'

Eliza grinned helplessly and nodded. 'It's Jay.'

Dottie stood and stared, hands on both hips. 'Well, that'll put the cat among the proverbial pigeons. On both sides.'

'Can't you be a little happy for me?'

Dottie moved over to the window and gazed out before turning back to Eliza. 'It will end in tears, my love. This sort of thing always does. Though I imagine it must be deliciously romantic.' She had spoken the last sentence in a wistful tone of voice.

'Would you talk to Clifford to smooth the waters?' Eliza asked.

Dottie shook her head. 'No, darling, I really can't. My advice is to put a stop to this before it goes any further.'

'I don't think I can.'

'Not willing to, more like. I don't blame you, honestly I don't. It must be irresistibly exciting, but he will never marry you. He'll marry one of his own kind.'

'I'm not so sure.'

'I am, and it will leave you with a tarnished reputation.'

'But I've already been married. I'm hardly a virgin.'

Dottie came across to sit beside Eliza on the sofa and took hold of her hand. 'People forgive a dead husband but they don't forgive a woman who has been cast aside, especially if the man concerned is not one of us.'

Eliza sighed. This was not what she wanted to hear.

'Honestly, darling. Put a stop to it, and soon.'

Jay had given Eliza the key to his study so that she could use it whenever she wished, either to take pictures of people, or to sort out papers for him when he wasn't there. She thought she might take individual shots of each member of the family, plus a few other individuals, though really the best shots she'd taken of people had always been out in the town or in the desert itself. Something about the wild seemed to make a person stand out in such sharp relief.

Indi had returned from her grandmother's, and Eliza was relieved that the old lady's dash across the desert on a motorbike hadn't left her more fragile than before.

'You must be happy,' Eliza said, as she set up her field

camera on the tripod in the study ready to photograph Indi. The Rolleiflex still wasn't back.

'I hated to see Grandmother fading like that,' Indi said. 'If I am honest I don't think she really is better. She is putting on a brave face, but she hardly eats a thing.'

'Didn't you want to stay on?'

'She insisted I came back here . . . So?' Indi said, after a short pause. 'You've been away for ages.'

Eliza thought about Jay and also her conversation with Dottie and managed to keep a composed face. 'I've been helping Jay with the water project. Some papers still need signing by the new investor before the funding can be released. It'll be any day now, and then the work will have to really pick up speed.'

'I'd love to see the progress.'

'I'm sure Jay would take you. Now, could you sit on the desk?'

'On the desk?'

'I'm after a relaxed shot.'

Indi went to perch on the edge of the desk. 'How about if I pretend to be reading a book?'

'Good idea.'

Indi picked up a book that had been lying open on Jay's desk and made a good fist of being absorbed in it.

'Now look up at me and smile.'

Indi did as she was asked and Eliza was astonished once again by the girl's beauty. Part of her wanted to raise the issue of Indi's relationship with Chatur, but as Jay had already dealt with it she decided to let sleeping dogs lie.

'Would you like one of me standing too?' Indi was saying.

'Maybe another with the book in your hand first.'

'*Hē bhagavāna,*' Indi said as she turned the page, 'why is Jay reading about toxic chemicals?'

257

'No idea,' Eliza said and changed the subject. 'Did you know your grandmother came to help when I was bitten?'

'She told me. It was odd, actually; she spoke a lot about you. But why all the fuss – people rarely die from a black widow's bite.'

'I think I had an extreme reaction. Jay was wonderful.' Eliza couldn't help but grin at the memory of his gentle care and consideration while she'd been ill.

'Oh, he would be,' Indi said, and gave a chilly smile that didn't reach her eyes.

'Indi, I –'

'Oh, don't worry; I can see it in your eyes. His too for that matter. But be warned, if I can see it, everyone else will too.'

'I'm sorry. We just started out as friends.'

'Don't be. I'm over it. But I wouldn't fall in love with him. You're not the first, Eliza, not by a long way. And Laxmi won't like it at all.'

'She doesn't know,' Eliza said, as calmly as her thumping heart would allow. In her mind she was remembering his legs tangled with her own, so dark against the white of the sheets.

Indi pulled a face, then shook her head. 'She may seem all kindness to you, but when it comes to her darling sons, they can do no wrong. Make no mistake, she will not allow it to continue. You'd better watch your step.'

Eliza examined her nails but didn't reply for a moment. When she spoke it was in a small tight voice. 'You mean not the first English woman?'

'Of course. But he must have told you about them. Isn't that what lovers do? Tell each other. And you're not a virgin anyway, so what does it matter? He usually likes the married ones. Over soonest.'

Eliza swallowed hard. How many had there been?

'Is that why Jay was reading about toxic chemicals?' Indi said.

'I don't follow?'

'To poison Laxmi.' She threw back her head and laughed, but Eliza was horrified. Jay had probably just been reading up on pyro.

At that moment Jay walked in. Eliza saw the anxiety in his eyes when he caught sight of her face.

'It's a joke, Eliza, just a joke,' Indi said.

'Something wrong?' he said, looking from one to the other.

Eliza shook her head. 'Just a joke I didn't get.'

He frowned. 'That's all?'

'Relax,' Indi piped up. 'Gosh, you're tense. Been doing something you shouldn't have, Jay?'

'Indira knows about us,' Eliza said, thinking it best to just come out with it.

He shrugged. 'It was bound to happen. Now, Eliza, where do you want me?' he said, as he turned away from Indi.

'Sitting at the desk. Is that OK?'

'Good idea,' Indi said. 'The Prince at his desk. The British will love it.'

Jay laughed, but Eliza knew exactly what he was recalling in his mind's eye. Just before they had left his palace to come back here she had found him pacing his study. He'd asked her to come to help with the papers that lay all over the room, but when she took a few steps towards him he'd picked her up and sat her on the desk. Then he'd kissed her neck.

'I thought you needed me,' she'd said, glancing at the papers.

'I do need you, more than you know.'

She laughed as he undid her blouse and then lifted up her skirt.

'Glad you're not wearing trousers,' he said.

She helped him slip off her underwear and then he removed his trousers. He bent his head and kissed her stomach. She threw back her head and gazed at the ceiling, no thoughts in her mind at all, just the sensation of his lips brushing her skin and his hands on her breasts. When it got too much to bear, she wrapped her arms around his neck and pulled him to her. The papers went flying and ended strewn across the floor as they made love. When it was over they were both so damp they'd gone to her room and she had wiped the moisture from his skin. Then he had done the same for her, although it hadn't ended there. He had washed her hair, gently massaging her skull afterwards. Indian head massage, he'd said. He had made her sit on a stool and had spent ages massaging her head, neck and shoulders until she felt as if her muscles were made of liquid. Then he'd carried her to the bed, where they'd made love again, although this time so slowly Eliza felt she had slipped outside herself.

She was in the process of learning what he liked, how he sighed when she touched him, how he liked her to move with him inside her, but he seemed to already know exactly what she wanted, even before she knew herself. For those last few days at his palace they hadn't been able to stop themselves. They had lived in their own world, safe from everything that might hurt them, and it had made everything beautiful. The sunsets were especially splendid, the dawns heart-breaking, the wind had carried the fragrance of frangipani and jasmine and the sun had shone. Her love for him, and her love for life and his beautiful palace, had expanded until that was all there was and all there would ever be. 'What is this?' she'd said. He'd replied that it was a result of his terror of losing her after she'd been bitten. He had to make her truly his.

'And you mine,' she'd said. '*Hamesha*.'

'Always,' he echoed.

Now, standing in the room with Indi and Jay, Eliza came to with a jolt. She knew she was reddening at the memory and wondered if she could ever look at a desk in quite the same way.

Jay had spotted the colour on her face and winked, but Indi had seen it too. 'For goodness' sake. If you want to keep it secret, no more lingering looks.'

Eliza had not been aware of lingering looks, but of course that was the thing about being in love. The sparkly sweet-scented madness that rendered you helpless – so wrapped up in that one person you became oblivious to everyone and everything else. Even though Eliza knew it was lunacy, she did not want it to stop. Not ever. She decided she must practise being more discreet, though at the back of her mind she wasn't really sure she wanted it to remain a secret. Surely if they explained that they loved each other Laxmi would understand? Then Indi's earlier remarks about Jay's previous love affairs came racing back. Was he really the type who fell in love at the drop of a hat and then got bored? As she asked herself that question, she looked at him and the love in his eyes shone out. No. He couldn't be that kind of man.

25

The following day Eliza was surprised when a handmaiden came to say that Clifford had asked to see her and was waiting in the *durbar* hall, wanting to talk with her.

Only ten in the morning and already hot, Eliza slipped into a summer frock she had made herself: vibrant green with white spots, a fitted bodice that had taken ages to get right, short sleeves and a crisp white collar. Then she made her way to the *durbar* hall, where she found Clifford walking the length of it with his back to her. She watched for a moment or two. How stiff his narrow shoulders were. She imagined him naked, and at the thought of his pale body she couldn't help the comparison with Jay, whose skin, when lit by a lamp, glowed like burnished copper. She pictured touching Jay in the way he loved, his body molten and moving in tandem with her so that they seemed to have been designed to fit.

She was sorry for Clifford, but when he twisted round to look at her, she shrank from what looked like triumph in his eyes.

'So, Eliza, you decided against Shimla.'

'You know I did. I still have things to do here.'

'Things to do, Eliza?'

Even though she realized he was trying to embarrass her, she refused to lower her eyes and held his gaze.

'So?' he said.

She drew in her breath. 'Clifford, I'm busy. Was there something?'

'Yes. Here's your camera back.' He handed Eliza a box.

'Thank you, Clifford. Was there anything else?'

'Oh yes. Most certainly. Your prints will be back soon.' He still showed no sign of moving.

'And?'

'Let us walk out to the courtyard.'

Outside it was already sweltering and Eliza began to perspire. 'Aren't you hot in that linen jacket?' she said.

'Don't worry about me, old girl. I'm used to the heat.'

They walked across to a wide flame tree and made themselves comfortable on a bench beneath it. The birds were sleeping now and all you could hear was the water falling from a small fountain and the *mali* moving slowly as he tended to the flowerbeds at the other end of the courtyard.

'So you're wondering why I've come.'

Eliza looked up at the endless blue of the sky and wished he'd leave. She wanted to be alone with her thoughts of Jay. She liked to go over each moment they'd shared, and when she did a little shiver of physical memory gripped her. She was becoming addicted to recalling moments too thrilling to share with anyone, though she knew they'd have to tell people something soon. And by *people*, of course, she meant Laxmi. She was lost in her thoughts when Clifford spoke again, and for a moment assumed she had heard incorrectly.

'Say that again?'

'Jayant Singh is likely to be arrested.'

She twisted her body towards him, thinking it must be a joke. He wasn't smiling.

'Why?'

He puckered his chin. 'Under suspicion of insurrection.'

'Don't be ridiculous. He's almost as British as you and I.'

'But not where it counts.' He thumped his chest. 'His heart is Indian through and through. Anyone caught circulating seditious papers can be imprisoned indefinitely. Anyone. No appeal. And for a member of a royal family to be active precludes their right to rule for ever.'

'But he wouldn't do anything like that,' she said, feeling heat at the back of her eyelids and pleading with herself not to cry.

'And you know that, how?'

'I just do. He's good and honest.'

'And you have been spending far too much time with him.'

She stiffened. 'That isn't any of your business.'

'Does his mother know?'

She looked away, knowing her eyes would tell him the truth.

'I thought not. She won't be best pleased.'

'Clifford, please don't say anything. I'm asking you as a friend.'

He gave her an ingratiating smile. 'We'll see.'

Eliza hated that phrase. That and *Let me think about it* or *I'll give it some thought* – the dismissive phrases her mother used to make her feel as if she were insignificant and whatever it was she had asked for was of little or no consequence. She got to her feet.

'You know what, Clifford. I bloody well don't care. Do your worst.'

He glanced up at the gallery that circled the courtyard, hidden behind *jali* screens. 'Never know who's watching. Personally I can't imagine anyone wanting to remain in a place like this. Don't give the silent watchers anything to gossip about. Calm down and sit down. That's not why I'm here.'

So that was why he'd led her out here. He had known they'd be in full view of the *zenana* and she would not wish to make a scene in front of them.

'Now smile and be a good girl,' he continued as he patted the seat. She took a deep shuddering breath and sat, though it only made her want to slap his smug face.

'So what has Jay done? Tell me exactly.'

'I can't say just yet.'

'You've no proof, have you?' She watched his eyes. 'No proof at all.'

'Eliza, be assured I have everything I need to put your Prince Jay behind bars for a very long time.'

Even though it was terribly hot, a chill passed through her. He had to be bluffing. Surely. She had a sinking feeling that seemed to be growing by the minute. First, all the things Indi had said about Jay's affairs with women, and now this. But still she could not believe what he was saying.

'Why tell these lies, Clifford?' she said. 'It won't make me care for you more.'

'I need you to take me to Jay's study without him being there. Can you do that? Is there a way we can do it without being seen?'

'Why?'

'There's something I need to check.'

She narrowed her eyes. 'You want me to help you prove he is disloyal to the British?'

'You can look at it that way. Or on the other hand it might prove that he is loyal.'

She snorted. 'And that this is some ridiculous trumped-up charge.'

'Exactly.'

'Who has accused him?'

265

'I can't tell you that.'

'Very well. I don't suppose I have much choice. Though I don't see the need for this ridiculous skulduggery.'

'You have the key?'

She nodded.

'He must trust you.'

They walked slowly through the long, thick-walled corridors, though for Eliza the cooler air meant scant relief. She unlocked Jay's door and they both went in. Clifford didn't look at anything but went to sit at the desk and pulled the typewriter closer. 'Where does he keep the paper?'

'In the second drawer down. Why?'

He didn't answer, but opened the drawer and pulled out a sheet and inserted it into the machine, slowly rolling it round to the top. The sound really irritated Eliza, who couldn't help but feel Clifford was dragging this out – whatever this was. He typed a few sentences, rolled the sheet of paper through and pulled it free.

'I think that's enough,' he said, as he got to his feet and pocketed the sheet of paper.

'What did you just write?'

'You can look. Nothing significant, I promise you.'

He handed her the sheet of paper and she read some nonsense about Kent being the garden of England.

'You're from Kent originally?'

'I am.'

'So what's Kent got to do with Jay?'

'Kent? Nothing at all. And now I must leave you.'

Eliza was puzzled. 'But you said you wanted to look round his study?'

'I've seen all I need to. Thanks very much.'

'Aren't you going to explain?'

'Another time.' And with that he gave her a cheery wave and left her not knowing what to think. Had she made things worse for Jay or had she made them better?

As if that was not enough, the very next day she was summoned to the outer rooms of the Maharajah. When she arrived he was already sitting on a small *gaddi* with Priya at his side. Standing facing him were Jay and Laxmi. Jay's rebellious stance – arms folded, legs wide apart – indicated that there was trouble afoot. In addition Chatur was there, sitting on a high-backed chair with his back against the wall.

'Thank you for coming,' Anish said, waving at Eliza to come closer but not indicating that she should sit. Priya didn't meet Eliza's eyes, and Jay simply nodded at her. Laxmi turned away, but Eliza had glimpsed that Jay's mother seemed to be looking very red-eyed. What on earth was going on here?

'You took it upon yourself to do this?' Anish was saying.

'I did. It was all my doing,' Jay said.

'And you, mother?'

'I –'

'She had nothing to do with it,' Jay interjected.

Laxmi shook her head but remained silent.

'And how were you able to get hold of the key if your mother did not assist?' Priya added, spitting the words in a disparaging tone and emphasizing the words *your mother*.

Jay looked at the ground before answering, then raised his head and met Anish's furious glare. 'I knew where she kept the keys to the jewel safe.'

'And the mortgage you raised on these family jewels? *My* inheritance, not to put too fine a point on it. Not yours.'

Priya made a sharp tutting noise, but Anish held up his hand as if to warn her to keep silent. If looks could kill, Priya's face would have had Anish dead on the spot.

Laxmi's shoulders heaved. 'It was I who suggested it. It is not Jayant's fault.'

Priya stood suddenly. 'Say that again!'

Laxmi squared her shoulders and stared at her daughter-in-law. 'I gave him the key! It was my idea to mortgage the jewels. The irrigation of our lands is crucial if the people are to survive another drought. You, Anish, were doing nothing. Your father would be ashamed of you. Don't you realize the British will accuse you of misrule unless you act, and then we'll lose everything.'

'Mother!' Anish said in a shocked tone.

'Mother,' Jay repeated, but more sadly. 'I can't let you take the blame.'

Priya sat down. 'Send her away. Do it, Anish.'

Laxmi stood her ground. 'I've warned you about this, Anish. You haven't gone far enough to reform the land revenue systems, nor have you agreed a fairer arrangement for land management. The people will rise up against us if we do nothing to help. You know the States Subject Conference is there purely to undermine the Princes.'

Anish looked at his hands and fiddled with the rings he wore, at least two on each finger. Priya glared at him with a sourer face than you could imagine, and that made Eliza feel sorry for Anish. He was weak and his wife despised him for it. He was also incredibly effeminate, and Priya did not give the appearance of a satisfied woman.

'You want the peasants to turn to the British instead of to us?' Laxmi said.

'Nonsense, mother. You're getting worked up over nothing,'

Anish said. 'And of course you weren't to blame for the theft of the jewels. This is Jay's responsibility, not yours.'

Priya snorted, loudly enough for them all to hear, and then spoke. 'So when will this so-called mortgage be repaid?'

'We had to extend when the first British investors dropped out, but we have others on board and the papers are due to be signed in a few days' time,' Jay confirmed.

'And how much do you owe?'

Jay swallowed visibly. 'Thousands, brother, thousands.'

Anish spluttered. He had turned bright red and then, clutching his chest, he winced as if in pain. Laxmi took a step forward but Priya stopped her before speaking bitterly.

'It has happened before. It will pass. That British doctor the Resident sent was useless. And your Mr Hopkins told my husband to lose weight and take more exercise. We wanted medicine.'

'Do not over-excite yourself, my son,' Laxmi said, with a sad shake of her head.

While Eliza watched, Anish turned a normal colour again and began to look better. She realized that Clifford must have assumed Anish would support Jay's arrest for stealing the jewels. That was what it had to have been about, not seditious papers at all, and Eliza worried that Anish would, indeed, press charges. But she didn't understand why Clifford had wanted to use Jay's typewriter to type a paragraph about Kent, and if it was about the jewels, why had Clifford spoken of disloyalty to the Crown?

Anish pointed at Jay. 'I hold you responsible and you alone. What does a woman know about these things? If the mortgage is repaid by the end of the week then I will over-look this, but if it is not I will divest you of your lands in return for the loss of the jewels. Is that clear?'

Eliza held her breath as Jay gave a sharp nod and then spoke. 'Why did you bring Eliza in here?'

'Because she is at the bottom of all this,' Priya said.

Anish ignored her. 'Because I need her to witness the papers I have had drawn up explaining what will happen if your mortgage is not repaid in time. Chatur will sign too.'

Eliza had been uncomfortable throughout the entire exchange of words but now let out her breath. The papers for the loans only had to be signed on time and then the mortgage would be repaid and all would be well. She glanced at Jay as if to say, should I sign? He simply nodded his assent and looked away.

Chatur smiled at Eliza, but it was a smile that left her with a chill in her blood.

26

Eliza was gazing out of the window hoping to see the courier arrive with her finished photographic prints from Delhi. It was already sweltering, but she loved seeing the monkeys leaping from tree to tree, and the vista across the flat rooftops of the gilded city still took her breath away, just as it always did. The cubic houses, close to the fortress walls, almost bleached of colour now, shimmered in the heat, and in the silver sky drifts of bright green parakeets swooped and dived.

She spotted a convoy of cars snaking up the hill. When the first car hooted its horn and halted, Clifford and another man climbed out, both of them wearing dark formal-looking suits. The car behind drew up and two British army officers climbed out of that one, both of them wiping their brows with white handkerchiefs. Whoever was in the third car remained in the car. Eliza watched a little longer as the men disappeared from view when they entered the castle, but then, puzzled, she ran down the main staircase, almost falling as she reached the last three steps.

Nobody was in the great hall and nobody was in the first courtyard. In fact the castle was strangely silent. She sat on one of the huge swings, sniffing the strongly scented jasmine growing close by, and kept an ear open for voices. The scents of cooking were already in the air: ginger, cardamom and coriander. With no desire to leave Rajputana, she had grown accustomed to spicy air and scented flowers.

She and Jay had not spoken of the future beyond making sure the first stage of the project was finished on time, and it looked as if that would happen the moment the papers were signed. Jay had also promised that once the first stage was finished he would take her to Udaipore, the best place to see the sky turn violet and the clouds appear before the heavens opened. While she was imagining that, she closed her eyes and opened them only just in time to see Jay walking between the two army officers towards the exit. He twisted back to her and mouthed the words *don't worry*. She froze. Of course she would worry. Jay held his back very straight and his chin up, every inch a royal, while the officers gripped him by the elbows. It was extremely upsetting to see and very clear to Eliza that Jay had been arrested. She turned round and saw Laxmi looking desolate but standing beside a triumphant Priya. Eliza ran to Laxmi.

'Can't we do anything?'

'We can put our faith in the gods.'

Eliza stared at her. 'This is insane. There must be something. I'll talk to Clifford Salter. I'm sure he will help.'

'It is your Mr Salter who has arrested my son.'

'But Anish said he would wait until the papers were signed. Jay has to go to Delhi tomorrow to sign them. How can he do that if he's under arrest? Why didn't Anish wait?'

Laxmi chewed her lip. 'This has nothing to do with the mortgage or the jewels. My son has been charged with attempted sabotage, writing incendiary papers against the British, and inciting rebellion, also against the British.'

Eliza stared at her. 'But that's utterly ridiculous. Of course Jay wouldn't do that. And sabotaging what exactly?'

'His own irrigation project.'

Eliza almost laughed. 'These are nonsense charges. You

must see that. I'm going to help.' And with that she took a step away, intending to run after the soldiers and Jay.

Priya smirked, but Laxmi caught her by the sleeve. 'Do not make a show of yourself and us.'

Eliza was fuming. 'That's all you care about? You're not going to react to this?'

'Not like this. If you run after them you are playing right into their hands. Behave with dignity and buy yourself time to think. You have much to learn. Now come with me.'

Eliza left Priya standing and followed Laxmi. When they arrived at the *zenana*, Laxmi indicated that Eliza should follow her into her sitting room. Unusually, Laxmi did not sit but rang the bell and then paced back and forth. Eliza had a million questions but out of respect for Laxmi held her tongue. It was extremely unusual for a royal to be arrested and Jay's mother must be feeling terribly worried. Either that or livid. Maybe both. So Eliza waited for Laxmi to speak. After about ten minutes, tea arrived and Laxmi finally sat down.

'I thought you would be a good influence on my son and now look at what has happened!'

Eliza was astonished. 'You blame me for this?'

'You recall what I said about Mr Salter being a suitable husband for you?'

'That was never on the cards.'

Laxmi ignored what Eliza had said and carried on with her train of thought. 'You will also recall me telling you I'd found a perfect marriage partner for my son?'

Eliza stared open-mouthed. 'You really want to talk about marriage while Jay has been dragged off like a common thief?'

'He was not dragged. Let us stick to the facts.'

And once again Eliza received the lecture about Jay's marriage prospects and how things would go for him if he married beneath him.

'Do you not care for Jay's happiness?' she said when Laxmi had finished.

Laxmi smiled. 'Romantic love passes as quickly as the life of a dragonfly. It is similarities of background that make a marriage solid. Too many differences will wreck it.'

'I am not so different from Jay.'

'Different enough. My son may think he loves you . . .'

'He said that?'

Laxmi did not reply. 'As I was saying, whatever he thinks he feels now is a result of lust, not of love.'

'How can you say that?'

'Because I have experienced it myself.'

Eliza drew in her breath, then let it out in a puff. 'Can we not talk about it now, please. What are we going to do about Jay being taken?'

'The two are connected, my dear.' Laxmi stared at her. 'Mr Salter has proof, I'm afraid. He showed me a pamphlet typed on Jay's typewriter. The letter "j" sticks, you see, and doesn't work properly.'

'He would never have done anything like that. Maybe somebody else got in there?'

'Be that as it may, they have a case against my son and the damage is done.'

'But it isn't fair,' Eliza said, almost in tears.

'This world is rarely fair, my dear. But I'm pleased to see you have faith in my son. Now I have an idea for a way out of this. If I tell you what I want you to do, will you promise to carry out every word?'

'Of course. I'll do anything that might help get Jay released.'

'You will not like it.'

All manner of thoughts rushed through her head but she nodded. 'I don't care. Just tell me.'

'You will need to be quick, because Priya is determined to convince Anish to ban you from the castle. Priya and Chatur are both determined in the same small-minded way. Neither of them wanted you here from the first, and both think you have been a bad influence on Jayant. And I have to say I am inclined to agree with them on that after all.'

There was a slight pause while Eliza took that in.

'Well, my idea involves you speaking to Mr Salter again . . . and perhaps a little more.'

Eliza stared at Laxmi as the woman explained her idea. When she had finished, Eliza could not speak. Surely this couldn't be the only way?

Shaken by Laxmi's idea, Eliza left in horror and went to her room to think, spending much of the rest of the day staring out of her bedroom window wondering how it had come to this. She recalled every moment she had spent with Jay. She had been sure that he returned her love: his tenderness and passion so unlike anything she'd ever experienced. All she wanted was to spend the rest of her life by his side, and that was something she had never expected to feel. Her work was to have been her life. But she and Jay were comfortable together, at ease in silence, and yet there was an edge and it was that edge that lent excitement to it. Sometimes she felt so tense, it was as if they were trying to tear each other apart during their love-making. It seemed to spring from the overpowering need to enter into each other's soul in the only way they knew how, as if they were attempting to make themselves one. Other times it was sweet and gentle and Eliza relaxed into her body in new and languid ways. Now she lay on her bed naked and knew it had not been lust driving Jay. He had said it himself. There was a sense of destiny at play here.

But then, right out of the blue, she remembered what he'd said about wanting a free India, in which Indians ruled their own country. Could he really have been responsible for the offending pamphlets after all?

Just as Eliza was thinking that, there was a knock at the door and she jumped – the knock interrupting her disloyal thoughts. She was tempted not to answer it but, thinking it might be news of Jay, threw on a dressing gown and opened the door.

'Indi?' she said when she saw the girl there. 'You look terrible. Has something more happened to Jay?'

Indi shook her head. Her eyes were clearly red from weeping. 'No. It is my grandmother. She is sick again and I must leave. She needs me . . .'

'I'm so sorry to hear that.'

'It is not why I've come. I have this for you.' She handed Eliza an envelope.

After Indi left, Eliza glanced at the stamp. It was English, but the handwriting was not her mother's. She slit open the envelope and found a single sheet of paper inside.

She saw immediately that it was from James Langton.

My dear Eliza,

I never thought it was sensible that you should up sticks and leave your mother in her time of need. While you took off for the other side of the world (on a whim, I might add), I myself have been away for several months on important estate business.

When I arrived home it was to discover your mother had suffered a stroke and is now in the General Hospital receiving treatment. The doctors believe it is not the first.

Eliza, I'm sorry to have to say this, but the signs were already there. The slurred speech may not have been entirely due to the gin as you asserted. After your husband's untimely death, you really should have remained at home to look after Anna. I have done all I can. You must come home immediately either to care for your mother, should she survive, or to make her funeral arrangements.

I myself am about to remarry and cannot continue shouldering the burden of your mother.

Sincerely yours,
James Langton

A slicing pain in Eliza's chest almost stopped her breath, the guilt over her father and Oliver now compounded by this. She had been a terrible daughter, abandoning her mother at the worst possible moment, and she felt utterly wretched. Her poor mother must be feeling terribly frightened, so of course she must return to look after Anna in her final days. There was no choice, and yet she couldn't help remembering how she had tried to persuade her mother to reduce her drinking. Had hidden the bottles, had watched over her, had stayed awake at night listening for the sound of her mother's frantic search for alcohol. Nothing had helped. Anna Fraser had been hell-bent on self-destruction, and how could she ever find the strength to give up the gin when she had nothing to take its place? Eliza had seen the way her mother used alcohol to block out her loneliness and the inner demons that had haunted her life. In her darkest moments Eliza also knew that her mother's alcoholism was an illness of mind, body and emotion. There was no medical help to be had, no organization to help; her mother had been left to drown in her own addiction while the rest of the world looked on and called her spineless. Eliza had thought her weak too – a mercurial alcoholic, impossible to manage. But maybe Eliza's father had not been blameless. Perhaps Anna hadn't lied and it wasn't his death that had triggered Anna's descent but his infidelity? And *more*. Whatever the *more* had been.

She went to her wardrobe and glanced inside, sniffing the scent of mothballs. She touched the silk dress Clifford had given her. So beautiful. So perfect. As she read the letter again, it occurred to her that she'd been living in a fool's paradise. Jay came into her mind and she shook her head. Though torn between helping the man she loved and her poor mother, dying alone and unloved, she knew where her duty lay. With one last look at the view from her window, Eliza began to cry.

27

Eliza had barely slept and in the morning her decision loomed large. In the end there really was just this one last thing she could do for Jay before she left for England. With a terribly heavy heart she would do what Laxmi had asked of her. First she dressed in a conventional European dress with a nipped-in waist and little collar, then she tied up her hair. After that she stepped into her best pair of high heels, dabbed on some rouge and a light lipstick, sprayed the last of her Chanel No. 5 behind her ears, and gathered her courage.

She had requested a car, and as she waited at the castle gates she thought of her time there, from the moment she had arrived, nervous and uncertain about what the future might hold, right up to the awful sight of Jay being taken away. The months had been filled with ups and downs, but more than anything she would always remember the joy that she could never have imagined possible. And yet here she was now and nothing had really changed.

The car arrived, and sooner than she might have wished she was deposited at the entrance to the Residency. Before she knocked at the door she glanced back at the town. This was an elegant area of smart *havelis* where the rich merchants lived and where a few British buildings stood resolute, surrounded by lush gardens heavy with the scent of flowers. She took a deep breath. If she tapped quietly the butler wouldn't hear and she would not have to go through with it. She wanted to turn back the clock: to return to the days she'd spent with Jay at his palace – the happiest days of her life – but there was no going back. There never was, no matter how much you railed or pleaded against the march of your own fate. And it was her fate that, after everything, she must do this. She didn't tap quietly but rapped on the door with her knuckles. What was the point of delaying the inevitable?

After the butler had shown her to the shade under the veranda at the back of the house, she arranged herself carefully and, sitting up stiffly, managed to control her emotions. She watched the birds pecking at the gravel path and looked up at the patches of blue between the branches of the frangipani tree. The place was a riot of flowers, and Eliza wondered how Clifford managed to use enough water to keep them so fresh. There was very little breeze and she was already feeling the heat. She glanced around, wondering if she could just get up and walk indoors. There would be a fan inside if nothing else.

The butler brought out a jug of iced lime soda and two crystal glasses on a silver tray.

'Master is coming,' he said, and gave Eliza a little bow.

She heard footsteps and twisted back to see Clifford, looking rather red in the face.

'Damn heat,' he said, as he sat opposite her. 'We'll drink this and then go in, if it's all right with you.'

'Absolutely.'

They didn't speak for a few minutes and Eliza enjoyed the feel of the cold glass against her overheated palm. She wanted to roll it across her forehead, where she could already feel the beginning of a heat-induced headache, but did not. It wasn't just the heat: Eliza's neck and shoulders were rigid with tension. Could she go through with this? Every cell in her body was telling her to leave, but she remained calmly seated, hoping none of the inner turmoil was showing.

'So, indoors now?' he said, and held out a hand to her.

She nodded and allowed him to escort her inside to the small sitting room where she had waited once before.

He indicated that she was to sit, so she sank back into a deeply overstuffed armchair with cushions that swallowed her. A mistake, she thought, and pulled herself up to perch on the chair's edge instead. It was essential to remain upright and in control.

'The summer will be hell, won't it?' she said.

'Well, I did offer you Shimla,' he said, his face impassive.

'I know.'

There was a long uncomfortable silence during which Eliza thought of ways to frame her speech. In the end she decided to just come out with it.

'Clifford.' She swallowed rapidly before continuing. This was it. No going back. 'I would like to take you up on your other offer, if it still stands.'

He frowned.

'What I mean is –'

'I think I know what you mean.'

'So?'

He looked completely taken aback, and for a moment Eliza thought she might be too late. She looked at him, hoping for some response, but couldn't read the expression on his face.

'Clifford, I'm saying I accept your offer of marriage.' She paused. 'If you will have me.'

He was still looking at her without speaking, but then he smiled. 'I knew you'd come round, old girl.'

Internally she winced at the expression but tried not to show how much she disliked it.

He got to his feet and then came across to where she still perched stiff, strained and sad. He seemed not to notice any of that.

He held out a hand to her and she allowed him to pull her up. 'You've made me a very happy man. I'll not let you down.'

She bowed her head for a moment and then met his gaze. Her throat felt tight and constricted. Could she say it or would it just come out as a strangled sound? With a puzzled expression he inclined his head as if he already knew there was more, but wasn't sure what.

'Is it about your mother? We can bring her out if you like. Or it won't be too long before I might be able to get a transfer to London. Whatever you want. Your wish is my command. Just fire away,' he said, now beaming happily as if nothing could spoil this moment for him. 'You have made me the happiest man on earth.'

He leant across to kiss her but she shook her head and pulled back, feeling guilt-ridden. She tried to clear her throat before speaking. 'I'm afraid there is one condition.'

There was a slight pause, and she heard the sound of some kind of hooting bird outside in the garden. Probably an *ooloo*, she thought. Perfect name for an owl. Strange the things that slip into your mind even at such a moment as this. She pulled herself together and summoned her courage.

'I will marry you,' she said, 'but I want you to release Jay with no slur on his reputation and no repercussions. All charges against him must be dropped and I need your assurance that he will not be arrested again.'

'I'm delighted you have decided not to throw your life

away on an Indian. But Eliza, you make this very hard for me.'

She swallowed. 'I'm sorry.'

He shook his head. 'I need time to think.'

'There is no time. He must be released today. He has to sign the agreements with his investors in Delhi. If he fails he loses everything. The irrigation project will fail.'

'He means an awful lot to you?'

'He means a lot to me, yes, but so does the irrigation project. He wants to do good, Clifford, you must see that. His brother has done nothing for the people, and when I first met Jay his life seemed so aimless. Now he has a purpose and it's a good one. You know he would never sabotage his own project. It makes no sense.'

'And the pamphlets?'

Eliza thought for a moment, and couldn't help feeling that Chatur was lurking somewhere near the bottom of all this.

'I think someone has framed him,' she said. 'If I were you I'd be looking to question Chatur.'

'You'd stake your life on that?'

'I would.'

'And you're willing to marry me in order to secure Jay's release.' He paused for a moment before looking right into her eyes. 'Eliza, I have one question.'

She nodded.

'Do you think you could ever love me?'

She could see the utter sadness in his eyes and gazed back at him, but with the memory of Jay etched within her whole being she could not say yes. 'I can promise to try.'

'Well, maybe that will have to suffice. I will need to speak to him again, but consider Prince Jayant a free man the moment I have. Do you realize this little arrangement between us must never be spoken of? It would ruin my reputation. You understand that?'

'Of course.'

'I mean it, Eliza. You can't even tell Jay.'

She nodded.

He went to his office to telephone, and when he'd made his arrangements he came back.

'So,' Clifford said. 'What about a little trip up to Shimla, just the two of us? We can go the day after tomorrow, as long as that gives you time.'

'Clifford, I'm going to England. As soon as I've packed.'

He frowned.

'Oh goodness! With everything else I forgot to tell you. My mother is terribly ill and in hospital. I have no choice but to go to her. She has nobody.'

He looked disappointed but he nodded. 'Of course.'

'I'm hoping to pick up some final copies of my photographs from the printers while I'm in Delhi.'

'Some are already on their way here, I believe, but you can always check while you're there. I have a few of the earlier plates here too. I'll help with your arrangements, and let me take care of the cost of a first class berth on the *Viceroy of India*. It's the fastest ship. Just get yourself to Delhi pronto. Your tickets will be delivered to the hotel and from there you'll take the train.' He paused. 'You know the Imperial?'

'I do, though I've never stayed there.'

'Your bill will be taken care of. All you need to do is wait for the tickets to arrive. Should only take a few days. I'll wire the shipping company.'

'I really can't accept all that.'

'I insist, and when you come back I'm sure Julian

284

Hopkins and Dottie will invite you to stay with them until the wedding. Do you have any idea how long you'll need to be in England?'

'As long as it takes, I suppose.'

'I have something for you,' he said, and opened a drawer in the mahogany desk opposite the door. He took out a small velvet-covered box and came over to Eliza. 'I hope it fits.'

She opened the lid and took out a gold ring studded with diamonds and rubies.

'It was my mother's. Do you like it?'

She nodded as she allowed him to slip it on to her finger, and ignored the tears pricking the back of her eyelids.

'I'll organize an announcement in *The Times*,' he said. 'There isn't a car available for a few days. Will the train do?'

She nodded again, and he didn't seem to notice that all she really wanted to do was curl up and die.

28

May

Clifford was a decent enough man, if a little lacking in sensitivity – he hadn't even noticed the despair that had crossed her face when she'd agreed to marry him. Or perhaps he had noticed but hadn't wanted to acknowledge it. He was a man content with his own view of the world, defined by his rigid stance on all things India. Eliza resolved to find a way to manage, but what if every time he touched her she would die a little death? She made an attempt to console herself, as if she could somehow force herself out of her true feelings. If it wasn't too late they'd have children: she could be a mother and give her children a comfortable life. That had to be worth something. And she'd carry on with her photography too.

But her soul cried out for the passion and joy she'd experienced with Jay. It was like being given a glimpse of paradise from an open prison door only to find the door slammed shut again. Maybe the euphoria wouldn't have lasted, but now she'd never know. As she packed the belongings she'd need for England it was with a tight, hard feeling in her chest. She wished she could pack away the memory of his hands on her flesh, his lips on her mouth, his voice and the way it made her stomach flip. It was impossible. She would never be able to parcel away her feelings. Nor would she ever forget the trace of sandalwood and limes. Nor the sight of his amber eyes. What a naïve fool she'd been to think there ever could have been a future with Jay.

She comforted herself with the knowledge that she hadn't let Laxmi down and that at least Jay would be free to finish his project. As she was thinking that, she heard a gentle knock at the door and Laxmi came in, her long scarf flowing loosely about her. It was only the second time she'd come to Eliza's rooms.

She held out her hands to Eliza. 'I will always be in your debt for what you have done today.'

Eliza swallowed the lump in her throat and gave Laxmi a little nod but, fearing to express even a little of her terrible inner loneliness, didn't go to her and simply gazed at the floor.

'I do know how hard it must have been for you,' Laxmi added.

Eliza looked up. 'You have no idea.'

'I think I do. You have done a deeply unselfish thing. You have freed my son and nobody else could have done.'

'I had no choice.'

'Maybe. But not all would have done it. You have shown your true worth as a woman. Had things been different I would have been proud to call you my daughter-in-law. My daughter.'

Eliza's tears welled up and sadness made her voice break as she tried to reply.

'Sometimes life leaves us with impossible decisions. I know you care deeply for my son and he for you,' Laxmi continued, 'but I hope you understand I have a duty as a mother.'

'Thank you for all your support while I've been here,' Eliza said, her throat still choked. She admired Laxmi so much, and yet she had been the one standing between herself and Jay.

'I'm so sorry it couldn't have ended on a happier note for you.'

'I'm going to England. My mother is very ill.'

'Well, my thoughts will go with you for a safe journey. I hope one day you will understand my position.'

Eliza could not reply.

'Come here, my dear.'

Eliza went to her and Laxmi wrapped her arms around her. Just when she thought she had done with crying, Eliza's tears fell again.

The overnight journey to Delhi began in the afternoon. The train was almost unbearably hot and the carriage was full of local people. She feared the power of the British Raj over these men and women and did not want to be a part of it, and yet, by marrying Clifford, she would become one of them and would have to keep her mouth shut. More and more she'd become aware that the British should get out of India. Her only hope was that the Nationalist movement would gain control without too much bloodshed. Like many others she felt certain it would happen, because really, the way things were how could it not?

Her dress was already damp from sweat and she was forced to constantly wipe her forehead too. She took off her engagement ring because her fingers were at risk of swelling; that was what she told herself. It came to her that her only hope of enduring the tediously slow train and cramped conditions was to think of all the beautiful photographs she had taken. Nobody could take that away from her.

The images seemed to pop up out of nowhere, and as

they filled her mind they kept on coming. First at the simple camp where she had stayed with Jay: the men wrapped in their early morning blankets, sitting cross-legged beside the small outdoor fire. The tiny ponds where boys tended their buffaloes. The lake at dawn and again at dusk. The faces of Rajput men and their camels. The jewel-like colours of the castle. The fairyland night-time illuminations. The way the light played on the water of the courtyard fountains. The parakeets and dragonflies. The concubines brushing their hair. The women with their upright posture, their dignity and their bright shiny clothes. The bazaars. The children. The huge liquid blue skies. The photographs of the royals and of Indi, who gazed out upon the world with eyes that seemed to know everything.

Then she thought of the rains she knew would be coming, and felt unhappy that she would not see the damson skies and thundering torrential monsoon. She had longed to be at Udaipore, the city of lakes surrounded by the Aravalli hills, and the hilltop fort from where they would have watched it all. She had never believed she would really leave India before the rains and yet here she was. Leaving. Her temples throbbing with pain, she couldn't shut out the sound of the train wheels clattering on the track, so brittle that the *clickety click, clickety click, clickety click* seemed to be coming from inside her own head. She clapped a palm over her mouth, fearful that the wail trapped inside her would wind its way out. This dark and empty time was taking Eliza from the man she loved and was forcing her to marry a man she did not. Over and over, her fading dreams were mocked by the sound of the wheels on the rails. *The man she loved, clickety clack; marrying a man she did not, clickety clack.*

289

Then her thoughts drifted to her mother lying alone in the hospital, facing death with no one who loved her. To have lived your entire life and be left with not one person by your side was a pitiful fate. However rotten a mother Anna had been, she deserved better. And though Eliza's heart clamped as if a vice was squeezing it, she would do what she could for her. At last she would be a dutiful daughter, thankful that at least she had one final chance to make amends.

When she arrived in Delhi the weather was awful and a kind of hot clammy mist hung over the town. At the Imperial Hotel her room was small but comfortable. She opened the bathroom door to see a rolltop bath tub standing on a black and white tiled floor along with the usual washbasin, lavatory, and a huge looking-glass on one wall. She left the heavy bedroom curtains open so that she could see the sky while she lay on the bed, hoping to snatch some sleep before the next stage of her journey. And she didn't know if that would be in a few days' time or if it might be sooner. Tomorrow she hoped to have a chance to pick up copies of some of her prints from the printers to take back to England to show Anna and maybe interest a local paper. Now all she could think of was finding a way to refresh her exhausted mind a little and give her aching body a chance to recover from the headache she'd had since leaving Juraipore.

Although the fan in her room worked, it really was just shifting hot air about rather than introducing a much-needed cool breeze, so after a while she drew the curtains to block out the light and then, still stiff and tense from the journey, lay down on top of a pale blue satin bedspread. But she kept twisting about in the attempt to find a relaxing position and couldn't stop thinking.

There would be little enough to look forward to, but it was only now, on the verge of leaving India, that she fully realized how much she had grown to think of it as home, just as she had as a child. At least when she came back to be with Clifford she would still be in India, for England could never touch her the way this wild, throbbing country did.

She slipped her engagement ring back on, then twisted it round so it looked like a wedding ring. The symbol of being taken. She couldn't help feeling as if she were owned, and removed it again. She thought back to when she had raised the subject of women's suffrage with Anna.

With a raised voice and a disgusted look her mother had been adamant. 'Women do not need a vote,' she'd said. 'That's what husbands are for. What do we know of politics?'

'Mother, can we not inform ourselves, make our own choices?'

'What you need, Eliza, is a husband, not a vote. And, as I've said many times before, one cannot have a career and be a wife. Women cannot have everything.'

Eliza had given up after that. Nothing would convince her mother, and some time after that she'd literally bumped into Oliver in the bookshop. And marriage had become a way out.

After an hour of thinking about the past Eliza got up again, washed and then dressed in clean clothes. If she couldn't rest, then she had to make a move.

The hotel ordered a driver and car for her and once outside she saw that the mist had lifted, which meant she just had time to see the new part of the city before the light faded. Her first stop would be to look at the architectural splendour of the new British centre of government. It had only been finished in February and this was her first chance to see it.

She hadn't expected to arrive at an imposing gravel road leading in the distance to an extraordinary series of domes and towers, in red, pink, cream, and gleaming white. As the car moved on through the tall archway Eliza was impressed by huge lawns dotted with trees on either side of a grand central drive, known as the King's Way, and a network of sparkling waterways that seemed to be following the route. The driver told her it was a mile and a quarter long, or maybe two miles, he wasn't sure, but he knew it was lined with black lamp-posts right to the end. All the buildings at the end of the drive were glorious but, like something from the Italian Renaissance, it was the Viceroy's palatial house that took Eliza's breath away. Suffused with light, the stonework actually shone. With all this brand new splendour it seemed that the British believed they would rule India for years to come.

This was the end result of that triumphant march into Delhi in 1912, celebrating the transfer of the seat of British power, the terrible day the bomb had been thrown at the Viceroy and the day David Fraser had died. Eliza gazed at the glittering fountains as the falling sun turned the sky a deep rose and wished she could enjoy this new city more fully; but it was tinged with too much tragedy for her. Then, as darkness fell, she asked the driver to show her the avenues radiating out from this central point, avenues lined with spacious bungalows in extensive flower-filled gardens. After that, on their way back to her hotel, the velvety sky deepened to black and the city itself exploded into a glittering marvel of lights, a twinkling earth-bound reflection of the heavens.

★

The next afternoon, after visiting the printers and finding the place closed, she was just about to enter the Imperial when, guided by what she couldn't tell, she twisted back. A fraction of a second later she heard a single burst of noise, as if thunder itself had been shot directly from a cannon. She gasped at the sight of a huge ball of smoke erupting from the lower window of the building on the other side of the street. The explosion didn't seem to echo but was followed by the sound of glass breaking and then of bricks or masonry crashing to the ground. Horrified, she watched flames creeping along the wooden frames of the windows on the first floor. Within minutes the glass was gone, and now tongues of orange and yellow were reaching out and licking the air. Through the dust and billowing smoke she couldn't see exactly what had been damaged, but it looked as if something had exploded inside the very building that held her photographic printers. Flames were tearing through the rest of the building, visible at all the windows on both floors. There was the sound of more windows shattering and a great whooshing sound, and then debris filled the air before raining down on the street below. Huge plumes of black smoke rose up into the sky, and the stalls around the building became powdered with ash, white smoke whisking between them.

She took a few steps towards the building, hoping no one had been hurt, or worse, but then she remembered the building had been locked up and nobody appeared to be lying on the ground dead or injured, at least not on her side of the street. Though she could hear coughing and spluttering, the only other sound was the crackle of the fire. A moment later a crowd of blackened ghoul-like creatures swarmed over to the Imperial side of the street; some with cuts on their arms and faces, clearly from flying glass. She watched for a moment to see if there were others who might need her help, but then heavy smoke stopped her. In the centre of the street it cleared and it was only then that she saw him, standing alone and covered in blue-grey dust. She ran forward, and as she did he saw her.

29

Jay gave her a weak smile. The next moment he crumpled right in front of her and fell to the ground. With her heart pulsing in her throat she ran across and knelt on the black gravel ground beside him, stroking his face and pleading with him to open his eyes. There was no response. She felt her chest tighten with fear as she spoke, repeatedly telling him that help would be coming and he was to hold on, that she was right beside him and she wouldn't let anything happen to him.

An official from the hotel came out to try to encourage her back inside in case of flying masonry, or even worse, but she refused.

'Help will be here soon,' the hotel concierge said, but then stepped away from danger.

She and Jay were alone in the street, but she could hear that the crowd behind them on the steps of the Imperial had found their voices and were either crying from shock and relief that they were safe or excitedly telling their stories. She drowned out their noise by focusing on Jay.

He was still breathing, and she took comfort in that, and he didn't appear to be cut anywhere. She wondered if something had hit him on the head? She didn't take her gaze from his face, as she sat watching for the slightest sign of movement. She heard bells ringing and a man moving the crowd away at the side of the street, and then, as a doctor in a white coat appeared, Jay opened his eyes, seeming to regain consciousness.

'I signed the papers,' he said, trying to lift his head. 'We did it.'

She looked at him and couldn't help smiling. 'You almost get killed and the first thing you say to me is that you signed the papers?'

He almost smiled back, but then he seemed to shrink back into the ground and was gone again. She had been holding back tears but now they began to spill.

'He's still breathing?' the doctor asked as he knelt beside Eliza.

'He hasn't stopped breathing at all,' she said, clutching at any chance of hope in the midst of this. 'What's the matter with him? He will be all right, won't he?'

'I can't tell yet.' He listened to Jay's chest, then glanced up at her. 'Breathing a little weak and heart racing. You know this man?'

'He's Jayant Singh Rathore, a Raja from Juraipore.'

'And you are?'

'A friend,' she said, but she wanted to say *I am the one who loves him.*

'Well, it's a hospital bed for him.'

'Can I come?' She paused. 'Please?'

'It's a little irregular, as you're not family, but as you seem to know him, then very well.'

At the hospital Eliza did not leave Jay's side. For the rest of that day and overnight she sat alone on a wooden straight-backed chair, trying very hard not to weep in front of anyone. *You have to live*, she whispered, as time distilled into this one moment. *You have to live. You cannot die.* That this strong, wonderful man could have been felled like this was unbearable, and she held on to the fact that he was young and healthy. If anyone could pull through surely it was he. But every hour that went by brought no sign of improvement. She watched for his grey cheeks to change in colour, or for the sign of blood returning to his whitened lips, or the slightest, just the very slightest, flutter of his eyelashes. But still there was nothing. He remained pale and barely alive.

As she sat she thought of Clifford. And then she thought of her mother, also lying ill in a hospital bed. Until that moment her mother had completely gone out of her mind. Whatever happened, she would still have to leave.

The next day she asked a nurse to organize a telegram to be sent to Laxmi and then the doctor sent her back to the hotel. She still had to eat and sleep, he said. And she tried to do both. She really did. But the food turned her stomach, and when she attempted to sleep she woke, hot and sweaty, her disturbed mind exploding with anxiety. And it was only then that she realized her prints might have all been destroyed in the explosion and the plates with them.

After just a few hours of this hopeless attempt at resting, she washed, changed her clothes and went down to the hotel foyer to ask if the tickets had arrived, praying that they had not. When the receptionist handed Eliza an envelope she tore it open. The train tickets were for that evening. In just two hours' time. She raced up the stairs, packed, and then a driver took her back to the hospital. She had to see Jay before she left. Had to know if he would be all right.

When she arrived the doctor took her aside. He led her into an office and indicated that she was to sit. 'He has recovered consciousness.'

She drew in her breath sharply and her eyes began to fill.

'He has sustained an internal injury but I have hopes he will recover.'

She covered her mouth to hide the trembling.

'He's very weak but he has been asking for you. Please don't tire him. Although I have explained a little of what happened, at the moment he remembers nothing of the fire. Please don't say anything that might upset him at this stage.'

She nodded, her heart swelling with a mixture of hope and fear.

'I'll let you have a few minutes and then I'll come and get you. He's still in a fragile state, you understand.'

She nodded and brushed her stupid tears away. He was alive. He would live. That was all that mattered. She wanted to run to his bedside but took several long deep breaths, got up from the chair and forced herself to walk calmly and with her head erect. She felt a lump develop in her throat but told herself to remain calm, as Laxmi would have been.

When she reached the bedside his eyes were closed and for an awful moment she feared the doctor had been wrong, and that he would not recover at all, but he must have heard her pull up a chair because he opened his eyes. His skin was a better colour now and so were his lips. She absorbed that quickly, all the time really only looking at his eyes for signs of recognition.

'Eliza.'

She swallowed the lump in her throat and her eyes blurred. His voice had been soft and low and it made her want to wrap him in her arms and hold him tight until he was strong again.

'Don't speak if it tires you,' she said.

'I don't know why it happened but suddenly Clifford Salter arranged my release.'

She reached out to him. He held her hand, raised it to his lips and kissed it. There was a long silence during which he closed his eyes and she continued to hold his hand.

'None of that matters now,' she said.

He opened his eyes and gave her a warm smile. 'We'll go away. Just you and I. We'll have a splendid camp before the rains and then go on to Udaipore.'

She blinked rapidly. 'My mother is ill. I'm on my way back to England.'

'When you're back, then?'

She nodded, knowing she could not tell him that when she got back she would be marrying Clifford, nor would she ever be able to explain why. Thank goodness she hadn't put her engagement ring back on. She reminded herself that right now she must not say anything that might upset Jay's recovery.

'I love you, Eliza,' he said softly. *'Main tumhe pyar karta hu aur karta rahunga.'*

'I love you too. For ever. With all my heart.'

They stayed like that, with her holding his hand and him so weak, and her trying to be brave. At least he's alive, she thought. Alive.

She heard a cough and twisted back to see the doctor appearing at the door.

He tapped his watch. 'Time's up, I'm afraid. He's very weak.'

She nodded and got to her feet, then leant over Jay and kissed him very gently on the lips.

'Goodbye, Jay.'

He didn't speak, but lifted his hand and traced her hairline with his fingertips.

Out on the street, devastated by what had happened and feeling completely wretched, Eliza ducked into an alley-way, where she crumpled and sank to the ground. She felt hollowed out, as if the solid parts of her had turned to liquid and were flowing out over the very edge of her world. Everything had been destroyed: her hope of an exhibition in October and the jeopardy the whole project would be in if her prints and plates had been fire-damaged. But far worse, her love and fear for Jay. She could never tell him the truth. She buried her face in her arms and, feeling that she would never wake from this nightmare, the sobs flooded out of her.

PART FOUR

'Only those who are ravaged by love know love . . .'

– Rumi, *Mathnavi*, 109

30

Gloucestershire, England

Eliza gazed at the big sky above the tree-lined hill behind her mother's house. Anna Fraser's home was a square residence, surrounded by broken dry-stone walling, and, standing on the corner of a narrow crossroads, its Cotswold stone glowed buttery in the late afternoon light. Eliza's gaze followed the beech-lined lane leading further down the valley and along the drive to James Langton's house. It was beautifully, refreshingly green, though Brook Park itself, a gloomy, turreted place, had seen better days. Eliza could see the top of the clock tower rising above the old stables, but the house itself was blocked from view by dark fir trees. She took one last look at the sky, picked up her case, found the spare key under a stone at the side of the hydrangea bush, and unlocked the peeling back door.

Inside was only silence.

She walked into the kitchen, where the washing-up had been piled up haphazardly, encrusted pans had been left on top of the cooker and the rubbish bin was overflowing. Was her mother here or still in hospital? She checked the living room and found it also in a mess. Had Anna been rushed to hospital leaving all this? She began to tidy up, planning to book a taxi to the hospital a little later, but then she heard a weak voice calling out.

'Hello. Who is there?'

It seemed that her mother must be upstairs. Not knowing what state Anna would be in, Eliza climbed the stairs cautiously and tiptoed across the landing to her mother's bedroom. The door was slightly ajar. She pushed it open and stepped inside the interior of the cold, dark room.

She made out her mother lying on the bed, fully clothed but very pale. 'I came home from hospital yesterday,' she said in a small voice. Eliza walked across to her and held her mother's left hand. 'What did the doctors say?'

'Oh, you know. This and that.'

She stroked her mother's hand, noticing how it trembled, then spoke in a low voice. 'Mum, I don't know. You need to tell me.'

'I'm so tired, darling, so tired. You call the doctor. He'll tell you. We'll talk later.' Anna's voice was as weightless as she herself appeared to be. She closed her eyes and Eliza carefully placed her mother's hand back by her side. It was as if Anna was somehow trapped inside her fragile body, and Eliza felt she couldn't reach her.

She opened a window, then went downstairs and found the family doctor's phone number in a small book on the hall table. She wondered if Anna even knew what was going on, but straight away called the consulting rooms. When the call ended she sat down on the floor with her head in her hands. Anna's hospital stay had revealed an incurable cancer and now there was nothing more the doctors could do. The stroke had been minor; it was the cancer that was killing her. *I hope you'll remain at home with her*, he'd said. *We wanted her to stay in hospital but she insisted on going home. She doesn't have long.*

The next day, while her mother slept, Eliza drowned her distress by walking. While she walked she thought of her mother and then of Jay and prayed that he would fully recover from his injuries. It would be too much to lose both of them.

She followed the lane, walking beside coppiced hedging cut back to encourage low growth, and noticing that the dips and hollows of the Cotswold countryside were at their best, gleaming in myriad shades of green. On the higher banks above the grassy verges, sheep were grazing in the patchwork of small green fields and above her the sky, with its mixture of blue, grey and white, glittered with moisture caught by the sun. She carried on up to the woods at the top of the hill behind the big house, where large trees marched across the horizon in a gloomy military manner. After passing through them she ran down the other side into the old bluebell woods, where as a child she would often roll in the beautiful sea of blue beneath a bright green canopy and where, later in the year, the smell of wild garlic drifted.

When she grew tired and her feet and legs ached from the exertion, she sat on a log and tried to imagine a future with Clifford. She still wanted to do so much more with her photography. Give a voice to the voiceless. That was the thing. In a more positive state of mind, she became brighter and remembered how her camera made her forget everything else. She decided she'd maybe walk to the valley on the other side of Cleeve Hill, and take pictures there, or follow the deep dark tree-lined road going down to Winchcombe, or perhaps even climb up to Belas Knap, the ancient long barrow that she had loved since childhood.

During the day walking soothed her brain; during daylight hours the present was manageable.

As May turned into June she was relieved that Anna had stopped drinking and seemed well enough to sit in the garden. One day as they sat out there with just a light breeze warranting a cardigan, she asked Anna about her stay in hospital.

Her mother gave a little laugh. 'It was quite nice.'

She had spoken lightly, as if she'd been talking about a short visit to Weston-super-Mare.

Eliza had decided to probe a little further and touched her mother's sleeve, as if to say, come on Mum, talk to me. 'They dried you out, didn't they?'

'I suppose. I haven't had a single drink since you came home.'

I wish this could have happened sooner, Eliza thought in the silence that followed. But now that her mother was more alert and at last confronting the truth there could be a chance of something, however small.

'I'm pleased you're a bit better,' Eliza said. 'Really pleased.'

'It's been lonely. I've been lonely.'

'I'm here now.'

No more was said then, but Eliza glanced at her fragile mother and felt sad at heart.

Still she cared for her ailing mother solicitously, and Anna's favourite occupation became sitting with Eliza and reminiscing about the old days.

'Do you remember the wonderful early days in Delhi?' Anna said one late afternoon when the shadows were lengthening.

Eliza thought about it. She remembered the monkeys everywhere, climbing on walls in the garden, scampering up trees and sometimes even coming into the kitchen to steal food. She had loved the monkeys.

'And the garden?' Anna said.

'All those bright flowers?'

'Yes, them.'

Eliza glanced at Anna and saw tears in her eyes.

'It was good, Mum, India was good. Do you remember all the shops in Chandni Chowk?'

Anna smiled. 'Selling everything.'

'Yes. Snake oil, Dad used to say.'

'He did.'

And so the days passed, but at night the loss of Jay disturbed her rest. Even her snatches of sleep were broken by dreams of explosions and she would see him covered from head to toe in black dust, sometimes dead, sometimes alive. At night she wrote letters. It was all she could do without waking her mother and she wrote many, many letters to Jay, that in the morning she tore up and stuffed into the old wood burner. When her mother complained of the smell she said, 'Oh, it's just the burner, just the burner getting old.' She had to do something to rid herself of the hurt, had to find a way to escape her own mind, but the questions kept spinning. What would really happen when she married Clifford? What if she could not stop herself shrinking back?

The constriction in Eliza's chest did not diminish.

But Gloucestershire's rolling hills and valleys were lovely, as they always were at this time of year, with the hedgerows bursting and all the trees fresh and green. The blue sky was a comfort to Eliza, as were the gently moist air and mild sunshine, so different from Rajputana's scorching heat and dry burning air. While her mother slept, she told herself over and over that it was for the best and that no matter how long it were to take she would stay with Anna.

As the dull, detached days passed, Jay's words repeated in

her head. *I love you, Eliza.* She told herself she would get over him. She would take beautiful photographs and that would heal her. She would be safe behind the camera lens. She would look out at a world that couldn't look back. She decided, as she had done as a child, that pain was better withheld, untouched, controlled, and while she might never experience true happiness again, she had her memories.

Anna ate almost nothing, but when Eliza suggested her mother might like to accompany her on one of her walks, Anna gave a little nod and suggested a picnic. They left the house by way of a gate at the back of the small garden that led to a cobbled pathway, skirting one of James Langton's orchards. As a child, one of Eliza's favourite pastimes had been to climb the gnarled apple trees and sit in the branches munching on stolen fruit. It had given her a secret kind of pleasure but had come to an end when James found her there, ordering her down immediately. He didn't approve of children climbing his precious apple trees. With a hammering heart she had scrambled down too fast and, though she had done it many times before, her foot had caught behind a branch and she had tipped out of the tree. Nothing broken, but she'd badly twisted an ankle and received a series of lectures about the evils of girls climbing trees.

Now, after a few hundred yards, the two of them veered off into the orchard and Eliza spread out an old tartan blanket for Anna to sit on. Eliza opened the lid of the small picnic basket.

'When did you get this?' she asked.

'I've had it for years.'

'We never used it?'

'Just once.'

'Well, at least we're using it now.' Eliza swallowed her distress at the thought that this was possibly the last time.

Then she remembered the other picnic. The one with James Langton. She glanced up at the sky where a few lazy birds were half-heartedly flying from one tree to another. The whole world seemed to have stilled, and Eliza took off her cardigan. 'Warm, isn't it,' she said.

Her mother's head was bowed.

'Mum?'

Anna looked up. 'I'm sorry.'

'For what, Mum?'

She flapped her hand. 'I don't know. The picnics we didn't have. Everything.'

'I survived, didn't I?'

Anna smiled, as if she'd suddenly thought of something and was bursting to share it with her daughter.

'Climb a tree. Go on, climb a tree.' She glanced about excitedly. 'There, that one. Climb that one.'

Delighted by her mother's sudden gaiety, Eliza got to her feet. 'You mean it?'

Anna nodded.

'Not sure if I still can,' Eliza said, as she estimated the height of the drop should she fall.

'I never knew where your grazed knees came from.'

'Until he found me in the tree?'

Anna nodded.

'Right. Here we go.'

Eliza managed to get a foothold easily and was up on her old favourite branch within moments. She tested to see if it was strong enough to bear her adult weight and deemed that it was. Then she edged along a short way and sat with her legs dangling.

Her mother's laughter carried up to her.

'I used to sing when I sat up here,' Eliza said.

'Sing what?'

'Childhood songs.' She began to sing *I do like to be beside the seaside* and after a while her mother joined in: the two of them singing at the tops of their voices until it ended in gales of laughter and a side stitch for Anna.

Eliza slid back down. 'You all right?'

Anna nodded.

'What happened with him?'

'James?'

It went suddenly quiet.

Anna looked at Eliza as if gauging how much to say. 'He's gone away with his new wife.'

'Well, let's not spoil a lovely day with thoughts of him. Let's eat.'

Her mother clapped her hands. 'I hope we have ginger beer. I love ginger beer.'

'I never knew that.'

'There's lots you don't know. Lots and lots.'

Eliza was glad that for the next couple of days her relationship with her mother carried on in the same vein, with Anna happier than Eliza had ever seen her. It was as if Anna's words were unstoppable, like water suddenly released from a previously blocked pipe. Then the postman called. Anna didn't receive much mail. In fact nothing had been delivered since Eliza's own arrival back home, but she spotted the Indian stamp the moment the postman gave it to her. She had been wondering if Clifford would write, and had lived in dread of hearing from him. For now, out of sight was out of mind. It was more than she could hope that it would contain news of Jay.

She heard her mother's shrill voice.

'Is there mail for me?'

The envelope was addressed to Anna, so Eliza handed it over the moment her mother followed her into the small hall. For a split second she had considered opening it herself first and then claiming she hadn't noticed it was actually for Anna.

Her mother took the envelope and went up to her bedroom, leaving Eliza perplexed. She hadn't recognized the writing, but surely the letter must have come from Clifford. Who else knew her mother's address, though why write to Anna and not to her?

When her mother didn't come back down, Eliza thought she must have decided to have a nap and set about spring-cleaning the old attic, the place Anna had stored all sorts of unwanted stuff. Eliza didn't mind the dust or the scent of sandalwood, though it had never seemed so pungent before. She'd expected the childhood scents to have been stronger, the way that colour was once so bright, yet despite that, it did feel like one of those lonely summer days when she'd run up the stairs to crawl beneath a dustsheet while her mother went outside to drink. After a while she would stand on tiptoe to peer over the bottom of the tiny dormer window to watch. The fields opposite the house had seemed so wide, inhabited by stout farmhands rubbing the small of their back as they straightened up.

She glanced out at them – they were only small rectangular allotments now – then she moved aside a few rolls of wallpaper and shifted some of the boxes. At the back an old-fashioned leather trunk had been pushed against the wall. It had metal studs and two canvas belts wrapped around the middle. She squatted down to undo the buckles, the key turned, and the lid was lighter than it looked.

She didn't know what she had expected, except perhaps for the trunk to be full, but, surprised to see a small bottle of sandalwood oil, at least she'd found the source of the aroma. There was a suitcase inside the trunk. She lifted it out and picked up the bottle to sniff it. The aroma, stirring the memory of his skin, seemed to spread around her as if it were he who had been carried on the air. She hurriedly put the bottle back down. She had told herself she would get on with her life, get over the loss of Jay, learn how to live again, and that would be an end to it, but she couldn't erase her feelings so easily. At least while she remained with her mother she did not have to confront the reality of her impending marriage. And though she had tried so hard not to think about Jay, when she realized this little piece of India had lived inside the trunk all these years, once again it occurred to her that a hidden hand had taken her back to India. It had to have been for a reason. It couldn't all have been for nothing.

A luggage label pasted on the front of the case showed a grainy line drawing of a grand building and a name: *Imperial Hotel, Delhi*. Inside it something rectangular had been wrapped in white paper and tied with string. She undid the string, then tore the paper and pulled it off to reveal a framed photograph of two people with a small child, now faded and stained. She turned it over and saw the name of a photographic studio in Delhi.

Later she went to Anna's room, wanting to ask about the people in the picture. Her heart sank when she opened the door; the bedroom reeked of gin. Eliza went over to Anna. She stroked her mother's thinning dark hair away from her damp forehead – so different from her own thick hair – feeling such unbearable sadness. No longer judging her mother, she felt only pity. She glanced around to see what had happened to the letter, thinking something in it must have upset Anna, and soon spotted it in the bin, torn in two. She pieced it together and read that Clifford had informed Anna about his engagement to Eliza. She had hoped there might be some news of the explosion in Delhi. Not that Clifford would be likely to tell Anna what had happened to Jay, but he might have mentioned whether her prints and plates were safe or not.

By the time the afternoon had dragged on and the shadows outside were lengthening, she was thinking of making something for supper when she heard the hiss of breath.

'You're leaving.' It was a statement, not a question, and spoken in a slurred voice.

'Not yet, Mum. Not for –'

Her mother interrupted. 'You always go. It's what you do.'

'And what you do is drink. Why? Why now? I thought you were happier.'

She waited for a reply, but her mother just snorted and looked away.

'Mum?'

'I haven't been happy since you were five.'

'But that isn't my fault,' Eliza said, fearing all the old recriminations were starting again.

'You read the letter?'

Eliza nodded. 'I would have told you about the wedding.'

Anna pursed her lips before she replied. 'And yet I had to hear it from Clifford.'

'I'm sorry. Really.' She held out a hand to Anna but, when her mother did not take it, let it drop.

Her mother coughed weakly, then began to speak. 'You were only five years old when I found out about your father.'

'About the gambling?'

'The whore.'

'You said there was more. In your letter. What more, Mum?'

Anna shook her head and closed her eyes. When she didn't open them again it seemed as if she had fallen asleep. It was dark now and getting colder, so Eliza found an extra blanket for her and then went downstairs.

Two days later Anna had not recovered enough to come downstairs. Eliza cared for her mother, fussing over her by day and, at night, leaving both their bedroom doors open in case Anna might need her. And then one night Eliza heard her call out. Eliza grabbed her dressing gown and quickly went through.

She turned on the bedside lamp in time to see Anna shaking her head. A slow, sad little shake.

'I have a small post office account in Cheltenham. A trifling sum but it will be yours.'

'Never mind that now, Mum.'

Eliza gulped back the lump in her throat as she watched Anna open her eyes, say something else, and then close them again. She carried on mumbling but it was impossible to follow her words. Eliza had an awful flashback to all the other times when she had been drinking. She took a deep breath. This was different. The room was terribly quiet but for Anna's laboured breathing, and they remained mostly silent. But then Anna groaned, drew her brows together and flapped her hands.

'Can I get you something, Mum?'

Anna smiled lopsidedly and when she spoke her voice was thin, more air than sound. Eliza tried to comfort her, but her mother just stared and then her eyes filled up.

'I did something wrong.'

'Please don't upset yourself. What does it matter now – ?'

'It matters.' She paused as the tears spilled over.

Not understanding, Eliza wasn't too sure what to say.

Anna brushed the tears away and tapped her hand, but then began to cough and was unable to speak for another moment or two. When she did, her eyes were fierce and her face had changed. Eliza's heart lost a beat as she saw a trace of Anna's old anger, but it was over in moments and all that was left was her hollow eyes and paper-thin skin. It was becoming harder to remember her any other way.

Anna grasped her hand and was trying to smile, but her eyes were red and watery. 'Please. It's too late for me, but if you . . .'

There was a short silence as Eliza attempted to figure out what she meant.

Anna began to cough again and Eliza held a glass of water to her lips. After she had taken a sip she made a small sound, not quite a cry, more like the whimper of a frightened animal, and then spoke again. 'You might put it right.'

'I don't understand?'

Anna took a breath, managed not to cough, and then spoke in an urgent, breathy voice. 'I want you to find your sister.'

Eliza's mouth literally fell open. Her sister? She didn't have a sister. There had only been the two of them for as long as she could remember. Surely she wasn't serious? She glanced at Anna, who had now fallen asleep and whose breath was very faint. Eliza watched for a few minutes and then crept downstairs.

Later Eliza brought down the bottle of perfumed oil to fragrance the room, but the smell of sickness hung in the air.

315

And when her mother smelt the oil she began to weep, so Eliza took it out and put it in the shed where it could upset no one.

She tried to ask about the sister she'd mentioned, but Anna seemed to have forgotten all about it, and so all Eliza could do was watch her mother looking at her as if she did not know who she was. Then out of the blue she whispered, 'Half-sister. Found her in the house once, dirty little thing.' After that she was too far away to say more and, as Eliza sat holding her hand, she watched her mother's life being erased.

Then, with no particular warning, and while Eliza was out of the room making a cup of tea, Anna's heart stopped beating. She was just sixty. Eliza stifled a sob and held her hand. Then she half sang, half sobbed one of her favourite childhood songs to her dead mother. After that she wept like she had never wept before. It had all been too late and now there could be no going back.

31

India, July

Armed only with the little photograph she had found, Eliza returned to India. She had been away for just over two months, though it felt like a lifetime. The house had not belonged to Anna, so once the death had been registered and the sad little funeral was over, Eliza no longer had a reason to stay.

To begin with she checked into the Imperial in Delhi and tried to track down the photographic studio where the photo she'd found had been taken. Sadly it was long gone, and Eliza wondered if she'd ever discover whether her mother had simply been delirious or if she had been telling the truth about the half-sister. The one thing that almost convinced her was that the man in the picture had a look of her father, though not at all the way she remembered him.

After Calcutta and Delhi she travelled on to Juraipore, where Clifford met her at the station. She asked him about the explosion in Delhi and was told that Jay had recovered from his injuries. She was immensely grateful for the news and thanked him for his kindness. But the heat was shocking and, although already pink, he flushed scarlet and she felt a little bit sorry for him. She had promised to try to love him but knew instantaneously that she never could. Before he delivered her to Julian and Dottie, he also explained that Eliza's prints and plates had not been lost in the explosion. Apart from one batch, they had already been sent back to him in Juraipore when the explosion happened. She breathed a huge sigh of relief, but when he kissed her she struggled to find a way to lock out all thoughts of further intimacy. With the smells of Rajputana rising unbidden in her nostrils, she managed better in shutting out her feelings of grief over Anna's death. It was all she knew to do, and yet she couldn't prevent a growing feeling of hopelessness.

The busy first couple of days at the doctor's house were passed in a small cocktail gathering, a tea party, and an evening of bridge. After that, as it was so hot, they did not go out, and though Eliza gave the illusion of functioning well, for her it seemed as if the very foundations of her life were being slowly eroded. Before long she almost forgot the smell of English moisture in the air and gave herself up to the dry air of the desert.

One morning, hot and feverish, she woke with a terrifying image in her head of herself as a red ball of fire encircled by a golden cage of flames. She began to sob and the doctor's wife heard her.

Dottie was motherly, although she had no children. She clucked over her husband and now she clucked over Eliza too. It was well intended, but Eliza longed to clap her hands over her ears and yell at her to go away and leave her alone. It wasn't really fair, as Dottie had always been kindness itself, but Eliza wanted to drown in her sorrow, not be comforted out of it. And though Dottie did her best to persuade Eliza to get dressed and come downstairs, Eliza turned her face to the wall, with silent rage consuming her.

A little later she heard the heavy tread of footsteps from the landing and then a light tapping on her door. She wanted it to be Jay and for one mad moment hoped that it was, and quickly sat up in her bed. When Clifford came in, she sank back down again and refused to look at him.

'Come on, darling,' he said. 'I'm so happy you're home but this really won't do.'

She didn't reply. Didn't even move a muscle.

'The Viceroy will be passing through next week. I really will need you in tip-top condition.'

She rolled towards him and opened her eyes. 'I'm not a bloody horse, Clifford.'

She could see the exasperation in his eyes but could do nothing about it. She wondered if he might know anything about a sister, but when she raised the subject he just looked blank and said Anna must have been delirious. There was nobody left to ask, so Eliza felt inclined to let it lie.

She put up with his wet kisses and luckily he expected no more, but when she thought of what was to come she felt sick. Every time he asked her to set the date she made an excuse. Too close to her mother's death. Too hot. Too late in the year.

When she wasn't feeling the slicing pain of being parted from Jay, she thought of her mother, crushed by life, and at the end a broken woman. It was unbearably sad. But then she wondered if her mother had ever really glowed with inner light. Had she ever been happy? If she had, was it David Fraser who had snuffed the light out, and had she herself been dazzled by her father and never really considered her mother?

A half-sister?

The words frequently slipped into her mind, leaving her restless. Another day passed and then another. On the following morning Eliza went into the bathroom, leant against the wash-hand basin and stared into the mirror. She gazed at her ashen skin and her lank hair and saw that the changes were not an improvement. She ran a bath and, afterwards, her spirits picked up.

The bedroom had been heavily curtained and Dottie had left it that way once Eliza claimed the light hurt her eyes. But now Dottie marched in carrying a box. 'Now, Eliza,' she said. 'This is for you, but first I am going to open the curtains. It's stuffy in here and you need light and air.'

Eliza glanced at the only shard of light visible in a small gap between the curtains; it stung like a knife in her eyes and she turned her back.

'I don't care,' Dottie said. 'Turn away if you must, but I am airing this room.'

Eliza heard the sound of the curtains being pulled back and saw light flooding the room.

Dottie came over to her. 'You've washed your hair.'

'Yes.'

'That's a start.' She patted Eliza's hand. 'Let's open the box.'

They sat on a small two-seater sofa by the window overlooking the garden. 'It's from Clifford,' Dottie said in a neutral-sounding voice.

Eliza opened the box, then a leather case inside it, and was surprised to find a new Leica Model C, 'Schraubgewinde', complete with a matched set of lenses and also a separate rangefinder that could be attached to the top of the camera.

'Isn't that thoughtful,' Dottie said. 'You could do a lot worse than Clifford.'

Eliza blinked rapidly and felt a glimmer of excitement. A new camera might make all the difference. 'But this would have cost the earth. I just can't believe it.'

'I know he's not the love of your life,' Dottie continued, 'but surely this proves how much he cares for you.'

'How do you know he is not the love of my life?'

'Darling, you told me, remember? Anyway, it's in the eyes. Always in the eyes. I've been there too, in my way.'

Startled by such an intimate confession, Eliza stared at her friend.

'Don't look at me like that,' Dottie said. 'He was a lowly non-commissioned fellow in the British Army, a Londoner, totally unsuitable . . . but I loved him.'

'I'm not judging you. How could I?'

'I don't usually tell many people this, so I trust you not to spread it around, but I became pregnant. The shame was destroying my mother, so I agreed to marry Julian.'

'And the baby?' Eliza asked, feeling uncertain.

'I miscarried.'

'I'm so sorry.' There was a moment's silence. 'You never had another?'

'Don't feel pity for me. For a long time I felt dead inside, but Julian and I have been happy since and I truly love him.'

'Would it be terribly impertinent to ask, why no children?'

'I'm afraid Julian can't.'

'Did you know that when you married him?'

Dottie shook her head, and her eyes filled with tears. Eliza put an arm around the older woman's shoulders. 'You know, when I was in England my mother muttered something about me having a half-sister.'

'Really? Have you any idea who?'

'None. I don't even know if it was true.'

'Well then,' Dottie said. 'Let me be your sister.'

They were sitting like that, both looking tearful, when Clifford came in.

'Goodness, Dottie, I hope you have not caught this crying disease of Eliza's,' he said.

Eliza pretended to laugh, while Dottie rubbed her tears away with her hands.

'Don't be ridiculous, Clifford,' Eliza said. 'There's nothing wrong with Dottie.'

'So? Like the camera?'

Eliza got to her feet and came across to him.

'I love it. Exactly the right make and model. Thank you.' And Clifford, looking pleased, gave her a peck on the cheek.

The camera turned out to be just what Eliza needed. Straight away she took photos of Dottie's beautiful garden, of the house, of Dottie herself, and then pleaded with Clifford for a servant to assist her when she went into town to explore the old city. There she took photographs of faces, flowers, food, of anything she could see. She thought she spotted Indi, but when the person turned it was not the girl; however, it only made her more determined to go back to the castle for her equipment.

One afternoon she wandered about aimlessly, then sat quietly in Dottie's garden bathed in sunshine, wondering how to broach the subject of visiting the castle to arrange the return of her belongings. When Clifford came striding towards her with a wide grin on his face she realized she should have chosen to sit in one of the wicker armchairs.

He sat down beside her on the bench but didn't speak. She watched him for a few moments, steadying herself by holding her hands together in her lap and managing to avoid shifting away from him.

'Well,' she said. 'What is it? You are clearly itching to tell me something.'

'Indeed, I am,' he said, and she faltered under his direct

gaze. 'The thing is, old girl, I've gone ahead and set the date.'

'Oh,' she said, and looked at her feet while rearranging the folds of her skirt. When she attempted to think of something else to say, her mind went blank.

'You don't sound very happy. I thought you'd be pleased.'

She blinked away the heat rising in her eyes and breathed slowly and deeply. He knew perfectly well she had been delaying and, if he didn't, he was even more thick-skinned than she had previously thought. She recalled how she had once thought he might be a sensitive man; how wrong she had been.

He was still waiting for an answer, so she looked up, but not at him, and seeing so clearly the vision of Jay in her mind's eye it was painful. The attraction couldn't be explained by reason alone, and it wasn't just that Jay was handsome and intelligent, it was his sensitivity too. The way he engaged with her, as if whatever she might say was of infinite interest to him.

'When?' she eventually said.

'October. Should be cooler weather by then. Not this damn, god-forsaken heat.'

'Where?'

'Here in Juraipore.'

Not here. Not right under Jay's nose! She fought to conceal her horror and, realizing that she had been twisting her hands in her lap, now stilled them. 'So soon?'

'We are not getting any younger and if we are to hear the patter of little feet . . . well, the sooner we start practising the better.'

He reddened and she tried to pretend she hadn't seen it by closing her eyes. It was July, so that meant she only had three months. As she thought that, the vision of Jay grew in intensity.

'I was hoping to be a photographer for a little longer. Before having children, I mean,' she said in a calm voice, as if it was a perfectly ordinary thing to suggest.

'Eliza, you are thirty now. We can't realistically put it off. So no, I think not.'

Her eyes shot open. 'But I was thinking of taking photographs all over the world. Paris or London at the very least.'

He reached out and grabbed her hand. 'You are not listening. I said no. You will be a wife and mother, and an eminently capable one at that. Rest assured it will keep you fully occupied.' He patted her hand and let it go. 'Best keep the photography for a hobby, there's a girl.'

Eliza got to her feet and feeling the steel inside her looked at him full on. 'If I am to marry you, Clifford, we need to get one thing clear. I will not be ordered to do, or not to do, anything. And tomorrow I am going to the castle to retrieve my belongings. I trust you will allow me a car, or would you prefer if I went by a camel with a pull cart? It's how I arrived, after all.'

She took a few steps away and heard him stand to come after her, but when she twisted back to look she saw that he had walked the other way and was leaving the garden.

When Chatur met her at the top of the long ramp leading to the main gate, all the words she had been practising flew from her mind. As he took a step towards her he waved a few sheets of blackened photographic paper, the type she used for her contact prints.

She frowned. 'What's this? Why is it black?' He held up his darkened fingertips and passed her the paper.

She sniffed. 'Why has it been burned?'

He displayed a sorrowful face. 'I am desolate. There was a fire.'

It was fire she smelt, but more than that she smelt lies and deception too. 'I don't believe you,' she said. 'Where?'

'Darkroom went up in flames and so did your bedroom.'

'You mean all my equipment and all my clothes?' Eliza spoke in a thin, hard voice, as if all the air had been punched out of her.

'Burned to a cinder.' He shook his head. 'Terrible pity.'

Eliza narrowed her eyes, tilting her head to one side so that he knew she doubted him, then wiped away the sweat beading at her hairline as the distress inside her worsened.

'When was this?' she asked.

Once again he gave her a sorrowful look. 'Only last night, and here you are the following morning. So close and yet so far. Such a pity.'

There was nothing to be gained from further argument, but something calculating about his eyes hardened her resolve. Unable to think of an adequate reply, her jaw stiffened. She glanced up at the mighty castle, then she turned her back on Chatur and climbed back into the car without saying goodbye.

Back at Dottie's house her resolve faded. It seemed that every time she climbed out of the well of despair something pushed her back down. She closed her eyes, picturing the depths of a real well. In Rajputana dark dank wells had been used for suicides as well as murders, and probably still were. It was enough to shake her out of the panicky moment, but still she felt shredded. Without her equipment and without her clothes, all she had was the remains of Oliver's nest egg, the monthly sums she had saved and the small savings fund her mother had left in a secure post office in Cheltenham. Hardly a fortune.

She felt so angry and frustrated she swore and stamped about her bedroom at Dottie's. Breathlessly hot and not knowing how to rid herself of such fury, she lay prostrate, face down on her bed, and thumped the pillow, wishing it was that devil Chatur.

Dottie must have heard her, because she came in and squatted down beside the bed. Eliza turned over to look at her and Dottie smiled encouragingly and asked what all the noise was about. Eliza flared at her. 'The bastards have destroyed all my equipment.'

'Who?'

'Chatur and the castle. They burned everything. I didn't believe it at first, but it is exactly the sort of thing they do. Well, Chatur would. I just don't understand how they knew I'd be going up there today.'

'My dear, maybe Clifford phoned to let them know you'd be going. You know . . . trying to help. Anyway, you can buy more equipment, can't you?'

Eliza shook her head, then added, 'My clothes have gone up in flames too. I only have these few things.' She pointed at the wardrobe.

Dottie smiled conspiratorially. 'No need for despair. Just get up and follow me.'

Eliza was puzzled, but she did what Dottie asked. The two women left Eliza's room and went through to a small room at the back of the house.

'What's this?' Eliza asked, looking round.

'The clothes in here are too small for me. I have put on a bit this last year or so. Such a shame, as one or two are really quite lovely. Try on as many as you wish and then take whichever ones fit.'

'You're sure?'

'I am unlikely ever to be so slim again. Most aren't very old, so you won't find them out of date.'

'We are roughly the same height, aren't we?' Eliza said.

'I may be a fraction taller, but we can take them up if need be.'

By the end of an hour Eliza was feeling sweaty but pleased to have picked out three blouses, two skirts and two dresses. Unfortunately, Dottie had no trousers, but anything else they could probably find in the heat-drenched bazaars. Dottie promised to send one of the Indian maids with Eliza so that if she wanted to buy Indian clothing at the bazaar the maid would pretend it was for her to keep the price down.

And this is exactly what they did. After two hours in the jungle of the bazaar and although the heat had been excruciating, Eliza managed to find everything she needed. Though the streets stank of fish and drains, she had enjoyed herself and, as they returned to Dottie's at the end of the day, the sky glowed bright pink before the sun finally disappeared completely.

32

Eliza and Dottie were absorbed in rearranging the library when they heard a rap at the front door. Though still early, a small fan already shifted the air and set the dust motes dancing in streams of sunlight. Even at this hour the heat was unbearable, and Dottie had explained that just before the rains, with no relief to be had, everyone turned crotchety.

'I'll go,' Dottie said, as she wiped her hands on her apron then stuffed it behind a cushion.

Eliza raised her brows.

Dottie smiled. 'Well, you never know.'

While Dottie was in the hall Eliza gazed out of the window at the giant peepal tree in the garden. She longed to be sitting beneath its shade and yet she knew that even the shade gave little relief when the air had become so dry it sucked the moisture from you.

A few minutes later Dottie returned, holding out a small white envelope. 'For you,' she said. 'From the castle.'

Eliza took it and as she held it in her hand she stared, aware of an unsettling sense of foreboding.

'Aren't you going to open it?' Dottie said with an inquisitive look.

'I . . . yes, of course. It's just . . .'

'Just what?'

'I'm probably being silly.' Once she had torn open the envelope, she drew out a single sheet of paper. As she read it she was aware that her legs had begun to shake. She sat down abruptly and read through again, but still couldn't quite take it in.

'Bad news?' Dottie asked, clearly curious.

'I'm not sure.'

'So tell me.'

Eliza hesitated, unsure whether to reveal the contents or not. Then after a moment she spoke. There was nothing to be gained from lying. 'Jay wants to see me. He's at a camp somewhere or other.'

Dottie paled and took a seat close to Eliza. 'Is that a good idea?'

Eliza shook her head.

'What does he actually say?'

Eliza passed the note to Dottie, who read it and then glanced up. 'How presumptuous! He thinks you will just drop everything.'

Eliza nodded. 'I can't go.'

'No.'

There was a long silence. Dottie was the first to speak again. She gazed at Eliza and gave her a half smile. 'You can't not go either, can you?'

Eliza hung her head, too full of mixed emotions to reply.

'So?' Dottie said. 'From what he says here . . .' She tapped the note, then handed it back to Eliza. 'You only have an hour before the car arrives to collect you.'

'I can't. Clifford would be furious.'

'Yes.'

'You'll hate me. You'll all hate me.'

'I would never do that. You're the first real friend I've made in Rajputana. I was so looking forward to you living next door, but I do understand, you know. I've seen you with Clifford: seen you shrink from his touch, even though you do your best to hide it.'

Eliza felt ashamed, but even his voice grated on her. She chewed the inside of her cheek before she spoke. 'If I go and Jay doesn't want me?'

'It's a risk. You should go, but if you decide you want to come back you must end it with Jay. Irrevocably. I am not being unkind but you have to make a decision and stick to it.'

Eliza got to her feet at the same time as Dottie, and the two women embraced.

'You've been very kind to me, Dottie.'

Dottie grinned. 'I'll always be here. And, in the meantime, I'll tell Clifford you have gone away for a little break with a friend of mine.'

As the sun rose higher in the sky, Eliza left to go to Jay. What would happen she didn't know, but not to go would be like turning her back on herself. During the journey images of him seared her mind and left her jumpy, the feelings of anticipation not quite overriding the fear that he might not even be there.

She wound down the window and a beggar smiled at her, so she threw some rupees out of the window for him and it seemed like an auspicious thing to happen. She smiled at herself. Was she already turning native, as the Brits would say? If she was, she didn't care. She felt free, the blood singing in her veins. Wonderfully, thrillingly native, that's what I'll be, she whispered, and the words bubbled about in her head until she became quite dizzy.

The feeling of nervous anticipation continued as they

passed a string of camels on their way out of a village. Further on she spotted farmers and young boys driving their bullocks onwards. Her driver carried on through villages of mud huts with thatched roofs, and it was only then that the doubts crept in. Eliza slapped at a mosquito whining around her face and her forehead felt hot to the touch. Too hot. What had she been thinking? Jay had clicked his fingers and she had come running. And now another voice was in her head. Her mother berating her, telling her not to be so stupid. But this was not a mere rap on the knuckles, but something much, much worse, and it went far deeper, back to the edgy discomfort of days when mothers were to be treated with caution and fathers were never to return.

Today her mind was a place of shadows, but as a scorching wind blew dust and flies in her eyes, Eliza snapped out of it. She wanted the sunlight, and more than anything she wanted to stand tall with Jay for all the world to see.

She also wanted to be like the woman she'd met in Paris, whose goal was to be a photographer, and while Eliza had understood she might one day marry she didn't feel as if she'd achieved enough. She didn't know how or when, but the fact remained that she still had to get her equipment back from the castle in order to see how much of it really had been ruined. And, whatever was to happen with Jay, she might still be able to mount her exhibition at the Imperial Hotel, even if she had to scale it down and do it alone.

The heat, leaden and unrelenting, was exhausting, but she kept a fixed smile on her face. The first sign they were nearing their destination was hazy smoke hanging motionless in the dazzling blue sky. She whooshed away a swarm of flies, then smelt burning charcoal and the sweet tantalizing aroma of roasting meat.

When the camp finally came into sight, she experienced the first signs of genuine apprehension: a racing heart and sweaty palms. The simple beauty of the desert shone, but an extraordinary striped red and silver tent had been erected and was now surrounded by a dozen flaming torches. Was this especially for her, or had he been planning to camp like this anyway? Was she central to this scenario or was she not?

She glanced around to see if she could spot Jay anywhere, but all she saw was a great burst of birds rising into the sky above the tent. For Eliza it was a moment of crushing disappointment. Perhaps he was still to arrive, she thought, as the driver helped her out and then carried her case in the direction of the tent. 'Wait,' she called out. 'I'll take it inside.'

'Your room is on the right,' the man said.

She was surprised. She had no idea tents could accommodate more than one room, but this was so large. The tent's flap had been pinned back and she parted the light muslin curtains at the entrance and found herself in a small vestibule. Fancy that, she thought, a tent with a hall! Then she drew aside a heavier curtain on the right and entered the room that was to be hers.

The whole of the interior was curtained in swathes of ruby-coloured silk, all gathered together at the top of the tent, rather like an old-fashioned circus tent might have been. But it was the bed that caught her eye. The frame was painted in gold and the bedspread and cushions were silver. Rose petals had been strewn over the bed and surrounding floor, which was carpeted in the most beautiful woven kilims she had ever seen. There was even a chaise longue, an armchair, a small table and a dressing table in there too.

She sat on the bed feeling amazed, but also a little bewildered. The room was fragranced, and as she sniffed the air she realized that there were oil burners in two corners and that it was rose and some kind of sweet orange she could smell. The whole thing was almost unbelievable. She thought of the simple picnic she had enjoyed with her mother and wished Anna could have witnessed this. And yet, as she continued to sit on the edge of the bed, she shivered with unease. Why had Jay brought her here? Maybe the note hadn't even been from him?

She heard a slight rustle and looked up. An unsmiling Jay stood silently just inside her room. An image of his hands moving fluidly over her body flashed in her mind and she felt a stirring within her. But he seemed as remote as the sun in an English midwinter and she blinked to stem the tears. What was he thinking? Why didn't he speak?

'So, you have recovered from the explosion?' she said, rather nervously.

He raised his brows.

'I mean, I heard you were well. Was it a bomb?'

Now he frowned. 'So we are to speak of bombs, are we? Maybe we might next move on to the weather?'

She twisted her mouth, unable to comprehend the meaning of his light sarcasm, then swallowed hard and met his gaze. There had been a time when she would have laid down her life for a glimpse of those black-lashed amber eyes; now it was all she could do not to shrink back.

'Eliza, why did you stay away? I had to hear where you were from my sister-in-law.'

'Priya told you?'

'She never misses a chance to assert her superiority, or to show she has access to private information. But Eliza, I tried to contact you.'

'I am sorry.'

'Never mind *sorry*. Tell me why.'

She sighed deeply and wished she could tell him about her deal with Clifford. Longed to say I did it because I love you. I did it for you.

It was still far too hot and she wiped the sweat from her brow. 'I am marrying Clifford in October,' she said, but she couldn't bear to look at Jay as she spoke.

He took a few steps towards her and she smelt the sandal-wood on his skin. It was unbearably evocative, but when he answered it was with an edge of anger. 'Is that all I meant to you, all we meant to one another? Damn it, Eliza, how could you?'

Eliza hated to waste these precious moments with him, yet, remaining silent and in torment, she became aware she was doing exactly that.

'Very well,' he said. 'I will be back tomorrow and when I am back I will arrange for your return to your fiancé.'

He almost hurled the words at her.

'In the meantime there is a handmaiden to help you.' And with that he left.

Eliza lay back on the bed and realized that the roof of the tent right above her bed was patterned with silver stars. She rolled on to her tummy and allowed the tears to fall. What was the matter with her? She had come this far because she loved him and now all she had done was turn him away. But the truth was that unless she actually broke off her engage-ment to Clifford she was not a free woman and, though not one to be bound by convention, she could not be so reckless or unfeeling. But what if Jay had gone for good? The idea of that brought on fresh tears.

She tried to tell herself she was fortunate to have known him; he had been in her life, however briefly, and she would find a way to treasure that by keeping the memory of him locked safely away. So what if they could never be together – she had known love and many had not; and yet when she thought about it, how well had she known him? How much was really him and how much was who she thought he was? Maybe it didn't matter. For, as long as she could recall his deep smoky voice, she would always have some part of him. He was the only man she had loved, apart from her father, and she could still feel her love for David Fraser no matter what he had done. She would never forget Jay's wild imperfect love, nor her galloping heart when he was near. She would never speak of it, never defend herself, and she'd learn how to live without him.

When the handmaiden came in, Eliza saw at once that it was Kiri.

'Madam.' The woman gave the usual palms-together greeting.

'Kiri, I am so happy to see you,' she said and stifled her distress.

Kiri came across and knelt on the floor beside the bed. 'Give me your hands, memsahib.'

'Oh, please don't call me that.'

'What should I say?'

'Eliza?'

The woman gave her a wry smile. 'I cannot. Will madam do?'

Eliza smiled despite herself. 'That will do nicely.'

'Let me bathe you and wash your hair. It will make you feel better.'

'Where?'

Kiri rose and pointed to one of the lengths of curtain that enveloped the room. 'We are having a bathroom. Come.' Eliza followed Kiri into a spacious bathroom with a polished metal tub, an earthen toilet and a carpeted floor. On a small table a heap of fluffy cushions lay ready, along with some towels.

'We will make you beautiful.'

'I am not sure that will help me now, but I'm feeling exhausted and maybe a bath will help.'

'Madam, it has been terrible at the castle since you are gone. He has been, how do you say, a bear with two heads.'

Sensitive to her own embarrassment, Eliza nevertheless asked, 'What do you think he feels for me?'

The woman laughed. 'You don't know?'

Eliza shook her head.

'If anyone mentions your name he leaves the room. If his mother speaks of a marriage to a distant Princess he roars at her. You only have to look at his face, madam. You see it there.'

As Kiri tenderly soaped and then oiled her skin, Eliza closed her eyes. And then, after her hair was cleansed of desert dust, Kiri went to the bathroom and came back with a beautiful blue-green silk robe that matched Eliza's eyes, and a pair of embroidered slippers.

She then indicated a spot on the opposite side of the bedroom.

'I am to go through there, Kiri?'

'Yes, madam, I cannot follow.' She lowered her eyes.

Eliza took a step forward. She should have expected it,

but it was only then that she realized Jay had not gone away and that he would be waiting for her on the other side of the curtain. She paused and glanced back at Kiri again, but the woman did not look up.

Eliza drew the curtain aside and, treading softly, went through. As she took in his side of the tent – the deep midnight blue embroidered with threads of copper – she didn't see Jay. The floor had been carpeted in blue but paler than the silk of the tent and, as she looked down, she saw his feet. He'd been standing just the other side of a tall wardrobe of some kind, its dark velvet curtains restricting her view. But as her eyes adjusted to the gloom – only candles and oil lamps lit the room – she saw him step forward.

'It's dusk now,' he said. 'I can turn up the lamps if you like.'

She shook her head. 'I can see.'

There was a prolonged silence as they stared at each other. Then he came across and she allowed him to lead her to a bed heaped with cushions.

'We'll just sit together. Is that all right?' he asked in a deeply choked voice.

It was a low bed and as they both adjusted their cushions neither spoke. Despite his dignity she could sense a gentle sadness in him that only served to amplify her own.

Once they were in a semi-supine position he reached for her hand.

'You didn't go?' she said.

Silence.

'Jay?'

He sighed deeply and then turned to her. 'Look at me, Eliza.'

She shifted her position so that she could turn her head and look at him full on. The grief in his eyes almost floored her, and feeling her tears welling she held on to herself.

Then as they gazed at each other, he smiled. 'Tell me the truth, sweetheart. For pity's sake, why?'

'Clifford?'

He nodded wordlessly, but it was the intensity of his eyes that loosened her tongue. She realized she was incapable of lying to Jay and that, now she was with him, she was dropping back into a place where she could be more truly herself.

'He promised to release you from prison with complete immunity from future charges.'

'If you consented to marry him?'

She nodded. 'In his defence, it really was your mother's idea. Please don't be angry with her,' she added when she saw his jaw stiffen. 'She suggested it to protect you, Jay.'

'Very well. If that's what you believe happened, let's talk about something else. I have seen Devdan. He admitted Chatur approached him to ask for his help in framing me over the incendiary pamphlets.'

'Why would Dev agree to that?'

'There were reasons.'

'Like what?'

'Eliza, I really can't say.'

She shrugged. 'And you don't feel betrayed?'

'I think Dev was placed in a difficult position.' He gave her a wry smile. 'Although there was also an inducement he couldn't resist. Chatur promised him a typewriter and a licence.'

'Oh God!'

'Chatur was actually behind it all. He had been wanting to get me out of the way for months, so he manipulated Dev.'

Eliza felt sick. 'I knew Chatur was cunning. But what about Dev?'

'I don't know. Truly. Up until now he's been a good friend. We have talked.'

'How can you be so blind? He's capable of anything.'

'It's his father who was like that, not Dev.'

'What did his father do?'

Jay shook his head. 'All I can tell you is that, whatever Dev's father did, it wasn't good.'

'So what will happen to Chatur?'

'Anish is exploring his options.'

'That's all?' she asked incredulously.

'For the time being. Now I want you to rest, eat and sleep and hopefully clear your head.'

But there was something else pressing on her mind.

'You know we can't sleep together while I am still engaged?'

He put a finger to his lips. 'Don't talk. Let's just lie here until it's time to eat.'

For two days the heat was devastating, and during that time they talked until it was even too hot for that, and then they lay side by side, indolent but not touching, Jay on his back with his hands clasped behind his head and her curled up nearby. The hours blurred together, filled with formless feelings for which there were no words.

'What is this?' she said, when they had been silent for some time.

He looked at her for a while. 'It's you and me. Need it be more?'

'It's so different. I don't know.'

'Do we have to call it anything?'

'I don't know that either.'

And then Jay told her the water project was almost finished and he had left it in the hands of a very regretful Dev. Eliza worried about Dev's apparent reformation, but when she questioned Jay he assured her that Dev would do nothing to harm the project. He also told her that the Delhi explosion she had witnessed had been caused by an old oil lamp left burning. It had set fire to badly stored chemicals, so there hadn't been a terrorist attack after all. Eliza was glad. It really would be too much to have witnessed two bombs, both in Delhi, the latter a shocking echo of the first.

They slept separately, each in their own section of the tent, but on the second night when she heard him moving around it was agony not to go through to him. In the hot stillness of the night she stiffened her resolve, and put up with excruciating longing. In the middle of the night she went out to look at the stars and saw the fire still lit and shining like a beacon in the darkness of the desert. She knew it was to keep wild animals at bay, and felt the crunch of earth beneath her feet as she quickly went back inside.

On the third morning she was sitting cross-legged by the fire, feeling deprived of sleep and waiting for coffee, when he came out, still in his robe. His skin glowed from the light of the fire and his hair was still wet from his bath, but she could see the fatigue in the dark shadows beneath his eyes. He hasn't been sleeping either, she thought.

As he squatted beside her the top of his robe fell open and she almost, but not quite, reached out to touch his chest. She wanted to feel his heartbeat connecting with hers and feel again the way his breath seemed to be hers and hers his, as it had once been before . . . Instead she asked him how

340

much of her equipment had been damaged by the fire at the castle.

He looked puzzled.

'Chatur told me a fire had destroyed my darkroom and my bedroom.'

'I have heard nothing about a fire. I would have been told.'

'So he duped me,' Eliza said.

'Sounds like Chatur.'

'Well,' she said, feeling her heart falter, but then, with her feelings under control, she carried on speaking. 'I have decided to write to Clifford.'

Neither of them had mentioned her engagement since she'd told Jay the truth, but it had been there all the time; a dark shadow they couldn't fully ignore.

'And?' he said, and she saw his eyes light up with hope. He's vulnerable too, she thought, despite all that strength and masculinity.

'The engagement. I'm going to break it off. Is there a rider who could deliver the letter?'

'I have just the man. He will go today.'

Eliza couldn't resist Jay's happy response and smiled at him. 'So leave me alone for an hour and it will be done.'

Once he'd gone she began to write and an extraordinary sense of hope filled her heart. The monsoon was nearing; she could feel it in the air and in her blood. Thank God. She didn't think she could bear the heat much longer and the rains would be such a blessed relief.

He came into the tent after the allotted time, but now with another man.

'Ready?'

She gave him a slight nod. 'Here it is.'

341

'This man will take it,' Jay said. 'And he'll let your friend Dottie know that you are safe.'

She smiled broadly as he took her hand.

'Now we must hurry. They need to pack up the camp before the rains and we – my lovely Englishwoman – we are headed for Udaipore.'

33

Udaipore

The leaden heat had been relentless but now, on their way to Udaipore, it was clear rain was imminent and the advancing storm was gathering momentum. The sky had darkened and, for the first time since she had come to India, back in November, Eliza saw the heavens become suddenly wild with movement as a mass of dark clouds swirled and billowed. It was exciting. New. Different. She wished she had her camera to catch the sight of dark, strangely lit clouds sliding over the distant Aravalli hills. And, at the first sign of a violent crash of thunder, Eliza felt her blood electrify as she rode behind Jay on his motorbike in the direction of the rains.

'What if it pours before we get there?' she shouted.

'We get wet!'

She laughed and, delirious with the joy of being close to him again, breathed his scent of sandalwood and limes. So much had happened before the rains, and here was another new chapter about to open up ahead of her just as the sky was about to open up too.

As they neared Udaipore, Eliza's level of expectation rose even further. She had longed to see the romantic city of lakes surrounded by the Aravalli hills stretching in multiple directions and now she would. Breaths of hot wind ruffled the grasses and, though dying to clap her hands and leap like a child, she had to hold tight to Jay. Eventually they reached a fortress appearing to rise out of the hilltop, as these places so often did. Jay pulled up, climbed down, and then helped her off. As she steadied herself she gazed at the archways, turrets and domes of the fort.

'This is the only place to really see the monsoon,' Jay said.

She looked down and could hardly contain her amazement when she saw a palace appearing to float on the mirror-like lake, the romance of its location utterly enchanting.

'Have you actually been inside the lake palace?' she asked, as if it might be an impossible thing that anyone might go there, that in fact it was real and solid.

He raised his brows as if to say, *Of course, what else would you expect?*

After gazing at the breath-taking panoramic view of the city and its surroundings, their small bags were taken inside and he escorted her to a covered pavilion with huge arches and columns, behind which the fort's palace lay.

'We will watch from here,' he said, as the first drops of rain began to fall.

'This is the start?' Eliza asked, and held out her hands to catch the first drops.

'It may be.'

The billowing clouds had now turned the most extraordinary shade of purple, and then, all at once, lightning filled the entire sky. It made her jolt and she held out a hand to him.

'Wonderful, isn't it?' he said.

'I can hardly believe a place like this could really exist.'

He laughed and squeezed her hand. She leant back against him and could feel his heart against her back.

'The entire place is surrounded by forests, lakes and, as

you can see, the hills. When the rain ceases I'll show you the lanes and alleyways of the old city.'

'The lake palace looks as if it has stepped out of the pages of a fairy tale.'

'It's the Royal Summer Palace.'

'Can we swim? After the rains?'

'If you don't mind the odd crocodile.'

One moment there were only a few drops of rain, but then they heard an almighty crash of thunder so loud it seemed as if the world shook with fright. And only then did the heavens open. Sheets of rain hammered down upon the town below them, smashing on to the lake, and everywhere the dry earth began to release an incredible aroma of long-held sweetness. She heard Jay speak but could not make out his words above the tumult.

They stood and watched for another hour, the rain still falling as if the storm might consume all the water in the world, and the sky still flashing continually. Soon the air had turned white with a curtain of rain so thick it obliterated the view of the town, the lake, and the palace. Only when the thunder ceased did he turn her round. Now that dusk was falling and with the depth of the rain she could barely see his face, but for his glittering eyes.

'Are you ready?' he asked. 'This is just a lull.'

'Yes. Let's go.'

As he led her back into the palace Eliza asked where the owner was and did he mind them being there.

'He's an old friend, and don't worry, it's all arranged.'

'You knew I'd come?'

'I hoped.'

Once they reached their room she took in an enormous four-poster bed, its curtains still open.

'Do you want to close them?' he asked.

She shook her head and walked over to the wide windows. 'Let's keep these curtains open too,' she said.

'And the windows open so that we can still hear –'

She laughed. 'You are such a romantic, Jayant Singh Rathore.'

'Is that a bad thing?'

She ran to him and flung her arms around his neck. He pulled her off him and led her away from the window towards the bed. When she lay back against the pillows he pulled up her skirt and then rolled down her stockings, his fingers touching her legs as he went. 'Silk?' he said.

'My only pair. Dottie gave them to me.' But she could not contain her laughter; as if the joy in her whole being had been long suppressed and now it had no option but to burst from her, taking her over, and making her shake and shudder. He laughed too, and before long she was laughing and crying at the same time and he was drying her tears. When she finally stopped he finished undressing her, then stared at her.

'So, so pale,' he said, 'like porcelain.'

Filled with the intoxication of the night, she was conscious of feeling released, from what she wasn't sure, but it was wonderful and like nothing she had ever experienced before.

'My turn, to undress you,' she said.

'I want to touch you first.'

She closed her eyes as his fingertips moved so, so gently over her skin, starting at her toes and ending with her eyelids, the sensation so exquisite she became completely lost in it. There was something about Jay that was eternal, like the land he came from, and, when she was with him like this, she felt drawn into his world, as if she too belonged in this space of everlasting moments and no time.

After she had undressed him, they made love. It was long and slow and Eliza had no idea how much time had elapsed. Outside the thunder crashed, providing a backdrop to her thumping heart, and when it was over she lay next to Jay, both of them sticky with sweat. She wondered if she needed to say something, but felt her love for him so intensely she dared not speak for fear of ruining the dizzy moment.

They were to make love more than once that night. As the storm continued to rage and the wind blew rain even through the edges of the window frames, they became urgent, and with the flavour of him on her tongue Eliza decided that these were the most exciting and beautiful moments of her entire life. The sounds they made could never be heard on the outside, consumed as it was by the monsoon, but she wouldn't have cared if the ear of the world had been on them. She thought of the people in the city below, all of them smiling with relief and delight that the rains had come, and wondered how many babies would have been made that night.

The next day, during a more prolonged lull, Jay took her down into the old city. She was amazed by how much the water had risen as they walked along the eastern shore of Lake Pichola, surrounded as it was by palaces, temples, bathing *ghats* and the soft ochres and purples of the wooded Aravalli hills.

But it wasn't just the lake. Rivers of water streamed down the narrow gullies and lanes that led down to the lake; everything was wet and glittering in the morning sunshine. He explained that the city was often referred to as the Venice of the East, and that its usually tranquil lakes were surrounded by gorgeous gardens.

'It's magnificent during the monsoon season and, as Udaipore has five major lakes, they all fill up. As you can see, the palaces look sparkling too.'

'This has to be the most romantic setting in all of India.'

He laughed and reached for her hand. 'We're in the right place then.'

'Is it all right to walk like this in public?'

'You care what people think?'

'I meant that it's different here. You're not supposed to, are you?'

'I don't think anyone cares. Once the rain comes a kind of wildness rises in the people. It gets into the blood and all the usual constraints fly out of the window.'

'I'm glad it's so much cooler now.'

He made a sweeping movement with his right arm. 'Look at it. This city was founded by the Rajput king Maharana Udai Singh II in 1559.'

'It is wonderful, but is that it?' she asked. 'Is the rain over?'

He looked surprised. 'I should certainly hope not. We need considerably more. This is just enough to rejuvenate the hills and turn them green, but we need to fill up our new lake at home.'

'Gosh, I'd almost forgotten.'

And he was right. The monsoon rains began to fall again and that second evening she noticed how much it had lightened his state of mind. How could she not have realized how worried he must have been that the rains might not come at all? Accustomed, as she was, to England's perpetual rainfall, it was so easy to forget that here it could signal the difference between life and death.

They passed another wonderful night together and spent much of it talking in the dark, the way that lovers do in the exploratory stage of a love affair. It was different to the way it had been when they had last been together at his own palace. This time they opened themselves up to more honesty than ever before. He told her how as a child in England he had cried into his pillow at night, how he had hated the bland English food and the terrible British snobbery. And he told her how sad they had all been when Laxmi lost her little girl, their sister.

'I think that's why we all became so fond of Indi. Not that she could ever take my sister's place. It was hard for Laxmi. Your child is an actual part of you. What do you do with the part that is lost?'

'I don't know if my mother ever felt like that,' she said.

She told him that she had never thought her mother loved her. And she told him that she had never enjoyed one moment of intimacy with Oliver and that she had dreaded going to bed at night. Once Oliver was asleep she used to go to the living room, where she sat up most of the night, and then she'd sleep in the day when he was gone. She cried and said she hadn't known it could be so different, and then, with the constant sound of the rain in the background, Eliza fell asleep.

They were interrupted early the next morning by loud knocking on their bedroom door.

Jay climbed out of bed, grabbed a robe and as he opened the door Eliza pulled the sheet over her head. She had never been so happy, but it was one thing for the servants to be aware of their relationship and quite another for one of them to see her undressed and lying in Jay's bed. She heard the door close and then Jay's footsteps. She was surprised when he didn't come back over to the bed, so she pulled the sheet from her face, only to see him standing stiffly at the window and staring out at the view in silence.

'What is it?' she said, her stomach tightening and her voice revealing a trace of anxiety.

He twisted back to her and held out a sheet of paper. 'Here,' he said in a dull voice. 'Read it.'

She slid out of bed and went over to take it from him, and then she read, hardly able to comprehend what this might mean for them.

'I'm so sorry,' she said.

'I have to go.' He looked at her so sadly a chill ran through her.

'Now? You have to go now?'

He nodded glumly.

'But you'll be back?'

'Let's sit down.'

'No, tell me.'

'As you have just read, Anish is dead and I have no choice but to go. Do you understand?'

'Of course,' she said, but knew she sounded like a sullen child.

'I may have to take the throne as quickly as possible.'

'But you'll come back?'

He shook his head again. 'I'm not sure I'll be able to. At least not immediately.'

'What about me?'

'We'll sort something out.' He put a wallet on the bedside table. 'In case you need money.'

'What? Sort out what?' she said, ignoring the money.

'Eliza, I don't know yet. All I know is there is a horse waiting for me and I must go.'

'You aren't going to ride in this weather?'

'Safer than the bike.'

'Safer?'

She sat down on the chair in the window and could hardly believe this had happened. 'You have lost your brother, and your mother and Priya must be terribly upset. I understand they need you.'

'It isn't just that,' he continued. 'If I don't do this the British will take over our kingdom. They have been itching to get rid of Anish and this may well be their chance.' As he began quickly to dress she watched numbly, knowing he was right and there was nothing she could do.

'And us?'

'Let's just see how the land lies. I'll arrange for a car to take you to my palace as soon as the weather allows. It's best you go there for now while things are in so much upheaval.'

'And then you'll come?'

'For a while, but I may have to live at the Juraipore castle, at least at first.'

'Will I go there too?'

He closed his eyes for a moment and didn't speak.

'Jay?'

He came over to her and held her tight but she pushed him away. 'You mean we won't even be able to live together. You will marry some Princess or other?'

Again he didn't reply.

She stared at him, horrified by what all this might mean, and longing for some words of comfort. Despite the pity she felt for his loss, a burst of anger shook her to the core.

When he still didn't speak, she turned and ran from the room and from the fort, but most of all from Jay. In blinding rain, she strode along the hilltop and, as tears scalded her cheeks, she did not care that she could barely see the ground before her. Lost in the darkness of the raging storm, she turned her anger against herself. What a naïve idiot she had been to have been seduced by a romantic location.

By the time she returned, soaked through and utterly bedraggled, he had gone. It was what she'd wanted: she couldn't have borne to see him again. But now that he really was gone, she felt as if her heart might split in two. She felt so soiled and ragged there was no hope of finding a way to soothe herself, no way to alleviate the hurt. The most wonderful time of her life had turned into the worst. It had felt natural to love Jay but it had led to this. Her solitary childhood had skewed everything that came after, but Jay had been able to reach her. How could she ever accept that it was over? As she stood alone in the bedroom they had shared, her spirits deflated, and her hopes shattered. What was she to do with the love that had suffused her entire being? Where was it to go? She thought of what he had once said – 'you have to be ravaged by love to truly know it' – but it was no consolation. She knotted her hands together, twisting and turning them in distress.

She refused food for the rest of the day and, as the light faded, she stared out of the window and watched the sky grow purple and then black. Maybe one day she might remember these nights in Udaipore and it would not hurt. Maybe one day she might finally forget the beat of his heart as they lay, skin to skin. He had touched her body but, more, he had touched her soul and now nothing was normal any more. With the stale dust of the desert gone and the earth softened by rain, it hurt to have shared the monsoon with him, and then for it to be lost.

34

On her first morning back at Jay's palace Eliza unpacked her small case, then stared around her at the room. She felt profoundly sad and sorely treated too, and had been pleased not to have to face Dev upon her arrival the evening before, especially after the long journey, during which they had been frequently hampered by intermittent rain. The blue Aravalli hills had been grown over by more green than before, and now the vista from her bedroom window also sparkled with fresh life. For a few moments it had been good to watch the opalescent dawn and the sun rising over Jay's land, but now her heart was heavy.

She pictured her arrival at the castle in Juraipore the previous November: the beautiful high-ceilinged room where she had first seen Jay with his hawk and thought him an intruder; the rooms where Laxmi had entertained her; the jewels, daggers, and priceless crystal-ware glittering in Jay's mother's cabinets; the marble bathrooms where the concubines had washed her hair; the tunnel she had crept through with Jay when they had been on their way to the Holi celebration in the town. She thought until her head was whirling, images and feelings crashing into one another, and then she stopped. To go any further hurt too much.

After she had dressed and breakfasted – Jay kept a skeleton staff even when he was away – she pulled on her boots and walked through the garden and orchard towards the newly completed lake. The scents from the still moist land almost made her reel and the air was wonderfully sweet. It was as if the rain had transformed everything; the wild flowers, the leaves on the trees, and the mossy aroma of the earth itself seemed to compete for her attention. But it was the sight of an enormous stretch of water shimmering in the morning light that made her gasp. The silvery lake had filled just the way Jay had hoped it would, the damming and fortifications had held, and Eliza could see that the sluices were all in place. When open, the water would run off along specially constructed channels across Jay's land and to the edges of several villages. It was a phenomenal success, and Eliza's heart lifted from seeing it and knowing the part she had played. She knew Jay intended to excavate the land for a further lake during the coming year and had plans for even more, and this had all started with her own chance remark the very first time he had brought her here.

She recalled that time, as she always did, with horror at the poor woman's awful fate, but also with sorrow at the memory of her very first stirrings of attraction for Jay. Wrapped up in herself, she gazed at the water, listening to the bleating of a flock of goats in the distance, and didn't hear footsteps coming up behind her, but then the person coughed and she turned round.

'So you are here,' she said and groaned inwardly.

Dev didn't answer immediately, almost as if he was making up his mind about what he ought to say. 'You will find what you are looking for here, if you allow yourself,' he eventually said, and she was surprised by it.

'I'm not looking for anything.'

'We're all looking for something. I saw you arrive last night. I thought I'd let you settle in.'

She remained still and, looking steadily, studied his face. Something about him was different. His bright look had dulled and he seemed troubled and tired. She hoped that Jay's trust in the man had not been misplaced, but still she found it hard to forgive his part in the plot to implicate Jay in wrongdoing.

'I thought . . .' he said, but then fell silent.

'Thought?'

'Marrying Mr Salter, aren't you?'

Her skin prickled with annoyance at the mention of Clifford's name and she answered curtly. 'Not sure how that is any concern of yours.'

Dev shook his head. 'It might have been better if you had never come back here.'

'To India . . .'

He nodded and she watched his eyes – she could see the barely concealed hostility in them, though she was aware that there was something more that hadn't been there before. She had made up her mind to try to see the best in Dev for Jay's sake, and though he didn't make it easy, she had to admit she was curious.

'You're looking after the estate for Jay?'

'My penance. I assume he told you.'

She nodded but didn't speak.

'Jay and I go back a long way. What I did was wrong, but he has forgiven me.'

She gazed at the ground and shook her head. 'I don't understand how you could have done it, especially when he has been so good to you.'

'It's complicated.' He said no more and, when she glanced up at him after that evasive answer, he turned his back and walked off.

Eliza returned to her room intending to repack her bag. She didn't want to stay on with Dev her only company, so she sat on the bed thinking. One thing was painfully clear: she must seal tight her heart and keep occupied, but, though there was no longer anything for her here, it was hard to leave, especially as the tang of sandalwood still lingered in the room. However, she eventually got to her feet and began to gather her clothes into a small pile at the bottom of the bed.

She looked out at the hot glistening day but, wound up inside, could not appreciate it. Despite her discomfort, she knew that she alone must be the one to decide her fate, not Clifford, not her mother, and definitely not Jay. She attempted to pack the bag, but why was it that items that had easily fitted in when she had left Dottie's house didn't fit in now? She took everything out and began again, then, once it was done, slipped in the wallet Jay had left for her. Although her instinct had been to throw it and its contents down the first well she passed, common sense had prevailed. Though she didn't want to be beholden to Jay, she might well need it.

Just as she zipped up her bag Dev opened the door. He looked different again, perhaps a little more vulnerable and certainly more diffident than before.

'Could we talk?' he said.

She frowned.

'Not much to say, is there?' she said, wanting to avoid spending time with him. While she had not enjoyed his contempt for the British when they'd met before, she did understand it, but this was not the time to argue the case for colonial departure or otherwise. In any case she pretty much agreed with him now.

He held up a hand. 'I'm afraid there is.'

'Oh?'

'Let's get some coffee and go on the terrace.' She thought for a moment. With her emotions in turmoil, sharing a coffee with Dev did not appeal, yet she found herself agreeing. She couldn't quite pinpoint what she saw in his eyes as he stood watching, but as she batted away a fly buzzing at her hairline, she wondered if it might be guilt.

They made their way to the terrace and, after a servant had brought out their coffee, she could see that something in Dev had changed. He looked smaller somehow and a little lost.

'You have never liked me,' she said.

'It wasn't you. I . . .' He paused.

'Then what?'

He hung his head for a moment or two and when he gazed up at her she saw his eyes were ringed with fatigue. 'I really don't know how to say this,' he said in a terribly miserable tone of voice.

She smiled. 'I have found that it is best to just come out with difficult things, whatever they are.'

As he inclined his head she wondered what could be so difficult.

'I may have told you my father died,' he said. 'Well . . .' He paused.

'You said he wasn't around,' she prompted. 'That it was just you and your mother.'

'He did something, but for years and years I could never really face it. Then you arrived on the scene and, when I had to face you, it brought everything back.'

'You're not making any sense. I know Jay told me your father had been in trouble.'

Dev shook his head, then glanced across at the over-grown garden. 'He ran away. We never knew where. Still don't.'

'But how is that anything to do with me?'

There was a long silence, during which Eliza fidgeted and Dev stared morosely at his fingers.

'So?' she eventually said.

Still nothing. She began to get to her feet.

'No, wait,' he said.

She looked at him. 'For goodness' sake, spit it out.'

'Where will you go?' he asked, indicating her packed bag.

'I thought maybe Jaipore, take a few photographs of the pink city. I also have to go back to retrieve as much of my equipment as I can.'

He stared at her as if he hadn't heard a word and then he spoke again. 'It was my father who threw the bomb that killed your father.'

She sat down with a thud. 'Say that again.'

'My father killed your father. I'm so sorry, Eliza.' He had spoken tonelessly, so much so that she had struggled to make sense of his words.

'Are you sure?'

This was the strangest conversation she'd ever experienced, and with her heartbeat wildly fluctuating she pressed her palm against her chest. What was this? What did he mean? Her mind went shooting off, so that she hardly knew what to think or how to feel. The desert spun around her and though the clarity was missing, a chilly sensation on her skin told her that there was truth at the heart of this.

Still. 'That can't be right,' she said.

He nodded and looked at her so sadly that she almost

reached out to comfort him, almost but not quite. Why was he saying this? Was it to undermine her? How was she supposed to respond? *My father killed your father.* My father. Your father. The words echoed in her head.

Eventually she found her voice. 'How long have you known?'

'That he threw the bomb? A few years, though I was told never to speak of it.'

'I meant how long have you known who I was.'

'Since Jay told me what had happened to your father.' He shook his head. 'As a child I needed to blame somebody for my father's absence, so I blamed the man he killed. I told myself he shouldn't have been in the way. Convinced myself it hadn't been my father's fault. Crazy I know, but back then it was the only way I could handle it.'

'And then when I came here?'

'It was as if the logic I had built up instantly crumbled. My father was a murderer and yours was dead.'

They remained silent for some minutes while Eliza allowed it all to sink in. After all this time . . .

'You never heard from him again?' she finally said.

'Nothing.'

'How did you know it was he who had done it? Was there proof? Maybe it was just rumour or conjecture.'

'One of the other conspirators informed my mother so that she would understand why he had had to flee. She explained most of it to me but told me he had gone because the British wanted to hang him. Only later did she really explain why.'

He sat looking so troubled that she had no option but to try and say something comforting, even though it seemed the wrong way round.

'Look Dev, you are not your father.'

'I don't know. I found out the whole truth when I was about thirteen or fourteen and sometimes I feel as if I must continue what he started. Then, when Chatur wanted my help, I knew it was wrong but I also felt sure it wouldn't stick and nothing would happen to Jay.'

'But he was arrested.'

'That was when I realized what an idiot I'd been and told Chatur I would reveal his involvement if he didn't persuade Clifford to release Jay.'

'And your own involvement would come to light too?'

'Yes. But there's more. Chatur knew, Eliza. Both he and Clifford knew about my father and Chatur threatened to tell you if I didn't help him. I felt ashamed. I didn't want any more people knowing, but I was also frightened for my father. That was why I really helped Chatur.'

'And he went to Clifford? Admitted that you were behind the pamphlets and not Jay? That it had been a mistake?'

'Yes, and he also explained that I'd never intended to distribute them and made out that it had just been a stupid prank on my part.'

'Clifford didn't arrest you.'

'No. Jay arranged for me to come here.'

'Why are you telling me now?'

'Because you will be gone and the chance might never arise again. I really thought you should know, and I suppose I needed to get it off my chest.'

'You know I saw what happened?'

He nodded. 'I'm so sorry.'

In some odd way she knew she must reach out and squeeze his hand and, when she did, she was rewarded with a smile of complete sincerity. But she couldn't help thinking

Clifford should have been the one to tell her. She would certainly call on him when she returned to Juraipore. Clifford had concealed the truth about who had been behind the bombing in Delhi all those years before and she wasn't going to let him get off scot-free.

35

The driver and car Jay had arranged back in Udaipore to take her to his palace were still at her disposal and, as she sat on the terrace, after Dev had gone, she decided to stay one more day. Dev's confession had cleared her mind and, as she stared at the sun-drenched landscape that lay quivering in the heat, she felt terribly sorry for what he had suffered as a child. But she was glad he had told her, and couldn't help feel as if the loose ends surrounding her father's death had at last been tied up. The morning had taken on a strange, unreal quality and, despite the rains, the atmosphere remained oppressive.

She wandered indoors, passed through a corridor with lacy, latticed marble screens, put down her bag, and went back to the grand room with the high windows, where the light streaming in from above gave the impression that the ceiling was actually the sky. So much had happened since Jay had first shown her this place, and she had to admit that she found it hard to leave. The walls were glowing golden and it was easy to imagine the grand old days when this had been an escape for the royal family. But Eliza knew Jay did not have the funds to restore the palace and that he had put everything into the water project. She was about to retrieve her bag containing the new Leica Clifford had given her when she saw Jay standing in the doorway.

'I didn't think you'd be here so soon,' she said. 'I thought you'd be at the Juraipore castle for longer.'

'Well, as you can see I am here,' he said. 'I'm glad I found you. I have managed to collect all your equipment from the castle and it will arrive this afternoon.'

She didn't speak, but looked at the air just above his head. Why was he talking as if everything was normal between them? Everything stilled and the air seemed to leave the room, leaving only heat.

'Eliza?'

'Thank you,' she said, her voice stiff. 'So the fire really was a fabrication.'

He nodded, then took a few steps towards her and, though she wanted to back off, she stood firm. 'How was your journey?' she said.

Up went his eyebrows. 'Must we be so British? Aren't there more important things to discuss?'

'You tell me.'

'Ah.'

They stared at each other until she finally broke the silence. 'So, are you to be Maharajah?'

He nodded.

'I see. Very well. I was just about to pick up my bag. If you could arrange for my equipment to be sent on, I would be very grateful.' She had not been able to keep a half-resentful tone out of her voice and she turned her back and began to walk off, but she heard him come up behind her.

'Eliza.' He reached for her hand but as she twisted round to look at him she shook him off.

'I trusted you, Jay. I have never really trusted anyone, but I trusted you.'

'You can trust me.'

She steeled herself to ignore the hungry expression in his eyes as he carried on speaking.

'You knew I might have to take over if anything happened to Anish.'

'Yes, I did. Silly of me to think anything had changed. Now, if you don't mind, I need to get going.'

'Eliza. It's different here. You know that. Personal desires do not come first, duty does.'

'Well, don't worry. This *personal desire* is going to make it easy for you.'

'Hear me out,' he said. 'There's more.'

'What more could there be, Jay? It's all perfectly clear.'

He almost seemed to wince as he shook his head. 'Stay here. Live here. I don't want you to leave. I'll be here as often as I can.'

Something hardened inside her and her jaw tensed. 'I won't be your concubine.'

'I'm not asking for that.'

'So exactly what are you asking? You know full well you'll have to marry a non-European in order to have legitimate heirs.' She knew she sounded bitter but she didn't care.

There was no reply.

'You think I'll live here for the rest of my life,' she continued, 'just waiting for your ever-decreasing visits?'

He looked thoughtful as he replied. 'I think you will have a beautiful place to live, a water project to manage if you wish, and a career as a photographer too.'

It was her turn to shake her head. 'Why didn't you tell me about Dev's father?'

'I believed it would upset you too much.'

'Turn me against Dev, more like.'

'And maybe a bit of that too. Look, what if I make over the entire place to you? Think, Eliza, you could own all this.' He made a sweeping gesture with his arm.

'You really believe you can buy me?'

'For heaven's sake, Eliza. You must know I didn't mean it like that. I just don't want to lose you.'

She sniffed at the air. 'Jay, you have already lost me. We have lost each other.' She stopped, and they were silent now. While she really wanted to be angry and flounce off, driven by her own righteousness, she simply could not.

'I'll never forget you, Jay, and I'll always love you, but this was never meant to be. I think if we are honest, we have always known that.' And now she held out a hand to him. He took it and pulled her close, and then he held her in his arms for the very last time. When they drew apart, tears blurred her vision and she saw that his eyes were moist too, and though she was tempted to soften, she forced herself to stay firm. Nothing good could come of staying. It might work at first, but over time it never could. She must start as she meant to go on; and the more she was able to control her emotions, the stronger she would be.

'You are a wonderful person, Eliza. Please don't ever forget that.'

She kept her eyes on his troubled face. 'I'll send word to Laxmi to let you know where to send my equipment.'

'Where do you think you'll go?'

'I need to see Clifford first, but after that Jaipore and then, well, I'll mount the exhibition if I can get hold of enough prints. It'll be earlier than I originally intended, and after that I'll probably have to go to England. I don't know yet.'

'You have the wallet I left you in Udaipore?'

She nodded. 'I didn't want to take it, but I see now I may need it to pay for the mounting and framing.'

'If there is ever anything. Anything at all, you will only have to say.'

He stopped speaking and she smiled at him through her tears, then turned on her heels and left. It made her feel sadder than she had ever felt, but there was no point postponing the moment.

36

When Eliza arrived at Dottie's house she was surprised to see cases and trunks piled up in the front garden and all the curtains closed. Dottie, bent over and counting the cases, looked frazzled, her hair falling loose from its pins and her cheeks red, but when she spotted Eliza, she straightened up and managed to smile.

'What's going on?' Eliza asked.

Dottie sighed deeply and brushed a few strands of hair from her eyes. 'We are being transferred.'

Eliza was puzzled. 'But why so soon? You haven't been here that long. I thought you'd be here for the duration.'

'There are rumours that Anish died because of the treatment my husband advised.'

Eliza snorted. 'That's ridiculous. He died because he was grossly overweight and downright lazy.'

Dottie shrugged. 'Either way, we are heading south. There was a time not so long ago that a doctor's word was law. Now it seems we can be removed at the drop of a hat. Anyway, enough of me. What about you?'

Eliza drew breath before speaking. She had practised the words, but that didn't make them any easier to say now.

'It's over with Jay.'

She watched Dottie's reaction, which appeared to be a mixture of pity and relief.

'And Clifford?' Dottie asked with a sad look. 'He's been lost without you.'

Eliza shook her head. 'I won't be going back to Clifford, but I do need to speak with him. Is he in, do you know?' She glanced across at Clifford's villa.

'I saw a car pull up earlier but I was a bit distracted.' She indicated the cases strewn around the place. 'We lost some valuables when we first moved up here and I really don't want it to happen again.'

'I'd better not hold you up, then, but I can lend a hand if you like.'

'Don't worry. It's all under control.' Dottie took a step away and looked up at the house. 'It is a pity, though. This is the nicest place I've ever lived. I'll miss it and I'll miss you too.'

She held out her arms and the two women embraced.

'I wish I could stay,' Dottie said as they parted. 'It's hard being a wife. Just when you start to put down roots, your husband's career digs them up again. The men don't mind. They have their work and the club. And I suppose it helps if you have children, but for me –'

'Oh Dottie, I wish I could help.'

Dottie shook her head. 'Whatever happens, Eliza, hold tight to your work.'

Eliza nodded. 'Thanks for everything. Keep in touch, won't you?'

Dottie smiled. 'Clifford will give you our new address. Take care, and good luck. I've loved getting to know you. You promise you'll carry on with your photography?'

'You bet.'

After Dottie had gone back indoors, Eliza walked across to the garden gate, a side entrance to Clifford's place. She didn't want to knock at the front door, rather she wanted to surprise him, hoping it would give her the advantage in what might well be a tricky exchange. She glanced up at the brilliance of the sky, shading her eyes as she did. As a child in India, cloud-spotting had been a game she and her father had used to play. Today, not a cloud in sight.

As she opened the gate it squeaked loudly and she saw straight away that Clifford was in the garden and had heard her. He stood, watering can in hand, immobile, almost as if frozen to the spot.

'Hello, Clifford,' she said, aware of a growing feeling of apprehension.

He seemed to collect himself and took a few steps towards her. 'I wasn't expecting to see you.'

She noticed that his cheeks had coloured and a flush was spreading down his neck. 'I don't suppose you were.'

He gave her a half smile. 'Are you back?'

'For good? No.'

'Ah . . . then?'

'Could we sit in the shade? It's rather hot standing like this in the sun.'

He indicated the bench under the peepal tree. 'That do you?'

She nodded and he called for the butler to bring them sweet iced *lassi*, and then they seated themselves.

As she settled on the bench, Eliza gazed at the garden. The recent rains had refreshed it and there was a slight breeze too. The grass was more luminous than before and the trees looked green; even the flowers had perked up. It's amazing how much difference water makes to life here, she thought. But she wasn't here to discuss water, what she wanted was answers, and no matter how unnerved she might feel, nothing was going to stop her.

'So?' Clifford said, twisting sideways so that he could look

369

at her. 'What do you mean by going off like that? And yes, I know who you've been with. I didn't for a minute believe that little fabrication of Dottie's.'

'I'm sorry.'

'I should think you are. And with Jayant Singh of all people!'

She didn't speak.

'Eliza, you must have noticed that these Indian chaps are effeminate, with all that jewellery and fancy garb.'

She stiffened and, having had enough of British arrogance and prejudice to last a lifetime, couldn't conceal her irritation.

'If you were ever to consider marrying an Indian you would be ostracized by both communities. Miscegenation is condemned on both sides, you know. I consider it a betrayal of Imperial principles.'

'I'm not prepared to discuss that with you. I have made up my own mind about the British in India and I will only say that I see things very differently. This is not our country, Clifford, it is theirs and they have a right to do things their way. As for Jay, that is between me and him.'

'So that's how you feel. I must say I am disappointed.'

'That's as may be. But now I need to ask you some questions and I'd appreciate some honest answers.'

He looked taken aback. 'I rather think I'm the one who should be asking questions. You, after all, were the one who ran off and then broke our engagement in a letter. You didn't even have the decency to tell me to my face.'

Eliza knew he had a point and was not without shame, but she was not to be deterred either. 'I'm truly sorry for it, but it wasn't planned,' she said, and met his gaze.

He sniffed. 'And what was the plan? Have a fling with the

Prince and then come crawling back to reliable old Clifford? I thought better of you.'

'There was no plan at all,' she said, rather sadly.

They were silent for a few moments and then he spoke again. 'I find it hard to forgive that you persuaded Dottie to lie for you.'

She didn't tell him it had been Dottie's idea. 'Please let's not bicker,' she said instead. 'I have more important things on my mind. And if we're talking of lying, why did you lie so blatantly about Jay's arrest?'

He gave her an uncertain look but didn't speak.

'You knew Jay was already being released when I came to you. Chatur had been to see you and told you there had been a mistake and that the culprit was Dev. I don't suppose Chatur admitted his own involvement, but you didn't arrest Dev, did you? Why not, Clifford?'

When she glanced at him she saw that he seemed to be studying her face, as if looking for clues that might tell him how much she really knew. She composed herself. Let him feel the unease, she thought.

Then after a moment she nodded. 'Yes. I know the truth. And what's more, I think I know why you let it happen.'

'And that was?'

'You knew I'd come running the moment you arrested Jay, didn't you?'

He gave a little shake of his head. 'It wasn't quite like that.'

'No more lies, Clifford. You counted on the fact that I would agree to marry you to secure Jay's release.'

'And yet I didn't need to persuade you. It was you who offered.'

She stared at him. 'More fool me!'

Clifford's jaw stiffened and he looked away.

'You also knew that if Jay was found guilty it would for-ever preclude him from ruling. But I think you guessed it was never going to stick.'

'I admit I'd smelt a rat from the start. Not only that, even before Chatur arrived to tell me it was Dev, the girl came running, telling me the truth and begging for Jay's release . . .'

She frowned. 'The girl? What girl?'

He got to his feet, took a few steps away and then twisted back and, looking at her, seemed unable to speak, as if he was turning something over in his mind.

'What girl, Clifford?'

'Indira, of course.'

'Indi? She wasn't in it too?'

'No. Dev had let slip to her what he and Chatur were up to. She'd never hurt Jay, though she might have wanted to hurt you.' He paused. 'Her own sister.'

The breeze dropped and everything in the garden stilled. Eliza could feel the beating of her own heart but her mouth had gone dry and she was unable to find the words she needed. What on earth was Clifford talking about?

'Indira is your half-sister,' he said, enunciating slowly as if he thought her a fool. 'She is your father's bastard.'

She stood, but her legs shook beneath her and she had to reach out to steady herself on the arm of the bench. 'You are making it up,' she said, 'just trying to provoke me.' But her voice was flat and something told her this was true. She thought of the photograph she had found in her moth-er's attic and, covering her mouth with her hand, kept wishing he would tell her it was just a joke, but he shook his head.

'I'm sorry,' he said. 'It's the truth.'

She felt like howling, but didn't want to give him the sat-isfaction of seeing he had been successful. In a way she didn't blame him, for she had hurt him and now it was his turn to hurt her. She forced herself to stand tall. Just as Jay was with her in every breath she took, she realized Indi had been too. She wondered how she could have been so blind.

'Are you all right?' Clifford said quite kindly, though nothing could pacify her now.

She turned on him, speaking angrily. 'Why didn't you tell me before?'

'I didn't want to hurt you. Truly. I genuinely cared for you.'

'I'm not made of glass.'

'She's illegitimate. You could hardly have been friends, let alone sisters.'

Eliza sat down again. 'I always wanted a sister. All my life I wanted a sister.' And then she remembered what her mother had said about turning the *dirty* child away. Her mother had turned Indi away; her father had been unfaith-ful. It was all true. Every accusatory word her mother had spoken had been true. Eliza had been ignoring Clifford as she thought this, but now, remembering what Dev had told her, her skin prickled.

'Indi is not the only secret you kept from me, is she, Clif-ford?' she said in an icy voice.

'I don't know what you mean.' He replied in an off-hand manner, and now he picked up some secateurs that had been lying on the grass and began trimming a nearby bush.

The burst of her own anger shook her. 'For Christ's sake, can't you be honest for once! You knew Dev's father was the one who threw the bomb that killed my father. That was why Dev agreed to help Chatur. He was frightened the truth would spread. He was frightened for his father.'

He paused for a moment and then his voice became more serious. 'I only wanted to protect you, Eliza. What good would knowing that have done? We had never been able to find the man.' He spoke calmly, as if the words were well rehearsed.

'And as for Indi, it wasn't up to you to decide.'

'I promised your mother.'

'And yet you arranged for me to come here, knowing Indira was here. Why did you do that?'

He didn't reply for a moment and looked nervous. 'I saw no reason for you to ever find out.'

'So who else knows? Indi obviously, but what about the others? Are they all laughing at me?'

He spoke, eyes down, his brow furrowed. 'I would never have let that happen. Nobody knows, Eliza. I promise you that. Indi only found out recently. Just before her grand-mother died she told Indi the truth.'

Eliza did not reply, but glanced up at the darkening sky and then bent forward, head in hands. It really was too much to take in. She didn't know how to feel about Indi, and had absolutely no idea how to deal with it either. She felt locked up inside and, needing to protect herself from such unfamiliar feelings, she felt the wall around her grow even more solid. She looked up. The garden had seemed so pretty, light and breezy; now it had become a place of shift-ing shadows.

She saw that Clifford was watching her. His face had changed and his stiff manner had softened.

'Was I really here to take photographs for the archive or was I an unwitting part of a conspiracy to spy on the royal family?'

'For the archive, of course. I have all your final prints.

I'll have the ones you choose sent up for framing and then they'll be delivered to wherever you like. Will that suit? And if you wish to complete the project then it will all be archived.'

'Thank you.'

'The prints will be at Dottie's. I don't imagine you'll be wanting to spend time here.'

'I must give you back the Leica.'

'No. It was a gift. I have no use for it.'

'That's very generous. Thank you. I'll repay you one day.'

He reached out a hand. 'Eliza . . .'

She shook her head. 'Don't come any closer.' If he said one more thing now she knew she would cry, so she got to her feet and very slowly and deliberately walked out of the garden.

Back at Dottie's the cases were being loaded up to be taken to the station. Dottie had put on her hat and came running across, calling out as she did.

'We are just leaving – did you get the address from Clifford?'

Eliza shook her head, and now that Dottie was close she seemed to realize something was up. 'Dear God,' she said. 'Whatever is the matter? You look as if you have seen a ghost.'

Eliza couldn't have spoken even if she had wanted to. She had come to India, to Rajputana, so full of expectations, but never in a million years with the thought that she might discover a sister.

'Take these keys,' Dottie was saying. 'There are two bedrooms, still made up. Not our furniture, you see. Stay as long as you need to. The rent is paid until the end of next month.'

Eliza nodded. 'Thank you. I still have to choose my final prints, so I'll do it while I'm here.'

'Just a sec, I'll write down our new address.' Dottie dashed inside and came back out with a folded piece of paper. 'I don't know what's happened to make you look like that, but if you ever need a friend, write to me. Visit. Whatever . . .'

Eliza swallowed the lump growing in her throat and wished her friend wasn't leaving. At the same time she realized she might never be able to speak of this.

Dottie held out her arms and they hugged, and then, after a few moments had passed, they let each other go and Dottie climbed into the waiting car and was gone. Eliza watched as the car disappeared into the distance. It had seemed terribly quiet while Dottie had been there, but now the noises of Juraipore assaulted her: children yelling, peasants selling their produce, the city folk going about their day. She covered her ears with her hands and ran indoors.

37

Eliza spent a restless night at Dottie's, her dreams ranging from being caught in wild desert fires to searching for the boiled sweets her father used to hide in his pockets; only when she looked up it was not her father's face she saw but that of Chatur. They say we deal with our problems in our dreams, but Eliza's were too numerous to ever be resolved. She had, however, woken with the clear resolution that she must speak to Indi, despite the way the thought of it made her feel.

When she had picked out the photographs for framing, she called at the castle and marvelled again at the view of the huge fortifications rising from the rock face under a light lemony sky, and the battlements appearing to spread for miles. As a liveried servant led her along corridors with polished stucco walls, softly glowing like the shells of eggs, she still didn't know if Indi would be there or back at the village. They crossed a flowering courtyard with a central fountain glittering in the sunlight and surrounded by a marble veranda, and then they went into a part of the castle she didn't know. Here the air smelt less of jasmine and more of cardamom and spice. The man told her this was the herb and vegetable garden, and they were in the part of the castle at the back of the kitchens.

'Through here,' he said, when the courtyards came to an end, and led her to semi-concealed stairs. They began the climb and carried on right to the top, where they continued through a bewildering series of connected courtyards enclosed by high walls and scalloped arches on every side. When they arrived at a small turret-like building he opened a door that immediately gave on to another steep, winding staircase.

'This way?' Eliza asked, feeling a little uneasy. The man nodded and began to climb. At the top he rang a rope bell attached to a pale blue door. Eliza hadn't known what to expect, but heard the tinkling of an anklet and was relieved when Indi herself appeared.

'These are your rooms?' Eliza said in surprise.

'My room.'

'Why here?'

'Come inside and you'll see.'

Eliza followed Indira into what would have been an octagonal chamber but for the part of it that was attached to the main building. In her overheated frame of mind, Eliza was relieved that a fresh breeze floated through the five tall narrow windows. This was nothing like the dark and gloomy corridors of the *zenana*, divided as they were into different apartments for Laxmi, Priya and the concubines. This was an enchanted place, light and fresh. Hypnotized, Eliza felt as if she was right up in the clouds.

'It was a lookout tower,' Indira said. 'Come and see the view.'

Eliza went across to one of the windows and could see a magnificent panorama of the entire town laid out below her and far into the plains beyond.

'It's small, but I love it up here. Once they put glass in the windows it became the only place I really wanted to be.'

There was no furniture other than a coloured *charpoy* loaded with cushions, a rug on the floor, a trunk and several square floor cushions.

378

Indira indicated they should sit but, unwilling to leave the window, Eliza remained where she could see the view. While she stayed there she could listen to the sound of goat bells carried on the wind, and hear the murmur of the trees, with the intoxicating fragrance of rose and jasmine rising from below. She saw distant splashes of bright colour and realized they were the women's scarves, flapping on the washing lines as they dried.

When she reluctantly moved away from the view she turned to face Indira and gazed at her for a few moments before lowering herself on to a cushion. 'I can see why you love it up here,' she said.

But what she wanted to say was, how dare you be my father's child? She knew such petulance wasn't going to help, and yet she still could not begin to unravel her mixed emotions.

Indira wasn't speaking either but sat folding and unfolding the long scarf she frequently draped over her head. Today she wore a simple skirt and blouse, sandals, and her hair was left loose. She looked as if she belonged in a turret, Eliza thought, a damsel waiting for rescue, and in many ways that's what she was. A feeling of pity washed over Eliza. This slight girl, with such tiny hands and feet, had not had the best start in life. Her grandmother had done all she could to make up for the absence of her mother and father, but could it ever have been enough?

At that moment Indi spoke. 'You know, then? I can see it in your eyes.'

Perhaps Indi had sensed a softening, Eliza thought, perhaps she had spotted an opening that Eliza herself had been unwilling, or unable, to find. She dug a nail into the fleshy part of her palm. 'I can't talk about it.'

They were both silent for several minutes, Eliza still listening to the sounds of the outer world occasionally drifting through.

'Tell me about your childhood,' Eliza eventually said.

'If you mean our father –'

Eliza flinched visibly.

'Sorry.'

'No. Go on.'

'I don't remember him.'

'And your mother?'

'I last saw her when I was not even three years old. I think she was a dancer but my grandmother would never speak of her. Said she had disgraced the family. I was fortunate my grandmother accepted me.'

Another awkward silence. It seemed that neither woman was finding this an easy conversation, and though Eliza needed to be here, at the same time she wished herself miles away. Anywhere would do, anywhere she didn't have to face the truth.

'So,' Eliza said, 'will you stay on here?'

'I won't go back to the village.'

'Jay will allow you to stay on?' There, she had spoken his name, without a trace of emotion. Neutral.

'Well, I suppose the answer is yes.'

Eliza shrugged, the pity she had fleetingly felt giving way to resentment again. 'There's something I wanted to ask,' she said, changing the subject. 'That stolen bottle of pyro. You didn't . . . well, what I mean is, you didn't have anything to do with Anish's death?'

Indi's eyes widened for a few seconds and then she burst out laughing. 'You mean did I kill Anish so that Jay would become Maharajah and you and Jay would be over?'

Indi's forthright reaction made Eliza feel a little ashamed at even having had such a thought.

Indi shook her head, the tears of laughter filling her eyes. 'I am not a murderer, Eliza. I may be many things but I am not that. I do have to admit I broke your camera.'

Eliza gasped. 'You really hurt me.'

'I'm very sorry for it. I thought it might encourage you to leave.'

'I thought we were friends.'

'I'm sorry.' She glanced down for a second. 'I didn't know who you were then.'

'So it was all right to hurt someone who wasn't your –' She stopped, couldn't say the word. 'But you did steal the pyro?'

'Chatur asked me to.'

'But why?'

'To make trouble for you. To make it seem like you'd be a risk to us all.'

'So Chatur did that.'

Indi nodded.

'I have very little power here, you know. I needed Chatur. I'm so sorry about not telling Jay. And now Priya has designs on him . . .'

Eliza was stunned. 'Priya?'

'She is accustomed to being a powerful woman at court, and it's quite normal for a Maharani to marry her dead husband's brother.'

'My God! I never knew. But he loathes her.'

'You still don't get it? Despite his vigour and strength, for us marriage has nothing to do with falling in love, as you call it – here it's about duty and family. Our marriages are arranged.'

Eliza sighed. Would she ever understand India? 'What about love?' she asked.

'People grow to love one another. That way it lasts.'

'But who can arrange a marriage for you?'

Indi shook her head. 'I am fond of Dev but I have no dowry, just my grandmother's house. You have seen it. A mud hut and worthless. I am completely alone in this world and I expect I always will be.'

Eliza nodded and suddenly realized how important it must have been for Indi to try to create an ally of Chatur. With no status or power of her own, she really had little choice. But Eliza decided she had to say something about her own relationship with Jay. It had been more than mere romantic love. She knew it, Jay knew it, and she wanted Indi to know it too.

'I love Jay,' she said. 'I always will.'

'And he, you, I am sure.'

'But Priya? That thought makes me feel quite sick.'

'All I can say is that Jay has always surprised us. He has his own views on life and he will only do what he believes to be right.'

'Whatever that might be?'

Indira nodded, and Eliza wondered how to progress the conversation and how she might be able to help the girl. Then she had an idea. 'Would you ever become involved in the independence movement?' she asked. 'Everything will change for ordinary people. I see now that self-governance is the only way ahead. I just hope it can be achieved peacefully.'

'Well, on that score Dev is very convincing. He has persuaded me that the world we all know is about to come to an end. Maybe not today, maybe not tomorrow. But it will.'

Eliza smiled. 'I assume you don't mean the end of the world. You mean British India?'

'Yes, that, but Dev believes the princely states will go too. Of course most of the Princes are fighting to preserve their seats of power. And who can blame them?'

'Jay will be a fair ruler while the kingdom lasts.'

There was a short pause, and in it Eliza guessed what was coming next.

'Tell me about him . . . tell me about your father, please, Eliza.'

Eliza took a breath, then sighed. She had always loved to remember her father, but now her feelings of love were so mixed up with anger and resentment she hardly knew where to begin. She recalled him taking her to watch pig-sticking and that she had hated it. There had been so much blood. Better, she had at first thought, was the time he had taken her on a shoot. They had waited on a high platform, but when the Viceroy had shot a beautiful elephant she had wept, much to her father's embarrassment.

'I loved my father,' was all she could say.

'And your mother?'

'His infidelity ruined her life.'

'You must resent me.'

Eliza looked at Indi, so alone. 'When Clifford told me, I was genuinely beside myself.'

Checked by a faint memory of her father, she paused, wondering if it was real. Or had she been too young to understand the significance of seeing her father holding the hand of an Indian woman.

'Angry at me?' Indi asked.

But Eliza was following her own train of thought and didn't reply.

'Angry at me?' Indi repeated.

Eliza sighed. 'At you, at my father, at Clifford for telling me. Worst of all was the anger I directed at my mother for allowing what my father had done to destroy her.' She paused. 'My mother had a drink problem.'

'I'm sorry.'

'And I blamed her for everything. I thought my father was perfect. Fool that I was.' She got to her feet; this was beginning to hurt too much. 'I think I maybe should go now.'

'So soon? Why not come up to the roof to look at the view?'

'So you can push me off?' Eliza said with a smile.

Indi looked blank and then she laughed as she stood. 'You never know. Come on. Up there, well, it's my way of seeing beyond my problems. And now, before the sun is at its height, is best.'

Indi took Eliza's hand and led her to what she said was a short cut. They climbed a few steps and went through a door at the top, and then it was as if they were really on top of the world. Indi spread her arms out wide and spun around on the spot, laughing and whooping as she did. 'Come on, Eliza, you too,' she called out without stopping. Eliza hesitated but then couldn't resist and the two women spun. It was exhilarating and, as every thought in her mind dissolved, Eliza felt free. She went faster and faster as this incredible countryside sped around her, and she knew that here, high above the city, anything could be forgiven, and that this girl who had so little was her own flesh and blood.

She heard the chime of bells and faltered, and was the first to stumble and land in a heap on the ground. How like life, she thought: it raises you up and then tosses you aside.

She watched Indira still spinning and whooping and spotted an eagle flying right above, in the bright expanse of the pale blue sky. Though hot and sticky, the breeze was drying her skin and in that moment, and despite all that had gone on, she felt that she would be happy again one day.

When Indi came to a standstill, without falling, Eliza got to her feet and went across to her. Then she held out her arms and hugged her sister. When they parted Eliza looked into Indira's sparkling green eyes.

'You are not alone,' she said. 'You'll have me, *bahan*, always and you'll never be alone again. I promise you that.'

38

Jaipore

The wide avenues leading through the arched gateways of the city of Jaipore were packed with soldiers and strings of camels decked out in silks, pompoms, and ribbons. Eliza passed through one arch and then another, the second a deep rosy pink and painted with intricate white flowers. She had remembered the pink city from her childhood and had prepared herself to be disappointed, but Jaipore was everything she had expected and more, the *havelis*, palaces and balconies all glowing with multiple shades of pink.

She had arrived at the height of the Hindu festival of Teej, and was lucky to find a vacant room beyond the typical cusped archways of a pretty *haveli* hotel right in the heart of the town. It was a little ironic that she was there during Teej, part of a series of three festivals during the months of the monsoon, and the time when women prayed to the goddess Parvati and to Shiva to seek blessings for marital bliss. Essentially a festival for women, Teej was all about a wife's love and devotion towards her husband: something Eliza was unlikely ever to achieve. The *love* was fine but she was a little uncertain about the principle of *devotion*.

She had seen the small red insects emerging from the earth during the rains, but hadn't realized that the festivals took the name Teej from those insects. But the *haveli* manager, a small man with piercing dark eyes and an excited air, had explained everything. She had learnt that while in northern India Teej celebrated the arrival of monsoon, in Rajputana it was also celebrated as a relief from the blistering heat of summer, and that this year the rain had come so late that the festival was running later than usual. The man was full of information, wouldn't stop talking in fact, until Eliza's head was spinning, but he went on to say that while fasting was essential during Teej, the festival was joyfully alive with the sights and sounds of women singing and dancing. Eliza decided to go out and see for herself, taking her new Leica with her.

As soon as she left the *haveli* she was faced with a town heaving with exuberant people. She gazed at swings that had been hung from the branches of tall trees and garlanded with marigolds. She still found it strange that these were swings for grown women, and not for children, but one look at the faces of women of all ages confirmed their delight. She noticed that their hands were decorated with intricate henna tattoos and their bodies were dripping with jewels. Either they are hoping for a mate, she thought, or they are praying for the health of the mate they already have. No woman wants to be dressed in relentless white for the rest of their lives.

Eliza found that a fairground had been erected a short distance from the *haveli*, so she opened up her new Leica, ready to capture the sight of a big wheel and rows of stalls selling dolls and fabric ornaments. Everyone in the whole town seemed to be there, the adults calling out to each other and laughing, while the children tore through the crowds creating mayhem wherever they went. Eliza asked people if they minded being photographed and most nodded and smiled, happy to be caught in their very best clothes. The funny thing was that every time Eliza took the photograph they seemed to suddenly turn serious. She photographed decorated and painted elephants lining the wide straight avenues, their *howdahs* dripping with silk, and further on she spotted tiny figures of Shiva and Parvati laid out on velvet cloths on the pavements and people crowding to buy them. How wonderful it must be, she thought, in one lonely moment, to be part of a community sharing your religious beliefs. Eliza had given up on God the day the bomb went flying through the air, taking her father for ever.

As the light grew lemony, dusk began to fall and the town, lit by hundreds and hundreds of tiny clay pots holding only oil and a wick, seemed to step straight from the pages of a fairy tale. The city palace glowed a deep rosy pink, and the hilltop forts loomed above the dark purple of the Aravalli hills. Eliza saw the beauty of it all, but for her it was beauty tinged with a deep melancholy: a recognition that she would never really be part of this. She couldn't help thinking of Jay and remembering all that had passed between them. She would always treasure the days she had spent with him but it was time to move on. And though a part of her felt like running away, she stayed to watch the dancing, and the sight of so many beautiful women moving as if their very lives depended on it lifted her spirits.

She was surprised when all of a sudden one of the women near to her grabbed her by the hand and led her into the heart of the throng. At first, embarrassed and clumsy, Eliza shrank from the exposure. She wasn't dressed for this kind of wild abandon, but after only a few minutes she allowed herself to let go.

That night she slept like a baby, and the next day decided to wear her nicest Indian clothes. She drew the line of dark *kaajal* around her eyes, just as the concubines had instructed her, and once again was amazed by the way the green of her eyes came to life. She applied a little rouge to her cheeks and lips and tied her hair with bright ribbons at the nape of her neck.

She would go down for coffee on the veranda and sit overlooking a lush garden and try to be happy. Then go for a stroll around the town. Today she would fit in, she promised herself.

She pushed open the heavy carved doors to the veranda but found the place deserted. Either she was too late or too early, and she wondered whether to look for somebody. But a butler came out to place a deep red rose in a vase on her table and then left. She was lost in her thoughts when she heard a man's voice. She remained completely still for a few moments. Surely it couldn't be him? She twisted to her side and saw that he was standing there, smiling, his amber eyes full of warmth.

'Jay?'

He put a finger to his lips and came closer, then knelt before her and took a small box from a pocket in his tunic. He opened it and held it out for her to see.

She stared at the most beautiful sapphire ring she had ever seen, then glanced at his solemn face.

'It turns out,' he said, 'that I cannot live without you.'

Eliza could not prevent her tears forming and, unable to fully comprehend that this was really happening, could only nod wordlessly.

'I'm so sorry to have put you through all this. I thought I was doing what was right. I want to say sorry and ask if you can forgive me.'

Eliza still could not speak for a moment. Then she smiled. 'Let us agree to forgive each other.'

'Come,' he said, as he got to his feet, then held out both his arms to her. 'You and I will build our faith in each other, through the dark times and the light.'

And then she went to him. While they held each other she could feel his heart against her own and knew this was good, even though the surprise of it still coursed through her. Afterwards they sat in silence for a while, the moment too precious to spoil with questions. The sun filtered through the trees and Eliza watched the birds flying about the garden and a couple of chattering monkeys swinging in the branches, and wanted to preserve the memory. For all of her life she wanted to be able to recall this one moment. Because it was perfect, and perfect moments didn't come around very often. There were questions floating in and out of her mind and soon she would ask them, but for now she held Jay's hand and experienced a sublime kind of peace, like knowing nothing could go wrong ever again. Minutes passed during which neither spoke.

He was the first to interrupt the silence. 'Have you already had coffee?'

'That's very down to earth, but do you know, I can't even remember. I seem to have lost the ability to think. In any case, I'm not thirsty now.'

'Then shall we walk, while it's still cool and quiet in the town?'

They left the *haveli* by way of a narrow alley, where only a few cats stretched indolently and failed to move out of their way. Then they went out into the streets of Jaipore. The early morning light revealed the beauty of the town. Everything seemed to shimmer, the pink of the buildings more delicate than they had been the day before.

Most of the shops were still closed, and as they passed the Palace of the Four Winds she asked the most pressing question.

'So how, Jay? How is this even possible?'

'My younger brother is to be Maharajah, with Laxmi as the Regent. She will have full control until he comes of age and I shall be her adviser.'

'Your mother agreed to this?'

'She's fond of you, Eliza, and when she saw how determined I was, she gave her blessing. The British too. We presented it as a *fait accompli* so that they didn't really have a leg to stand on.'

'And what about Priya?' She pulled her mouth down at the corners and raised her brows, intending the question to tease him. 'I thought she was to be your wife.'

He made a face. 'Never. Priya will be forced to take a back seat now, though I doubt Laxmi will insist she dresses in white and is sent back to her family.'

'I feel rather sorry for her.'

He put an arm around her shoulders. 'And I like you for it.'

'What's happened about Chatur?'

'He has been divested of power and made to leave the castle. I have appointed a new *dewan*.'

'Hurrah to that!'

'Now, the most pressing question is where shall we be married? Do you have a place that's special to you?'

'You really do mean you gave up being Maharajah for me? Are you sure?'

He laughed. 'Don't change the subject. Where? You can have a fairy-tale wedding here at the city palace – the family are friends of ours – or we can have a quiet affair in Delhi. The city palace lies at the heart of Jaipore and is rather wonderful. You'd think it was the actual city if you didn't know better, and it has everything from gardens of cypresses and palms to stables. There are weavers whose sole occupation is to weave silk clothes embroidered with gold flowers, and they are just for the elephants. The Maharajah has tamed cheetahs we could use in our marriage procession.'

'Enough!'

'You choose Delhi?'

She nodded. 'The city palace sounds extraordinary and must be every young girl's dream, but I think a fairy-tale wedding would be rather a sad affair for me, with no family.'

He stood still and looked into her eyes. 'Except for Indi.'

'She told you.'

He nodded. 'I should have realized. You have the same eyes.'

'Sort of, though mine are the colour of ponds and hers shine like emeralds.'

'Your eyes are beautiful and you are beautiful . . . Do you remember I once told you that you, Indi and I were linked, but I didn't know in what way?'

'And that it was our destiny to come together? Is that what this is all about?'

'Who knows? Life has a funny way of working out in unexpected ways.'

'It is good though, isn't it? You and me. Us?'

He laughed. 'It is wonderfully good. And good for Indi too. As she is now going to be my sister-in-law I can take responsibility for her dowry.'

'You couldn't before?'

'Not very easily. We are bound by certain traditions, as you know.'

Eliza felt so happy she couldn't stop smiling. 'I'm so pleased you have forgiven her. I did worry what would happen.'

'And I know a certain young firebrand whose mother will no longer be able to stand in the way.'

'Dev?'

'The very one.'

She experienced a sudden flash of anxiety. 'I'm worried you might one day resent me. You know, for giving up the chance to rule.'

'You worry too much. I think everything in India is going to change before too long, and far more than we realize now. Anyway, I have enough on my hands with the water project.'

'Yes.'

'By the way, I need to bring you up to speed on that. I've had some new ideas and, more importantly, I have the permission to dam the river I talked about. It will make a huge difference to what we're doing. And don't forget I'll be working as an adviser with Laxmi too. But enough of all that. Have I told you how gorgeous you look today and that this is a very auspicious time for an engagement?'

'Have I told you that you really have the most amazing eyelashes for a man?'

He batted his eyelashes at her and then laughed.

'And yes, I know it's the festival of Teej. I'll have to pray for a happy ending!'

'You'd look amazing with henna-painted hands,' he said, and then paused. 'So what's happening about your exhibition?'

'I still haven't got a venue.'

'What about in the main hall at my palace? We'd need to fix the floor, of course, but the light is terrific and if we send out the invitations in good time we should get a crowd.'

'Really? Oh, thank you. I'd love that.'

'My pleasure.' He paused and smiled at her. 'So, how many children shall we have?'

'Two perhaps, maybe three?'

'I was thinking at least five.'

She swallowed. Should she tell him now or wait a little longer, until she was certain? She hesitated, but then began to speak in a serious voice. 'Actually, on that point I do have something to say.'

He looked suddenly grave. 'We don't have to. I mean, if you want to focus on your career, and don't want –'

'No, you idiot. Stand still and listen. I'm late. Only a week, so it's too soon to really know, but we may have already started on number one.'

He looked up at the sky and thumped his chest and then he began to roar with laughter. She threw back her head and laughed with him, and only out of the corner of her eye did she see the merchants opening up and hear the tinkling of anklets as the women passed by, all the locals smiling at the sight of Jay and her laughing with such wild oblivion.

The sun rose in the sky and for the first time Eliza experienced the matchless perfection of life: each moment, each fragment of joy to be savoured, and when sorrow came, as it surely must, she would face it with an open heart, and know she would survive. She looked around her at the exotic pink city and knew she had, at last, moved on. And while she would always love her father, despite his faults, and would always feel a degree of regret over her mother, the future was what mattered now: her career, her love for Jay, and nurturing the next generation. Her mother had been wrong. There was no reason a woman should not have it all, and Eliza vowed that in the days and years ahead she would prove it. Not only would she follow a career she loved, she would also have a real family of her own, including the sister she had always wanted. She raised her head to the heavens. Be happy for me, Mum, she whispered. Be happy.

Epilogue

Three months later

Shubharambh Bagh

On a cool October day, the date set for Eliza's exhibition finally arrived. She rose early, leaving Jay still sleeping, and, wrapping her robe around her, she wandered through the corridors of his palace – now her home. Eliza loved the luminous light of the early morning and often explored on her own before anyone else had risen. She frequently had to pinch herself at the fortune that had brought her to this point. She and Jay had married quietly in Delhi and she was now growing accustomed to the idea of becoming a mother in another few months. What's more, she had finished the project for Clifford's archive and had been paid accordingly. And though Clifford had never actually admitted it, she had come to believe that while his personal intentions towards her had been honourable, he'd really had an ulterior motive in placing her at the castle, and that had been to keep an eye on the royals and report back while also photographing them.

When she arrived in Jay's huge reception hall, with the high windows and newly repaired floor, she gazed at the seventy-five photographs she had hung over the last couple of weeks. Jay had rolled up his sleeves and, working together, they had presented her work in the best possible light. Every picture was framed elegantly in black and they had been placed equidistantly along the entirety of one wall. The proud faces of the royals stared out, but so did the faces of the villagers, the children, and the poor. Each moment had been captured, sometimes in a soft grainy image, sometimes in harsh sharp light, and sometimes in shadow. Each picture was a work of art in its own right and Eliza was proud of what she had done. Against the opposite wall and in complete contrast to the black and white photographs, bright red perfumed roses in ten porcelain vases now lifted their blowsy heads to the light breeze and, in between them, chairs painted white were ready for those who wanted to sit and gaze. Eliza walked along the wall checking each photograph, straightening one, touching the surface of another, ensuring each one hung exactly as it should, and then she went upstairs to wake her husband.

That afternoon Eliza slipped into a long black dress, loose over her expanding tummy, and Kiri, who had come to live with them, dressed her hair with one of the red roses. Over her shoulders she wore a white silk shawl and when Jay came in and saw her he whistled.

'Well, my darling, you are even more beautiful than your pictures.'

She grinned with pleasure. He was wearing a traditional Rajput outfit, a dark *angharki* or coat, deeply cut out in the front, in black, red and white and, fresh from the bath, his hair was still damp. She went to him and stroked his cheek. 'You look pretty impressive yourself.'

There was a knock at the door and Jay went to open it.

Indi took a few steps inside. 'I've just tidied up the roses,' she said. Indi had been responsible for arranging the flowers and organizing the canapés for the opening party, and was now dressed in a red silk dress in the European style. 'Are you ready? I think I heard the first car pull up.'

As Eliza glanced at Jay she felt a rush of nerves. What if people didn't come? What if nobody liked her work? What if all they came for was to gawp at the Prince's English bride?

'I'll go down,' Jay said. 'Better if you make an entrance once the place has filled up.'

She nodded wordlessly and he came across to kiss her forehead. 'It will be fine. I promise. Haven't we sent out invitations to half the world?' He turned. 'Come on, Indi, let's go down.'

Jay was right. Invitations had been sent to photographic studios in Delhi, Jaipore and Udaipore. The *Times of India* had been invited, as well as the *Hindustan Times* and the *Statesman*, along with all the nobles of Jay's acquaintance and businessmen too. Eliza had also insisted on inviting the locals to view the photographs and join the opening party. Even Dev would be there, now that it was clear that Clifford would not be arresting him.

On her own in the bedroom she shared with Jay, Eliza glanced in the full-length mirror. Though her skin glowed with health and her eyes sparkled, she couldn't calm the butterflies in her stomach, but at least she could hear that more vehicles were arriving now. After half an hour of pacing the room, Eliza glanced up when Kiri appeared at the door to give her the message from Jay that it was time. She took a few deep breaths.

'Madam?' Kiri said. 'You are ready?'

Eliza nodded and swallowed her nerves, then, walking like an Indian queen, she made her way to the top of the grand staircase that led to the hall. She stood gazing at her feet for a few moments, feeling hot, her heart pounding.

When she felt brave enough to glance down at the gathered crowd she was astonished to see that the hall was full of smiling people with upturned faces and all eyes were on her. As she took her first steps, a loud cheer broke out. She blinked back the tears and felt as if her heart might burst, as the cheering carried on until she reached the bottom, where Jay stood waiting.

'Let me introduce you to Giles Wallbank,' he said, as she went up to him.

'How do you do,' a smiling blond man said, and held out his hand. 'I must say these photographs are really quite extraordinary. We'd love to publish a selection in the *Photographic Times*. Would that suit?'

She gave him a broad smile. 'Nothing would give me greater pleasure.'

'We'll talk later, and I'll have a contract drawn up as soon as possible. Now I must leave you to enjoy your success.'

After the man had wandered off, Jay held out a hand to her and then whispered. 'Look at the reaction,' he said, and indicated the people nodding their heads as they gazed at the photos and the queue waiting to talk to her.

Eliza would never forget this day as long as she might live. She had come to India uncertain about herself and nervous of her abilities as a photographer. She had come not really knowing who she was. All that had changed. She did not know what might lie ahead, but for now there was nothing more that could make her life more perfect – apart from one thing. And that was the safe arrival of their child. She looked into Jay's eyes, the reflection of her soul, and she had to blink even harder than before.

'You did it, my love,' he said. 'You really did it. And I couldn't be prouder.'

Author's note

The books that I found particularly useful while research-
ing this novel include the following titles:

Ahmed Ali, *Twilight in Delhi*, Rupa Publications Pvt
Ltd, 2007

Rustom Bharucha, *Rajasthan: an oral history*, Penguin
Books India, 2003

Diwan Jarmani Dass, *Maharani*, Hind Pocket Books Pvt
Ltd, 2007

Sharada Dwivedi and Shalini Devi Holkar, *Almond Eyes,
Lotus Feet*, HarperCollins, 2007

Henri Cartier-Bresson in India, Thames & Hudson, 1993

Caroline Keen, *Princely India and the British*, I. B. Tauris &
Co. Ltd, 2012

Amrita Kumar (ed.), *Journeys through Rajasthan*, Rupa &
Co., 2011

Antonio Martinelli and George Michell, *Palaces of
Rajasthan*, India Book House Pvt Ltd, 2004

Gita Mehta, *Raj*, Minerva, 1997

Lucy Moore, *Maharanis*, Penguin Books, 2005

Hugh Purcell, *The Maharaja of Bikaner*, Rupa Publications
Pvt Ltd, 2013

Sweta Srivastava Vikram, *Wet Silence: poems about Hindu
widows*, Modern History Press, 1975

Thank you

Words can never convey how grateful I am to everyone at Penguin/Viking for the level of support I continue to receive. Thank you so much, Venetia, Anna, Rose and Isabel. Huge thanks to Lee Motley for this gorgeous cover and to all the sales and rights teams who work so hard and achieve so much. Thanks also to my superstar agent, Caroline.

I wouldn't have been able to write this book without the help of everyone I met in India, so a massive thank you to Nikhil Pandit, Director, TGS Tours & Travels Pvt Ltd, Jaipur, Rajasthan, for organizing the trip so brilliantly. I am hugely grateful to Thakur Shatrujeet Singh Rathore, Thakurani Maya Singh, Thakur Jai Singh Rathore and Thakurani Mandvi Kumari at Shahpura Bagh for their generous hearts and the time and attention they gave me. It was not only a truly wonderful place to stay but it was also the history of Shahpura that inspired this book. Thank you also to Thakur Praduman Singh Rathore at Chandeleo Garh, a magical and peaceful retreat. I'll never forget the dinners on the roof beneath the stars. Thank you to everyone at the Pal Haveli in Jodhpur, and also to Thakur Man Singh and Thakur Prithvi Singh, the owners of the Narain Niwas and Kanota Castle in Jaipur. Thanks also to our wonderful and endlessly patient drivers and guides.

I can't end without thanking all my lovely family for

putting up with me, and in particular my husband and 'super-chef', Richard, who has been inspired to cook amazing Indian food.

Rajasthan is a magical land and writing this book has been a wonderful experience. More than anywhere I have ever been I hope one day to return. So perhaps, above all, my thanks go to India itself and in particular Rajasthan. And, in case anyone is wondering about the spellings in the book, I have used Jaipore, Udaipore and Rajputana as they would have been spelt at the time the book is set. Juraipore is, of course, entirely fictional.